Jonathan CHYNOWETH [of Cusgarne]
m. Anne Tregear (1693–1760)

Jonathan (1710–77)
m. Elizabeth Lanyon (1716–50)

Robert (1712–50)
m. Ursula Venning (1720–88)

Jonathan (1737–1806)
m. Joan Le Grice (1730–1804)

Hubert (1750–93)
m. Amelia Tregellas (1751–)

Elizabeth (1764–99)
m.(1) Francis Poldark
(2) George Warleggan

Morwenna (1776–)
m.(1) Rev. Osborne Whitworth   m.(2) Drake Carne
(1764–99)   (1776– .)

Conan (1796–)   Loveday (1801–)

Garlanda (1778–) ⎱
Carenza (1780–)   ⎰ Morwenna's
Rowella (1781–)   ⎰ younger
m. Arthur Solway   sisters

- -

Tom CARNE (1740–94)
m. Demelza Lyon (1752–77)

Luke WARLEGGAN (1715–1800)
m. Bethia Kemp (1716–44)

Nicholas [of Cardew] (1735–1805)
m. Mary Lashbrook (1732–)

Demelza (1770–)
Luke (1771–)
Samuel (1772–)
William (1773–)
John (1774–)
Robert (1775–)
Drake (1776–)

Cary Warleggan
(1740–)

George (1759–)
m. Elizabeth Poldark (née Chynoweth)
(1764–99)

Valentine (1794–)
Ursula (1799–)

The Stranger from the Sea

When the seventh Poldark novel, *The Angry Tide*, ended in December 1799 it seemed as though this saga which had delighted millions on TV screen and printed page must die with the century. But time is proof against mere calendar change and lives continue whether chronicled or not. So when in 1810 King George III became mentally ill and a Regency was proclaimed, Poldarks and Warleggans were affected by this national event and by the Regent's unexpected decisions regarding the prosecution of the war with France.

It is at this turning-point that a new generation takes the centre of the stage in the persons of Jeremy and Clowance, children of Ross and Demelza.

Their concerns of head and heart, and the presence in all their lives of an enigmatic stranger from the sea, unfold against a background which ranges from Wellington's lines in Spain to a Midsummer Night in Cornwall, from a ball in London to a brush with the Preventive men.

As the new generation moves forward into the industrial age, Winston Graham fills in the past, portrays the present, and hints at the future as only a master storyteller can.

by the same author

Ross Poldark
Demelza
Jeremy Poldark
Warleggan
The Black Moon
The Four Swans
The Angry Tide

Night Journey
Cordelia
The Forgotten Story
The Merciless Ladies
Night Without Stars
Take My Life
Fortune is a Woman
The Little Walls
The Sleeping Partner
Greek Fire
The Tumbled House
Marnie
Grove of Eagles
After the Act
The Walking Stick
Angell, Pearl and Little God
The Japanese Girl (short stories)
Woman in the Mirror

The Spanish Armadas

The Stranger from the Sea

A Novel of Cornwall
1810–1811

WINSTON GRAHAM

COLLINS
St James's Place, London
1981

William Collins Sons & Co. Ltd
London · Glasgow · Sydney · Auckland
Toronto · Johannesburg

British Library Cataloguing in Publication Data

Graham, Winston

The Stranger from the Sea: a novel of
Cornwall 1810–1811. – (Poldark; 8)
I. Title
823′.912[F]   PR6013.R24

ISBN 0 00 222616 2

First published 1981

Photoset in Garamond
Made and Printed in Great Britain by
William Collins Sons & Co. Ltd Glasgow

Book One

Chapter One

I

On Thursday, the 25th October, 1810, a windy day with the first autumnal leaves floating down over the parks and commons of England, the old King went mad.

It was an event of consequence not only to the country but to the world. Among those it directly affected were four Cornishmen, a merchant, a soldier, a diplomat and a doctor.

Of course it was not the first time: twenty-two years earlier he had gone insane for a long enough period to bring the legislative affairs of the country to a standstill. Again in 1801 and in 1804 there had been short periods of aberration, enough to give rise to anxiety on the part of his doctors and his ministers. To begin with, this latest attack seemed little different from the others. Except that he was older, and nearly blind, and that his favourite daughter was dying . . .

The first symptom was that he began to talk. All through the day – non-stop – and most of the night too. One sentence in five was rational, the rest were irrelevances strung together like rags on a kite, blowing as the wind took them. He addressed his sons: those who like Octavius were dead he thought alive; those who were alive – and there were many of them – he thought dead. He laughed aloud and crawled under the sofa and was brought out with the greatest difficulty.

The Whigs tried unsuccessfully to hide their gratification. The Prince of Wales was devotedly of their party, and if he became Regent he would at once dismiss the Tory mediocrities who had clung to office for so many years. The long sojourn in opposition was nearly over.

Napoleon too was gratified and made no greater attempt to hide his pleasure. The Whigs were the party of peace: those who did not secretly admire him were at least convinced that it was futile to wage war on him. They agreed with him that he could never be beaten and were anxious to come to terms. They would be his terms.

II

Almost exactly four weeks before the King's illness, three horsemen were picking their way down a stony ravine in the neighbourhood of Pampilosa. The second in line was a middle-aged man, tall, good-looking if a little gaunt, wearing a riding habit and a cloak of good quality but well worn and of no particular nationality; the two others were younger, small, wiry, ragged men in the uniform of the Portuguese army. There had been a road, a dusty track, since they set out in the early morning from Oporto, but lately it had deteriorated and become so overgrown that one only of the two soldiers could pick it out among the scrub oak, the cactus, the boulders, the rotted trees. He led the way.

As dusk began to fall the older man said in English to the man behind: 'How much farther?'

There was talk between the soldiers. 'Garcia says the Convent of Bussaco should be but three leagues or so distant now, senhor.'

'Will he find it in the dark?'

'He has never been there, but there should be lights.'

'If it has not been evacuated. Like all else.'

'At the request of your general, senhor.'

They rode on, the small sturdy horses slipping and sliding down the rough descent. All the way they had come across deserted farmhouses, burnt crops, dead animals, overturned ox-carts, the trail of evacuation and destruction. There had been corpses too, teeming with flies, usually old people who had collapsed in flight. But it was clear that the countryside was not as deserted as it seemed. Here and there foliage stirred; figures appeared and disappeared among the olive trees; several times shots had been fired, and once at least the balls had flown near enough for discomfort. The peasants were fleeing from the invader but many of the men were staying behind to harass him as best they could. The *Ordenanza*, or militia men, were also in evidence; in woollen caps, short brown cloaks and threadbare breeches, armed with anything from butchers' knives to old blunderbusses, and riding wild ragged ponies, they arrived suddenly in clouds of dust or wheeled against the skyline blowing briefly on crescent-shaped horns. Twice the Englishman had had to produce his papers, in spite of his Portuguese escort. He did not fancy the fate of any stragglers of the invading army. But then the behaviour of the invading army had invited every sort of retaliation.

It was a mild September night but no moon. A few mist clouds drifted across the spangled stars.

They reached a dried-up river bed beneath a cliff, and the leading soldier dismounted and cast about him like a bird dog seeking a new scent. The Englishman waited patiently. If they were lost they could sleep well enough in their cloaks; a night among the stunted chestnut trees would do no one any harm, and they had food and water to last.

Then a bent figure emerged from behind a clump of aloes. Indistinguishable as to age and sex, it approached cautiously and there was whispered talk. The soldier turned and said:

'We are closer to the convent than we thought, senhor, but it will be necessary to make a detour. The French army is directly ahead of us.'

There was a pause.

'Which way ahead of us?'

'West, senhor. They are a great host. They have been

pursuing the English all day. This man advises keeping to the river bed for half a league, then crossing between the hills to the Bussaco ridge. The French artillery are in the valley.'

The Englishman fumbled in his pouch and found a coin to give to the stunted figure who had saved them from stumbling into the enemy lines. Since he had a fair appreciation of the value of his own freedom, the coin was a large one, and the ragged shadow was suitably overcome, and went off bowing backwards into the darkness that had hatched him. In the present chaos, the giver reflected, when civilization had broken down, a plug of tobacco might have been more valuable.

The riders followed the advice they had been given, moving all the time very cautiously among the great boulders, lest the warning turned out to be more general than precise. Ever and again the leading soldier would halt his horse and listen for the tell-tale sounds that might warn them they were running into an encamped enemy. It took an hour to reach the turning to which they had been directed. It was a moot point whether to stop there for the night, but clearly the greater distance they could put between themselves and the French, the safer they could rest. The idea of reaching the convent at Bussaco was dropped; it seemed likely that the French would already have occupied it.

As the evening advanced a cool wind got up off the sea, which was only a few miles distant, and the riders made better use of their cloaks. They began to climb, first among hillocks, then diagonally up and across a sharp and rocky ridge. As they reached what appeared to be the top, with the gorse and heather waist high around them, the leading soldier again stopped. They all stopped and listened. A very peculiar sound, like a wail; it could have been women's voices keening, but was not. It could have been some sort of flute – a shepherd piping to his flock – but it was not.

The horses came up with each other. The two soldiers argued together. The one who spoke English said:

'We must turn farther north, senhor. That is the French.'

'No,' said the Englishman. 'I do not believe that is the French.'

'Then what?'

'Let us see for ourselves.'

'No, no! We shall be captured! We shall be shot down!'

'Then wait here,' said the Englishman. 'Or follow me but slowly, fifty paces behind. Then if I am wrong you can still see to your own freedom. The French will not follow you far at night.'

'And for yourself, senhor?'

'I have an idea what this – noise – is.'

He edged his way across the heather towards a rocky bluff that could be discerned in the dark because it cut off the stars. His escort came after him at a distance. They had gone some quarter of a mile when they were halted by a challenge. The Englishman reined in his horse and stared at a solitary figure holding a firelock directed at him. Then he saw three other men part hidden behind bushes, their guns also at the ready.

He said sharply, in English: 'Friend. Name Poldark. From Oporto with despatches. And Portuguese escort.'

After some moments the first musket was lowered and a stocky bonneted figure came slowly forward.

'Let's see yer papers.'

The Englishman dismounted and fumbled in his pocket, produced a wallet and handed it over. Another of the soldiers appeared with a shaded lantern, and they bent over it together.

'Aye, sir. That would seem in order-r. Who would ye be wishing to see?'

'Who's your commanding officer?'

'General Cole, sir, o' the division. Colonel McNeil o' the battalion.'

'What are you, infantry men?'

'Second Battalion, Seventh Fusiliers. Sergeant Lewis.'

'I'll see your colonel.'

The two Portuguese soldiers had also dismounted and their white teeth glinted in the dark as they were greeted by their allies. They walked their horses along the ridge of the escarpment and were soon among a mass of soldiery taking their ease, talking, chatting, but cooking nothing, the few fires being sited so that they should be little seen at a distance.

'My escort were greatly alarmed at the noise they heard,' said Poldark presently. 'What were your pipers playing?'

Sergeant Lewis sniffed. 'It was some old Scottish lament. It comforts the men to listen to the wistful music now. Tomorrow's morn we shall all be more martial.'

They came to a clump of tall cedars. Their great trunks had been used to support a temporary headquarters where tables had been put up and a lantern burned. Lewis disappeared, and returned with a tall man who came forward and then stopped, stared and swallowed.

'Poldark, Poldark!' he said. 'So it's Captain Poldark himself! I should never have supposed that there were more than two of that name!'

The other had stopped too. Then he laughed. 'So it's the same McNeil! Well, I'll be hanged!'

'Which you never were,' said McNeil; 'fortunately for your pretty wife. However much some folk thought you deserved it!'

They shook hands after a fractional hesitation. They had never been friends, because twenty years ago they had been on opposite sides of the law. But they had respected each other and come to a mutual understanding, and indeed to a certain wary liking.

Well, it was all far behind. In a cross-fire of conversation they exchanged news. Captain Poldark had landed at Oporto, not with despatches as he had claimed but on a special mission as observer on behalf of the government. When he reached Oporto he was told that Wellington had been retreating with his army for three weeks and that he would be better advised to re-ship to Lisbon and make his contacts there. But by the time this was discovered the sloop on which he had come had sailed and he had decided, against all advice, to ride overland.

He did not elaborate at all on what his mission was and Colonel McNeil did not press him. After exchanging polite news about Cornwall – the Bodrugans and the Trevaunances, the Teagues and the Trenegloses – they strolled a hundred yards to the edge of the bluff, from which they could see the whole of the Mondego Plain. A great company of glow-worms had come to inhabit it. Everywhere the lights twinkled.

'The French,' said McNeil laconically.

'Massena commands?'

'Aye. Wellington decided today to go no farther, so we have encamped up here and watched the army, the host, filling up the valley below us. Columns of dust have been blowing across the plain and into the foothills all day. The odds, of course, are not more than two to one against us; but of our forty thousand half are untried Portuguese. Ah, well, tomorrow will show . . . It was five to one at Agincourt, was it not.'

'Well, yes. But here we have no pompous beribboned knights to confront but an army of revolutionary France forged by a genius.'

'No doubt it will be a harder fight, but all the better for that. When do you ride on?'

'Not tomorrow, if this is happening.'

McNeil looked at his companion. Ross Poldark was dressed as a civilian, perhaps for a greater degree of safety traversing a country at war. But then he had no reason to be a soldier, having long since taken on a new cloak of respectability; indeed become a Member of Parliament. Now he was getting up in years, grey at the temples, no

15

fatter, but more lined. He was of the lean kind that feed their bellies with their discontent.

'You intend to stay?'

'Of course. I have a rifle. An extra gun can hardly be despised.'

'Did not Henry say, "The fewer men, the greater share of honour"? All the same, I believe we can spare ye a wee bit by the way.' McNeil screwed in his greying moustache and laughed. It was a subdued guffaw compared to the noise Ross remembered.

'Are we lying so quiet to deceive Massena into thinking there are fewer of us than there really are?'

'Aye. I do not think he knows our Second or Fifth Divisions have caught up with us yet. That will be pleasant – to surprise him. It is always pleasant to have some good troops up your sleeve.'

Poldark pulled his cloak round him as the night breeze blew some fog off the sea.

'And you, McNeil. When we saw you in Cornwall you were a captain in the Scots Greys. This change to a line regiment . . . ?'

McNeil shrugged. 'I have neither money nor influence, Poldark. At the best I could have become a major had I stayed with my old regiment. Here – in the – the crucible of the Peninsular war I have already made the most important step – though as yet only a Brevet Colonel. But in the natural wastage of war I shall expect soon to have my rank confirmed.'

They stood silent, looking down on the diadem of lights, while more mist drifted in and dispersed among the sharp hills and the tall trees. McNeil took it as a natural expectation that the wastage should not include himself. Ross Poldark, equally naturally, welcomed the risks of battle that for him offered no preferment except the possible preferment of death.

Ross said: 'One thing you said, Colonel. Perhaps I misheard you. Did you say – did I hear you say that you could not suppose there were more than two of my name?'

'You did.'

'Why not one? Who else is there? *Do* I misunderstand you, then?'

'You do not at all. There's a Poldark in the Monmouthshires. I saw his name but the other day in the commissary lists. I thought once to seek him out but you'll appreciate we have not had much time on our hands!'

Ross eased the foot that now often pained. 'Is he in this army?'

'He must be. The 43rd are part of Craufurd's light division. They should be immediately on our left.'

'Far?'

'Half a mile. Do you wish to see him? Is he a relative?'

'I suspect so.'

'Then I'll get a man to go with you after supper. I take it you'll sup with us first?'

'Gladly.'

III

They had supped off cold food and the night was quiet, except for the scraping of the cicadas and the soughing of the wind. Once or twice the keening of the pipes grew out of the dark, a dree sound, mourning as if for the slaughter on the morrow, yet quietly stirring, both a lament and an incitement. Down below in the plain the roll of drums sounded. It was as if the French were making no secret of their power – the power that had decimated all the other armies of Europe – so that the knowledge might seep into the minds and hearts of their opponents and sap their courage before dawn broke. The English knew there would be a battle tomorrow, for Wellington had said that this was as far as they would retreat – and what Wellington said he always meant. But the French could not know whether the army encamped on the slopes above them might not have done the wise thing and slipped away before morning, leaving no more than a rearguard to delay their advance. It had happened often enough in the last few years. The British victory at Talavera last year was the exception, not the pattern.

It was near midnight when they had finished eating, and as a soldier led Ross through the lines many men were already asleep – or at least they were lying down wrapped in their cloaks. They were all, it seemed, fully clad; no one bothered to take greater ease knowing the day ahead. Groups lay on elbows or squatted, quietly talking. McNeil had mentioned Agincourt, and Ross remembered the play he had seen at Drury Lane in which the king went round visiting his soldiers on the night before the battle. Remarkable that this Scottish soldier should be able to quote a line or two. There had been a Cornishman, Ross remembered, in that play. No, no, the king had been mistaken for one by calling himself Leroy . . . Did Shakespeare suppose *that* was a Cornish name?

It was more than half a mile, and Ross was limping by the end of it. He rode a horse longer than he walked these days. Then it was an asking and a questing, a seeking among dark and sprawling figures, the thumb jerked, the finger pointed. Ross's escort moved like a small Scottish ferret from group to group. At last a man sat up and said:

'Yes, I'm Poldark. Who wants me?'

'One of your own blood,' said Ross. 'Who else?'

There was a startled oath, and a thin man scrambled to his feet. He had been lying, his back propped against a tree, his scabbard across his knees. He peered in the uncertain starlight.

'By the Lord God! It's Uncle Ross!'

'Geoffrey Charles! I never thought I should have the good fortune to meet you in this way! But I'm conceited enough to believe that no other person with such a name exists in the British army!'

'By God!' Geoffrey Charles embraced his kinsman cheek to cheek, voice and tone light with pleasure, then held him by the biceps in a firm examining grip. 'It is too *much* to believe! Just when I was thinking of home – here, with the snap of a finger, as out of a magic bottle, comes the person I remember best of that motley crew – and, with one exception, value most highly! God save us! It can't be possible!'

Ross explained his presence.

'Then should you not go at once to Wellington instead of frittering your time discovering an unimportant nephew? Go and see Old Douro and then when he is done with you, I shall be happy to talk!'

Ross hesitated, unwilling to explain the precise nature of his presence here, uncomfortable indeed that, stated in a few sentences, it might not commend itself to his nephew at all.

'Geoffrey Charles,' he said. 'I am sent here for the value of my observation rather than my communication, and I suspect General Wellington has not a little on his mind tonight. What I have to say to him will not help him win or lose the battle in the morning and can be as well said after as before.'

'You are staying?'

'Of course. Wouldn't miss it. Can you use another sharpshooter immediately under your command?'

'My command, *mon Dieu! C'est à ne pas y croire –*'

'Well, I see you are now a captain. And that, since I have so long been a civilian, gives you a seniority I'd be willing to accept.'

Geoffrey Charles snorted. 'Uncle, you do yourself no sort of honour, since I understand you have been in and out of a number of scrapes during the last ten years! To say nothing of your membership of that talk-house in Westminster! However, if you wish to be by my side in any little action which may take place to dissuade the French from climbing this escarpment . . . well, I'll be happy to accommodate you!'

'Good, then that's settled.'

19

'You've seen the French encamped below?'

'Colonel McNeil gave me the opportunity.'

'So you'll appreciate that there could be at least a chance of your *never* being able to deliver your message to Wellington?'

'It's a risk my conscience will entitle me to take.'

Ross was by no means sure that he would be welcomed by the General. He had a letter of authority. But Wellington had a very personal and clear line of communication with the Foreign Secretary, who happened just at the moment to be his brother, and he might well suspect this semi-military civilian unexpectedly visiting his headquarters of being here on behalf of other members of the Cabinet who thought less well of him. It was not far from the truth, though the thinking was not Ross's own.

They had squatted together by now on the soft pine needles beneath the trees. A batman brought them a hot drink that passed for coffee, and they sat chatting easily together like old friends.

They had not seen each other for four years, because Ross had been himself abroad when Geoffrey Charles returned after Corunna. Ross was startled at the change in his nephew. When he had last seen him Geoffrey Charles was a young cadet, eager, full of fun and high jinks, drinking and gambling his small allowance away, always in trouble and always in debt. Now he looked lean and hard, all the puppy fat gone, face sun-tanned and keen, handsome in a rather hard-mouthed way that only the army or fox-hunting can produce. A campaigner who by now had seen more war than Ross had ever seen. Not so much like his father as he had once given promise of becoming; perhaps the thin line of dark moustache made a difference, as indeed did the indentation in the jaw.

'Well, well, my dear life and body, as Prudie would say! I should never have supposed you were so well disposed to me after our last meeting, Uncle! Are you rich? I doubt it.

It was never in the character of a Poldark to become rich, however much fate might favour him. Yet you met my urgent needs like a lamb. And they were not small! You got me out of a scrape! Indeed, had you not so helped me I might never have seen Spain and Portugal but have been dismissed the army and spent salutary years vegetating in Newgate!'

'I doubt it,' said Ross. 'You might have suffered some loss of preferment; but in time of war even England cannot afford to let her young officers go to prison for the sake of a few guineas.'

'Well, had the worst come to the worst I suppose I should have swallowed my pride and asked Stepfather George to bail me out. All the same, your generosity, your forbearance, allowed me to escape the moneylenders without that humiliating experience.'

'And now it seems you must have mended your ways – Captain Poldark.'

'Why do you suppose that, Captain Poldark?'

'Your preferment. Your grave appearance. Four years of very hard soldiering.'

Geoffrey Charles stretched his legs. 'As for the first, that was easy, men do not make old bones in the Peninsula, so one is given a place as it becomes vacant. As to the second, my gravity, if you observe it as such, is largely due to the fact that I am wondering how to compose a letter to Aunt Demelza if her husband comes to hurt under my command. As to the third, four years of soldiering of any sort, as you should know, dear Uncle, does not breed mended ways of any sort. It encourages one in unseemly behaviour, whether with a woman, a bottle, or a pack of cards!'

Ross sighed. 'Ah, well. I shall keep that from your relatives.'

Geoffrey Charles laughed. 'But I'm not in debt, Captain. In the most singular way. Last month before this damned retreat began the regiment had a donkey race; there were high wagers on all sides, and I, fancying my moke, backed myself heavily and came in a neck ahead of young Parkinson of the 95th! So for the first time for twenty-odd months I have paid off all my debts and am still a few guineas in pocket! No! Twas lucky I won, else I should have been gravelled how to pay!'

Ross eased his aching ankle. 'I see someone has been chipping at your face.'

'Ah yes, and not so engagingly as yours. *Ma foi*, I could not imagine you without your little love-token, it so becomes you. I lost my bit of jaw on the Coa in July; we had a set-to in front of the bridge. But it could have been worse. The surgeon gave me the piece of bone to keep as a lucky charm.'

Chapter Two

I

The night had worn on, but they dozed only now and then, still exchanging the occasional comment, the quip, the reminiscence. As dawn came nearer they talked more seriously about themselves, about Cornwall, about the Poldarks.

Geoffrey Charles had taken the death of his mother hard. Ross remembered him as a pale-faced youth calling to see him in London one afternoon and saying that this happening, this loss, had changed his attitude towards his future. He was no longer content to go to Oxford, to be groomed pleasantly for the life of an impoverished squire in the extremest south-west of England. To be under the tutelage of his stepfather, whom he disliked, for the sake of his mother, whom he deeply loved, might be acceptable. The former without the latter was not. He wanted to make his own way in the world and felt he could ask no more favours of Sir George Warleggan. His immediate wish was to leave Harrow as soon as he could and join the Royal Military College at Great Marlow as a cadet. Ross had tried to persuade him otherwise; he knew enough of the army himself to see the difficulties of a young man without personal money or influence; he also knew Geoffrey Charles's already expensive tastes and thought his nephew would find the life too hard. Although three years at Harrow had toughened him, he had been much spoiled and cosseted by his mother when he was younger, and some of that influence still showed.

But nothing would change his mind. It seemed to Ross that the real driving force was a wish to distance himself from Cornwall and all the memories that Cornwall would revive. He had to keep away, and distaste for his stepfather was only a partial reason. So the thing had gone ahead. It had meant a good deal of correspondence with George – which was difficult – but at least they had avoided a meeting. George had been quite generous, offering his stepson an income of £200 a year until he was twenty-one, thereafter to be raised to £500. Geoffrey Charles had wished to spurn it; Ross had bullied him into a grudging acceptance.

'I'm not thinking solely of myself in this,' Ross had said, 'in that the more you receive from him the less you'll need from me! But George – George owes something to your mother – and your father – and it is elementary justice that he should discharge it.'

'To ease his conscience?'

'I have no idea what will ease or disarray his conscience. To take this allowance from him would seem, as I say, a form of elementary justice in the widest sense. If it eases his conscience I am happy for his conscience. But it is much more a matter of an equitable arrangement arrived at for all our sakes. Certainly it would have pleased your mother.'

'Well, if you feel that way, Uncle Ross, I suppose I'd better fall in.'

So in that bitter February – bitter in all senses – of 1800. In time, of course, Geoffrey Charles had recovered his high spirits. He had taken to his new life with a will – even during the year of temporary peace – and George's allowance, which came to him fully in 1805, had not prevented him from running into debt, so that Ross had twice had to bail him out of dangerous situations – the last time to the amount of £1000. However, it had not impaired their relationship.

Geoffrey Chalres yawned and took out his watch, peered at it by the light of the stars.

'Just on four, I think. In a few minutes Jenkins should be round with another hot drink. We should break our fast before dawn because I suspect they will be at us in the first light. Before that I want to introduce you to a few of my friends.'

'I cut no pretty sight in this civilian suit.'

'I've talked often about you to my closest friends, Anderson and Davies. In your own quiet way you have become quite a figure, y'know.'

'Nonsense.'

'Well, judging from letters I sometimes get from England. Your name crops up now and then.'

'Letters from whom?'

'Never mind. Incidentally, you have scarce told me anything of Cornwall.'

'You haven't asked.'

'No . . . Not from lack of interest . . . But sometimes, when one is bent on the business of killing, a whiff or so of nostalgia is not a good thing.'

'Tell me about Wellington.'

'What d'you want to know that you don't already know? He's a cold fish, but a great leader and, *I* believe, a brilliant soldier.'

'It's not the general opinion in England.'

'Nor always among his own men. Even here there are Whigs enough who see no hope of defeating Napoleon and greet each withdrawal we make with a nod as if to say, "I told you so."'

'The English,' Ross said, 'are weary of the long war. The distress in the North and the Midlands is acute. The government seems to spend as much thought to putting down revolution at home as to defeating the French.'

'The English,' said Geoffrey Charles, 'frequently make my bile rise. When we got home after Corunna we were treated as if we had let our country down and run away! They spoke of John Moore with contempt, as if he had been a bungler and a weakling! I dare say if he had not died they would have had him up for a court martial!'

'Many are arguing different now,' said Ross. 'Defeat is

25

never popular, and it takes time to judge all the circumstances.'

'They sit on their fat bottoms,' said his nephew, 'your fellow MPs do, swilling their pints of port and staggering with the aid of a chair from one fashionable function to another; they issue impossible instructions to their greatest general; and then when he dies in attempting to carry them out they rise – they just have strength to rise – in the House and condemn him for his inefficiency, at the same time complimenting the French on their superior fighting skill!'

'It's said that Soult has put up a monument to him in Corunna.'

'Well, of course, one military commander appreciates another! That is an act of courtesy that the English cannot pay to their own – if he should happen to die in defeat instead of – like Nelson – in victory.'

Ross was silent. This son of his old friend and cousin, Francis, a rake and a failure, whom he had sincerely loved (by a woman he had also loved) had grown and changed in mind as well as body since they last met. Ross had always had a softer spot for Geoffrey Charles than could be justified by the relationship. This meeting confirmed and strengthened it. He could hear Francis talking; yet the sentiments were more like his own.

'And Wellington,' he prompted again. 'As against Moore?'

The younger Captain Poldark rubbed fretfully at his injured jaw. 'Old Douro is a great man. His troops will follow him anywhere. But Moore we loved.'

The batman arrived with another cup of steaming coffee.

'So, as we're in the mood now, tell me about Cornwall. You say my favourite aunt is well.'

'On the whole, yes. Sometimes of late she suffers from a blurred vision but it passes if she spends an hour or two on her back.'

'Which she will not willingly do.'

'Which she does not at all willingly do. As for the children . . . Jeremy is now but an inch shorter than I. But I believe most of that growing took place a while ago. When did you last see him?'

'I did not return to Cornwall after Corunna. I was so angry that our retreat – and Moore's generalship – should be looked on in the way it was looked on that I threw out the thought of going down there and having to justify what in fact needed no justification . . . So, it must be all of four years – Grandfather's funeral, that was it. Jeremy must have been about fifteen. He was as tall as I then, but even thinner!'

'He still is.'

'And his bent, his way in life?'

'He seems to have no special wish to join in the war,' said Ross drily.

'I don't blame him. He has a mother, a father, sisters, a pleasant home. I trust you don't press him.'

'If this struggle goes on much longer we may all be forced to take some part.'

'*Levée en masse*, like the French, eh? That I hope will not happen. But I would rather that than we gave in to Napoleon after all these years!'

Ross cupped the mug, warming his hands on the sides while the steam rose pleasantly into his face. Something was rustling in the undergrowth and the younger man stared at the bushes for a moment.

'We have many noxious things round here,' said Geoffrey Charles. 'Snakes, scorpions . . .' And then: 'If we negotiate with Napoleon now it will only be like last time over again – another truce while he gathers breath and we give up our overseas gains. I know this campaign is unpopular, but it's vital to keep it in being. Is it not? You should know. The government is so weak that one loses all confidence in it. If only Pitt were back.'

'I think the government will persist while the old King lives.'

'That's another hazard. He's seventy-odd, and they say he's recently been ill.'

The sound of drums made rattlesnake noises distantly from the French camp.

'And Clowance?' asked Geoffrey Charles, as if aware that time was growing short. 'And your youngest, little Isabella-Rose?'

'None so little now. Neither of them. Clowance is almost seventeen and becoming somewhat pretty at last. Bella is eight, and very dainty. Quite unlike Clowance at that age, who was something of a tomboy. Still is.'

'Takes after her mother, Captain.'

'Indeed,' said Ross.

'And Drake and Morwenna?'

'Bravish, though I've not seen them for a year. They're still at Looe, managing my boat-building works, you know.'

'It was a good move, getting them away, and I'm grateful for the thought. They had too many memories around Trenwith. Dear God, to think at one time I intended to settle down at Trenwith as a country squire and to employ Drake as my factor!'

'You still may do the first, if this war ever finishes.'

'Something *must* be done about this Corsican, Uncle. It's appalling to think after all this time the fellow is only just turned forty. The trouble with genius – whether good or ill – it starts so young. Have they any more children?'

'Who? Drake and Morwenna? No, just the one daughter.'

A messenger came hurriedly through the dark, picking his way among the sleeping figures. He passed close by them but went on and into the tent fifty yards away.

'Message for Craufurd, I suppose,' Geoffrey Charles said. 'I suspect we should break our fast now. That drum-roll is spreading down in the valley.'

'I have not much ammunition,' said Ross. 'I could do

with a mallet also, for I had not expected to fire as much as I now hope to do.'

'I'll get Jenkins to get them for you. We don't have such things, but the 95th are close by. Thank God, we're well equipped as to firelocks and the like. And a fair supply of ball for the cannons.' Geoffrey Charles sat up and massaged his boot where his foot had gone to sleep. 'And while we're about it, about this talk of bullets, perhaps I should inquire after the health of a man who certainly deserves one, though he'll take good care never to come within range . . . I'm speaking, of course, of Stepfather George.'

Ross hesitated. 'I've seen him once or twice in the House of late, but we avoid each other, and altogether it's better that way. Nor do I often see him in Cornwall. I hope the days of our open conflict are over.'

'I haven't see him since '06, when Grandfather died. The same day, no doubt, I last met Jeremy. It was misty-wet and a very suitable day for a wake. George looked a thought pinched then, growing old perhaps before his time.'

'He took your mother's death hard, Geoffrey.'

'Yes. I'll say that for him.'

'As we all did. You know I was – more than fond of your mother.'

'Yes, I did know that.'

'Although I'd seen little enough of her since she became Mrs Warleggan, she left – a great gap in my life. Her death – so young – left some permanent emptiness. As I know it did with you. But George surprised me. For all that occurred, all that happened in the past, I can never think anything but ill of him; but his sorrow and *dismay* at your mother's death was surprising to me. Perhaps I shall not ever think quite so ill of him again.'

'Well . . . He has certainly not remarried.'

'I have to tell you,' Ross said, 'that since Mr Chynoweth's death Trenwith has been neglected. As you know, after your mother's death, George made his permanent home at his parents' place at Cardew, but he maintained a small staff at Trenwith to look after your grandparents. I don't imagine he visited them more than once a month, just to see things were in order. When your grandmother died I believe nothing changed. But after Mr Chynoweth went George virtually closed the house. The new furniture he had bought for it in the 'nineties was all taken away to Cardew, the indoor staff disappeared. So far as I know, much of the grounds are overgrown. The Harry brothers live in the cottage, and I suppose see to the house and grounds as best they can. Harry Harry's wife may do something too, but that is all.'

'And George never comes?'

'I think he would not be George if he *never* came. He turns up, they say, from time to time to make sure the Harrys cannot altogether relax; but I don't think his visits are any more than about three-monthly.'

Geoffrey Charles did not answer for a while. The stars were appearing and disappearing behind drifting cloud or fog.

'I suppose the house is legally mine now.'

'Yes . . . Well, it will be when you come home to claim it. I feel guilty in not taking more active steps to see to its condition; but so often in the past my intrusion on the property has led to bitter trouble between myself and George. While there were people to be considered, such as your Great-aunt Agatha, or your mother, or yourself – or Drake – I felt bound to interfere. But where a property only is concerned . . .'

'Of course.'

'Much of the fencing that George put up has gone, either with the passage of time, or villagers have stolen it for firewood; but on the whole I gather very few of them venture on the property. They have a healthy respect for the two Harry bullies, and maybe a certain feeling that in due course it will be occupied by a Poldark again and so not treated too rough. But the house is in bad repair. Clowance went over the other day.'

'Clowance? What for?'

'She's like that. I was home at the time and I scolded her for taking the risk of being caught trespassing. But I think I could as well have saved my breath. Of course she was upset that I was upset, and appreciated the reason. But she tends to be impulsive, to act by instinct rather than reason – '

'Like her mother?'

' – ah – yes, but not quite the same. At the back of *everything* Demelza did – all the times she did apparently wayward things – and still does! – there's a good solid reason, even though in the old days it was not a reason or a reasoning I could agree with. Clowance is more wayward in that respect than Demelza ever was, because her behaviour seems to be on casual impulse. She had no *reason* for going over to Trenwith, she just took it into her head to go and look at the house, and so did.'

'At least she was not caught.'

'That,' said Ross, 'unfortunately was Clowance's defence. "But, Papa, no one saw me." "But they might have," I said, "and it might have led to unpleasantness, to your being insulted." "But it didn't, Papa, did it?" How is one to argue with such a girl?'

Geoffrey Charles smiled in the darkness. 'I appreciate your concern, Uncle. If I am ever out of this war, or have a long enough leave, I'll get rid of those two Harrys and Clowance can wander about Trenwith to her heart's content . . . She said it was in bad condition?'

'You can't leave a house four years, especially in the Cornish climate, and not have deterioration. Of course . . .'

'What were you going to say?'

'Only that little if anything has been spent on Trenwith since your mother died. While your grandparents were alive George maintained the place with the minimum of upkeep; so in a sense it is ten years' neglect, not four.'

'So it's *time* I was home.'

'In that sense, yes. But this is where you belong now. If we can with our small resources harness the Spanish and Portuguese efforts to resist, it ties down a disproportionate part of Napoleon's strength. And even his resources are not inexhaustible. It has been a desperately wearying trial of strength and endurance. D'you realize that Clowance can never remember a time when we were not at war with France? Except for that one brief truce. No wonder we are all weary of it.'

'Weary but not dispirited.'

It looked as if fog was thickening in the valley. Unless it dispersed before dawn it would be of great value to the attacking side.

'Look, Geoffrey Charles, meeting you in this un-expected way has brought home to me more acutely my neglect of your affairs – '

'Oh, rubbish.'

'Not rubbish at all. I am particularly culpable because, nearly thirty years ago, a similar state of affairs occurred in an opposite direction. I came back from the American war when I was twenty-three. My mother had been dead a dozen years or more but my father had only just died. But he had been sick for a while and the Paynters were his only servants, and you can imagine how ill they looked after him. Your grandfather, Charles Poldark, did not get on too well with his brother and seldom came to see him . . . I would not want you – when you come back – to return to the sort of chaos and ruin I returned to.'

Geoffrey Charles said: 'Hold hard, there's Jenkins. I'll go and tell him your requirements. Let's see your rifle.' This was examined. 'A good weapon, Captain, that I'll wager you did not pick up in Oporto.'

'No, Captain, I did not.'

'What is it exactly?'

'A rifled carbine, with Henry Nock's enclosed and screwless lock. You see the ramrod is set lower in the stock to make it easier to withdraw and replace when loading.'

Geoffrey Charles frowned at the mist. 'Some of the sharpshooter regiments have got the Baker rifle. Not us yet. We still handle the old land pattern musket. It serves.'

There was silence for a while.

Ross said: 'In the American war thirty years ago there was a man called Ferguson – Captain Ferguson of the 70th – he invented a breech-loading rifle. It would fire six shots a minute in any weather. It was a great success . . . But he was killed – killed just after I got there. I used one. Splendid gun. But after he was killed nobody followed it up. Nobody seemed interested.'

'It's what one comes to expect of the army,' said the young man. He bore the rifle away and soon came back with it. 'That is attended to. Breakfast in ten minutes. Then I'll introduce you to my friends.'

'By the way . . .'

'Yes?'

'Regarding your stepfather. You said he had not married again.'

'True. Has he?'

'No. But I received a letter from Demelza shortly before I left. In it she says that there is a rumour in the county that George is now – at last – taking an interest in another woman.'

'*Mon dieu*! Who is she?'

'Unfortunately I can't remember the name. It's no one I know. Harriet something. Lady Harriet something.'

'Ah,' said Geoffrey Charles significantly. 'That may explain a little.' He scuffed the ground with his boot. 'Well . . . I suppose I should wish him no ill. He was my mother's choice. Though they lived a somewhat uneasy life together – undulating between extremes – I believe she was fond of him in her way. So if he marries now at this late age – what is he? fifty-one? – if he marries again now I can only say I hope he is as lucky a second time.'

'He won't ever be that,' said Ross.

A few minutes later they were called to breakfast: a piece of salt beef each, a dozen crumbly biscuits – perhaps with weevils but one could not see – and a tot of rum. Ross met the other men who were Geoffrey Charles's friends. They were light-hearted, joking, laughing quietly, all eager and ready for the mutual slaughter that lay ahead. They greeted Ross with deference, and a friendliness that deepened when they learned he was not content to be a spectator of the battle.

While they were eating a spare, dour figure on a white horse, followed by a group of officers, rode through them. There was a clicking to attention, a casual, dry word here and there, and then the figure rode on. It was Viscount Wellington making his final tour of the front. He had nine miles of hillside to defend, and his troops were spread thin. But they had the confidence that only a good leader can impart to them.

Ten minutes after Wellington had passed, the drums and pipes of the French army began to roll more ominously, and, as the very first light glimmered through the drifting mists forty-five battalions of the finest seasoned veterans in Europe, with another twenty-two thousand men in reserve, began to move forward in black enormous masses up the escarpment towards the British positions.

Chapter Three

I

The second courtship of George Warleggan was of a very different nature from the first. A cold young man to whom material possessions, material power and business acumen meant everything, he had coveted his beautiful first wife while she was still only affianced to Francis Poldark. He had known her to be unattainable on all accounts, not merely because of her marriage but because he knew he meant less than nothing in her eyes. Through the years he had striven to mean something to her – and had succeeded on a material level; then, less than a year after Francis's death, he had seized a sudden opportunity to put his fortunes to the test; and with a sense of incredulity he had heard her say yes.

Of course it was not as straightforward as that, and he knew it at the time. Long before Francis's death the Trenwith Poldarks had been poverty-stricken; but after his death everything had worsened, and Elizabeth had been left alone to try to keep a home together, with no money, little help, and four people, including her ailing parents, dependent on her. He did not pretend she had married him out of love: her love, however much she might protest to the contrary, had always been directed towards Francis's cousin, Ross. But it was *him* she had married and no other: she had become Mrs George Warleggan in name and in more than name, and the birth of a son to them had given him a new happiness, a new feeling of fulfilment, and a new stirring of deeper affection for her.

It was only later that the old hag, Agatha, had poisoned

his happiness by suggesting that because Valentine was an eight-month child he was not his.

For a cold man, preoccupied with gain, interested only in business affairs and in acquiring more power and more property, he had found himself suffering far more than he had believed possible.

Although a marriage undertaken on one side to acquire a beautiful and patrician property, and on the other to obtain money and protection and a comfortable life, should certainly not have succeeded beyond the terms for which it was tacitly undertaken, it *had* been, had *become* successful. There had been an element of the businesslike in Elizabeth's nature, and a wish to get on on a material level, which had responded to his mercantile and political ambitions; and he, taken by that response and by much else that he had not expected in her, had found himself more emotionally engaged with each year that passed. That they had quarrelled so much at times was, he knew now, all his fault and had arisen over his unsleeping jealousy of Ross and his suspicions about Valentine's parentage. But then, just when all that was cleared up, when there had seemed an end at last to bitterness and recrimination, when, because of the premature birth also of their second child, his doubts about Elizabeth and about Valentine had been finally put to rest, just then when the future was really blossoming for them both, she had *died*. It was a *bitter* blow. It was a blow from which he had never quite recovered. His knighthood, coming on top of his bereavement, instead of being the crowning point of his pride and ambition, became a sardonic and evil jest, the receiving of a garland which crumbled as he touched it.

So in the early years that followed he had become very morose. He lived mainly at Cardew with his parents, and when his father died he stayed on with his mother, visiting Truro and his Uncle Cary daily to supervise his business interests and, almost incidentally, to acquire more wealth. But his heart was not in it. Still less was it in the social side

36

of his parliamentary career. To enter a room with Elizabeth on his arm was always a matter of pride, to go through the repetitive routine of soirées and supper-parties, to perform alone a social routine he had planned for them both, was something he hadn't the heart to face. Nor any longer quite the same ambition. Unlike his rival and enemy Ross Poldark, his entry into Parliament had never been concerned with what he could do for other people but with what he could do for himself. So now why bother?

Several time he thought of resigning his seat in the House and being content to manipulate the two members sitting for his borough of St Michael; but after the first few bad years were over he was glad he had not. His own membership brought him various commercial rewards, and he found his presence in London enabled him to keep in closer touch with the movement of events than any proxy alternative he could devise.

Both his father and mother pressed him to remarry. Elizabeth, in spite of her high breeding, had never been their choice. They had always found her personally gracious and had got on well enough with her on a day to day basis; but to them she had the disadvantage of being too highly bred without the compensating advantages of powerful connections. Anyway, it was terribly sad she had gone off so sudden that way, but it was a thing that happened to women all the time. Being a woman and a child-bearer was a chancy business at the best of times. Every churchyard was full of them, and every evening party or ball contained one or another eager young widower eyeing the young, juicy un-married girls and considering which of them might pleasure him best or advantage him most to take to second wife.

Therefore how much more so George! *Rich*, esteemed in the county – or where not esteemed at least respected – or where not respected at least feared – a borough monger, a banker, a smelter, and now a knight! And only just turned forty! The catch of the county! *One* of the catches of the country! He could take his pick! Some of the noble families might not perhaps yet quite see it in that light, but they were few, and, as he progressed, becoming fewer. To grieve for a year was the maximum that decorum would dictate. To go on year after year, getting older and steadily more influential, and yet growing each year a little more like his Uncle Cary whose *only* interest in life was his ledgers and his rates of interest . . . It was too much. Nicholas, who had started all this from nothing, who had laid the foundations on which George had built his empire, who had seen all that he worked and planned for come to fruition and to prosper, had died the month after Pitt, and, as he lay in bed with his heart fluttering at a hundred and sixty to the minute, it had come to his mind to wonder why some sense of achievement, of satisfaction, was lacking. And he could only think that the circumstance disturbing his dying thoughts was his son's failure to react normally to a normal hazard of married life.

When Nicholas was gone Mary Warleggan continued to prod George about it, but with growing infrequency. What elderly widowed woman can really object to having her only son living at home, or at least be too complaining about it? After all, George had two children, and even if Valentine was growing into a rather peculiar boy, this would no doubt right itself as he became an adult; and she did see a lot of her grandchildren. Valentine spent most of his holidays at home, and little Ursula, the apple of her eye, was at Cardew all the time.

The situation also suited Cary. He had always disliked Elizabeth and she had disliked him, each thinking the other an undesirable influence on George. Now she was gone uncle and nephew had come even closer. Indeed in the first year of widowerhood Cary had twice saved George from making unwise speculative investments; George's grasp of the helm was as firm as ever, but the bereavement had temporarily deprived him of his instinct for navigation.

That time was now long past. Lately George had even recovered some of his taste for London life and for the larger scale of operations he had been beginning in 1799. He had found a friend in Lord Grenville, one-time prime minister and now the leader of the Whigs, and visited him sometimes at his house in Cornwall. In the endless manipulation of parties and loyalties and seats which had followed the death first of Pitt and then of Fox, George had gradually aligned himself with the Opposition in Parliament. Although he owed his knighthood to Pitt, he had never become a 'Pittite', that nucleus of admirers of the dead man notably centring round George Canning. He was convinced that the weak and fumbling Tory administration was bound to come down very soon, and his own interests would be better furthered by becoming a friend of the new men than of the old.

True, some of them had crack-brained schemes about reform and liberty, fellows like Whitbread and Sheridan and Wilberforce; but he swallowed these and was silent when they were aired, feeling sure that when the reformers came to power they would be forced to forget their high ideals in the pressures and exigencies of cabinet office. When the time came he might well be offered some junior post himself.

But George still had no thought of another marriage. Such sexual drive as remained to him seemed permanently to have sublimated itself in business and political affairs. Of course over the years he had not lacked the opportunity to taste the favours of this or that desirable lady who had set her cap at him, either with a view to marriage or because her husband was off somewhere and she wanted to add another scalp to her belt. But always he had hesitated and drawn back out of embarrassment or caution. The opportunity to sample the goods before buying never seemed to him to exist without the risk of later being pressed to purchase; and as to the second sort, he had no fancy to have some woman boasting behind her fan of having had him in her bed and perhaps cynically criticizing his prowess or his expertness.

There was one day he seldom missed visiting Trenwith, and that was on the anniversary of his marriage to Elizabeth. Though the wedding had in fact taken place on the other side of the county, he felt it suitable to spend a few hours in her old home, where he had first met her, where he had largely courted her, where they had spent most summers of their married life, and where she had died – even though it was a house that had always been inimical to him, the Poldark family home which had never yielded up its identity to the intruder.

He rode over with a single groom on the morning of June 20, 1810, and was at the church before noon. It was a glittering, sunny day but a sharp draught blew off the land and made the shadows chill. Chill too and dank among the gravestones, the new grass thrusting a foot high through the tangle of last year's weeds; a giant bramble had grown across Elizabeth's grave, as thick as a ship's rope. He kicked at it with his foot but could not break it. 'Sacred to the memory of Elizabeth Warleggan, who departed this life on the 9th of December, 1799, beloved wife of Sir George Warleggan of Cardew. She died, aged 35, in giving birth to her only daughter.'

He had brought no flowers. He never did; it would have seemed to him a pandering to some theatricality, an emotional gesture out of keeping with his dignity. One could remember without employing symbols. Besides, they were a waste of money; nobody saw them, and in no time they would be withered and dead.

He had taken care that she should be buried far from any of the Poldarks, particularly from that festering bitch Agatha who had ill-wished them all. He stood for perhaps five minutes saying nothing, just staring at the tall granite cross, which was already showing signs of the weather.

The letters were blurring, in a few more years would become indistinct. That would never do. They would have to be cleaned, re-cut, cut more deeply. The whole churchyard was in a disgraceful state. One would have thought the Poldarks themselves would have spent a little money on it – though certainly their own patch was not as bad as the rest. The Reverend Clarence Odgers was a doddering old man now, so absent-minded that on Sundays his wife or his son had to stand beside him to remind him where he had got to in the service.

Nankivell, the groom, was waiting with the horses at the lych-gate. George climbed the mounting stone, took the reins, and without speaking led the way to the gates of Trenwith.

The drive was nearly as overgrown as the churchyard and George resolved to berate the Harry brothers. It was a big place for two men to keep in condition, but he suspected they spent half the time drinking themselves insensible. He would have discharged them both long ago if he had not known how much they were feared and hated in the district.

Of course they were waiting for him at the house, along with the one Mrs Harry, whom rumour said they shared between them; all smiles today; this was his one *expected* visit of the year so they had made an effort to get the place clean and tidy. For an hour he went around with them, sometimes snapping at their explanations and complaints and apologies, but more often quite silent, walking with his memories, recollecting the old scenes. He dined alone in the summer parlour; they had prepared him a fair meal, and Lisa Harry served it. She smelt of camphor balls and mice. The whole house stank of decay.

So what did it matter? It was not his, but belonged to the thin, arrogant, inimical Geoffrey Charles Poldark now fighting with that blundering unsuccessful sepoy general somewhere in Portugal. If, of course, Geoffrey Charles stopped a bullet before the British decided to cut their losses and effect another panic evacuation like Sir John Moore's, then of course the house *would* come to him; but even so, did it matter what condition it was in? He had no further interest in living here. All he was sure was that he would never sell it to the other Poldarks.

When the meal was finished he dismissed the Harrys and went over the house room by room, almost every one of which had some special memory for him. Some he thought of with affection, one at least with concentrated hate. When he was done he returned to the great hall and sat before the fire Mrs Harry had prudently lighted. The sunshine had not yet soaked through the thick walls of the old Tudor house. He had not decided whether to stay the night. It was his custom to lie here and return on the morrow. But the bedroom upstairs – his bedroom, next to Elizabeth's old bedroom – had looked uninviting, and not even the two warming-pans in the bed were likely to guarantee it against damp. The year before last he thought he had caught a chill.

He looked at his watch. There was time enough to be back in Truro, if not Cardew – hours of daylight left. But he was loath to move, to wrench at the ribbon of memories that were running through his brain. He lit a pipe – a rare thing for him for he was not a great smoker – and stabbed at the fire, which broke into a new blaze. It spat at him like Aunt Agatha. This was old fir; there was not much else on the estate except long elms and a few pines; not many trees would stand the wind. It was after all a God-forsaken place ever to have built a house. He supposed Geoffrey de Trenwith had made money out of metals even in those far-off days. Like the Godolphins, the Bassets, the Pendarves. They built near the mines that made them rich.

The first time he had seen Aunt Agatha was in this room more than thirty-five years ago. Francis had invited him from school to spend a night. Even then the old woman had been immensely old. Difficult to believe that she had survived everybody and lived long enough to poison the first years of his married life. Years later she had been sitting in that chair opposite him now – the very same chair – when he had come into this room to tell his father that Elizabeth had given birth to a son, born, prematurely, on the 14th February and so to be called Valentine. She had hissed at both of them like a snake, malevolent, resenting their presence in her family home, hating him for his satisfaction at being the father of a fine boy, trying even then with every ingenuity of her evil nature to discover a weak spot in their complacency through which she could insert some venom, some note of discord, some shabby, sour prediction. 'Born under a black moon,' she had said, because there had been a total eclipse at the time. 'Born under a black moon, and so he'll come to no good, this son of yours. They never do. I only knew two and they both came to bad ends!'

In that chair, opposite him now. Strange how a human envelope collapsed and decayed, yet an inanimate object with four legs carved and fashioned by a carpenter in James II's day could exist unchanged, untouched by the years. The sun did not get round to the great window for another hour yet, so it was shadowy in here, and the flickering cat-spitting fire created strange illusions. When the flame died one could see Agatha there still. That wreck of an old female, malodorous, the scrawny grey hair escaping from under the ill-adjusted wig, a bead of moisture oozing from eye and mouth, the gravestone teeth, the darting glance, the hand capped behind the ear. She might be there now. God damn her, she was more real to him at this moment than Elizabeth! But she was dead, had died at ninety-eight, he had at least prevented her from cheating the world about her birthday –

A footstep sounded, and all the nerves in his body started. Yet he contrived not to move, not to give way, not to accept . . .

He looked round and saw a fair tall girl standing in the room. She was wearing a white print frock caught at the

43

waist with a scarlet sash, and she was carrying a sheaf of foxgloves. She was clearly as surprised to see him as he was to see her.

In the silence the fire spat out a burning splinter of wood, but it fell and smoked unheeded on the floor.

'Who are you? What d'you *want*?' George spoke in a harsh voice he had seldom cause to use these days; people moved at his bidding quickly enough; but this apparition, this intrusion . . .

The girl said: 'I am sorry. I saw the door open and thought perhaps it had blown open.'

'What business is it of *yours*?'

She had a stillness about her, a composure that was not like excessive self-confidence – rather an unawareness of anything untoward or wrong.

'Oh, I come here sometimes,' she said. 'The foxgloves are handsome on the hedges just now. I've never seen the door open before.'

He got up. 'D'you know that you're *trespassing*?'

She came a few paces nearer and laid the flowers on the great dining table, brushed a few leaves and spattering of pollen from her frock.

'Are you Sir George Warleggan?' she asked.

Her accent showed she was not a village girl and a terrible suspicion grew in his mind.

'What is your name?'

'Mine?' She smiled. 'I'm Clowance Poldark.'

II

When Clowance returned to Nampara everyone was out. The front door was open, and she went in and whistled three clear notes: D, B^b, A, then ran half up the stairs and whistled again. When there was no response she carried her foxgloves through the kitchen into the backyard beyond, filled a pail at the pump where twenty-six years before her mother had been swilled when brought to this house, a starveling brat from Illuggan, and thrust the flowers into the water so that they should not wilt before that same lady came in and had time to arrange them. Then she went in search.

It was a lovely afternoon and Clowance was too young to feel the chill of the wind. Spring had been late and dry, and they were haymaking in the Long Field behind the house. She saw a group standing half way up the field and recognized her mother's dark head and dove-grey frock among them. It was refreshment-time, and Demelza had helped Jane Gimlett carry up the cloam pitcher and the mugs. The workers had downed tools and were gathered round Mistress Poldark while she tipped the pitcher and filled each mug with ale. There were eight of them altogether: Moses Vigus, Dick Trevail (Jack Cobbledick's illegitimate son by Nancy Trevail), Cal Trevail (Nancy's legitimate son), Matthew Martin, Ern Lobb, 'Tiny' Small, Sephus Billing and Nat Triggs. They were all laughing at something Demelza had said as Clowance came up. They smiled and grinned and nodded sweatily at the daughter of the house, who smiled back at them.

'Mug of ale, Miss Clowance?' Jane Gimlett asked. 'There's a spare one if you've the mind.'

Clowance had the mind, and they talked in a group until one after another the men turned reluctantly away to take up their scythes again. Last to move was Matthew Martin, who always lingered when Clowance was about. Then mother and daughter began to stroll back towards the house, Clowance with the mugs, Jane bringing up the rear at a discreet distance with the empty pitcher.

'No shoes again, I see,' said Demelza.

'No, love. It's summer.'

'You'll get things in your feet.'

'They'll come out. They always do.'

It was a small bone of contention. To Demelza, who had never *had* shoes until she was fourteen, there was some loss of social status in being barefoot. To Clowance, born into a

45

gentleman's home, there was a pleasurable freedom in kicking them off, even at sixteen.

'Where is everybody?'

'Jeremy's out with Paul and Ben.'

'Not back yet?'

'I expect the fish are not biting. And if you look over your left shoulder you'll see Mrs Kemp coming off the beach with Bella and Sophie.'

'Ah yes. And Papa?'

'He should be back any time.'

'Was it a bank meeting?'

'Yes.'

They strolled on in silence, and when they reached the gate they leaned over it together waiting for Mrs Kemp and her charges to arrive. The wind ruffled their hair and lifted their frocks.

It was a little surprising that two such dark people as Ross and his wife had bred anyone so unquestionably blonde as Clowance. But she had been so born and showed no signs of darkening with maturity. As a child she had always been fat, and it was only during the last year or so since she had left Mrs Gratton's School for Young Ladies that she had begun to fine off and to grow into good looks. Even so, her face was still broad across the forehead. Her mouth was firm and finely shaped and feminine, her eyes grey and frank to a degree that was not totally becoming in a young lady of her time. She could grow quickly bored and as quickly interested. Twice she had run away from boarding-school – not because she particularly disliked it but because there were more engaging things to do at home. She greeted every incident as it came and treated it on its merits, without fear or hesitation. Clowance, Demelza said to Ross, had a face that reminded her of a newly opened ox-eye daisy, and she dearly hoped it would never get spotted with the rain.

As for Demelza herself, her approximate fortieth birthday had just come and gone, and she was trying, so far with some success, to keep her mind off the chimney corner. For a 'vulgar', as the Reverend Osborne Whitworth had called her, she had worn well, better than many of her more high-bred contemporaries. It was partly a matter of bone structure, partly a matter of temperament. There were some fine lines on her face that had not been there fifteen years ago, but as these were mainly smile lines and as her expression tended usually to the amiable they scarcely showed. Her hair wanted to go grey at the temples but, unknown to Ross, who said he detested hair dyes, she had bought a little bottle of something from Mr Irby of St Ann's and surreptitiously touched it up once a week after she washed it.

The only time she looked and felt her age, and more than it, was when she had one of her headaches, which usually occurred monthly just before her menstrual period. During the twenty-six days of good health she steadily put on weight, and during the two days of the megrim she lost it all, so a status quo was preserved.

In the distance Bella recognized her mother and sister and waved, and they waved back.

Clowance said: 'Mama, why do Jeremy and his friends go out fishing so much and never catch any fish?'

'But they do, my handsome. We eat it regularly.'

'But not enough. They go out after breakfast and come back for supper, and their haul is what you or I in a row-boat could cull in a couple of hours!'

'They are not very diligent, any of them. Perhaps they just sit in the sun and dream the day away.'

'Perhaps. I asked him once but he said there was a scarcity round the coast this year.'

'And might that not be true?'

'Only that the Sawle men don't seem to find it so.'

They strolled on a few paces.

'At any rate,' said Clowance, 'I've picked you some handsome foxgloves.'

'Thank you. Did you call at the Enyses?'

'No . . . But I did meet a friend of yours, Mama.'

Demelza smiled. 'That covers a deal of ground. But d'you really mean a friend?'

'Why?'

'Something the way you used the word.'

Clowance brushed a flying ant off her frock. 'It was Sir George Warleggan.'

She carefully did not look at her mother after she had spoken, but she was aware of the stillness beside her.

Demelza said: 'Where?'

'At Trenwith. It was the first time ever I saw the front door open, so in I went to look in – and *there* he was in the big hall, sitting in front of a smoky fire with a pipe in his hand that had gone out and as sour an expression as if he had been eating rigs.'

'Did he see you?'

'Oh *yes*. We spoke! We talked! We conversed! He asked me what damned business I had there and I told him.'

'Told him what?'

'That he has the best foxgloves in the district, especially the pale pink ones growing on the hedge by the pond.'

Demelza flattened her hair with a hand, but the wind quickly clutched it away again. 'And then?'

'Then he was very rude with me. Said I was trespassing and should be prosecuted. That he would call his men and have me taken to the gates. Said this and that, in a rare temper.'

Demelza glanced at her daughter. The girl showed no signs of being upset.

'Why did you *go* there, Clowance? We've told you not to. It is inviting trouble.'

'Well, I didn't *expect* to meet *him*! But it doesn't matter. There's no harm done. I reasoned with him.'

'You mean you answered him back?'

'Not angry, of course. Very dignified, I was. Very proper. I just said it all seemed a pity, him having to be rude to a neighbour – and a sort of cousin.'

48

'And what did he say to that?'

'He said I was no cousin, no cousin of *his* at all, that I didn't know what I was talking about and I'd better go before he called the Harry brothers to throw me out.'

Mrs Kemp was now approaching. Bella and Sophie were making the better pace on the home stretch and were some fifty yards in front.

Demelza said: 'Don't tell your father you've been to Trenwith. You know what he said last time.'

'Of course not. I wouldn't worry him. But I didn't think it would worry you.'

Demelza said: 'It isn't worry exactly, dear, it is – it is fishing in muddied streams that I hate. I can't begin to explain – to tell you everything that made your father and George Warleggan enemies, nor all that happened to spread it so that the gap between us all became so great. You surely will have heard gossip . . .'

'Oh yes. That Papa and Elizabeth Warleggan were in love when they were young. Is that very terrible?'

Demelza half scowled at her daughter, and then changed her mind and laughed.

'Put that way, no . . . But in a sense it continued all their lives. That – did not help, you'll understand. But –'

'Yet I'm sure it was not like you and Papa at *all*. Yours is something special. I shall never be lucky enough to get a man like him; and of course I shall never be able to be like *you* . . .'

Bella Poldark, slight and dark and pretty, came dancing and prattling up with a story of something, a dead fish or something, large and white and smelly they had found near the Wheal Leisure adit. She had wanted to tug it home but Mrs Kemp would not let her. Sophie Enys, a year younger and outdistanced on the last lap, soon contributed her account. Demelza bent over talking to them, glad of the opportunity to wipe something moist out of her sight. Compliments from one's children were always the most difficult to take unemotionally, and compliments from the ever candid Clowance were rare enough to be specially noted. When Mrs Kemp joined them they all walked back to the house, Jane Gimlett having preceded them to put on tea and cakes for the little girls.

The eager flood that had caught up with Clowance and her mother now washed past them and left them behind, in the enticing prospect of food, so the two women followed on. They were exactly of a height, and as they walked the wind, blowing from behind them, ruffled their hair like the soft tail feathers of eider ducks.

Demelza said: 'Then you were allowed to leave Trenwith unmolested?'

'Oh yes. We did not part so bad in the end. I left him some of my foxgloves.'

'You – left George? You left George some foxgloves?'

'He didn't want to have them. He said they could wilt on the damned floor of the damned hall, for all he cared, so I found an old vase and filled it with water and put them on that table. What a great table it is! I never remember seeing it before! I believe it will be still there when the house falls down.'

'And did he – allow you to do this?'

'Well, he didn't forcibly stop me. Though he snarled once or twice, like a fradgy dog. But I believe his bark may be worse than his bite.'

'Do not rely on that,' said Demelza.

'So after I had arranged them – though I still cannot do it so well as you – after that I gave him a civil good afternoon.'

'And did you get another snarl?'

'No. He just glowered at me. Then he asked me my name again. So I told him.'

Chapter Four

I

It was said of William Wyndham, first Baron Grenville, that one of the flaws in his distinguished parliamentary career was his passion for Boconnoc, his eight-thousand-acre estate in Cornwall. Bought by William Pitt's grandfather with part of the proceeds of the great Pitt diamond, it had come to Grenville by way of his marriage to Anne Pitt, Lord Camelford's daughter.

A man of austere and aristocratic tastes, a man not above lecturing many people, not excluding the Royal Family, on their responsibilities and duties, he was wont to ignore his own once he was two hundred and fifty miles from Westminster and settled in his mansion overlooking the great wooded park, with his own property stretching as far as the most long-sighted eye could see.

It was here, not in Westminster, that George Warleggan had first met him. Sir Christopher Hawkins, who had been a good friend to George as well as making money out of him, had represented to Lord Grenville that if his Lordship needed another spare man in addition to himself for the banquet held at Boconnoc to celebrate Trafalgar, the member for St Michael, who had been a knight for five years and was of influence in the Truro district, might make a suitable guest. George had accepted the invitation with surprise and alacrity. It was just about the period when he was beginning to emerge from the long shadow cast by Elizabeth's death and when his personal ambition was stirring again.

No one, not even George himself, would have claimed that in the succeeding five years he had become an intimate of Lord Grenville – becoming a close friend of Lord Grenville's was considerably more difficult than to become one of the Prince of Wales – but he was accepted as an occasional guest in the great house. And they met at Westminster from from time to time. Grenville acknowledged him as a useful supporter and a neighbouring Cornishman. Bereft of his helpmeet, George had done little personal entertaining, but in the summer of 1809 he had given a big party at Cardew and had invited Lord and Lady Grenville. Grenville had refused, but it was a note written in his own hand.

It was the following year, a month after George's annual pilgrimage to Trenwith and about a month before Ross had yielded to pressure and accepted the invitation to go to Portugal, that the Grenvilles invited George to a reception and dinner at their house, and it was on this occasion that he first met Lady Harriet Carter. They sat next to each other at dinner, and George was attracted, partly physically, partly by a sense of the unfamiliar.

She was dark – as night dark as Elizabeth had been day fair – and not pretty, but her face had the classic bone structure that George always admired. Her raven hair had a gloss like japan leather; she had remarkably fine eyes. She was dressed in that elegant good taste that he recognized as the hall-mark of women like his first wife.

One would have thought it unlikely to meet anyone at Lord Grenville's table who was not socially acceptable, but sometimes, in his seignorial role as one of the largest private landlords in the county, his Lordship thought it meet to include among his guests a few local bigwigs (and their wives) who in George's opinion were not big at all. This was clearly not such a one.

Conversation at the table for a time was concerned with riots in the north of England, the depreciation of the currency and the scandal of the Duke of Cumberland; but presently his partner wearied of this and turned to him and said:

'Tell me, Sir George, where do you live?'

'Some thirty miles to the west, ma'am. At Cardew. Between Truro and Falmouth.'

'Good hunting country?'

'I've heard it so described.'

'But you don't hunt yourself?'

'I've little time.'

She laughed – very low. 'What else is more important?'

George inclined his head towards his host. 'The affairs of the kingdom.'

'And you are concerned with those?'

'Among other things.'

'What other things?'

He hesitated, a little nettled that she knew nothing about him. 'Affairs of the county. You do not live in Cornwall, ma'am?'

'I live at Hatherleigh. Just over the border – in England.'

They talked a few minutes. Her voice was husky and she had an attractive laugh, which was almost all breath – low, indolent and sophisticated. You felt there wasn't much she didn't know about life – and didn't tolerate. He found himself glancing at her low-cut gown and thinking her breasts were like warm ivory. It was an unusual thought for him.

As another course was served a man called Gratton leaned across the table and boomed at him: 'I say, Warleggan, what sort of stand do you take on Catholic Emancipation? I've never heard you speak about it in the House!'

'I speak little in the House,' George replied coldly. 'I leave oratory to the orators. There are other ways of being valuable.'

'Yes, old man, but you must have an opinion! Everyone has, one way or t'other. How d'you vote?'

It was a ticklish question, for, on this as on so many other domestic subjects, George differed from his host and was at pains to hide it for the sake of his personal good. Gratton was a ninny anyhow and deserved to be taken down. But George was not quick-witted, and he was aware that Lady Harriet was listening.

'To tell the truth, Gratton, it is not a subject on which I have extravagant feelings, so I vote with my friends.'

'And who are your friends?'

'In this company,' said George, 'need you ask?'

Gratton considered the plate of venison that had just been put before him. He helped himself to the sweet sauce and the gravy. 'I must say, old man, that that's a very unsatisfactory answer, since it's a subject on which governments have fallen before now!'

'And will again, no doubt,' said Gratton's partner. 'Or will fail to stand up in the first place!'

'Mr Gratton,' said Lady Harriet, 'what would you say to emancipating the Wesleyans for a change? Now the Prince of Wales has taken up with Lady Hertford I suspicion we shall all be psalm-singing before long.'

There was a laugh, and talk turned to bawdy speculation as to the nature of the Prince's relationship with his new favourite.

Lady Harriet said to George in a low voice: 'I take it, Sir George, that your fondness for the Catholics is not so great as that of my Lord Grenville?'

He had appreciated her turning the subject and suspected it had been deliberate.

'Personally, ma'am, I care little one way or the other, since religious belief does not loom large in my life. But for the preference I'd keep them out of Parliament and public service. They've bred traitors enough in the past.'

As soon as he had spoken he regretted his frankness and was astonished at his own indiscretion. To say such a thing in this company was folly indeed if he wished, as he did, to remain on the Grenville political stage-coach. He cursed himself and cursed this woman for provoking him into speaking the truth.

He added coldly: 'No doubt I offend you, but I trust you will look on this as a personal confidence.'

'Indeed,' she said, 'you do not offend me. And in return I will give you a little confidence of my own. I hate all Catholics, every last one. And William, I fear, knows it.'

William was Lord Grenville.

All things considered, George found he had enjoyed his dinner more than any for a long time. It was as if he had put on the spectacles he now used for reading and looked through them onto a more brightly coloured world. It was disconcerting, but far from disagreeable. He distrusted the sensation.

Ah well, he told himself, it would all soon be forgot. There were many soberer matters to be attended to. But a few days later, rather to his own surprise, and having thought all round it a number of times, he put a few discreet inquiries in train. There certainly could be nothing lost by knowing more on the subject. It could be, he told himself, an interesting inquiry without in any way becoming an interested one.

So came some information and some rumour. She had been born Harriet Osborne and was a sister of the sixth Duke of Leeds. She was about twenty-nine and a widow. Her husband had been Sir Toby Carter, who had estates in Leicestershire and in north Devon. He had been a notorious rake and gambler who had broken his neck in the hunting field and had died hock deep in debt. He had even squandered the money his wife brought him, so the Leicestershire estate had had to be sold and she was now in possession of a part bankrupt property in Devon, her only income coming from an allowance made her by the Duke. There were no children of the marriage.

This far information went. Rumour said that husband and wife had not hit it off, that she was as mad on hunting as he and that he had locked her in her room two days a week to prevent her riding to hounds too often. There were other unsavoury whispers, most, it must be admitted, about Sir Toby.

All this was quite sufficient to put a man like George right off. The *last* thing he wanted was a turbulent married life; if for one moment he now thought re-marriage an acceptable, or at least contemplatable, estate, there were twenty pretty and docile girls who would fall over themselves for the chance. To take a dark and aristocratic widow with a slightly sinister history . . .

In any case, he told himself, writing the subject out of his own mind, he would never gain the Duke's permission for, or acceptance of, such a marriage. The Warleggan name might make the earth shake in Cornwall, but it counted for little in such company as Lady Harriet frequented. Her father, he discovered, had been Lord Chamberlain of the Queen's Household. It was a dazzling circle to which she belonged. Too dazzling.

But that was half the temptation.

The other half was in the woman herself, and here George found it difficult to understand his own feelings. Once or twice in the night he woke up and blamed his encounter with Clowance Poldark.

By every rightful instinct he should have detested that girl on sight. Indeed he did, formally and overtly. He had been as rude to her as he knew how, and she had taken absolutely no notice. He had glared at this daughter of the two people he disliked most in the world and had vented his spleen on her. But at the same time some more primal and subconscious urge had found her physically, startlingly, sexually, ravishing. This had only made its way through to his conscious mind later, when the image of her plagued him, that image of her standing before him in the gaunt dark hall, barefoot, in her white frock, the sheaf of stolen foxgloves on her arm, the candid grey gaze fixed on him with unoffended, innocent interest. Of course in his wildest moments – if he had any – he had *no* sort of thought of her for himself, no thought of there *ever* being anything between them except the bitterest family enmity. Yet the impression of her youth, her freshness, her ripe innocence, her sexual attraction, had wakened something in him that made him think differently from that day on. The years of austerity no longer seemed justifiable. There was something more to life than the scrutiny of balance sheets and the exercise of mercantile and political power. There was a woman – there were women – women everywhere – with all that that meant in terms of instability, unreliability, anxiety, jealousy, conquest, success and failure, and the sheer excitement of being alive. The memories of his life with Elizabeth came seeping back, no longer tainted with the anger and dismay of loss. Unknown to himself he had been lonely. His encounter with Harriet Carter came at an appropriate time.

For a while still, and naturally, as befitted so cautious a man, he did absolutely nothing. He was not quite sure how he should proceed even if he ever decided to make a move. A widow was not a spinster. She was more her own mistress. Yet it seemed improbable that she would agree to any union without the full consent of her family. And it was not likely that that would be immediately forthcoming.

And yet. And yet. To be married to the sister of a duke! And money was not sneezed at even in the great houses. If she were truly as poor as his reports told him, the Duke might be glad to get her off his hands. A lot depended on the approach. In any event *he* did not wish to play his cards too soon. How could one judge of a single meeting? How contrive other meetings without declaring one's interest too obviously? At length he took his problem to his old friend Sir Christopher Hawkins.

Sir Christopher laughed. 'Before heaven, there's nothing easier, my dear fellow. She is at present staying with her aunt at Godolphin. I'll ask 'em over for a night and you can dine and sup with us.'

So they met a second time, and although there was a

numerous company there was opportunity for conversation, and Lady Harriet soon received the message. It made a difference to her. Her brilliant dark eyes became a little absent-minded as if her thoughts were already idly turning over all the implications of his presence. She talked to him politely but with a slight irony that made him uncomfortable. Yet she was not unfriendly, as she surely must have been if she had decided at once that his suit was impossible.

· Her aunt, a pale tiny woman who looked as if the leeches had been at her, also received the message, and to her the message was clearly distasteful. The Osborne family of course had considerable property in Cornwall, and it could have been that Miss Darcy knew him and his history too well.

So the second meeting ended inconclusively. But it was not one of total discouragement. And a hint of opposition always braced George whether he was trying to gain possession of a woman or a tin mine.

Business took him to Manchester in September, and he was gone a month. He had only been north of Bath once before, when he visited Liverpool and some of the mill towns in 1808. These new mushroom towns of Lancashire excited him with their belching chimneys, their seething, smoky streets, the crowds of grey-faced cheerful workers tramping over the greasy cobbles into the mills and factories. Here was money being made, in new ways. Factories, new factories, were springing up everywhere, employing twenty workers in one place, a thousand in another, and with every variation in between. The vitality of a place like Manchester was attracting the most enterprising of the working orders, who came in from town and countryside hoping by hard work, intelligence and thrift to become one of the employers instead of one of the employed. A few succeeded – enough to inspire the others – and when they did so succeed climbed virtually from rags to riches in a half-dozen years. It was an inspiring sight, and George did not much notice, or at least was not affected by, the other side of the picture. The horrible conditions in which most of the millhands both lived and worked was a natural by-product of industry and progress; it literally was part of the machinery, the human element which drove and operated the looms, the bobbins, the spindles, the flying threads, the warp and woof of cotton manufacture which created riches where none had ever been before.

He knew, of course, that half the labour force was under eighteen years of age, that Irish parents sold their children to the mills, and that the workhouses of England disposed of their pauper children in the same way, that many children of ten years old and less had to work sixteen hours a day. Several of his more sentimental Whig colleagues, such as Whitbread, Sheridan and Brougham, had made speeches on the subject in Parliament and created a great fuss about it, so he could hardly be in ignorance of the statistics. But while he regretted them in principle he accepted them in practice and saw no way of altering a situation which industry had created out of its own dynamic.

However, on his second visit he saw more, could not fail to see more, of the poverty and distress which his colleagues talked about and which had led to protest meetings and riots in the new towns. And now it was not just the distress of the exploited, it was the distress of the manufacturers themselves, faced with over-production and the closure of the European markets by the new edict of Napoleon, which had almost put a stop even to the smuggling in of manufactured goods via Heligoland and the Mediterranean ports. Many of the mill-chimneys no longer smoked, and a worse hunger than ever before stalked the towns. Beggars and child prostitutes infested the streets.

George stayed with a man called John Outram, who represented a pocket borough in Wiltshire but who had property in the north. Outram was convinced that only peace with France would save the manufacturing interests from disaster. But this, it seemed, was as far away as ever. The obstinate, pedestrian group of Tories who ran the country, and who were supported not only by the King but by the sentiment of much of the country itself, would not negotiate yet again with the great Corsican. They persisted in the delusion that somehow, if they held on long enough like a battered old bulldog with its teeth locked, they could defeat him – or he would defeat himself – or he would die – or some other piece of good fortune would occur to get them out of the mess they were in. In the meantime a quarter of manufacturing England starved.

Outram said if only one could see peace in a year there were outstanding pickings to be had in Manchester at this time. A dozen big firms he knew personally were on the verge of bankruptcy. Five had already crashed – and that of course was not counting the plight and the fate of many of the small ones. A hundred thousand pounds laid out now would be worth a million next year – if there were only peace. But what chance *was* there?

George licked his lips. 'If the King were to die . . .'

'Ah, Prinny would change it all, I know. He's committed to turning these nonentities out of office. We'd have a negotiated peace in six months. But there's little real chance of that. The King is seventy-three, but they say he's as vigorous and hearty as a man of fifty. Perhaps more vigorous, if the truth be told, than his eldest son!'

'It comes of living a better life,' said George coldly.

'I've no doubt,' said Outram, looking sidelong at his friend. 'I've no doubt. Though personally, over the years, I wouldn't have minded being in Prinny's shoes. You must admit he's had the pick of the crop in every field! Ha! Ha!'

While he was in the north George took time to examine some of the opportunities that existed. He hadn't the least intention of investing any of his money in this area while the future remained so unpredictable, but it gave him pleasure to see some of the businesses and properties which, if not already officially on the market, could be picked up cheap one way or another at this time. It interested his keen brain to see how mills and factories operated, how they balanced the price of their goods against their operating costs, how much of those costs went on the human factor of wages, how much on the machines they worked. It stimulated him to consider in what ways he could have improved on the organization; and sometimes the primitive book-keeping amused him. It would have shocked Cary.

Each time he thanked the anxious owners for their time and trouble and said he would consider the matter and write later. Of course he never wrote. But in the bow-window of his sunny, autumnal bedroom in Knutsford, he made careful notes of what he had seen, and filed away for future reference all the information he had been given. One never knew when such things would come in useful.

He returned to Truro on the evening that Ross Poldark met his cousin's son on the wooded hills behind the convent of Bussaco.

II

Among the later acquisitions to George's personal coterie was a man called Hector Trembath, the notary who eleven years before had picked up the pieces of Mr Nathaniel Pearce's ruined practice and tried to put it together again. This had not been easy, for when there has been fraud and dishonesty in a firm, clients shy away even though the owner of the practice is quite new. George, seeing in the young man a useful ally and if necessary tool, had befriended him and helped to set him on his feet. As a result Trembath was altogether George's man. In appearance he was tall and slim, with a lisp and a mincing walk that made some people think he was not entitled to the wife and two children he claimed. Being of a good education and gentlemanly appearance, he could go into company where such men as Garth and Tankard, George's factors, would have been out of place. And he was never reluctant to undertake errands of inquiry or negotiation. It was he who had reported on Lady Harriet Carter.

He waited on George on the morning following George's return and reported further. It appeared that Lady Harriet had returned home to Hatherleigh, and there was going to be a sale of both stock and farm, including her husband's horses and her own. It was to take place the following week. When George expressed doubt as to the likelihood of this tale, Trembath produced the advertisement in the newspaper and the notice of sale.

George said: 'But this is taking place under a writ of *Fi-Fa*. That means – well, of course you know what it means!'

'A forced sale, Sir George. On the direction of the sheriff. It means everything must go.'

George turned the money in his fob. The feel of gold coins between his fingers was always pleasurable. 'I can scarce believe that the Duke would permit such a thing! His own sister! It's monstrous.'

'It may be, Sir George, that she has refused help. That is what I gathered.'

'From whom?'

'I chanced to get acquainted with her farm manager . . .'

Trembath looked up coyly, and George nodded his approval.

'. . . who says that Sir Toby Carter's debts were so horrific that nothing can be saved. The worst has only become known since the Leicestershire estate was sold. I think it is her Ladyship's wish to accept help from no one until the whole debt – or as much as possible – is liquidated.'

George was reading the sale notices. 'But some of her own possessions are listed here. At least, they must be hers . . .'

'I think she is' Trembath coughed 'liquidating the memories also, as you might say.'

George said: 'These horses. "Tobago, Centurion, Lombardy, the property of Sir Toby Carter. Dundee, Abbess, Carola, the property of Lady Harriet Carter. Dundee the prize-winning steeplechaser of sixteen hands, eight years old, in superb condition, one of the finest hunters ever bred in Devon . . ." What is a steeplechase?'

'It's a form of obstacle race,' said Trembath. 'Over hedges, streams, gates, etcetera, always keeping the church steeple in view. I confess I should not have known myself if I had not asked. It is become fashionable in Devon and –'

'Yes, yes,' said George. He went to the window, hands behind back, and viewed the scene. Below, a handcart was being dragged over the cobbles by two gypsy women and followed by some mangy dogs. Two things George very much disliked were gypsies and dogs. He would gladly have whipped the former out of town and hung the latter in the nearest barn. He did not mind horses. In a detached way he was fond of them, since they provided the only means of transport on land, apart from one's own legs. He liked their powerful, muscular quarters, their warm animal smell, the readiness with which they allowed themselves to be utilized by man. He wondered idly if Harriet Carter were over-fond of dogs as well as of horses. It was a horribly common complaint among the landed gentry. Perhaps it was the commonest complaint of all English folk.

He was aware that young Trembath was still talking. He was sometimes inclined to prattle. At thirty-eight he should have grown out of the habit. 'What's that you say?'

Trembath recoiled a little. 'Er – Walter, the farm manager, said Lady Harriet was very put about, whether to allow Dundee to go. She was much distressed, but in the end thought it the only thing to do. They say he'll fetch a pretty penny.'

'How much?'

Trembath looked startled. 'Sir?'

'How much would it cost? Have you any idea?'

'The horse, sir? I have no idea. It will be at auction, of course. The price will depend upon how many people bid for him.'

'That I do happen to know. But, let me see, when did I buy a horse last? That should give one some idea.'

'I think, Mr Warleggan, that this is likely to be a special price.'

'Well, let it be a special price. And do you – does your friend know what will happen, what Lady Harriet's intentions are once the property is sold?'

'No, Sir George. Would you like me to inquire?'

'Discreetly, yes. Tell me, when there is a sale of this sort – under a sheriff's writ – will the vendor be present at the sale?'

'Oh, I think that is a matter of personal choice, as you might say. I was at a sale in Tresillian last year, of this nature, sir, of this nature, and the vendor stood beside the auctioneer all day. But in the case of a lady of delicate sensibilities . . .'

'Well,' George said, 'we shall see.'

III

The sale took place on Tuesday the 2nd October. No reserves were placed on any of the items, and as a consequence many of them went very cheaply indeed. Not so, however, Dundee, who fetched one hundred and fifty guineas. A thin, effeminate, youngish man who gave his name as Smith, was the buyer. Lady Harriet Carter appeared briefly for the sale of the horses but was not visible during the rest of the day. Sir George Warleggan, of course, was not present.

Until the estate was finally settled, William Frederick Osborne had offered his sister a dower house near Helston called Polwendron, and had suggested that when Harriet chose to live in London, as he trusted she would now do most of the time, she should live at 68, Lower Grosvenor Street, which he shared with his mother. Harriet thanked him and moved to Polwendron. She had no particular fancy for the West Country, she wrote, the hunting was not good enough, but William should know she was none too taken with London life either, where the only grass to be seen grew among sooty cobbles and too many of the smells were man-made.

In mid-October a groom arrived at Polwendron leading a black horse and delivered it to the house, with a note.

The note ran:

Dear Lady Harriet,

It came to my Notice through a mutual acquaintance that in painful Circumstances to which we need not refer again you were yourself recently parted from a Friend. This, I am sure, caused distress on both sides, and in recollection and in commemoration of our several delightful Meetings, I am endeavouring to repair that distress by returning your Friend to you. I think you will find he has been well cared for and is in good health. I have not rid him myself for fear of finding myself unwittingly involved in a Steeplechase, which is an occupation on which I as yet lack instruction.

I have the honour to be, dear Lady Harriet,
Your most humble and obedient servant,
George Warleggan.

It was a letter on which George had spent the best part of a day, destroying one draft after another. In the end he flattered himself it was exactly right. Only at the very last moment had a stirring of humour induced him to add the last sentence. Now he felt the letter would not have been half as effective without it.

The groom came back empty-handed. Lady Harriet was not at home. But the following afternoon a ragged young person without livery of any sort brought a reply.

Dear Sir George,

When I returned home yesterday eve Dundee was cropping the grass on my front lawn. Having read your letter, I do not know whether to be more overcome by your splendid Generosity or by your quite improper Presumption. Regarding the former, I must confess that my reunion with my hunter was of a touching nature which could not have left a dry eye, had there been an eye to see. Regarding the latter, my over-impulsive decision to sell Dundee was largely inspired by a wish to put behind me certain unpleasant Memories which this horse will always invoke – more so, certainly, than by any conscientious or earnest wish to see my husband's Creditors utterly satisfied.

However, since your act can only have been inspired by kindness of heart, and since I regretted the sale as soon as it had gone through, I am indebted to you, Sir George, for enabling me to recover my best Hunter in such an agreeable and untedious way. My indebtedness, naturally, can only be Moral, and not Financial, and I am accordingly enclosing my Draft on Messrs Coode's Bank of Penzance for one hundred and fifty guineas. Should you have had to pay more than this from the anaemic, prating fellow who bought it at the auction, pray tell me the amount and I will reimburse you further.

Again thanking you, I am, Sir George,
Yours etc.
Harriet Carter.

George read the letter almost as often as he had drafted his original note. After leaving it a day he wrote back.

Dear Lady Harriet,

I am happy to have your letter of the 19th and to learn from it that, even though I may have been presumptuous in returning your horse without your prior permission and consent, yet that I did not err in supposing this reunion to be something you desired in your Heart. Indeed it is a compliment to me to know that I estimated your feelings rightly.

But, since this was intended as a Gift – a light Gift and to be treated lightly but not to be rejected – I am distressed that you should deplete my pleasure by more than the half in introducing the question of *Payment*. If it is more blessed to give than to receive, then I do not think you should take away from me the greater part of the beatitude. I venture to return your Draft, and have the honour to subscribe myself, madam.

Your humble and obedient servant,
George Warleggan.

There was a week's delay, then a note came back.

Dear Sir George,
Did I not in my first letter speak of your improper presumption? – the cause of the offence lying in the greatness of the Gift: from a gentleman to a lady of the briefest Acquaintance. How much more improper, therefore, would it be for the lady to connive at such presumption. I am therefore returning the Draft to you again, and beg of you, if you value that little friendship we have so far achieved, not to return it a second time.

Riding Dundee yesterday, it seemed to me that the change of Ownership, brief though it had been, and his sudden and unexpected return to me, had in part at least purged out association of its ugly memories, and that my obligation to you was therefore the More. So let it be. The thought is all.

I am, sir, yours etc.
Harriet Carter.

George waited a few days. He made no attempt to pay in the draft, and had no intention of doing so – at present. But it did cross his mind that this way he might hedge his bets and, as it were, get the best of both worlds.

Eventually he wrote again:

Dear Lady Harriet,

So let it be. The thought is all. But since the *greatness* of my presumption lies in the smallness of our Acquaintanceship, might not the error be atoned for in some part by a resumption of that Acquaintance, thereby reducing by each meeting some of my offence? In such a way Acquaintanceship may become Friendship, and, as we are now neighbours – or would be in a county of larger estates – this is surely no more than a natural progression? Would you permit me to call?

I am, dear Lady Harriet,
Your humble servant and admirer,
George Warleggan.

George read this through many times before he sent it. He thought: what phrasing; how I have progressed! Twenty years ago I would not have *known* how to *begin*! Ten years ago, with all the culture that Elizabeth brought, I could not have done it. But there it is; evidence of maturity, a growing elegance of thought; a blacksmith's grandson has become a courtier! Even Lady Harriet's friends could not have done better than that.

At length he sent it off, reluctant to part with it to the last. As the groom clattered away on his fifteen-mile ride, Cary Warleggan came into the parlour with news just received from London that the King had gone mad.

Chapter Five

I

On the 10th of November Demelza had just finished making her weekly saffron cakes and was wondering how long it would be before Ross was home to taste them. In all their years together he had so far only been absent from home once at Christmas. In 1807 he had travelled with the Earl of Pembroke on a special mission to the Austrians. He had not in fact ever got to Vienna, having been sent flying home from Copenhagen to report that France was intent on forcing Denmark into war with England. But then, no sooner was he in London than he was despatched again to Portugal as part of a mission to try to encourage the Royal Family to leave Lisbon and seek safety in Brazil.

That Demelza had not minded so much. She had heard he was safe back in London and knew precisely what the second mission was – in any event it was an honour to be so chosen and the dangers did not appear too great. But this latest invitation had reached him in Cornwall, and although he did not go into details his attitude showed that it was of a more secret and risky nature, and of such a kind that he was a little dubious about taking it on. However he had gone, and apart from a letter telling her of his arrival in London, nothing since. She presumed he was still in Portugal. There had come news recently of a British victory there – but followed by a continued withdrawal from the country recently liberated. It was all very confusing. And disquieting.

Of course Ross was a noncombatant, a civilian, a visitor, someone whose business it was to observe, not fight. But in battle the dividing line tended to get blurred. In any event she knew too well that it was not in Ross's nature to steer clear of conflict if he happened to become accidentally – and patriotically – involved.

So what it amounted to was this: at *any* time, at *any* moment in *any* day, while she was in the still-room rearranging the jars, while she was decorating the raisin cake, while she was scolding Isabella-Rose for getting into a temper, while she was rubbing her teeth with a mallow root to clean them – at *any* of these moments Ross might be dying of wounds on some dusty hillside in Portugal, sick of a fever in a hospital and unable to hold a pen, just safely returned to London and writing to her now, or jogging on a coach between St Austell and Truro on the very last stage of his journey home.

It was necessary to continue to live every hour as it came, prosaically, steadily, concentrating on domestic things, life in the house, at the mine, in the villages, arranging and preparing meals, seeing that there was enough ale, ordering coal and wood against the coming winter – and, as the lady of the manor, so to speak – being available to listen to complaints, resolve little difficulties, help the needy, be a sort of nucleus for the Christmas preparations whether in the church or the surrounding countryside.

And, if a horse clattered unexpectedly over the cobbles, it was really rather stupid to let one's heart lurch in sudden expectation.

The 10th November was a quiet, heavy day, and Jeremy had gone fishing again with Paul Kellow and Ben Carter. In the winter, instead of staying out till supper-time, they usually returned at dusk, so Demelza decided she would take a stroll down to the cove in the hope of meeting them as they returned.

It was only a month now from the eleventh anniversary of Elizabeth's death, and to Demelza the time had flown. Indeed, stretching it a bit further, it seemed no time at all since, in the darkest period of their married poverty, she had walked down to the cove and gone out fishing while heavily pregnant with Jeremy, and had nearly lost him and herself as well. Now *he* was out fishing, tall, slender, nineteen years old, elusive, artistic, not taking life seriously, a harder person altogether to understand than Clowance.

The first decade of the century had been a good one, her relationship with Ross back to the early days, warm and full of laughter, intermittently passionate, always friendly. Into that sort of companionship they had been able to draw their two eldest children so that, in spite of occasional disagreements, the accord in the house, the outspokenness, and the unstressed affection was notable. Only lately perhaps, over the last year or so, had an element of unsympathy grown up between Ross and Jeremy.

Ross too, she thought, had been thoroughly happy – or at least as near happiness as so uneasy a man could well achieve. After the tragedy following her first visit to London, and after Elizabeth's death, he had wanted to give up his seat in Parliament. He had felt himself compromised by his duel with, and killing of, Monk Adderley. He had told Lord Falmouth that in any case he felt himself useless at Westminster, a place that was just a talking shop, where words were more important than deeds. Lord Falmouth had not taken his complaints too seriously, and when he got home she had added her arguments for his staying on.

It was the right decision, for soon afterwards opportunities for travel and unorthodox service to the Crown came along. It was not Lord Falmouth's doing but was the result of the impingement of his restless personality on his friends in Parliament. 'Why don't we send Poldark?' was a sentence that was heard more than once in Government circles over the next few years. To begin, he had been invited to take part in a mission to report on the conditions in which English troops lived in the West Indies. He was away six months. The following year he had gone abroad again, though this time only to Norway. So further missions had developed, of which this last to Portugal was the fifth.

It suited him well. Though passionately attached to Cornwall, and wanting in principle only to live there, to run his mine, to love his wife, to watch his children grow, the restless adventurous streak would not be stilled. Since most of the missions in a time of war involved some danger, this suited him too. And he felt his usefulness in the world.

He had made little money. But over the years they had continued sufficiently affluent to live a comfortable life. As he said to Demelza, the most important thing was to strike a balance: poverty and riches each in their own way caused unhappiness. With money, the way to be happy was to continue to have almost enough.

When she reached the shore there was no sign of the boat. A spot of rain fell on her hand, and the gulls screamed and nagged at her. A lump of cloud like a sack of potatoes hung over the sea. Then she saw, far out, twin sails low down on the horizon.

It was funny, she thought, complete ease, complete satisfaction was never much to be found. There had been many changes around them in the last few years, changes in the neighbourhood. Sir John Trevaunance had died, and Unwin Trevaunance, in the money at last, had lost no time in selling Place House. It had been bought by a rich merchant called Pope, who had made money in America, a thin pompous man with an insufferably high collar and a voice like a creaking hinge. After one sight of the new owner Jeremy had re-christened Place House, the Vatican.

Mr Pope was fifty-odd, with an attractive young second wife called Selina and two daughters by his first wife, Letitia and Maud. Letitia was plain and eighteen, Maud a year younger and pretty. All three women were ruled with an iron rod.

Dr Choake had died, and Polly Choake had moved back to Truro, where there was more life, and especially more whist. She had not sold Fernmore but had let it to some cousins of hers called Kellow. Charlie Kellow, the father, was associated with coach-building and with two of the new enterprises that were just beginning to run stage-coaches about the county, and was as much away as at home. Enid Kellow was a dark cramped woman with eyes that didn't focus, so that one was never sure what she was looking at. There were three children: Violet, fair and pretty and ill; Paul, handsome and slight and too mature for his nineteen years; and Daisy, dark and vivacious and amusing.

So, Demelza tried to tell herself, how lucky they were, now Jeremy and Clowance were growing up, that people had come into the district with new and young company, to give variety to Ruth Treneglos's children and the children of the miners and village folk. She told herself this without a great deal of conviction because she didn't feel that any of the newcomers were quite up to the standard of her own family.

This, no doubt, was a strange feeling in one who had lived the first fourteen years of her life in the extremest squalor. But no doubt it was a common emotion among all parents. (No one is ever good enough for *our* children.) These newcomers . . . well, the Popes were, even Ross agreed, pretentious; quite unlike the Trevaunances, the Bodrugans, the Trenegloses, who, whatever their faults, were natural and down to earth. *They* never cared a damn about impressing anybody, being totally convinced that their own behaviour was right.

As for the Kellows, there was an unhealthy streak. An older daughter, it seemed, had died of the consumption, and Violet was in a fair way to do the same. Daisy was charming but *hectic*; she seemed to want to live twice as fast as anyone else in case her life was half as long. And Paul was a little effeminate and greatly conceited with his own looks and opinions and he had too much influence over Jeremy.

They had only been in the house a year when Paul Kellow, then sixteen, had discovered an old mine shaft on the cliffs between Nampara and Trenwith which dropped sixty feet to a beach and a rocky inlet. (It was not far from the Seal Hole Cave of which Demelza still had wild dream memories.) Here, with the help of his father, he had built a ladder and nailed it to the side of the shaft so that there was access to the inlet at all tides. It was known already, and it would for ever more be known, as Kellow's Ladder, and here Paul kept his own boat – an old-style lugger that his father had picked up for him fifth hand from St Ives, and which he used for less respectable ventures to Ireland or France.

The gig was coming in swiftly now. It was clinker-built and sturdy, ideal for use from a tidal beach. Ross had had it constructed in his boat-building yard in Looe five years ago, and he and Jeremy and Drake had sailed it round on two lovely summer days in June when the sea had been as calm as Dozmare Pool and light had danced off the rippling bow wave, and the ugliness of war had seemed a universe away. Since then Ross had used it scarcely more than twice, but Jeremy was always in it.

It *was* strange, Demelza thought, the number of days they spent fishing. Yet it was a harmless occupation. Jeremy had done well enough at Truro Grammar School – better than his father – but he hadn't wanted to go on to Oxford or Cambridge. Nor had he wanted to go into the Army or Navy, though he turned out for training with the Volunteers twice a month, of course, and certainly would fight with the best to fend off an invasion. But so far he seemed to lack enterprise and direction.

Perhaps, Demelza thought, he had grown up under the shadow of a very positive, active, dominant father. Though Ross had been the very reverse of harsh or demanding, indeed, had been far more indulgent than she was, you cannot change a personality, and if it is a very strong one its mere presence affects those around it.

She decided not to appear to be standing and waiting like an anxious mother, so climbed the rough path which would take her to the gorse-grown headland leading back to the Long Field. Half way up she apparently saw *Nampara Girl* for the first time, waved, and they all waved back. She stopped as they came slowly into the cove, dropping the lug sail and then the main sail, drifting gently, oar-steered towards that part of the beach where there was more sand than pebbles. Then she walked slowly back to meet them.

As they came in Ben Carter jumped into the water and pulled the boat a few feet up the sand. Jeremy followed and began to trot towards her. Ben Carter was that Benjy Ross Carter whose face had been scarred in a manner not dissimilar from his namesake's by the mentally deranged Reuben Clemmow that gale-ridden March night a quarter of a century ago. He was the second of the local boys who was devoted to Clowance, and it had to be admitted that Clowance took him a little more seriously than she did Matthew Martin. With his rangy figure and tight, intensely dark-browed, mobile face, with its short unfashionable beard, there were plenty of village girls ready and willing to take him very seriously indeed, but so far, with his twenty-sixth birthday not far distant, he had not been caught.

'Mother,' Jeremy said as he came up, 'I rather think we would better prefer not to see you just at this very moment, if you don't mind, for we have a cargo, an unexpected cargo aboard that will not pleasure you. Do you think you could be a good girl and walk away while we unload it?'

Demelza instinctively glanced past him towards the boat. In spite of the lightness of his words, Jeremy looked a little pale, and moved to block her view.

'What is it?'

'A little something we have picked up in the sea. A triviality, no more.'

'Tell me.'

He shrugged. 'Two dead men.'

'Oh, Judas . . . Where were they? . . . floating?'

'No. On a raft. Drifting slowly inshore. Near Trevaunance.'

She said: 'I have seen dead men before.'

'I suppose. I thought to save you the pretty sight.'

She walked past him and down to the boat. The great beach of Hendrawna, just on the other side of Damsel Point, was of course a place of constant reception for the flotsam of the sea. Throughout the centuries this iron coast had been a graveyard for ships, and even when the wrecks occurred twenty miles away the currents would often carry some of the booty onto one of the largest and flattest beaches in the country. So constant watch was kept by the villagers for any sign of treasure trove, and beachcombers tramped the high-tide mark twice daily, picking through the leavings of the sea. There had been nothing since like the great tragic wrecks of 1790, and, apart from a coal ship in '97 which had been a great boon to the villagers, pickings in recent years had been scanty. There had been little noticeable difference brought by the long war except an increase in the supply of corpses – an increment everyone except the most hardy could well have done without. Sometimes these, when new and recognizable, were given a decent burial in the churchyard, but more often than not they were shovelled in in the sandhills just too deep for the gulls to get at them.

Demelza went towards the boat disliking what she might see, though common sense told her that if the bodies had been too bloated the boys would not have picked them up.

Benjy Carter was back in the gig by now and, with Paul Kellow, was bending over the bodies which were lying in the stern. She could see the legs, both in tattered blue

76

trousers, the bare feet. She kicked off her own shoes, pulled down her stockings and threw them out of the sea's reach, scrambled aboard, skirt dripping. One man was dark, swarthy, and cut about the head; he seemed also to have bitten his tongue . . . The other looked younger, with a mass of tawny hair; the rags of a shirt only partly hid a strong white chest.

Paul Kellow straightened up and pushed the hair out of his eyes.

'Well, Mrs Poldark,' he said, pointing to the fair man. 'I believe this one is still alive!'

II

George Warleggan waited two weeks for a reply to his last letter to Lady Harriet; none came, so he felt he could delay no longer in putting himself at the centre of events during this constitutional crisis. He posted to London and reached there in the third week of November.

He found political London seething. Five years or more ago, following his new policy of edging himself into the favour of the future ruling party of England, he had resigned from White's Club and joined Brooks's, that traditional home of the Whigs. It contrived now to be a hot-bed of rumour and speculation. On the one hand he saw serious discussion and negotiation in progress, a lobbying for position, a hard bargaining for posts in the possible – indeed probable – new government. Those, however, who had no special axe to grind regarded the crisis as splendid entertainment and a sort of daily lottery. Fresh news of the King's health was awaited each morning and heavy sums were wagered as to the number of days it would be before he had to be restrained in a tranquillizer. Club wits when playing cards and laying down the king took to saying: 'I play the lunatic!' One older member when in his cups even imitated the Prince of Wales imitating the King at his most imbecile twenty-odd years ago.

The Lords Grey and Grenville, George knew, had been prised respectively from their northern and western estates and were in Town. Sheridan and Moira and Adam were in constant attendance on the Prince of Wales – who this time was being notably more circumspect. Spencer Perceval and his Tory ministers continued to hold the portfolios of office in their incompetent but tenacious hands and to hope that something would turn up.

The only good news in the last few weeks was that the French under Marshal Masséna had suffered a severe setback at a place no one had ever heard of called Bussaco. The British had repelled a force of double their strength and beaten them into a headlong retreat with six or seven thousand casualties. (The Whigs were trying to minimize this news, and later information, that Wellington was once again retreating, gave them the satisfaction of arguing that the victory had been greatly exaggerated.)

All this was interesting to George; and if Wellington were being unsuccessful it was specially pleasing to him personally, for he had gone out of his way to accommodate that gentleman when he was seeking a place in Parliament three years ago; Wellington had sat for St Michael for a few months and had then casually left it. George had been very unfavourably impressed by his obvious lack of any desire to be made a friend of.

But the constitutional crisis and the opportunity for some parliamentary advantage if or when Grey and Grenville came to power – perhaps with luck even a baronetcy which could be passed on to Valentine – had not been the total or even the main reason for his postponing his courtship of Harriet Carter. Central to his decision was the lure of the factories in Manchester.

The three physicians, George learned, who were attending on the King were Sir Henry Holford, Dr Baillie and Dr Heberden. A fourth, who came twice a week and

78

on whom the Queen relied for advice, was Mr David Dundas, the Windsor apothecary. This for the time was all, for when he recovered his sanity in 1788 George III had made his family swear they would never again call in 'the mad doctors', as he called them, for they had treated him so ill and put him into a strait-jacket. Chief among these tormentors was Dr Francis Willis, who ran his own private asylum in Lincolnshire. The King in fact no longer had any reason to fear this particular gentleman, as he had been gathered up by time; but there were, unfortunately for His Majesty, two sons, John and Robert Willis, who carried on their father's fell trade. The Queen had been resisting government pressure for several weeks but at last was giving way.

So these six gentlemen were now the six most important men in the kingdom. On their reports and prognostications the gravest and most far-reaching decisions had to be taken. With the King incapable of signing Orders in Council, the government of the nation simply could not function. Even Parliament itself could not be prorogued and could envisage the horrid prospect of having to go on sitting indefinitely. But if a regency *were* created and power vested in the Prince of Wales, and *then* the King recovered, the regency would at once become invalid and the King, who had hated his eldest son with an all-consuming hatred since the boy was seven, would be furious and perhaps sent into a new decline. Also the old King was very popular in the country, partly because he was old, partly because his old-fashioned bulldog opinions reflected the popular sentiment of the day, partly because he lived a good life, cared for his wife, and stood for a morality which people admired even when they didn't observe it themselves. Whereas the Prince of Wales was widely unpopular and despised; so that no political party which tried to rush events or appeared to be setting the legitimate king on one side without good reason could expect a smooth ride at the hustings.

The official reports of the doctors were all hopeful of an early recovery. Spencer Perceval said they were, and as Prime Minister it was his duty to acquaint Parliament with the news. After all, people said, why shouldn't it happen again as it had happened before? Twenty-two years ago a Regency Bill had been in active preparation, with Pitt making discreet arrangements to retire into private life, and the King had suddenly come round. It was bound to happen again. Or was it? Nearly a quarter of a century later? A man well into his eighth decade?

The other and lesser George was irritated by these official reports. It was quite clear to him that, since Perceval and his colleagues would be turned out of office when the King was officially superseded, they would set the best face on all and every medical report they received in order to put off the evil day. What of the unofficial reports? Prinny was a member of Brooks's, but had kept clear of it since his father's illness became known. Rumour in the club said that he had himself visited his father once and that the old man had not recognized him. It was said that the King hugged his pillow and called it Princess Octavius, that he denounced his wife as an impostor and claimed Lady Pembroke as the Queen.

How to be sure? Or if not sure, how to be surer than most people, sure enough to invest large sums of money on the outcome? Once it became certain that a Regency would be established the value of the Manchester properties would be quadrupled overnight.

Chapter Six

I

By the time Christmas came Stephen Carrington had established himself as a personality in the community of Nampara, Mellin and Sawle.

Seeing them carried up the stream-bordered track to the house that day, the one man so obviously dead, the other so near it as to make the difference barely perceptible, Demelza had thought him too far gone for recall. She had hurried ahead to the house and sent Gabby Martin flying to bring Dr Enys. By luck Dwight was nearby and was able to superintend the first aid. The sailor was carried upstairs, stripped and covered with warm blankets; warming-pans were put at his feet, and his hands rubbed with spirit, while a drop or two of brandy was tried upon his lips. Dwight said the man was faintly breathing, and he stayed with him until that breathing became perceptible to all. Then he went down and sipped a little port with Demelza and patted her hand and said he would come again as soon as he had broken his fast in the morning.

But by morning the rescued man was conscious and able to speak. By afternoon he was eating light food and sipping a cordial. By the following day he was out of bed.

Stephen Carrington, gentleman. From Gloucestershire, where he had some interest in shipping and trade with Ireland. He had left Bristol in a barque bound for Cork. They had been dismasted in a great storm; the ship had begun to sink; one of the boats had capsized and he had taken to a life-raft with the mate and a lascar sailor. They had drifted for days – or so it seemed. The mate had died.

The lascar sailor had lasted almost as long as Carrington but not quite.

Youngish. Demelza would not have put him beyond thirty. A West Country accent but different from Cornish. He was clearly a very strong man, for Dwight found he had two broken ribs, yet he was soon moving about the house and farm as if nothing had happened. He had a broad face, particularly across the brows, and his leonine hair and bright blue eyes made him handsome. All the younger maids clearly thought so. As did Clowance. Wearing one of Ross's old suits, for Jeremy's were not broad enough, he made himself useful in any way that came along, friendly, cheerful, liked by everyone.

He was not penniless – there had been money in a belt about his waist – and he offered Demelza two guineas to pay for his keep. She refused. So he spent some of it up at the kiddleys getting on good terms with the miners.

Having lived in the company of gentlefolk for twenty-five years but never been precisely one of them herself (though she enjoyed their company – occasionally – and admired some of their attitudes and came to adopt what she liked of their behaviour as her own), Demelza had razor-sharp perceptions about them. Far more so than Ross, who hardly bothered to notice. And she was not quite sure what to make of Stephen Carrington.

Two days before Christmas he asked if he might stay till the end of the year.

'Dr Enys tells me that me ribs are not yet healed, and it would be a great favour t'have a few more days in such pleasant company.'

'We shall be quiet for Christmas with my husband away, but you'd be more than welcome to be with us.'

He scratched his head. 'To tell the truth, Mrs Poldark, though me body's almost healed, the shipwreck's given me mind such a shaking up – being so near death, as t'were – that I'd be glad to have a little time more to rest and refit. I'm everlasting grateful.'

So Christmas came. There was a party at the Trenegloses and another one at the Popes, and a third, though restricted as to size, at the Kellows. To all these Stephen Carrington went. Demelza had given a party last year, so she made the excuse that Ross wasn't home. Caroline Enys, impulsive as ever, having decided against doing anything, suddenly made up a party to see out the old year. 'My two little brats are really too young to appreciate anything but sweetmeats and jellies, so let 'em go to bed and we'll celebrate Saturnalia. Or eat oaten cake if you prefer it.'

In fact they did a little of both. Although Killewarren had no very large room, the company dispersed itself about four or five. In one they played dice, in another they jigged to Myner's violin, in a third they helped themselves to goose and capon and pheasant, or syllabubs and chocolate cake, in the fourth they sprawled around a big fire and told stories. When midnight came a groom tolled the stable bell and the candles were blown out and everyone foregathered and, with appropriate grunts or squeals, dug for raisins in the great flat bowl of lighted brandy.

When the fun was over and she had kissed Dwight and Demelza, Caroline said: 'Why *does* that man still go a-hunting? I love him dearly but he does try us hard.'

'Tis in the blood,' Demelza said. 'I can't imagine why, for the other Poldarks s'far as I know have stayed quietly at home most of their lives. But it seems he tasted adventure too early and can't rid himself of the flavour.'

'As a civilian,' Dwight said, 'he's not likely to be at much risk; he may be home any day.'

'That's what I tell myself,' Demelza said, a little tremulously, moved by the occasion, the brandy, the warmth of the fire, and more particularly by the warmth of her two dearest friends.

'And where is Verity this year?' Caroline asked, perceiving the emotion she had stirred and trying to allay it.

'At home. Her stepdaughter Esther is coming to stay.'

'Will Andrew be there?'

'Senior? Oh, yes. He has been retired four years, greatly to Verity's relief.'

Caroline picked a hair off Dwight's coat. 'And this young man Jeremy fished out of the sea. Did he do it with a hook and line? Mr Carrington is, I agree, more than a little handsome. Better dressed and with a fashionable haircut he would not look at all out of place in a London ballroom.'

'They're Ross's clothes he's wearing.'

'Ah well, Ross has the sort of distinction that allows him to be shabby if he chooses. So does Dwight, but I won't let him choose.'

'You should try influencing Ross.'

'That I wouldn't dare! How long is he staying?'

'Stephen? I'm not sure.'

'We may be off to London next week, Demelza.'

'What? *Both* of you? But you only came back in October! All this *travelling*. I better prefer to stay in one place.'

'It's a small matter sudden,' Caroline said. 'Dwight has just received a medical invitation and he has thoughts of accepting it.'

Demelza looked at Dwight and Dwight looked back at her and smiled.

'Ross will be back by then,' he said.

'He'd better be. Otherwise I'll think all my – friends have deserted me.'

'Why don't you come with us to London?'

'What, and maybe cross coaches? – him going one way and me the other? No, thank you. But thank you all the same.'

The guests were dispersing to their various rooms again. Stephen Carrington as he left the room was linking little fingers with Clowance. Jeremy had Maud Pope in tow. The fair young Mrs Pope was standing reluctantly beside her elderly husband, politeness masking discontent.

'Tell me,' Caroline said, two gloved fingers on Demelza's wrist. 'Tell me, woman, what are you going to do about Clowance?'

Demelza looked startled. 'About her? What's wrong with her?'

'Only the complaint that attacks us all at that age. She's growing up. *And* getting prettier. It's a not uncommon phenomenon.'

'What should I do? Send for the Fencibles?'

'Not *en masse*. Seriously, it is a problem that will one day concern me but not yet for almost a decade. I bred late. And for me it will not be so difficult. I'll take my two little drabs to London and dress them in fine silks and see if there is any quality dancing attendance. And by quality I do not mean the length of a gentleman's pedigree or the whiteness of his ruff.'

'I'm glad,' said Demelza. 'Oh . . . as for Clowance . . . what can I wish her? A life one half so happy as mine has been? With the man of her choice. Let her choose, Caroline. She must do that for herself.'

'So, I hope, will Sophie and Meliora when the time comes. Dwight would insist on it if I did not. But it is the *extent* of the choice that matters. I want my children to have had a passably close look at fifty men before they drop their anchors. What concerns me a little, my dear, is that Clowance's choice, unless we take steps to amend the situation, will be limited to a half-dozen, if that. You say she does not care for the receptions and balls given in Truro?'

'Those two or three she has been to, no. She better prefers galloping across the beach on Nero . . . But Caroline, if she is suffering at all it is from the indecision of her parents. Ross does not care for these occasions – and often is away when he should be home. And I . . . well, I can never *see* myself in the situation of an anxious mother launching her daughter into a succession of soirées, parties, balls. Even though I have been Mrs Ross Poldark so long I do not think I have the – the confidence or authority . . . Certainly not without Ross.' She stopped and frowned into the fire. 'But even if I *had*, should I *want* to? Surely not. My daughter is not a – a cow at a country fair with a bow of pink ribbon round its neck waiting for inspection from those who are interested in putting in a bid. She deserves something different from that!'

Dwight laughed. 'So you see, Caroline.'

His wife said: 'I see nothing but an obstinate mis-understanding of my meaning. Of course Poldarks are unique and to themselves, apart. No, no, I intend no irony. No one could see you or Ross pursuing the conventional *rounds*, as it were. It would be a perversion of all you stand for in the county. Nevertheless, daughters – and sons for that matter – should be given the opportunity of seeing a fair sample of the opposite sex before they choose. And, since I see you are both against me, I can only add that it was my wide acquaintanceship with the landed youth of Oxfordshire that made me all the more instantly aware of the sterling qualities of Dr Enys.'

'Landless and penniless as I was,' said Dwight. 'I don't really believe calculation or deep perception entered into it with either of us, Caroline. We saw each other. And when we'd done that we'd eyes for no one else.'

'There you put your finger on it all,' said Demelza, helping herself to port and trying to convince herself. 'Of *course* it is better that every daughter and every son should meet as many as possible of their own age. But who's to say the twenty-third man you meet has anything to commend him over the third? If with the third the fire has been lighted, no extra numbers can put it out. And if in all you only have six to choose from . . . will the choice be any worse? I don't know. I saw only one. But then I was different. I was beyond measure lucky.'

'Consider Ross,' said Caroline. 'The luck didn't run just one way.'

Demelza patted her hand. 'We can argue about that.'

86

'Well,' said Caroline, 'it is good for old friends to have something to argue about at twenty minutes before one o'clock on the first of January, eighteen hundred and eleven. I'm tired of toasting "Death to the French", for I've been doing it for nearly two decades. So let us toast to ourselves – and absent friends.'

II

Early January was fine and still in Cornwall, with the ground soft and damp and no bite to the air. All the unrelenting savagery that the weather and the sea were capable of was withdrawn, held in abeyance, scarcely to be considered as a serious threat. No sun came through; the days passed under grey, mild, still skies. Compared with two weeks before, a little daylight seemed to have crept into the afternoons.

One day Stephen Carrington said to Clowance: 'This house. This Trenwith House that you say is near and belongs to your cousin – which way is it?'

'Just past Grambler. You know, the village. About four miles.'

'Could we walk there? They tell me it is more than two hundred years old, and I am interested in old buildings.'

Clowance hesitated. 'Well, officially it belongs to my cousin Geoffrey Charles Poldark, but his stepfather, Sir George Warleggan, actually takes care of it for him, and Sir George does not encourage visitors.'

'Does he live there?'

'Oh no. Just two gamekeepers who care for the place for him. But he is not friendly with our family, and my mother has forbidden me to go there again.'

Stephen thrust a hand through his thick hair. 'Well, I have the greatest respect and admiration for Mrs Poldark, and I should be the last to encourage you to disobey. She is a very beautiful woman.'

'Who? My mother? Yes, I suppose so . . .'

'Had you not noticed? Perhaps not, for you are very like her.'

'I think I am very *un*like her – different colouring, bigger bones, different shaped face . . .'

'No, no you take me wrong. I mean that Mrs Poldark for a beautiful woman is the least conceited about it that ever I've met. Almost unaware – after all these years still a little surprised when a man's eyes light up with – with admiration. It is in that I mean you are like her. You are . . . unaware.'

'If that is intended as a compliment,' said Clowance, 'then I'm obliged to you.'

'The more I struggle the deeper I flounder,' said Stephen. 'So let me say again, I should not wish to encourage you to disobey your mother, see. Shall I go ask her if we may go? You will not come to no hurt in my company.'

'I'll not come to no hurt on my own,' said Clowance. 'But asking Mama wouldn't profit you. I'll take you to the gates if you like, and if they're open we can proceed to the bend in the drive so that the front of the house may be seen.'

By now it was eleven, and for the first time for several days the clouds were thinning to show the disc of the sun like a six-shilling piece lying on a dusty floor. They went by way of the cliffs, since Clowance knew if they went up the valley past the mine the bal girls would be sure to see them and start tongues wagging. This was a way much frequented by people in the old days before the Warleggan fences were put up, but even though in recent years the fences had fallen or been pulled down the route was not as much used as formerly. Much of it was overgrown with gorse, and part of the cliff had tumbled.

The sea was uninteresting today, flat as a pewter plate. Even the gulls were uncommunicative. Everything was silent, waiting.

Clowance said: 'My father told me once that there was a

way into Trenwith no one but he knew. He used to play there with his cousin, who was killed in a mine.'

'Did he say where twas?'

'It was somewhere along this route – an old mine tunnel. It ran under the kitchens and came up by a well-head in the courtyard. When George Warleggan lived there with his wife a dozen or more years ago he barred my father from entering the house, so Papa gave him one or two unpleasant surprises.'

'And then what happened?'

'I believe they came to blows more than once.'

'Was that how your father got his scar?'

'How did you know he had one?'

Stephen put his hand out to help her over a boulder. 'That drawing of Jeremy's. Tis of your father, isn't it?'

Clowance disdained the hand and climbed quickly after him. 'Before he was married Papa fought in America. That was where that came from.'

'And Ben Carter has a similar one.'

'Yes . . . Of a sort. Why do you say that?'

Stephen did not at once reply. His face was turned towards the sea, where a thin line of an unexpected wave was moving under the surface towards the cliffs.

'Ben Carter is crazy for you, isn't he.'

Clowance's eyes did not flicker. 'I think he has a taking.'

'And you?'

She half smiled. 'What d'you mean? And me?'

'I mean have you a similar taking for him?'

'If I had or if I had not, should I be obliged to confess it to you?'

'No . . . I shouldn't've asked. No . . .'

They walked on and came to some rotting posts, which was all that was left of George's stout fencing.

'Whose sheep?' asked Stephen as they entered the first field. 'Does Warleggan farm here?'

'No, they'll be Will Nanfan's or Ned Bottrell's. They rent these fields from Sir George's factor.'

89

'They're forward – the ewes, I mean. They'll be dropping soon. I was brought up on a farm, y'know.'

'No, I didn't know.'

'Often used to help the farmer with his lambing.'

'Did you . . .'

'Yes . . . A farm near Stroud.'

They walked on.

Clowance said: 'As soon as the lambs come they'll have to be taken out of these fields.'

'Why?'

'The gulls would get them.'

'What, these gulls?'

'No, the big black-backed ones. They're big as geese themselves. Even near the village the lambs won't be safe . . .'

Now they could see the grey chimneys of Trenwith sheltering under the fall of the land.

'There,' Clowance said, stopping. 'That's your house.'

'But this is not the front way, this surely is the back.'

'Yes. I changed my mind.'

They gazed a few seconds.

Stephen said: 'You ride that black horse splendid.'

'Nero? He's an old friend.'

'Every morning. On that beach. Like the wind. I wonder you don't fear to stumble in the pits.'

'He's sure-footed.'

'Well, I tell you, it's a splendid sight.'

'Papa calls it my constitutional.'

'What does that mean?'

'I'm not sure. Some word he has picked up in London.'

There was silence.

Stephen said: 'No chimneys smoking.'

'I told you. The Harrys – that's the caretakers – live in the lodge.'

He said: 'Can I ask a favour of you?'

'It depends.'

'I'd like to see the house. Will you stay here, wait for me ten minutes while I look around?'

She was quite decided. 'No. But if you want I'll come with you.'

'What will Mrs Poldark say?'

'Perhaps she need not know.'

III

They went into Trenwith House. There was no lock or bolt on the door. The air inside was sour with damp. In the great hall wood ash from an uncleared fire had blown across the stone flags and lay thick on the table. Stephen admired the huge window with its hundreds of separate panes of glass. They moved into the winter parlour, which was also furnished. There were fewer cobwebs here, as if the Harrys had made an effort to keep one room clean.

He said: 'Where is your cousin?'

'With the army in Portugal.'

'And when it is over – if he survives – this is his inheritance . . . Some people have the luck, by God!'

She had slipped off her cloak. Under it she was wearing a primrose frock, only a shade different from the colour of her hair. She sat in one of the armchairs and picked at a thorn which had got into her sandal. 'Do you – did you have no inheritance?'

'*No* . . . Nothing. Miss Clowance . . .'

'Yes?'

'You know maybe . . . maybe you can guess why I took the liberty of inquiring for your feelings for Ben Carter.'

'Do I?'

'I hoped you did. It's because I have a great fondness for you meself.'

She stared at the lattice of winter sunlight falling on the worn carpet. There were still two pictures on the walls.

'You heard . . . ?' he asked.

'Yes, I heard.'

He said: 'I have been telling a lie to your mother.'

'In what way?'

'If I tell you me feelings for you, then I cannot do it under the shadow of a lie. I must tell you the truth. I told Mrs Poldark that I was in some way of business in Bristol, that my ship – *my* ship, note – was struck by a storm, that it went down and that the mate and me and Budi Halim, took to the raft and were as you found us when Jeremy picked us up. That's not true.'

'No?'

'No. It was not my ship. I'd no interest in her. I come from Bristol, sure enough, but as a seaman, see, just with an education better than most, thanks to the Elwyns, who adopted me. The *Unique* was not carrying a cargo to Ireland and struck by a storm. There was no storm. She were a privateer, fitted out in Bristol by a half-dozen merchants, and I was a gunner aboard her. We sailed to the French coast looking for plunder. We found some but before we could turn with it we ran foul of two French naval ships – like sloops only smaller . . . We have the heels of most men-of-war. *Had*. Not of those. They gave chase and sunk us off the Scillies. No mercy given. We were destroyed.'

She re-fastened the buckle of her shoe.

'Why did you tell my mother different?'

He shrugged. 'I was none too proud of me trade. I sought for something more, giving the impression of being something more. That's not a thing to be proud of neither, is it? But that's the way I thought, on impulse so to say, on the spur of the first meeting. And then of course I had to keep up the story . . .' He looked at her. 'I'm sorry, Clowance. I could not lie to you.'

'I'm glad.'

She stood up, trying her weight on the shoe, went to the window, frowned out at the rank weeds in the courtyard.

'I'm glad,' she said.

He came up behind her, put a hand on her arm. Her hair was hanging across her face, and he kissed her hair where it lay on her cheek. Then he turned her towards him and kissed her on the mouth. They stood together and then she quietly released herself.

'That was nice,' he said.

'Yes,' she agreed simply.

He laughed and caught her to him again, smiling as they kissed but soon losing his smile. His hands began to move up and down her frock, lightly but informingly, touching her thighs, her waist, her arms, her breasts, like someone exploring with quiet anticipation a fine and beautiful land shortly to be conquered.

She freed her mouth and said: 'I think it's time we went home.'

'Dinner will be two hours yet.'

'It was not dinner I was thinking of.'

'No. Nor I . . .'

Her frock had a wide neckline, and with two light fingers he slid it off one shoulder, began to kiss that shoulder and the soft part between shoulder and neck. He felt her give a deep sigh. Slipping the frock an inch further exposed the top part of her breast, that part that had suddenly lifted and filled with her breath. He began to kiss it.

Just before his hands reached up to the frock again she put her own fingers on his face, smoothed it lightly and then pushed it away.

'Enough.'

Satisfied with his success, aware of the dangers of going too fast and too far, he released her.

'Sorry if I've offended.'

'You have not offended.'

'Then glad I am not to have to be sorry.'

She shivered as she pulled up the shoulder of her frock, as if the chill of the house had suddenly affected her. She took up her cloak and he helped her on with it, putting his

93

face close to hers as he did so. Then he kissed her neck again.

She moved away. 'What was that?'

They listened. 'Maybe a rat,' he said. 'In no time they'll make such a house as this their own.'

'I should not wish to meet the Harrys. They would not dare touch me but they could be rough with a stranger.'

'Let 'em try . . . Clowance.'

'Yes?'

'Can we come here again?'

'It depends.' They moved back into the hall.

He opened the outer door and peered out. 'On what?'

'All sorts of things.'

They went out. The heavy latch clicked as he closed the door behind them.

'When Mrs Poldark tires of me,' he said, 'which must be soon, I have thoughts to stay on a while in the village – perhaps try to find work. There's naught taking me home. Me mother cares nothing. Me father I never knew, though surprising as tis, they were proper wed. He died at sea. I am just happy to be here – on solid ground for a change, and among such – such delicious people.' He moved his tongue across his lips.

'You cannot eat us all,' said Clowance.

He laughed. 'M'ambition is strictly limited.'

There was still no one about. Long pale shadows moved with them over the fields.

They reached the cliffs again. Three fishing boats had appeared, punctuating the misty sea.

'Let us stay here awhile,' she said.

'Why?'

'Never mind.' She knew that her face still gave away the emotions she'd been feeling, and had no relish for arriving at Nampara until she had quite recovered.

'Shall you care,' he said, 'whether I go or stay?'

'So many questions, Stephen, so many questions . . . Now may I ask you one?'

94

'Of course.'

'How many girls have you left pining for you in Bristol?'

He laughed, pleased with the question. 'How can I answer that? There are girls – have been girls – I'm twenty-eight, Clowance – how could there not have been? Only one was important, and that ended five years gone. That was the only one that was important – until now.'

She looked at him very candidly. 'Are you telling me the truth?'

'You must know I am. Me dear. Me love. Me beautiful. I wouldn't – couldn't deceive you in this.'

She turned away from him, aware that the emotions she had sought to subdue were returning.

'Then,' she said, 'if you would be so kind, Stephen, would you walk on ahead of me? I will follow you . . . in a little while.'

Chapter Seven

I

Ross reached Chatham early on Saturday morning, the 12th January, 1811. He had survived the bloody encounter at Bussaco with no more than a scratch on his shoulder, but had caught the influenza which was raging in Lisbon when he got there and so had missed the early ships home. He posted at once to London, and his first act when he arrived was to send off the letter to Demelza he had written while lurching in the wind-blown waters of Biscay.

Having slept nine hours in a comfortable bed, he breakfasted and went through drifting snowflakes to see George Canning at Brompton Lodge, Canning's new house. It was in the village of Old Brompton, less than half an hour's walk from Hyde Park Corner and set among orchards and market gardens; though the fields and lonely lanes in between were much infested by footpads and highwaymen. Canning was in and received him eagerly, listened to his report, and at once asked Ross to repeat his account to the Foreign Secretary, Lord Wellesley, and the War Minister, Robert Dundas. This Ross agreed to so long as it was done quick; his only wish now was to rejoin his family.

His friendship with George Canning had ripened through the years, until Ross now accounted him his best friend in London; and he knew it was Canning who had been behind most of the later missions he had been invited to undertake. At present Canning was in the wilderness, out of office and out of favour both with his own party and with the opposition; but no lack of immediate popularity could prevent him being a power in the land, both as an orator and as a statesman. Ten years younger than Ross and coming from a quite different background, he had a political genius that Ross could not hope to match but none of Ross's military training (when fighting a duel with Lord Castlereagh recently his second had had to cock the pistol for him because he had never fired one before).

Yet they had much in common; the nonconforming, scarred, bony Cornishman and the part-Irish, witty, sharp-tongued statesman. They each had a certain arrogance – neither suffered fools gladly or even silently, so they made enemies; they both had an intense, almost obsessive loyalty to friends that persisted through all vicissitudes; they were both reforming radicals by temperament yet Tories of necessity. They had both been staunch followers of Pitt; they both believed in Catholic Emancipation and both had rejoiced when three years ago slavery had been abolished throughout the British colonies. Particularly and absolutely, they both had a great sympathy for the lot of the common people but a conviction that the active prosecution of the war must for the time being take precedence over all.

That was Sunday. Canning's beautiful wife was at their country home in Hinckley with their ailing son, so he insisted that Ross should spend the day with him. He told Ross of the King's insanity, of the fact that on December 19th – over a month ago – Spencer Perceval had at last been forced to introduce a Regency Bill. Although people always said the King was improving, the fact remained that the government could not pass a single measure without his consent, and it was difficult to get a rational signature from a man who fancied himself an animal out of Noah's Ark.

Since then there had been bitter disputes and wrangling both in and out of the House because the Tories wished to restrict the Prince's powers, at least for two years. It all confirmed the Prince's bitter hostility to his father's government, and he had been heard to say after receiving one communication from them: 'By God, once I am Regent they shall not remain an hour!' So the Whig party was coming in on a four-fold platform: Peace with France; the surrender of the dispute with America; the Emancipation of Ireland; and the abolition of tithes. Samuel Whitbread, the brewer's son turned statesman, was likely to become Foreign Secretary, with powers to negotiate the peace, and Lord Grenville was almost certain to be Prime Minister.

So would come peace, said Canning bitterly, another patched-up peace like the peace of Amiens ten years ago, a pact which had given the French back half their colonial empire and allowed Buonaparte just the breathing space he needed before setting out on his next round of conquests. So must come the withdrawal of a discredited Wellington from Portugal and the abandonment of that country to the French.

'It *must* not happen,' Canning said. 'But I do not know how it may be stopped from happening . . . I saw Perceval only yesterday. He still puts on a brave face about the King, but, in confidence . . . well . . .'

'D'you think the Prince immovable?' Ross said.

'Immovable in his detestation of the present government, yes. I had hopes for a while of Lady Hertford. She is, I believe, leading him to a soberer way of life. As you know, I am *persona non grata* with the Prince; but I took an opportunity and spoke to Lady Hertford on this subject. She feels there is nothing she can do for the present government, for it has been denounced past recall.'

'And the Prince is in favour of all the policies the Whigs are in favour of? Even peace?'

'So it would seem. Apart from the Whig party itself, all his personal advisers, Adams, Moira, the Duke of Cumberland, Sheridan, Tyrwhitt . . .'

'Sheridan?'

'There perhaps lies a faint hope. As you know, he is one of my oldest friends, but of late we have seen little of each other. He is the Prince's most intimate friend, but he is not popular with the Hertfords and they may well have influenced the Prince against him. Also, of course, he is now seldom sober . . .'

There was a pause. Ross eased his ankle.

Canning said: 'You must not go home yet, Ross.'

'It is past time.'

'Not, at least, until this crisis is past. It has been the very devil keeping members of all persuasions in London this fine frosty winter when hunting conditions have been so good. The severer weather that you see today has but now struck us. If – during the next few weeks – I can count on your vote in the House, this will bring those I can absolutely rely on to fifteen. Where many issues are delicately balanced, such a group can wield a deal of influence.'

'Influence to what end?' Ross asked impatiently. 'It cannot turn an issue which will be decided entirely by the King's illness and the Prince's whim. If I could see a way where, by staying at Westminster, I could influence the question of peace or war, I would stay. But it is out of our hands.'

'Well, stay a week. Two weeks. Stay here with us. Joan would wish it if she were here. To see the Bill through. And to tell your story to those in high office. Please. It is your duty. Otherwise the purpose of your mission is unfulfilled.'

II

George Warleggan had agonized his way through Christmas and the New Year. It was not in his nature to gamble – except on near certainties – this was the problem. Yet if he waited much longer the opportunity must surely be lost. Others could see as clearly as he, others would step in and snap up the Manchester properties if he did not. They might already be gone. In London there was no way of knowing one day from the next what might be happening in the northern cities.

The official reports of the doctors were still hopeful. Spencer Perceval had announced only that week in Parliament that he had just been to see the King himself and that they had conducted a perfectly normal conversation with no sign of mental alienation or confusion on the King's part. Yet the Regency Bill was making slow but inevitable progress; the politicians could not wrangle for ever. Nor could they wait. Nor could George.

And then by chance one day he heard of someone who might help him to decide, who might be induced to advise him without knowing he was doing so; a Cornishman – very unexpectedly in London at this time. Even that unexpectedness was significant.

Ever since his imprisonment in a French prisoner-of-war camp soon after the outbreak of war Dr Dwight Enys had made a particular study of mental ailments. Having seen the effect of starvation and vile conditions on many types of healthy men, he had been struck by the wide differences of stamina between them, the strange ability some had to rise above their privations and the equally strange incapacity of others. Many apparently of the strongest went under; others of greater obvious frailty lived through it all. And he had come to the conclusion that it was the mental approach that made the difference: the essential determination of the mind to dominate the body. When he had been rescued Dwight Enys had practised this discipline on himself, much to his new wife's indignation, since she saw him constantly over-taxing his strength.

All that was now past, but in 1802, during the brief peace, he had gone to France with his great friend Ross Poldark, who was trying to trace any surviving relatives of Charles, Comte de Sombreuil, who had been killed in the abortive landing at Quiberon in 1795; and while over there Dwight had met a Dr Pinel, the director of an asylum called Bicêtre. Dr Pinel told him that in 1793, being then strongly imbued with the new principles of Liberty, Equality and Fraternity, he had decided to release a dozen madmen from their filthy cells and see what happened to them. Two died because before they were released their feet had been gangrened by frost, the other ten gave no trouble at all and six of these finally went back into the world quite cured. Since those days Dr Pinel had given the inmates as much freedom as possible and nowadays regularly dined with them. It was a new approach to the treatment of lunacy, and when he returned to England Dwight published a paper on his experiences and what might be learned from them.

As a result of this publication, he learned of the existence of Mr William Tuke, a Quaker merchant of York, who had opened a mental home ten or more years ago and, though pursuing a different and more Christian path than Dr Pinel, had arrived, as it were, at the same door. Restraint was reduced to a minimum, the patients were given work to do and healthy outdoor exercise. Dwight went up to see him and toured the madhouse. He was enormously impressed. Two years later he met the Doctors Willis and inspected thir asylum. He was now pressing, as George very well knew, for some reasonable hospital for the mentally deranged to be built in Cornwall, perhaps in Truro next to the Royal Cornwall Hospital which had been opened in 1799.

But why was he in London now? That was what George wanted to know. Dr Enys was notorious for the reluctance with which he left Cornwall and his village patients. It might be he was here in deference to his wife's wishes, since Caroline always spent a part of the autumn in London staying with her aunt, Mrs Pelham. But this was January. Unless he was doing something in some medical capacity Dwight was always a fish out of water.

George's relationship with the Enyses had been fairly good but never close over the years. He had disliked Dwight thoroughly in the early days when the young man, without a practice or money, had unhesitatingly taken the poverty-stricken Ross Poldark as his personal friend when the Warleggans had made it clear to him that he must choose between them. But Caroline had always been friendly with Elizabeth, and after her marriage to Dwight the couples had often met. Caroline, with her usual charming arrogance, had completely failed to accept that her loving friendship with Ross and Demelza should in any way constrict her social visits to Trenwith, and it was Dwight who had been summoned to Elizabeth's bedside on her premature confinement, had delivered Ursula, and later, along with Dr Behenna, had watched helplessly while Elizabeth slipped away.

In the intervening years George had occasionally been invited to dinner at Killewarren. Now and then they met in Truro. Once, when Ursula broke her pattern of abounding good health, Dr Enys attended her in the absence of Dr Behenna. It was the sort of relationship which in no way inhibited George from calling at Mrs Pelham's house. If the fact that it had never in all these years happened before made the visit unusual, that was a small point to set beside his need.

By a fortunate chance as George clopped into Hatton Garden a chair was drawing up outside the house, and Caroline got out with her eldest child, Sophie. George quickly dismounted and flung the reins of his horse over a hitching post. The street was crowded and for a moment Caroline did not notice the caller.

When she turned and saw him she raised an eyebrow and said: 'Sir George, what a surprise! To what do we owe the honour? Is there an R in the month?'

'My dear Caroline, I called to see if Dwight were in; but it is the more pleasure to find you and looking so charming. And your daughter . . . She's well, I have no need to ask.'

'Well, thank you. As are we all. But can it be your visit means you are not? Otherwise . . . ?'

Once again he avoided the irony. 'No, no. Passing. Just passing by.'

They went in. Dwight was in a small study off the main parlour and was reading a medical pamphlet. They all talked for a while, and Caroline ordered tea. She also invited George to sup with them, which he accepted. Over tea they discussed the constitutional crisis, the progress of the war, the latest plays, the iniquities of recruiting sergeants, the heavy frosts of the last two days, and the need for increased cleanliness in London's streets.

Caroline's invitation gave George time, and he was grateful not to have to bring up too soon the real object of his visit. But when they went into supper there was a horrid complication. Not only Caroline's aunt, Mrs Pelham, was there but another man, tall and ramshackle, called Webb, and two young soldiers (whose names George instantly forgot) yellow-skinned as Chinamen from their fevers in the Indies. And also there was a girl . . . the last time he had seen her . . .

'Have you met Miss Clowance Poldark?' Caroline asked him. 'Ross's daughter. She came up with us for a few days.'

'I – er – ' George said. 'Yes, briefly, once.'

'We almost quarrelled over some foxgloves,' said the girl, smiling.

'Indeed.' He bowed stiffly and went to his place at the table.

Over supper conversation was casual, and he wondered by what pretext he might afterwards get Dwight alone. The girl was in grey, looked paler than he remembered her; but the long fair hair was the same, the grey eyes, the young high bosom. She was not unlike in build, though better looking than, that other girl he had once had suppressed feelings for: Morwenna Chynoweth – then Whitworth – now Carne.

'Do you know the Duke of Leeds?' he asked Caroline in an undertone, while his other partner, Mrs Pelham, was talking to Colonel Webb. It was a sudden impulse of his to ask this; though contrary to his nature to betray his inclinations on any subject to more people than was vitally necessary, it did seem to him that disclosing the one interest might cleverly mask the other and real reason for his coming.

'I would not claim to know him,' said Caroline, in a louder voice than he would have liked. 'I've met him once or twice. My aunt probably does.'

'I met his sister in Cornwall recently.'

Caroline looked at him over the tip of her wineglass.

'Harriet Carter, d'you mean?'

'Ah . . . so you know her?'

'Oh yes. Passing well. We've hunted together.'

'She's living near Helston now, since her husband died.'

'I didn't know that. I knew she'd been left badly off.'

'Yes,' said George.

A footman refilled their glasses, and then Mrs Pelham broke with her neighbour and conversation became general – chiefly on how Prinny would measure up to his responsibilities when he became Regent. But later Caroline returned to the subject herself.

'Is Harriet Carter the Duke of Leeds's sister or half-sister? I never remember.'

'Nor I,' said George, knowing nothing about it.

'Oh, I expect they're of the same marriage. Willy's only about thirty-five. But there are younger ones about.'

'Indeed,' said George.

Caroline considered the heavy, formidable man beside her. It was quite difficult actively to *like* George, but she found him interesting; and there was sufficient of her uncle in her to appreciate what he had done, how far he had climbed, the extent of his achievement. She had never actually witnessed that side of his nature which could be ruthless and vindictive; and sometimes she thought there was a better man inside him struggling to get out. Even when Elizabeth was alive he had seemed to her a lonely man, though no doubt it was a loneliness brought about by the sourness of his own humours.

He and Ross, of course, could never mix; even with the abrasive element of Elizabeth gone, they were oil and water. Sometime, she thought ironically, when she was far gone in drink to give her courage, she would chide Ross on his dismissive attitude to money, which went in her view too far the other way.

She said: 'So you wish to meet the Duke, is that it?'

A faint flush showed on George's neck. 'Oh? Well . . . You think your aunt knows him?'

'Yes, I believe she does.'

'Then I should be honoured . . .'

Caroline waved away a plate of sweetmeats that had been offered her. 'You like Harriet?'

'I find her agreeable.'

'She rides like the devil, George. Did you know that?'

'Yes.'

'Are you serious?'

'Serious? I don't know what you mean.'

'Never mind. It was a light-hearted question. You have other reasons for wishing to meet the Duke?'

'No,' said George.

'I admire honest answers,' said Caroline.

Supper ended and the ladies retired. Clowance had been very quiet, answering only with quiet modesty the gallantries of one of the anonymous young soldiers, but occasionally she glanced across at George, as if assessing his person and his presence there. In return he looked at her but in such a way that he hoped she did not notice, taking in her fresh young looks, the roundness of her arms, golden in the candlelight, the heavy, firmly shaped lips that some young man no doubt was already tasting, the ripe young body.

The men drank port and talked about the wagers that were being laid at Brooks's as to the constitution of the new government. After a long time they rose to join the ladies. George let the other three men move off and then called Dwight back.

'That Clowance is with you – does it mean something has happened to Ross?'

'No, he is on a mission to Portugal.'

'That I know. But not back yet?'

'Not back yet. There can be many reasons for a delay. Caroline thought it would be good for Clowance to see a little society.'

'Is her mother or brother not here?'

'No. She came with us.'

'And are you staying long?'

'Perhaps two weeks.'

George said: 'Is it true, Dwight, that you came to London to see the King?'

Dwight raised his eyebrows but for a moment did not speak. 'I cannot imagine what may have given you that idea.'

'My informant said he had it on good authority.'

'You must know, George, that London is a hot-bed of rumour. Especially at a time like this.'

'All the same I was surprised to hear you were in Town, knowing how you dislike it – and January is not your usual month.'

'True.'

'Well,' George said, 'it is none of my business, but if you have seen his Majesty I hope you receive due recognition. It could help towards setting up your Cornish mental hospital, if it were to be known.'

'If it were to be known and if it ever happened.'

'Of course. My friend told me the Willises are close friends of yours.'

'*Close* friends? Hardly. Colleagues at the most. I don't approve of their methods.'

'But you may have discussed the King's condition with them?'

'I have discussed the King's condition with some of my

colleagues. That would not be putting it too high.'

'And are they as optimistic of his recovery as the reports suggest?'

'I hardly knew that the reports were so optimistic. Certainly everyone hopes the King will recover.'

'Amen,' said George.

'But . . .'

'But what?'

'It was not important,' said Dwight.

They moved towards the door. George said: 'I must take my leave now. I don't wish to disturb the others, so pray thank Caroline for her gracious hospitality, and Mrs Pelham too. And thank Caroline also, if you please, for the generous offer she made me at the supper table. I shall be delighted to accept it.'

'What that is I don't know; but of course . . .'

Dwight rang for George's cloak and hat.

George said: 'What do *you* personally consider are the chances of the King's recovery, Dwight?'

Dwight turned the doorknob between his fingers. 'Why are you so interested?'

'It may determine the future of England.'

'The war, you mean.'

'The war. The conditions in the north. Even the future of Europe.'

Dwight said: 'My own opinion is that the King will not recover.'

George licked his lips. 'Even though he has regained his reason thrice before.'

'Then he was younger. Each time the chances of a full recovery are less.'

'And a partial recovery would not enable him to stop the Regency Bill?'

'Parliament must judge that.'

'They say he has periods of lucidity still.'

'Oh yes. Has had from the beginning. But they don't last. Naturally I may be quite mistaken but I shall be much surprised if they ever do last long enough for him to be able to resume his conduct of the affairs of state.'

George heard the footsteps of the manservant.

'You judge from the reports of the other doctors or from personal observation?'

Dwight said: 'I believe it to be a complaint of the blood. Various symptoms suggest it. It is more common among men, though it can, I suspect, be carried, dormantly, as it were, through the female side. Ah, Chambers, will you see Sir George to his horse.'

Chapter Eight

I

George left next day for Manchester. If while he was away Mrs Pelham arranged some introduction for him to the Duke of Leeds, that was unfortunate. Financial affairs must come before affairs of the heart. Especially since one might influence the other.

It was necessary to move fast. Although he resented Dwight Enys's closeness of professional manner – and quietly resolved in return that, if or when it came time for a subscription list to be opened for the proposed mental hospital in Cornwall, a similar closeness – of his, George's, pocket – should be the order of the day; nevertheless Dwight had been proven right so often in medical matters that he was prepared to be influenced by what Dwight had said at this meeting. He was absolutely convinced that Enys had seen the King – however he appeared to dissimulate. Without such personal contact he would never have been so definite.

In Manchester he found the position scarcely changed since his visit of September. With the West Indies and South America as their only outlets, manufactured goods were piled in warehouses, unable to find buyers in a saturated market, while all embattled Europe cried out for them. Last month, December, there had been 273 bankruptcies, as against 65 four years ago. Weavers' earnings were less than half that of agricultural labourers. Skilled cotton operators were working a ninety-hour week for 8s.

Of course there was hope of a change. But nobody had the money to invest in a hope.

Except George.

At a knock-down price he bought a firm of fine cotton spinners called Flemings. Two other firms – Ormrod's – who were calico printers – and Fraser, Greenhow – builders and engineers – he arranged should receive large credits through Warleggan's Bank to enable them to keep afloat – this not by a straightforward loan but by the purchase of a substantial interest in his own name so that he owned a big share of the stock. He made three other smaller investments, and bought, at far below cost, commodities which could only rise when peace came. Altogether he invested seventy-two thousand, three hundred and forty-four pounds, which was almost every penny of realizable capital he possessed.

He returned to London in bitter weather after a week, satisfied that he had made the necessary provisions just in time.

Unfortunately his meeting with the Duke of Leeds, which occurred three days after his return, did not come off so auspiciously. His lordship clearly looked on Sir George as a middle-aged parvenu. Mention of Lady Harriet's name made his intentions obviously clearer than he had intended, and they were as clearly resented. The Duchess was more gracious, but only perhaps because it wasn't *her* sister or because she was too absent-minded to care. A pretty young woman, she kept wandering in and out of the room followed by two servants searching for a key she had lost.

But George, while setting a black mark against the Duke for his haughty manner – a mark incidentally which would never be forgotten – was not too put down by it. He knew that money talked even in the highest circles, and if and when the Manchester investments brought their proper return, which must be within the year, he would altogether be worth probably half a million pounds. Even the Leeds family, for all their great connections, could not ignore that. Harriet would not, he dared swear. With or without the Duke's ungracious permission, she should marry him in the end.

II

With politeness but with increasing impatience Ross stayed on in London. He had of course written again to Demelza. He was not only anxious to be home but bored with his days at Westminster, where everyone seemed far more concerned with what they could get out of the constitutional crisis than either the prosecution of the war or the starving weavers of the north. That all three problems were inter-related he fully admitted, but that the last two should be half submerged in the scramble for political power disgusted him.

A meeting was arranged for him with the Foreign Secretary, but this in itself was a difficult and delicate encounter. In the first place he did not care for Wellesley. His brother, the recently ennobled Viscount Wellington, was stiff-backed, austere, lacking in warmth, but he had the magic of a soldier of the very highest gifts. Wellesley, by ten years the elder, might well have done fine work in India but was far too authoritarian for England, and some thought him lazy as well as pompous. A wit had said that you couldn't see Wellesley out walking without feeling that he expected to be preceded by the tramp of elephants.

Foreign Secretary, most people thought, was the position Canning should have held, but he had been excluded from it by factional jealousies and his own misjudgements.

A delicate meeting therefore on two counts, for Ross had gone to Portugal only in a semi-official capacity as an 'observer', with the sanction of the government but not at its behest. Canning, Dundas and Rose were at the back of it, and Wellesley had at first tried to obstruct the visit on the grounds that there was ample official information available about Portugal without sending out spies.

Fortunately Ross had not heard this word as applied to himself, but he knew of Wellesley's general reluctance, and he could be as stiff-backed as the next. However, the nature of the report he had brought back showed so clearly his admiration for the disposition and behaviour of the British forces in the field that Lord Wellesley expressed his appreciation and promised that the whole Cabinet should have copies of it before the week was out.

Perceval also was complimentary and sent a note to say so, but Canning was still not satisfied.

'We're preaching to the converted, old friend. You must speak in the House on it.'

'I could not,' said Ross, 'or would not.'

'Why not?'

'Until the Regency Bill is through no one is in the least interested. Anyway, if you were to circulate this report to every member of the House, do you seriously believe it would alter their thinking? Or convince those who were not already of that mind? They wouldn't bother to *read* it. If I stood up and caught the Speaker's eye, how many would stay to listen? D'you suppose that Whitbread or Wilberforce or Northumberland would be one whit influenced by anything I said – one whit less certain that England is going to lose the Peninsular war?'

Canning bit his thumb. 'It is a point that has been pricking at my mind all week. The question is, what to do about it.'

'Call it a day and let me go home.'

Canning said: 'Preaching to the unconvertible is little more use than preaching to the converted. It is the waverers who matter. And then only the waverers with influence. I have been thinking, I have been thinking for some time that you should tell this story to Lady Hertford who no doubt could be prevailed upon to repeat it to the Prince. But I am not at all sure. It's possible that this is an error on my part. Nothing is one half so convincing at second hand, is it. Well, is it?'

'No, I should think not.'

'So therefore it should be first hand. Am I not right? There is really only one person who must hear this report, and that is the Prince himself.'

III

As January waned the winter hardened and the Thames froze. The trees around Brompton were stiff with rime. Horses slithered and snorted in the icy lanes, their breath like dragons' in the sunless air. Birds dropped dead among the apple trees, foxes crept into the corners of the barns for shelter, the pall of London smoke, undisturbed by wind, kept its distance in the east.

Ross occupied much of his time amending and revising his report so that it should read clearly and without ambiguity. He wrote a third time to Demelza, apologizing for but not explaining the delay. It was a very long letter, the longest he had ever written her, and in it he said quite a substantial part of what was in the report but in more colloquial terms. It helped him, he found, to see it through her eyes.

In vain he argued with George Canning that even if this meeting, this anomalous meeting, could be arranged, the Prince of Wales would long since have made up his mind from his own ample sources of information as to the advantages and disadvantages of withdrawing from the Peninsula. Ross also pointed out that the Monarch (or his deputy) could certainly invite some statesman to form a government with whose policies he was in *general* agreement, but beyond that he could certainly not control every item of policy once the Cabinet was formed. Canning retorted that on the contrary Pitt, though a King's man, had had to resign office ten years ago because he wished to emancipate the Catholics, an act the King vehemently opposed. In other words, no statesman, not even Grey or Grenville, could negotiate peace with France if the

Prince Regent did not wish it. Sway the Prince, influence him in his thinking, and you might yet prevent the final disaster.

And how, Ross asked, did anyone imagine that a single account by a virtually unknown Member of Parliament sent out to observe the course of the war, would be likely to 'sway' in any remotest way the mind of the Heir Apparent? Canning wryly agreed. But drowning men, he said, clutched at straws: was it not worth clutching at this straw for the sake of the cause they all so much believed in? And after all, was there not also another saying, that a last straw could break a camel's back? Sheridan, for all his old allegiances, was, he now knew, on their side. Lady Hertford also. A great mass of the ordinary people of the country would deeply resent giving in to Buonaparte after all these years of bitter struggle. Did it matter so much if Grey or Grenville took office if, so far as making peace was concerned, their hands were tied?

Strings, said Ross in wry disgust, who would pull the strings to arrange this meeting? Not Wellesley, said Canning, he was too much an interested party. It must be Sheridan. No one else could contrive it. For it must be done privately so that no one but the Prince's closest friends knew.

In the last few days of the month the weather relented, and the ice-bound countryside became a quagmire. Ross went several times to the House when an important vote was pending, and heard Canning speak. Canning had an astonishing mastery of the Commons, one of the most difficult things to achieve, and equally difficult to maintain. A sudden silence fell on the rowdy chamber when a great or influential speaker rose; but what he had to say was subjected to as close a scrutiny as if he were a nobody, and if the subject-matter did not live up to his reputation the noisy interruptions would soon break out. Certainly not with Canning this time; he spoke for seventy minutes and received an ovation at the end. Later when

Ross moved among a crowd of members to congratulate him, Canning smiled and said in an undertone:

'I have just heard, old friend. Tomorrow evening at seven.'

'Where?'

'Holland House. Ask first for Sheridan.'

That would be the 29th. Ross nodded grimly and would have turned away but Canning drew him back into the circle of his friends – Smith, Ward, Huskisson, Bowne and the rest – as if to preserve him from the dangers of pessimism and doubt. Ross had met the Heir to the throne twice at receptions in recent years and had formed a very poor opinion of him. The country, he thought, was in a very bad way if it was going to be governed by, or be under a government which depended for its existence on, this fat pompous dandy. He was held up to almost universal ridicule and contempt, and the lampoons printed about him were of unsurpassed sarcasm and savagery.

Only last week Ross had paid a penny for a pamphlet which ran:

Not a fatter fish than he flounders in the Polar sea.
See he blubbers at his gills; what a world of drink he
    swills!
Every fish of generous kind scuds aside or shrinks
    behind;
But about his presence keep all the monsters of the deep.
Name or title what has he? Is he Regent of the sea?
By his bulk and by his size, by his oily qualities,
This (or else my eyesight fails) this should be the Prince
    of Whales.

There were a few, of course, who thought different. In his own arbitrary, haphazard way he had favoured architects, actors and writers more than any other prince in memory; but his spendthrift, dissolute life, the sheer aimless self-indulgence of his existence, offended Ross almost as much as it did the mass of English people. The thought of making his report to such a man seemed to him an essay in the sourest futility.

The Regency Bill must become law by the fifth or sixth of February. Canning had heard whispers that all was not concord in the Whig camp. Lords Grey and Grenville, having drafted suitable replies for the Prince to make to the resolutions of the House of Commons, found their elegant and sonorous prose discarded, and quite new and almost intemperate replies sent in their place, such as could only have been drafted by undesirable intimates of the calibre of Sheridan and Lord Moira. They had thereupon sent a dignified letter of remonstrance to the Prince, pointing out that, on the eve of their appointment to lead the country, it hardly became him to ignore their counsel and to take note instead of his secret advisers.

This had not at all pleased the Prince, who was very unused to remonstrance. However, there was little Prinny could do about it now. He had made it quite impossible for himself not to get rid of the present government – and there was no one else. Lansdowne – Canning said – was too young and had no experience of office, Tierney was quite unreliable, Sheridan a drunk, Ponsonby a nonentity. The Prince would have to suffer the lectures and make do.

'I'd like you to stay till the Bill becomes law,' Canning went on. 'Not respecting what happens between you and the Prince. It is a crisis, Ross, that transcends the pettiness of some of the people taking part in it. There is even a week yet for the King to recover! When it is over, when it is all done, when we have lost the day, then you may return to your Cornish acres, and I will undertake to make no further claims on your friendship for a twelvemonth! Will you agree?'

Ross smiled. 'It is not my Cornish acres I am anxious to see but my Cornish wife.'

'Well, you can be with her by mid-February – scarcely more than three weeks' time. You will come to the Duchess of Gordon's next Friday?'

'What on earth for?'

'It's her soirée at the Pulteney. All the leading people will be there, both in government and prospective government.'

'I'm not one of the leading people.'

'I think it's important you should be present. Disagreeable though social events may be, they do fulfil an important function in the governance of this country.'

'By then,' said Ross, 'I may be in disgrace.'

'For what?'

'Who knows? Not keeping a civil tongue in my head to his Royal Highness? Assaulting one of his flunkeys? Wearing the wrong colour cravat?'

'The last is the worst offence,' said Canning. 'I've known men languish in the Tower for less.'

IV

Seven o'clock seemed an unpropitious hour, but presumably it was considered better if he presented himself after dark. God only knew, he thought, why there should be any need for secrecy: he was not carrying some private communication from the Czar of Russia. Presumably during this crisis everyone would be scrutinized and his influence weighed, even to the butcher carrying meat in at the back door.

The butcher, come to think of it, was likely to be of much the greater influence, since he ministered to the royal stomach.

Exactly on seven Ross was shown into the magnificent waiting hall by a blue-and-gold-liveried manservant, his cloak and hat taken, a glass of fine canary put in his hand. The great room was empty, and he stared unadmiringly at its rococo decoration. The Prince, a florid man, clearly had a taste for the florid in architecture. Like the later kings of France. Was there to be a parallel here?

The squeak of a door announced a stout elderly man

who weaved unsteadily towards him, heels clacking on the polished floor.

'Captain Poldark? Good day to you. I'll take ye in in a matter of minutes. The Prince is with his secretary attending to a communication he has just received.'

They shook hands.

'Correspondence greatly increases when the throne is so near.'

'Of course.'

'The weather is milder, praise be to God. The cold touches up my liver confounded hard.'

They stood in silence. The older man coughed in an infirm manner.

'A drop more canary? Or would a brandy suit ye better?'

'Thank you. I'm more than accommodated.'

Another silence. 'The Prince is very much set about with business, as you'll understand. He would, I assure you, have been much happier if his father had recovered.'

'So should we all, Mr Sheridan.'

'Well. Ah well. All the same, those are not sentiments I would recommend ye to express in this house, or not perhaps sounding so heartfelt about them.' Sheridan steadied himself against a chair. 'Tact is of the essence, Captain Poldark. Tact. I have already built up your reputation as a military strategist, so I'm relying on ye to be a social one too!'

Ross smiled. 'The first's quite undeserved, so I don't know how I shall measure to your standards in the second . . . But if you're busy pray don't wait. I can keep my own company until sent for.'

'No, no. No, no, no. But if I may I'll join ye in a glass.'

It was ten minutes more before Ross was ushered into the presence. The Prince was in a smaller room, sitting at a richly veneered table examining a snuffbox. He was wearing a dressing-gown of olive green silk embroidered with silver thread; under it a white cravat, brilliant canary waistcoat, white silk breeches. Although a year or two younger than his visitor he looked an old man by comparison, an elderly hen as compared to an eagle. Everything about his face, the lines, the pouches, the pitted skin, showed the evidence of soft living and self-indulgence.

Ross bent over the jewelled hand.

The Prince grunted.

'My father,' he said, 'is a great collector of snuffboxes. I thought to give him this one. It might comfort him in his affliction. They say it belonged to Henry of Navarre.'

There was nothing Ross felt like saying in comment on this, so he did not speak.

'Perhaps, Captain Poldark, you are not a collector? Or perhaps only a collector of information?'

'Your Highness?'

'I understand you are recently from Portugal, to which certain ministers in my father's government elected to send you to obtain an independent picture of conditions there.'

'That is correct, sir.'

'And you have a report to make?'

'I thought your Highness had already seen it.'

The Prince of Wales looked up for the first time. His eyes, though swimmy, were shrewd and assessing. And not altogether friendly.

'You are primarily a soldier, Poldark, a man of action rather than a man of letters? I found your report interesting but not at all well written. I flatter myself I am some small judge of style in literature. However, I am told that you talk more easily and perhaps with a better sense of the use of words.'

'I'm not an orator either, sir. I can only hope to add a few observations to what is already set down – and of course to answer any questions you may see fit to put.'

The Prince still fingered the snuffbox.

'At least you don't promise too much. That's something. The older I get the more I'm surrounded by people who promise too much. It's the disease of the courtier, a curse bestowed upon kings and princes.'

Ross again held his tongue.

'D'you know, I too would have wished to be more a man of action than I have been allowed to be. D'you know that? This war – this war has dragged on . . . When it began I was a young man. Nothing would have pleased me more than to have led an army in the field – to have taken some *active* part in a campaign.' He contemplated the thought with satisfaction, nodding his big head in agreement with the words. 'I'm not a coward. Good God, I'm not a coward. Nor is my family without military antecedents. But – because I am heir to the throne I am allowed no active part at all! I must be – cocooned like some expensive and irreplaceable silkworm, so that when my father eventually dies I am available to take his place: to sign documents, to appoint ministers, to help preserve the body politic of England! But *personally*, for *myself*, as a human being, I am deprived of the satisfaction of achievement to further the greater good – or at least the greater stability – of the nation. And although you may envy me the luxury of my sheltered life, Poldark; indeed you may; I envy you the freedom of being what in fact you are – a soldier, a politician, a man of action; we might even say, using the word in its less offensive sense, an adventurer.'

'I adventure on my own behalf only in mines, sir,' Ross said drily. 'As for the rest, through my life, occasions have presented themselves.'

The Prince yawned and stretched his fat legs. He was wearing silver buckle shoes and white lisle stockings with openwork inserts.

'And now you have been presented to me, eh? When did you first meet Lord Wellington?'

The question was sharply put. Ross hesitated a moment. 'Wellington? . . . After Bussaco, sir. But briefly. He had much to occupy his attention.'

'You must have met him before?'

'No, sir.'

'And Wellesley?'

'I have seen him at receptions. Once we exchanged a word in the House. Until last week. Then I presented this report to him.'

'And Canning?'

'Oh, Canning I know well, sir. Have known for seven or eight years.'

'Yes, so I thought. So I thought. This – all this – has very much the smack of Canning's contriving.'

'All . . . *this*, your Highness?'

'Yes, and do not look down your long nose at me. You know what I mean. Canning should be called Cunning! He considers himself too big a man to be out of government, so when he is out he constantly tries to interfere and run a little government of his own. What possible other purpose could your visit to Portugal have had when the government is receiving its own perfectly adequate accounts of all that is going on there?'

'I asked that, sir, before I went.'

'Oh? And what were you told?'

'That an independent report might be of value by someone who has nothing to lose or gain and who, rightly or wrongly, has earned some reputation over the years for – impartiality.'

The Prince turned the snuffbox over and ran his finger along the bottom. 'It has been repaired – but skilfully. I don't think my father would notice, do you?'

Again Ross did not reply.

'You have a stiff back, Captain Poldark.'

'Sir?'

'I say you have a stiff back. Don't pretend you don't understand me . . . Well?'

'Well, sir?'

'Well, sir, say what you have to say. Elaborate on this report. Tell me what you saw, what you found, and what you deduced. Pray give me a sample of your eloquence.'

Ross swallowed. It was in his mind to bow and excuse himself and stalk out. To hell with this fat fop and his dandified manners and his lisle stockings and his snuffboxes. If this was the future King of England, then God help England. This interview was taking its predestined course.

But . . . this was not a *personal* matter on which he was being granted an audience. If he walked out, it was not *he* who lost. If he stayed, if he persevered in face of this discourteous invitation, nothing would be won, surely nothing *could* be won from this paunchy prince; but *he* would have done all that could be done. He could not reproach himself later – as he had a number of times in his life, when his pride – perhaps a false pride – had induced him to act in a way that cut out any hope for the cause he was promoting. It was not a time now to consider personal inclination. The issues were too large.

He began to speak – awkwardly, haltingly, at first looking at the Prince, who continued to finger the snuffbox – then away from him, at a statue to the left of the sofa on which his Highness was sitting. It was a statue of some Greek god; probably Titan, he guessed from the beard and the horn. He tried to forget the living man, who might or might not be listening, and address the man in stone.

He talked for perhaps ten minutes, barely pausing; and during the last five with some feeling as the subject took hold of him. He eventually stopped and looked down. The Prince had put the snuffbox away, and his head was on his chest. His breathing was steady. Ross stared at him with growing anger and contempt. The other man opened his heavy lids and sighed and said:

'Is that the end?'

'That is the end . . .'

'They were right, Poldark, you do talk well once you're started. It helped me to a pretty nap.'

Ross swallowed, trying to contain himself.

'Then, sir, I have failed as I expected to fail. If I may now have leave to withdraw . . .'

'No, you may not.'

Ross waited. A French clock struck the hour.

The Prince said: 'What do you mean, you expected to fail?'

'I expected that you would not be interested.'

The Prince yawned. 'I have been told that at Bussaco General Merle reached the top of the ridge almost unopposed. Why did Wellington allow that?'

'He had too long a line to guard, sir. They were not unopposed, but they came up sudden through the fog, and we had not sufficient fire power at that point to hold them.'

'Why was the defensive position so extended?'

'Because otherwise it would have been turned.'

'So the battle nearly ended in disaster to begin?'

'No, sir. Wellington was holding troops in reserve for such a situation. From his position he could see the whole ridge but because of the dawn fog little of the ground below. As soon as he saw the French break through to the top he sent in the 88th Foot – and I think some of the 45th; there was a bloody fight which went on best part of twenty minutes and then the crack French battalions were driven off the ridge, with something like two thousand casualties.'

'Were you involved in this?'

'No, sir, I attached myself to my nephew's company which was a part of Major-General Craufurd's 43rd.'

'The 43rd,' said the Prince, and yawned again. 'Then you were more than an observer in the further stages of the battle.'

'Yes, sir. In that charge later in the day on General Loison's Division. I confess I have never seen men better led or more fierce towards the enemy. You see, General Craufurd when ordering them to attack shouted that they were to avenge Sir John Moore.'

'Moore,' commented the Prince. 'Another failure!'

'All who fought with him believe otherwise. They say he was given impossible orders from London.'

'That would not surprise me. That would not surprise me at all. All the same, he was defeated. As Wellington himself is now admitting defeat.'

'Not defeat, sir. A tactical retreat. With such superior forces against him he would soon have had his flank turned and his communications cut.'

The Prince took out his own snuffbox and pushed a little snuff into each nostril.

'That is not how I have it reported, Captain Poldark. I am told the British Army became a rabble, intermingling with the rabble of refugees all fleeing for Lisbon before the triumphant French. It is the usual story: inefficiency, bad generalship, careless officering, ragged, drunken, plundering soldiery!'

'Perhaps, sir,' said Ross coldly, 'you have later and more detailed news than I.'

'No doubt I have. No doubt at all.'

'Nevertheless before I left for home I saw some of the defensive positions prepared round Torres Vedras and I cannot imagine, having seen the valour of our troops *and* of the Portuguese – now properly led and trained for the first time – I cannot imagine that the French will ever take them. I'll wager my head Lisbon is safe.'

The Prince of Wales at last rose from his chair. It was a major upheaval and peculiarly uncoordinated, large areas of bulk levering themselves up in unrelated effort. One could even imagine all the joints giving out, the utter indignity of a fall. But presently it was achieved and he was upright, heavily breathing, began to pace the room, his thin shoes *slip-slop*, *slip-slop*.

'Defence, defence. That's all our generals ever think of, even at their best! All we can ever do is land in some outlandish country of Europe, subsist for a while on the patriotism of the natives, deal the French a few pinpricks, and then retreat in ignominy either to prepared defences or to our very ships! How can this bring Napoleon down? I ask you!'

Ross stood and watched him. 'It's no easy question to answer, sir. Indeed, it may be best to accept the inevitable and bow the knee to Napoleon.'

'Ah, so you agree then with what most sensible men think!'

'I don't know what most sensible men think, your Highness.'

'Don't fence with me, sir.'

'Well, we are after all an unimportant island attempting too much, are we not? . . . straining our resources to no effect, wasting our blood and treasure in trying to restrict the expansion of the great French nation. They already own most of Europe. Without our pinpricks they will soon own the rest . . . Since you do me the great honour of asking my opinion . . .'

He waited. The Prince did not speak.

'Since you do me the great honour of asking my opinion, then personally I should be deeply grieved to see the first decade of this century end in England's complete humiliation, and indeed in our abdication of responsibility to the many peoples in Europe who look to our help; but you, your Royal Highness, must – above all men – accept the responsibility of choosing the destiny of your country, and we, your subjects, will accept the decision. As, indeed, will History.'

The Prince dabbed his nose with a handkerchief which had been worked in the now inaccessible town of Ghent.

He said: 'Insolence can come in many forms, Captain Poldark. As a soldier you must be aware of that. Do you speak your mind in Parliament?'

'I seldom speak in Parliament, sir.'

'Not surprised at that. You should take lessons from friend Sheridan. When he was at his best – which alas is time enough – he could . . . but no matter. No doubt you're doing your duty as you see it. Perhaps you will give me leave to do the same.'

'Sir, that is what I said.'

The Prince resumed his heavy-slippered pacing. Ross eased his leg. The stertorous breathing came near, went away again.

'Poldark.'

'Sir?'

'Come here.'

His Royal Highness was standing at a desk. As Ross went over he opened a drawer, took out a parchment about three feet by two; unrolled it, spread it on the desk, trembling jewelled fingers winking.

'See here. This is the plan sent back to me of the dispositions of the defences before Torres Vedras. Explain them to me.'

Ross screwed up his eyes.

'Wellington is an incorrigible blunderer,' said the Prince. 'So say all my best advisers. The Tories think different – but then they would, being responsible for having put him there, and the Foreign Secretary his brother. I wait to be convinced that Wellington is not an incorrigible blunderer.'

Ross said: 'If all that I have said up to now, sir . . .'

'Never mind that. Explain this map to me. In fact, perhaps you do not know, I have despatches to say Masséna is no longer investing Lisbon but, having tested the defences, is retreating. Some assure me that this is only to take up a better position and to place us in a worse. Others say that winter and hunger and disease are doing Wellington's work for him – as possibly he calculated they would. But I am not without military knowledge. If you have aught to say on this matter, pray say it before you leave.'

Chapter Nine

I

The Duchess of Gordon did not have a town house but when in London lived at the famous Pulteney Hotel, and it was here she was to give her reception. The Beautiful Duchess, as she was known, had been a Monteith and was almost as much admired for her wit as for her good looks, but by 1811 she was in her early sixties which perhaps explained why the Duke lived separately in New Norfolk Street.

All the same she was impeccably and inextricably linked with the higher reaches of the British aristocracy and everyone who was anyone would be there – which, Ross said, meant the place would be insufferably crowded and unthinkably hot. Besides, although he kept some clothes permanently at his old lodgings in George Street, he had no smart new elegant suit available and appropriate for such an occasion. George Canning said it was all the more correct that, recently returned from active service in Portugal, he should wear something sober and restrained – perhaps even battle-stained! That way he would be distinguishable from the fashionable gentlemen of Westminster and the court. He was himself, he said, making no effort to dress in the latest fashion. Women – ah, women, that was different. If his beloved wife were here . . .

It was Friday, the first of February. The bitter cold had quite relented and some of the mud and slush had dried off the cobbles. Straw had been laid across Piccadilly outside the hotel, and a carpet and an awning put out. Lanterns flickered on decorated poles, and menservants in white wigs and scarlet coats kept back the people pressing in to see. There was already a big crowd when the two men arrived. In the street there was the strange mixed smell of cold unwashed humanity, horses, horse dung, damp straw and smoking lamps; one passed into the foyer already warm with candles and heavily scented with perfumes; servants took cloaks, women touched hair hastily in the long gilt mirrors, one by one joined in the procession crocodiling towards the salon where the Duke and Duchess waited for them to be announced.

Splendid blue Scottish eyes but rather cold met Ross's momentarily as he unbent from her glove; the tiara and the necklaces glittered, these latter on skin now best covered; a fixed gracious smile dimpled the still rounded cheeks; his name was murmured and he was past, a drink offered him which he accepted before he realized it was sweet white wine. 'Come,' said Canning, 'I know this place, it will be cooler and less noisy in the music room.'

An hour passed in idle talk. Canning excused himself and then rejoined him. Three men had spoken to Ross about his report and congratulated him on it. No one, it seemed, knew anything of his visit to the Prince – which was as well since the meeting had accomplished nothing.

When he returned Canning said: 'There's few enough of the Opposition here. Indeed there's a rumour they've at last been given leave to form the new Administration and are at work on it tonight. An unfortunate thing for the Duchess's soirée, and I've no doubt it will be an unfortunate thing for the country at large.'

Ross was only half attending for he had spotted a familiar figure in the doorway whom he had no desire to see either here or elsewhere: Sir George Warleggan. He was with an elegant woman of about forty Ross had never seen before. He inquired of the other and altogether more admirable George now standing beside him.

Canning said: 'That's Lady Grenville. Agreeable creature – much less needlessly austere than her husband.

But this is what I mean: they are here without their men; Lady Grey is in scarlet by the piano; Mrs Whitbread is with Plumer Ward; Lady Northumberland is on your extreme right.'

Ross was peering to his extreme right but not at the woman Canning indicated. There was a tall fair girl in white with braided hair. The frock was low cut across the bust, had gathered sleeves to just above the elbow, and a silk bow under the bust with long flowing ends. She had grey eyes, and a fringe fell lightly on her forehead. She was talking to, or, more properly, being talked to, by a burly young man in a silver coat of irreproachable quality and cut. The young man Ross had seen before somewhere. The young woman, by the strangest chance, bore a strong resemblance to his elder daughter. He stared and blinked and looked away and then stared again. His eyes went across the rest of the group and he saw two people he really did know.

'By the Lord God!' he exclaimed, swallowed, and smiled at Canning's surprise. 'Forgive me, George! There are old friends here whom I must greet.'

He slid among the talking chattering groups, avoided a waiter with a tray of wine, excused himself when Sir Unwin Trevaunance tried to stop him, and came presently up against the fair girl in white.

'Miss Poldark,' he said.

She turned, half smiling at something the young man had said, then her face after a moment's hesitated surprise became suddenly radiant.

'*Papa!*'

He took her by both elbows but with tact resisted the desire to crush her in his arms. Instead, he held her quite firmly at a three-inch distance and kissed her first on one cheek, then on the other and then rather selectively on the mouth.

'Papa, Papa! We didn't know you were *home*! When did you come? Why didn't you *tell* us! Are you well? You look well! But how *are* you? Does Mama know? How *lovely*! I *never* expected this . . .'

'And could I expect *this*?' he said. 'You, *here*, in London. Is your mother here? How did it come about? Dwight! Caroline!'

So the greetings went, questions half asked, answers half listened to. In all this the young man in the silver coat seemed about to withdraw, when Caroline said:

'Ross, have you met Lord Edward Fitzmaurice?'

They bowed to each other. Ross said: 'I know your brother, sir. Henry Lansdowne.'

'Yes, sir. And I think we've met in the House.'

'You spoke last year on Catholic Emancipation.'

The young man had a craggy face.

'Among other things! My brother tells me I am on my feet altogether too much. I believe now he has inherited he is not altogether sorry to be out of the hurly-burly.'

'Is he here tonight?'

'No. He was to have come but is involved in some political discussions which I believe are going on.'

'Indeed,' Ross said drily.

'And you, sir,' said Lord Edward. 'I have just had the great pleasure of meeting your daughter.'

'So have I,' said Ross.

'Ah yes, but not quite for the first time!'

They talked for a few moments more, liking each other, and then Caroline took Ross's arm and led him gently away, telling him of things in Cornwall, asking him of things in Portugal. They were returning to Cornwall next Thursday, she said, perhaps they could all go together? But Clowance, Ross said, to find her *here*, and at such a gathering. Clowance, who liked nothing better than to be barefoot and ride her big horse and to act the tomboy! Had Demelza agreed? Had Clowance wanted? Was it her, Caroline's, suggestion? And what, for God's sake, was Dwight doing here in February?

'Peace,' said Caroline, and Dwight smiled and shook his

head. 'Peace,' said Caroline, 'when we are home Demelza will explain how it came about; there is nothing to worry about, everyone is well, and if you will now come home with us and tend to your broad acres – '

'Narrow acres,' said Ross.

'And see to your family and your mine and leave these sporting expeditions to other men, we shall all be happier.'

'Fitzmaurice,' said Ross, looking round.

'Yes, Fitzmaurice,' said Caroline, 'who clearly has taken a fancy to your charming daughter. It will do no harm.'

'But Clowance,' Ross said and frowned. 'Isn't it Petty-Fitzmaurice?'

'Well, it's an old family, and no doubt they can choose for themselves. His brother was simply known as Henry Petty until he succeeded last year. Lord Edward is twenty-seven. And not bad-looking and clean-living like his brother and of good repute. What more could you ask?'

'For what?' Ross asked, startled.

'For a friend for your daughter. Is it so surprising? Let the attraction run.'

'So long as it runs in the right direction.'

'Ross, are you being parental? Not surprising – we shall all be in due course! But Clowance is, I believe, far too clear-headed to be influenced in any way by the claims of eminence or title.'

At that moment the clear-headed Clowance was discussing foxes.

'I don't believe it,' said Fitzmaurice, laughing. 'How is it possible?'

'I don't know, sir. Perhaps I live closer to the ground than you.'

'At the moment, Miss Poldark, you look far too astral to be anywhere *near* the ground! And please, I beg of you, do not call me sir.'

'What may I call you then – sir?'

'Lansdowne is my brother's new name, and he says he can scarcely get used to it yet. But I was born Fitzmaurice and am likely to die the same, since luckily my brother is married and already has issue. The names my parents gave me at holy baptism were Edward John Charles, and if I dare not ask you to call me by any of these, since it would presume an intimacy on *my* part towards *you*, I trust our acquaintance may soon become of sufficient depth to permit it.'

Clowance opened her eyes wider at this Westminster eloquence.

'Mine is Clowance,' she said. 'I believe I have only the one name.'

'Clarence,' said Fitzmaurice. 'Is that not a surname?'

'No, Clowance. C-L-O-W . . .' She smiled. 'There is one old . . . very old man who lives near us in Cornwall who insists on calling me Clarence, but I assure you it is not.' Into her mind as she spoke, making her smile broader than it would have been, came the thought of Jud Paynter – almost immobile now – sitting like a partly squashed beetle outside his dirty cottage in Sawle, chewing tobacco and spitting and refusing to accept the fact that he had not heard her baptized as Clarence. The contrast with this brilliant, elegant society was almost too much for her.

Fitzmaurice said: 'Well, *this* old man, Miss Poldark, will make no such mistake in future! Even so, if I may venture to say so, it's an unusual name to me. Is it common in your county?'

'No. There are no others I know of.'

'Has it a meaning? I mean in your Cornish language.'

'Yes, I believe so. I believe my mother told me it meant "Echo in the Valley".'

'Echo in the Valley,' said Lord Edward, looking at her. 'That is indeed an appropriate name.'

II

'Dear Ross,' Caroline said, 'on these occasions you do not

so much look like a fish out of water as a cat *in* water. What may I do to entertain you?'

Ross dabbed his face and laughed. 'Explain to me why my dearest woman friend should have such different tastes from my own.'

'Oh . . . that's difficult, isn't it. But let us say that of course I know we see here a selection of men and women who are vain, self-seeking, arrogant, over-dressed, avaricious and shallow. But they are little different in this respect from other people, except that they have more possessions, and perhaps possessions are a corrupting influence.'

'Stop there, stop there!' said Ross; 'for the first time in my life I've heard you utter a radical statement!'

'Of course I'll not stop there! My lecture's not half done. It's true you may also come across a greater simplicity, even a greater generosity among *some* of the poor. *But* among *most* of the poor and the base you will also find a greater brutishness, an ignorance, a lower level of understanding of so very much that is *important* in life. Many are poor because they have had no chance to be anything else, but most are poor because they are of a lower order of intellect, feeling, taste, comprehension. It's an inescapable fact!'

Ross smiled at her. 'I think you've been sharpening your arguments on Dwight.'

'And blunting them on you, my dear. I know.'

'Tell me,' Ross said, 'Demelza *suggested* Clowance should come with you? Is that it?'

'Let her explain herself; you'll be seeing her soon, I trust. And stop looking over my shoulder. Clowance is perfectly safe with that distinguished young man. He's unmarried, I believe. Who are you to say no if he wishes to make her a titled lady?'

'There's small risk of that. I am more concerned that she will be . . . ' He stopped.

'Unsettled by moving in such high company? D'you

wish her, then, to keep only the company of miners who are shaved once a week and can't sign their own names?'

'Sometimes, Caroline, I could strike you.'

'I know. I would rather like it. But seriously . . . ' She too paused.

'Can you be serious?'

'Seldom with you. But girls – all girls – need a broadening of experience which is so often denied them. Clowance deserves it. If she doesn't have a good and steady head on her shoulders she wouldn't be Demelza's daughter, or yours.'

Another man who was just then looking over someone's shoulder at Clowance was Sir George Warleggan. He had caught sight of Ross, safe back, one unhappily presumed, from his damned Portuguese adventure. Now he saw the daughter.

'My dear Lady Banks, this is the night of decision. I have it from Lady Grenville that her husband, the Baron, in company with Earl Grey and others close to them, are in process of making history! The new government will be announced tomorrow.'

'Well, the delays have been interminable already,' said Lady Banks, patting her crimped hair. 'Sir William has been fumin' and frettin' to get home to his estate. I don't care what you say, things are never the same without the master there – but he is being *chained* here, virtually chained, by a quite excessive sense of duty! *And* we're missin' all the best weather for huntin'!'

George, who knew that Sir William was remaining in London hoping for a sinecure, and had seen him being uncharacteristically polite to Samuel Whitbread only yesterday, inclined his head.

'Like me,' he said, 'your estates are far from London and this compounds the aggravation. One cannot go home in a couple of days and then return. What is your normal travelling time to Yorkshire?'

As he spoke Clowance happened to turn and their eyes

met. Clowance smiled at him. George looked away; then he changed his mind and looked back and nodded in acknowledgment. He assessed whom she was with, recognized his importance, his youth, his interest in her; his mind flickered with sudden sick jealousy over all the possibilities. So Ross, for all his hypercritical disclaimers of position and property for himself, was not above dragging his eldest brat up from Cornwall, dressing her in a revealing frock so that her wares should not go unnoticed, and introducing her to one of the most eligible bachelors in Great Britain. If Demelza's daughter by any chance should marry into such a family there would be no containing the arrogance of the Poldarks now or for ever after. All the same, George thought spitefully, Edward Fitzmaurice was not born yesterday. Far more likely if, in spite of his high reputation, he should try to sample the goods without buying. In that case, good luck to him.

'My dear Lady Banks,' he said, hastily shutting out from his mind a thought of the goods Fitzmaurice would be sampling, 'modern methods of making up the turnpike roads are ever advancing. These two Scotsmen – what are they called? – have laid roads like no one before; perhaps in a few years our journeys will not be so tedious.'

Something tapped him familiarly on the shoulder. It was a fan – a woman's fan. Over the years of his success George had developed a high sense of dignity, of decorum, and he turned in some displeasure, though careful to show nothing in his expression lest the person who tapped should be of an eminence to excuse her licence.

'Sir George, isn't it? I thought I couldn't mistake my benefactor . . .'

A tall young woman with hair so black that in the winking candlelight it had a bluish sheen. It was not in George's nature to flush easily – but he felt colour come to his neck as he bent over her glove.

'Lady Harriet! What a pleasure! What a delight! And what a *surprise*! I had thought you in Cornwall!'

'Where I wish I still could be. Or Devon, preferably, where the hunting is better. But business to do with my late husband's estate – or lack of estate – has called me here.'

George stammered and then remembered his manners, introduced the stout middle-aged Lady Banks. While polite conversation was made his eyes moved over the company to see if her brother was there – a relief that he was not at least immediately apparent – then back to Harriet Carter. Two months had passed since they had met; he took in what he saw greedily but assessingly. This was the young woman about whom he had already made the provisional moves and approaches to take her to his bed. Already he had plunged half his fortune in speculative but wise ventures in the north so that he should be a in a stronger position financially to gain her. To *gain* her. To *possess* her. To have her lying naked beside him, the sister of a duke. It was extraordinary! His eyes went over her. She would be heavier in the leg than Elizabeth, rather thick of ankle, he suspected, though it was hard to be sure. Sturdier than Elizabeth, stronger of breast and thigh; *good* shoulders, visible tonight, splendid shoulders, not broad but strong, alluringly rounded and shadowed; *delicious*.

He took a grip of himself, became himself again, smiling at her, talking respectfully; where had this strange sexual urge come from? It was not like him: he should be measured, careful; was it again that tempting damned Poldark girl who had set him off?

Could it be also – did he not detect – that Lady Harriet's attitude towards him tonight was more forthcoming – or at least less reserved – than it had been in Cornwall? This was the first time they had met, of course, since he had made her the gift of her horse, since the exchange of the letters. It was not only by this act, but also by his looks earlier, that he had made his intentions plain to her. So she had had time – plenty of time – to think, to reflect on the prospect of what he appeared to be offering her, and the prospect, it seemed, was not altogether unpleasant. The thought of an alliance with the grandson of a blacksmith could not, if that tap on the shoulder meant anything, be altogether repugnant to her. Nor could he, George Warleggan, personally be totally without appeal. The thought warmed him. But what of the Duke?

'Is your brother, the Duke, with you tonight, Lady Harriet?'

'He was to have come but there is much to-ing and fro-ing behind the scenes and he is caught up in it. Not that it is quite in his nature to be the political animal my father was, but he seems to have become a little entangled. So I came with my sister-in-law. This party is grossly short of men.'

Another woman spoke to her then and conversation became general. Harriet was wearing a full-skirted frock of turquoise silk, very much off the shoulders, and the necklace and ear-rings she wore to match were quite clearly an heirloom. That was one of the most curious characteristics of the aristocracy, George reflected. They were 'poor' or 'bankrupt' or had 'fallen on hard times', but there was always something coming to hand from an aunt or an entailment or a precatory trust. George had never been poor, for his father had begun to accumulate money soon after he was born, but he knew of a different sort of poverty than that at present being endured by Lady Harriet. It made her no less attractive.

Suddenly the other woman had turned away with Lady Banks and Harriet was speaking to him again.

'What? What was that?' he said.

'Sir George, you are being absent-minded with me. To a woman that is one of the unforgivable sins.'

'I ask your pardon. But you were not absent from my thoughts. What was it you said?'

'I said that I understood you called to see my brother last month.'

'That is so, Lady Harriet.'

'And my name was mentioned?'

'Since I had had the great favour of meeting you last year in Cornwall I could not fail to bring to his notice such a pleasurable occurrence.'

'Did you have other business with my brother?'

'Business, ma'am? None at all.'

Her eyes left his for a few moments, seemed to wander round the room. But they were not concerned with what they saw.

'Sir George, my father is dead. So is my husband. I am a widow of a sufficient age. I do not look on my brother as being *in loco parentis*.'

'I am happy to know that.'

A faint cynical smile played around her mouth. 'But that being said, Sir George, that is all.'

'All?'

'For the time being. Let us meet again in Cornwall.'

George licked his lips. 'But that may be *weeks*. Pray let me attend you while you are in London.'

She thought for a moment. 'That could be so.'

III

Clowance said: 'No, I live on a farm – a small estate, if you care to give it so grand a name – with my father and my mother and my brother and sister. We derive our living – or most of it – from a tin mine called Wheal Grace – which was named after my grandmother. My father is also in banking and in shipbuilding, all of which should make us rich, except for the fact that my father is so often away that nothing is quite attended to in time and our way of life is quite comfortable but never opulent.'

'Your father,' said Lord Edward, 'is, I suspect, that rare type of radical who practises what he preaches. I know that he and my brother see eye to eye on most of the home issues of the day. As it happens, birth has given me a certain amount of position at an early age, and my brother, of course, a great deal more. Well, position brings responsibilities and I do not think he intends to abdicate any of them. In so far as any fall to me as his younger brother, nor shall I. Miss Poldark . . .'

'Yes?'

'Will you come to tea tomorrow? I should like you to meet my aunt, Lady Isabel Fitzmaurice. My mother died when I was nine, so Aunt Isabel has for long taken her place. She entertains a few picked guests on Saturdays about six. I should be there, of course.'

'You're very kind, Lord Edward,' Clowance said, 'but I fear I cannot come. I have promised to go with Mrs Enys to the theatre. We are to see – '

'Perhaps Sunday, then? That would be rather a different event, because of the day, but it could be arranged in very much the same manner.'

Clowance nervously fingered the shoulder of her frock. 'Lord Edward, I have just met my father after three months, when he has been away and in some danger. He would think it strange if I absented myself in this way. You do appreciate, of course, that I am not accustomed to this social life in London . . .'

'Of course,' said Edward Fitzmaurice, a little stiffly. 'I do understand that.'

Dr Dwight Enys had been in earnest conversation with a clear-eyed good-looking small man, and when the opportunity arose he beckoned to Ross and introduced him as Humphry Davy. A Cornishman and a Fellow of the Royal Society, discoverer of nitrous oxide and first isolator of the elements of potassium and sodium, he was the brightest light in the scientific world of the day. Dwight had begun a correspondence with him ten years ago, and they had met three or four times. Davy was a little dandified for Ross, the voice without a trace of West Country accent, and drawling. Then Davy excused himself and the two friends were temporarily alone. Ross and

Dwight had no secrets from each other (or Dwight only one from Ross and that long buried in the dark December of 1799) and complete trust in the other's discretion, so their talk was frank and open. After discussing Portugal, Ross told his friend of his visit to the Prince of Wales and Dwight explained the reason for his being in London.

'He's a man of great vigour for his age – great physical vigour. But the brain that controls that vigour is sadly deteriorated. It shows too in his near blindness. I believe his insanity to be in the line of his royal descent.'

'How so?'

'Probably some hereditary weakness – even perhaps going as far back as the Stuarts. It has emerged every so often through the generations: the pain in the limbs, the wild excitability, the delusions, the intense depressions. The symptoms are much the same, though of varying severity. Of course, not many of his forbears have lived as *long* as he has . . . In this one reads history as much as medicine.'

'And you do not expect recovery?'

'No . . .'

'Well . . . there we are . . . But it is a sad day for England now this fat fop is to become Regent.'

'With such a life of self-indulgence, he seems unlikely to make old bones,' said Dwight. 'And then what?'

'Queen Charlotte? They say she's a warm, impulsive creature. A lot will depend on whom she marries.'

Someone was playing a piece on the Broadwood pianoforte, but only those closest to the instrument were attending. Caroline came swiftly across the room, her auburn hair lifting from her shoulders as she moved. With drink the company had become more animated, and she slid with great elegance among the glasses held aloft, the multi-coloured suits, the bare shoulders, the sweating footmen with balanced trays.

She said: 'Can you hear it? Amid all this noise. Dear Alexander, though rather aged now, always insists someone shall play his great composition at every one of his wife's soirées. What do they call it? "Cauld Kail in Aberdeen". It's said it's still all the rage in Scotland.'

They tried to listen.

Caroline said: 'So you see, Ross, Clowance and Lord Edward Fitzmaurice have now separated. You had nothing to fear; she is in no danger of being contaminated.'

'Who is she talking to now?'

'Ah, more aristocracy, I fear! That is Susan Manchester, one of the Duchess of Gordon's daughters. But possibly with her there is less risk?'

'A pretty woman,' said Ross, refusing to be provoked.

'All her daughters are, and she's married 'em off spectacularly. Charlotte, the eldest, is Duchess of Richmond, Susan is Duchess of Manchester, Louisa is the Marchioness Cornwallis and Georgiana is Duchess of Bedford. Her only failure was Madelina who could find no one better than a baronet.'

'And doesn't she have a son for Clowance?' Ross asked.

'There is one knocking about, and unwed, but unfortunately I don't see him here tonight.'

Ross broke off these sardonic pleasantries, his eyes catching sight of a movement by the door.

'Sorry, Caroline . . . What I *do* see here tonight . . . quite suddenly . . .' He stopped and frowned.

'What is it?'

Ross nodded his head towards a stout man talking to the Duchess of Gordon. 'Whitbread. Just arrived. And Northumberland with him . . . Does that mean the new Administration is formed?'

'Where is your Mr Canning? He's likely to know.'

'I don't think anyone knows – yet, except those two gentlemen.'

Clowance came to her father's side and took his hand in hers. He smiled at her.

'I shall come home with you on Thursday,' he said.

'I'm glad.'

'And race you across the beach.'

'Maybe.'

'And I promise to stay at home for at least a week telling stories to Isabella-Rose.'

'I would not mind one for myself.'

'I thought you were too old for that.'

'It depends on the story.'

He said: 'Perhaps you've stories to tell me instead?'

She looked up at him. 'What makes you say that?'

'Seeing you here was a great surprise. I wondered what had occasioned it.'

'One day I'll tell you.'

'One day?'

'Soon . . .'

'How did you find Lord Edward?'

'Very – agreeable. He asked me to tea.'

'What did you say?'

'I said no. Was that correct, Papa?'

'If that was what you wished, that was correct.'

'Yes . . . I *think* that was what I wished.'

George Canning came quietly up behind them, and Ross introduced him to Clowance.

Canning drew Ross a little aside and said: 'This is the end. Spencer Perceval is to be dismissed in the morning. There is nothing more we can do. You may resort to your beloved Cornwall; Perceval can no doubt return to his legal practice – where he was a much richer man than as leader of the government. Ah well . . . for my part, since I was not in office before, I shall miss very little – except that in harrying the new administration I shall do it with a greater sense of mission . . . I am in essence a political animal, Ross, as you are not. You will be happier out of it all.'

'Not happier,' said Ross, 'with a solution that gives everything away.'

'It's an ill wind: our spinners and weavers will be less hungry. Perhaps somehow we shall learn to exist with the Corsican brigand. Poor Wellington!'

'Poor Nelson,' said Ross. 'Not to mention John Moore and ten thousand others.'

'I don't know,' said Canning bitterly. 'Perhaps their death is their glory. It shouldn't matter to them that they fought for a lost cause.'

They were standing in the wide double doorway of the music room and could see into the great salon. Some just perceptible change was coming over the company. A few minutes ago, such was the babel it was impossible to make oneself heard at anything below a subdued shout. Now it was different. There was *news*. News had been brought by Whitbread and Northumberland. People were still talking, but with less animation. Glances were being exchanged, the most important people were being watched – behind fans, over the tops of glasses. Whitbread was talking animatedly to two Whig friends, emphasizing something repeatedly with his hand. Was this news of government or of battle? Lady Grenville had been listening to Lord Northumberland. Abruptly she gave him her hand. He bowed. She swept across the room – not towards the music room but towards the entrance of the hotel. It seemed that she was leaving. The Speaker of the Commons, Mr Abbott, was accompanying her. Lord Holland hurried after them.

Loud conversation died away altogether. Murmuring took its place. Lord Fitzwilliam had gone across to Whitbread, who immediately turned to him and repeated his story. Whitbread's face, pale when he entered the salon, was now flushed – and not, it seemed, altogether with the heat. The Duchess of Gordon, concerned lest her soirée should be still more put out of joint, turned to ask a question of the burly, blustering Lord Kensington, who had been laying heavy bets on the outcome at Brooks's. Kensington laughed and shrugged his shoulders.

'They're out!' he said in a loud voice. 'By God, they're out!'

His bellow seemed to relieve the tension; more people

crowded round Whitbread to hear his tale. Whitbread angrily shook his head and made to leave. Whatever else he had come to this soirée for, it was not to satisfy the gossips.

Presently Robert Plumer Ward detached himself from the group around Northumberland and strolled towards Canning. Plumer Ward was an easy-going fellow, on friendly terms with everyone, a man who greatly enjoyed being in the know.

'Well?' said Canning testily, as he came up. 'What did that mean? What is surprising about it? Perceval must know his fate by now.'

'*They*'re out, George,' drawled Plumer Ward. '*They*'re out. Can you believe it? After all this fuss. According to the story – and it comes direct so there can be little chance of mistake – according to Northumberland, he and Grey and Grenville and Whitbread and the rest were deep in conclave in Park Street when who should come to call on them but William Adam, with a message, he said. Lords Grey and Grenville, in that godly-minded way they have, sent out to Adam that they could not at present see him. Adam replied that the message he brought was from the Prince of Wales. Lords Grey and Grenville replied that they still could not be disturbed for it was for the Prince of Wales they laboured, forming the new Government which was to be the first government of his Regency. Adam thereupon sent in word that they should spare themselves all the trouble, for the Prince had decided that no new administration was to be formed and that he had decided to continue with his father's ministers! What d'you think of *that*, eh? What d'you think of *that*?'

There was silence.

Ross said: 'Does that mean . . .'

'It must be false!' whispered Canning. 'It is a lie spread about to deceive us!'

'For what purpose? Who would benefit?'

'But the Prince has been an ardent and committed Whig for thirty years . . .'

Plumer Ward said: 'The Prince is no fool, for all his excesses. He must have been having private thoughts these last few weeks. Who knows what he has been thinking? Is it perhaps – has he come to the conclusion that there is a vast difference between being virtually on the throne and being the discontented eldest son?'

'I shall not believe it' said Canning, 'unless – until . . .'

Plumer Ward said: 'I'm told Grey and Grenville have now gone to seek an audience. But if Prinny has made up his mind it will not avail.'

'That means . . .' said Ross again; and got no further.

'It means,' said Canning, 'it *may* mean that our cause is not altogether lost.'

IV

Lady Harriet Carter said: 'There is a white lion in the Tower, brought back by Sir Edward Pellew. I wonder if he feels at all out of place in a building which has housed half the about-to-be beheaded lions of England. I suppose it is a symbol of progress that neither Lord Grenville nor Mr Perceval run any risk of languishing there while the other is First Lord of the Treasury . . .'

'Yes,' said George, taking out a handkerchief and wiping his hands.

'Are you quite well? You have gone pale.'

'Yes, I am quite well. It is very hot in here.'

'If this story is true,' Harriet said: 'if what they say is true it will blight more than one high hope of office. Did you have any?'

'What? What was that?'

'Any hope of office? You're a Whig more than anything, ain't you?'

'Yes,' said George.

'And did you?'

'No. I expected no office.'

'Then you have little to lose or gain. For my part I

should not relish any occupation which would keep me in this rowdy metropolis when there are so many broad and unspoiled acres to enjoy in the shires. Cornwall depresses me; it is so harsh and grey and windswept; but my aunt makes great play of the fact that there are several fine days a year.'

'Lady Harriet,' said George, and swallowed.

She looked at him with her great dark eyes. 'Don't say it, Sir George . . . yet.'

'What I have to say, Lady Harriet, is something quite different from what I had intended. Unexpectedly I find it will be necessary to leave London almost immediately. Indeed, I think, if you will excuse me, I will go now.'

'Go? Where?'

'Business matters.'

'So important?'

'Unfortunately for me there are other considerations besides politics involved in the Prince's decision. I – I fear I must attend to them.'

They looked at each other for a long moment.

'Then,' she said coldly, 'I must return to my sister-in-law in the other room unescorted, must I not. Good night, Sir George.'

'Good night, Lady Harriet. Perhaps . . .'

She smiled. He bent over her hand. His own hand was hot and unsteady, but it was not love of woman that shook him.

He turned and pushed his way unceremoniously towards the door.

Book Two

Book Two

Chapter One

I

Jeremy Poldark was an amiable young man who had grown up in the comfort and stability of a family home where casual manners hid deeper affections and where quarrels almost always ended in laughter. As a consequence, whatever powerful emotions might slumber within him, they had had no inducement yet to stir. Although conceived when his father was waiting to stand trial for his life and born at a time when his parents' financial stringency was at its most acute, he seemed to have none of Ross's dark, radical pessimism and little of Demelza's brilliant impulsive vitality. Perhaps more than any other of his family he had a true Celtic sense of *laissez-faire*.

One thing moved him to anger: cruelty to or neglect of animals; and one thing, apart from a talent for sketching, interested him deeply.

This interest dated back to a day when he was just ten and a half years old. It was the morning of the 28th December, 1801, and he had ridden on his new Christmas pony with his father to see Lord de Dunstanville at Tehidy. His father was a partner in the Cornish Bank of which Lord de Dunstanville was the principal shareholder, and Mr Stackhouse was there and Mr Harris Pascoe and a Mr Davies Giddy.

It was the first time Jeremy had ever ridden such a distance with his father and he was very proud of himself. He had worn a brown corduroy riding suit, new also for Christmas, and a tricorn hat secured by a cord under the chin to preserve its position in the gusty wind. It was a fine open day, with north-westerly clouds beating up from the horizon and hurrying off over the land towards France. The sun, like a handicapped painter, splashed colour on the landscape when and where it could. After the men had gone into the drawing-room to talk, little Lady de Dunstanville, with her daughter Frances and Mr Giddy, who was not here on banking business, had walked out with him onto the terrace, talking and laughing and looking expectantly down the long drive towards the gates. Frances Basset, a plain but pleasant girl of nineteen, had explained to her young guest what they were waiting for.

A young engineer attached to one of the Camborne mines, Trevithick by name and a leading man in the development of some strange contraption called a 'high pressure' engine, had taken one of his machines, which were designed primarily to pump water out of the mines, and put it on *wheels* and claimed that it would *move*.

There was much scepticism. People knew only a means of propulsion derived from a living animal with four legs whose hooves planted at irregular intervals on the ground as it moved created traction. Most argued therefore that, even if such a clumsy device as Trevithick proposed could ever be employed to move the wheels, the wheels themselves would not have sufficient grip upon the road to move the vehicle. The wheels would of course spin round. In any event, it was doubted that they would ever even be got to spin.

In this elevated company in which young Jeremy now found himself there was a somewhat greater faith than generally obtained, for Mr Giddy had been one of the chief encouragers of the young engineer, and Lady de Dunstanville had actually been present, and had worked the bellows, when one of the models had been persuaded to run round a room.

They all, therefore, waited on the terrace, for Mr Trevithick had said he would that day fire his machine and drive it the three miles from Camborne Church Town to Tehidy, where Mr Giddy and Lord and Lady de Dunstanville would be waiting to receive it with all proper acclaim.

As time passed and no engine appeared, they all agreed rather sadly that between a model eighteen inches high and an actual vehicle of the road over ten feet tall a wide gap of trial and error existed. When Lord de Dunstanville and Captain Poldark and the rest came out of their meeting and there was still no sign, it was concluded that the attempt, for what it was worth, had been a failure. Captain Poldark was invited to stay to dinner, but he excused himself saying that his wife was expecting them home. Smiling he tapped Jeremy on the shoulder and presently, after a glass of canary, they mounted and rode away down the drive.

Jeremy's pony was frisky after his rest, and though he tried to talk to his father, telling him what he had been told, most of the time they were separated by a few prancing steps; and they had been on their way from the gates for almost a mile when they beheld a sight which Jeremy was not to forget.

Something was crawling towards them over the rough uneven track. It was like a grasshopper on wheels with a tall proboscis held high in the front and sending out puffs of intermittent smoke. The wheels by which it moved were four in number, but many other wheels, some cogged, some plain, turned as well in the body of the monster. It cranked and rattled and coughed, and from every joint *apart* from the proboscis emitted more smoke and steam both white and black. And perhaps the most extraordinary thing of all was that, clinging to the machine, careless of heat and danger, were about twelve dirty men shouting at the top of their voices, while a couple of dozen more followed hallooing in the wake.

The noise was so great that Ross had to dismount and hold the heads of the horse and pony while the procession passed. Many waved to them, including the tall bulky figure of the inventor, and his companion Andrew Vivian. Jeremy sat his pony awestruck. He had never imagined anything like it in his life. It was opening the door to a new world.

The Poldarks had not long since passed an inn, and when Ross remounted they sat there watching the chattering clanking steaming monster recede. Presently the inn was reached, the engine came to a lumbering stop, and everybody slid and tumbled off it and went inside. After a few minutes they had all gone, and there beside the inn the strange machine was left smoking and simmering to itself.

Ross turned his horse's head. 'So they have done it. A great achievement. Let's be on our way.'

'But, Papa, if we could go back and look – '

'We shall see it again. If this is a success, have no fear.'

So they rode home as a few more clouds gathered to mark the turn of the winter's day. But they did not see it again, for, it seemed, there was an admirable roast goose at the inn as well as excellent ale, and the roistering company stayed for a meal before going on to Tehidy. In the meantime, nobody had remembered to put out the fire under the boiler of the engine, so the water evaporated and the boiler grew red hot and set fire to the wooden frame of the engine. Then a man came hammering at the door of the inn and the company streamed out to see the brilliant new machine collapsing in a great bonfire which left in the end only twisted metal, a few wheels aslant and a heap of smouldering coal.

II

One reason why Ross had not wished to stop was that there was some slight feeling between Trevithick and himself. Trevithick and a young man called Bull had put up the engine for Wheal Grace when Trevithick was only twenty-one, but over the years he had failed to come over to maintain it, and when the two engineers had themselves parted company Ross had chosen to continue to do business with the more reliable one. Trevithick had disliked this and had said so in no uncertain manner. Since Bull's death Ross had managed with the help of Henshawe and other local men. Ross bore Trevithick no ill will for his remarks, but, as they had not met since, he found himself a little embarrassed in the matter of jumping down from his horse and congratulating him on his new achievement.

Not so Jeremy, who thought of nothing else for days. To him that strange machine he had seen was not just an assembly of nuts and bolts and cylinders and pistons and condensers; it was alive; as much alive as a horse or a man; it had a personality, a dramatic character of its own, deserved an individual and honourable name. To start it, he learned, you had to light a fire in its belly and put in coal; then presently it began to simmer and hiss, and all the intricate joints became animated: the miracle of its life began. The very way it moved, seeming to sway a little from side to side as if endeavouring to walk; the *steam* that issued from everywhere, like sweat, like a dragon's breath; *moving*, making its own way across the countryside.

All this was breathtaking: he had seen a vision.

Thereafter he kept anxious watch in *The Sherborne Mercury* for any mention of his hero; but by now Trevithick was more out of Cornwall than in it, and news that he had put his new toy to practical ends came from Wales, where he had constructed a loco-motive which ran on a tramroad. The great engineer, James Watt, now in his late sixties, predicted disaster; for he himself still used engines with boiler pressures of little more than two or three lbs per square inch above that of the atmosphere; Trevithick was making boilers to work at 60 lbs, and talking of 100 lbs! An explosion, Watt predicted, must come sooner or later, with severe loss of life. One only had to experiment by soldering up the lid of a pan of water and putting it on the fire. Safety-valves were not enough.

It was not until seven years later, on his first visit to London with his father and mother, that Jeremy met the engineer. At that time Trevithick, not content with having driven one of his fire-engines clanging and chuffing through the streets of London in 1803, had now with some of his friends taken a field in north London between Upper Gower Street and the Bedford Nurseries, had palisaded it off and put down a circular railroad, and there advertised an engine (called Catch-Me-Who-Can) and was charging 1s. for admission to all who were curious enough to come and see – with a free ride included for those hardy spirits who dared to travel in the shaky carriage attached. It was a deliberate show – an attempt to gain the attention and the interest of the public.

Ross at that time was much preoccupied because he was going to – or hoping to – make one of his excessively rare speeches in Parliament – on the reform of the House of Commons; but Jeremy was so persistent that he agreed they should view the spectacle. Demelza, always fascinated by anything new, was almost as eager, and they had spent a morning there, and had all ridden on it at a speed of almost twelve miles an hour. Trevithick happened to be in attendance, and he greeted them like dear friends – as indeed they were, so far from home. Forgetful of any past resentments, he took endless trouble explaining to the boy of seventeen how his engine operated.

By now, however, there had been fatal accidents, just as Watt had said there would be; one engine had blown itself to pieces in Greenwich, killing four people and injuring others. On the morning they visited the site there were only a dozen people in the compound, and only two others would venture to take a ride. Ross said as they left: 'It is a wondrous novelty, but I would not like a son or brother of mine to be involved at this experimental stage.'

Jeremy said: 'Mr Trevithick tells me all the boilers are fitted now with two safety-valves instead of one.'

'I don't know whether I wish it will come to something

or not,' said Demelza. 'I suppose I have galloped faster than that but it does not *feel* so fast. With a horse you don't fear its wheel will come off!'

Jeremy said: 'Mr Trevithick says there is a shortage of horses because of the war. He feels there is a big future for the steam carriage.'

Ross said: 'That may be. But I don't think the time is ripe for it. I don't think people will want it.'

Jeremy sighed. Even his father, who was such a clever and infallible man, could not understand the magnetic potentialities of this new invention. Once again, though now so much older, Jeremy felt the strange conviction that there was a life – a sort of magic life – in the heart of this steaming, smoking monster. It was not just a machine devised by man. Man was breeding something new, a creature to serve him but a creature of whim, of individuality. No two could ever be alike.

He wondered even if Mr Trevithick saw it as he did, felt the fascination in quite the same way. In any event, in the succeeding years his father turned out to be right. Whatever the ultimate potential of this invention no one, for the time being, was the least bit interested in developing it further. And so everything had lapsed. The last Jeremy had heard of Mr Trevithick – in 1810, that was, shortly before he picked up Stephen Carrington from the sea – the inventor was ill and in debt and thinking of returning to live in Cornwall.

But in the meantime another matter was concerning Jeremy. Stephen had left Nampara on the 20th January but had moved only to take a room with the Nanfans who lived near Sawle Church, and a few days later he came to Jeremy with a proposition.

It seemed – and he confessed this shamefacedly – that the story of his being a small trader between Bristol and Ireland was not true. He had in fact been aboard a privateer when it had been sunk by the French; but, finding himself in such a house and tended on by such genteel and respectable women as Miss Poldark and Mrs Poldark, he had been afraid to tell them this. Not that there was anything illegal in privateering, but he did not know how the Poldarks would look on it. He had, he said, already confessed the truth to Miss Poldark, but not yet to Mrs Poldark.

But there was a little more to it than that. The privateer, the *Unique*, before it was caught and destroyed, had already made one capture: a small lugger with a few ankers of brandy aboard. Captain Fraser had not thought it a sufficient haul to take home so he had left the lugger at Tresco in the Scilly Isles to pick up on his way back with whatever other prizes he was able to find. Well, instead he had picked up a French warship. Stephen alone survived, and would like to go and collect the lugger. Could Jeremy help?

Jeremy said: 'D'you mean take you out there?'

'Yes. You saved me life in that handsome little gig. Twould be very suitable and gracious if you could help me now repair me fortunes.'

'You have papers? You could get the lugger released?'

'Nay, there'll be no papers. Two old brothers, Hoskin by name, are seeing to her for us. Captain Fraser did business with them before, and no doubt if I live I shall do business with them again. It's all a question of trading.'

They were sitting on Jeremy's bed in his room in Nampara. Stephen had called to see if there was any word from or news of Miss Clowance, but Demelza was in Sawle. Jeremy had been out in the yard seeing to a sick calf. A flurry of hail had driven them indoors, and with Isabella-Rose and Sophie Enys running wild downstairs Stephen had asked if he might have a word in private.

'What crew would you need to sail your lugger home?' Jeremy asked.

'Two. Three better, but you could manage with two.'

'Well, you want two for *Nampara Girl*. That means we should need four to go out in her.'

'That's the size of it. I thought if Paul Kellow had a mind to go. And maybe the other one that pulled me out – Ben Carter, is it?'

Jeremy hesitated. He didn't think Ben had particularly taken to Stephen Carrington. The reason was plain: Stephen had made a great set at Clowance, and Clowance, if Jeremy was not in error, was rather taken with him. Ben, however little hope he might entertain on his own account, could not help being jealous.

Stephen misunderstood the hesitation. 'I'll pay you well for your trouble. The lugger's French built, but I reckon she'd sell for £80 any day. And then there's the cargo.'

'Oh.' Jeremy made a dismissive gesture and got up. 'That's not it. I'd like to help . . . When would you want to go?'

'Sooner the better. I wouldn't trust the Hoskins beyond three months. You'd take a profit – a share in the profit on the brandy, eh? What d'ye think?'

'I think,' Jeremy said, 'the other two might be glad to have a little something. But that can wait.'

'Not too long, I hope,' said Stephen, and laughed.

Jeremy looked at the hailstones bouncing on the window-sill, gathering in little ridges and beginning to melt.

'It would be necessary to tell my mother.'

'Of course. Whatever you say. But mightn't she say no?'

'It isn't a question of yes or no, Stephen. It's that we aren't a family from which I can absent myself for one or two nights without saying what I am about. In any event she'll not mind the Scillies.'

'Your father is safely home?'

'Yes, thanks be to God. We heard this a.m. She is gone now to tell some of our friends.'

'Then perhaps it will be a good time to tackle her when she comes back.'

'Why?' Jeremy was genuinely puzzled.

Stephen laughed again and patted him on the back.

'You're a lucky man.' When Jeremy turned he added: 'T'have such a mother. T'have such a home. There seems to be no stress, no conflict in it. Have it always been so?'

'No . . . Not always.'

'Is it so when your father comes home?'

'Yes. Oh yes, I think so . . . Then we are a complete family.'

'But it hasn't always been so?' Stephen was persistent.

'There were times when I was very young when I remember feeling – torn. Torn by passions and emotions; I didn't understand them, but they were – in the house. My father and mother never *bicker*, Stephen, never *pick* at each other as I see so often in other houses. But when they quarrel it is over something important, and then it is – important.'

Stephen picked up his hat. 'I shall look forward to meeting Captain Poldark. But I trust . . . before then?'

'Probably before then,' said Jeremy.

III

That evening he told his mother.

She smiled at him with the utmost brilliance. 'Do you *want* to go?'

'I think so.'

'What is a privateer, Jeremy? I'm not certain sure.'

'Isn't it a ship owned privately by one or more investors in time of war which gets . . . isn't it called Letters of Marque? . . . so that it can make a tilt at the shipping of the other country – the one you're at war with?'

'I wonder how your father will think of it.'

'Of privateering?'

'Yes. And Stephen. Stephen's a great charmer . . . But I knew his first story was not true.'

'Why not?'

'There had been no storm for fourteen days before you picked him up.'

'I can't remember the weather so far back. How do you? I scarcely remember what it was like yesterday.'

Demelza helped herself to the port. She was getting light-headed as well as light-hearted.

'Well, there it is. He says he will be detained in London a few more days – your father, that is – but will return at the earliest possible moment. I wonder if he will see Clowance? They cannot know he is safe returned because he is not staying at his usual lodgings. He is stopping with Mr Canning. Is there a Mrs Canning? I hope they meet. I mean Clowance and your father. Maybe they will cross coaches, as I was afeared to do. Thank God he is back in England. It is hard to stop worrying; you can't turn it off sudden like a tap. I heard of a man once who survived the most utmost perils and then slipped on a banana skin.'

'Mother,' said Jeremy.

'Yes, my handsome?'

'Did you send Clowance because . . .'

Demelza said: 'I didn't *send* Clowance. She went.'

'It is unlike her.'

'Yes, it is unlike her. But people often do things that are unlike themselves. What is being true to oneself, I wonder? I never know. Sometimes there are three people inside of me, all wishing different. Which is me? What are you like inside, Jeremy? Are you like that? I never know. Sometimes you worry your father. Is there something special you want to do with your life?'

'Maybe.'

'*Is* there? Do you know what it is?'

'Not exactly. I'm not sure . . . Are we a trouble to you, Mama?'

'Just a little. Just a small matter troublesome. Dear life, what it is to have a family! . . . As for Clowance, you must give her leave to be wayward. She is growing up.'

'We all are.'

'Alas.'

'Why?'

'Why what?'

'Why alas?'

'I think I like you all at a certain size. Like hollyhocks. Before the rust starts.'

'Well, thank you, Mother. Your compliments fly on all sides of me.'

The light from the candles danced a jig as Mrs Kemp put her head round the door.

'Isabella-Rose is waiting to go sleep, ma'am. She waits to say good night.'

'Very well, Mrs Kemp. Thank you, Mrs Kemp. Tell her I shall come rushing up to her the very moment I can, Mrs Kemp. Which will be in a hundred seconds or thereabouts, give or take a few.'

Mrs Kemp blinked at this flow of words and left. Demelza finished her port, stretched her fingers towards the fire and flexed them. 'I feel like playing the spinet. I feel *very* much like playing the spinet. That's if Bella has not thumped all the life out of it. D'you know, Jeremy, I b'lieve I need a new one. I shall ask your father for one when he comes home.'

'What, a new spinet?'

'No, a pianoforte. They are – more brilliant. They can make the music fade and swell. This old machine, much as I love it, is worn out.'

'Bella would like that.'

'We must stop her thumping. Mrs Kemp does not believe she is musical really at all . . . January is not a time for sailing, Jeremy. Would this trip not wait until the better weather?'

'Stephen says not.'

'Do not rely on him too far, my lover.'

'Stephen? What makes you suppose I should?'

'Because it was just in me to say it. Pay no attention.'

'I always pay attention to you. Especially when you are in your cups.'

'*What* did you say?'

'I'm sorry, Mama. It was not intended that way. But I have a superstitious feeling that so often you are right.'

'Well . . . I try not to judge too quick on such a matter. I believe it is good to go cautious. Test the measure; make sure it balances. Then one is not surprised – pleasantly or unpleasantly.'

Jeremy stirred one of the logs with his boot. 'If Paul can get away I think we should leave about Wednesday; that's if the weather is reasonable and you would allow it. I should like to be there and back before Father returns.'

'If you have to go – go now,' said Demelza. 'Hurray, I should like that also!'

Chapter Two

I

They left on the Wednesday at dawn. Paul Kellow had been able to come, and after hesitation Ben Carter agreed too. Demelza sometimes remarked that winter in Cornwall set in on January 18; but this year, aside from the occasional gusty wind with hail showers, nothing unkind developed such as was occurring upcountry. The air came persistently from the north-west, preventing frost; and primroses and snowdrops were out.

All the same, the sea was restless, and they kept well clear of the saw-toothed coast. As they passed Hell's Mouth and crossed the Hayle Estuary Paul Kellow waved an ironical salute. The St Ives fishermen were out, dotted all over the bay and rising and falling in the swell like seagulls. More vengeful cliffs with the white gauze of spray drifting at their feet; the sands of Sennen, and then the deep-tangled waters of the Land's End.

Stephen came up beside Jeremy, as he was tightening a rope round the cleat on the mainmast. 'At this pretty rate,' he shouted, 'we should be in afore dark. Jeremy . . .'

'Yes?'

'We have not decided how we shall divide coming home. Will you come with me?'

'I had thought Paul probably. Is it important?'

'Not important, no. But Paul has to be back by Friday at the latest. I don't know how long . . .'

'I would have thought we could have made it well before then. But I can come instead of Paul if you think that better.'

Stephen took a last bite at the pie he had brought. When his mouth was half empty he said:

'The brandy is contraband.'

'Of course.'

'Also the *Philippe* couldn't be brought safe into your cove, I'd guess. Also she is a prize, and your father be due home shortly. I do not know how he would look on all this. Of a certain, I'd not want to embarrass him.'

Jeremy finished securing the rope, gave it a tug. 'What do you suggest?'

'I had thought at first I might take her back to Bristol; but I'd rather prefer to rid meself of the cargo here; and if there was a likely buyer for the lugger, twould be better to dispose of her too. I doubt whether you or any of your friends would wish to help me sail her up there and come home by land!'

'I'd assumed we were all coming back to Nampara . . . Well, there's little enough money at St Ann's, I agree.'

'That's what I thought. That's what the Nanfans told me. But there's St Ives, Penzance, Falmouth, Mevagissey.'

'My father's cousin lives in Falmouth,' said Jeremy. 'She is married to a retired Packet captain and he might know who would be a likely purchaser . . . But you're suggesting, then . . .'

'That we should take her to one of the Channel ports. Twould take us no longer than bringing her back to Nampara, and if we was lucky the business would be completed in a couple of days. Indeed, if you wanted to go home and leave me there, no doubt I could manage.'

A larger wave than they had previously seen came riding in behind them, and the little gig lurched and sidled like a restive horse. Ben Carter at the tiller brought her up a bit more to keep the wind steady on her starboard beam.

Jeremy shouted. 'Do you have any contacts on that coast? One cannot, you know, just arrive in a port with twenty ankers – or whatever it is – of contraband brandy.'

'I thought to try Mevagissey,' said Stephen. 'There's one or two I know – by name if naught else – who'd be glad to take the stuff. What are the gaugers like in that area?'

'I've no idea.'

'In St Ann's?'

'Not easy. There's a man called Vercoe. Been there for years. And gets ever sourer.'

'Don't he take a little on the side? Most of 'em do.'

'Not as far as I know. Of course it goes on – the Trade goes on, but I have never heard of him or his men being willing to turn a blind eye.'

'Well . . . that makes it all the more sense to try Mevagissey, or thereabouts. Would you be willing?'

They sighted the Isles of Scilly well before dusk, even in that short day. There being little cloud about and the sun not setting until 4.50, a long twilight followed and they were able to pick their way among the dangerous reefs and islands of Crow Sound and to tie up in the little Tresco harbour opposite the island of Bryher. This was no easy place to be with any sizeable vessel, for it was deeply tidal and was a prey to currents and Atlantic swells. But for something as small as *Nampara Girl* the small granite curve of the jetty offered protection enough. It was full tide at this time, and the great valley of water separating the two islands looked like a tide race, swelling and formidable.

'At low tide,' said Stephen, 'I've *waded* across. Could you believe it?' And turned. 'There she is.'

He pointed at a vessel riding at anchor in the harbour alongside a couple of rowing-boats and a skiff.

'Oh, she's trim,' said Paul, 'if I'd been your captain, I'd have settled for her, not gone whoring after bigger game.'

'We was eight in the crew,' said Stephen. 'Divide *that* prize up and you don't have enough to share. That's how he looked at it, God rest his soul.'

'Where are your friends?' Jeremy asked.

'Up at that there cottage where the light is showing. Look you, will you allow me to go up on me own? I think if the four of us come knocking on the door the Hoskins may get out a musket thinking it be the French!'

The other three made the vessel good for the night, having heeded Stephen's warning that by midnight it would be sprawling on its elbow in the sand, then went ashore and sat on the stone jetty smoking and talking to some islanders who emerged from the shadows curious to know what their business was. They were reticent, again on Stephen's instructions. Time passed and the inhabitants drifted away and they put on their cloaks against the chill wind. It was an hour before Stephen returned, carrying a storm lantern.

'All is well. We shall spend the night with the bastards, leave at dawn. Watch your step, I think I disturbed an adder.'

Jeremy said: 'You wouldn't come across an adder at this time of year.'

'All right. All right.' Stephen's voice was gruff, with a trace of anger in it; as if his meeting with the Hoskins had not gone too smoothly. This was borne out when they reached the cottage. A filthy old man with tin-grey hair stood at the door, watched them suspiciously as they trooped in. A single tallow candle guttered beside another old man who had a growth the size of a goose egg on his forehead and who was counting coins. Neither spoke to the new arrivals. The first brother slammed the door after them and put up the bar. The room smelt of urine and stale tobacco. There'll be bugs in here, thought Jeremy: we'll all be spotted pink before morning.

'Well, sit you down, sit you down,' said Stephen heartily, his own temper recovered. 'We can have the use of this room, but they've no food. Small blame to them as they wasn't expecting us. We have some of our own left, Ben?'

'In this bag,' said Ben Carter. 'Two loaves and some

butter that Mrs Poldark gave us. Three smoked pilchards. An apple. A square o' cheese.'

'Good. Good. Now, old men, leave us be, eh? We'll not steal your house, nor your money. I'll wake you at dawn so as you can count your spoons before we leave.' Stephen laughed. 'It's warmer in here than out in that wind. You're not all froze, I hope. Right, Nick and Simon, that's all.'

The man with the tumour tied his bag, and the coins clinked. 'I doubt ye've the right,' he said.

'Never mind that, never mind that, it's all settled,' said Stephen. 'Night, Nick.'

The grey-haired man by the door shuffled towards another door. 'Aye, it's settled. For good or ill, it's settled. Come, Simon.'

The two brothers went slowly out. As they left Simon said whiningly to the other: 'I doubt if he's the right, Nick, I doubt if he's the right.'

II

They left to return just as dawn was splitting open a bone-grey sky. While they slept, and scratched and slept, the tide had sucked itself out of the great channel and had again filled up, so there was little to suggest it had ever changed. Only the observant would have noticed the seaweed a foot higher on the sandy beach than it was yesterday evening. The observant – among them Jeremy – also noticed the swell had grown.

Paul Kellow and Ben Carter in *Nampara Girl* left first. Then Jeremy and Stephen Carrington in *Philippe*, watched by the two glowering Hoskin brothers who had come down to the jetty to see them off. '*Bastards*,' said Stephen, 'we're ten tubs of brandy short. I tackled 'em but they would admit nothing.'

Jeremy was not attending. What interested him most was to see how this French-built lugger responded to sail and helm. It was like trying a new horse. He had no fears for *Nampara Girl* with Ben aboard; he was a better sailor than any of them. For him the appeal was to bring *Philippe* home, which had made him instantly agreeable to Stephen's suggestion.

About an hour after dawn clouds assembled and the wind backed south-west and began to pipe up. For the course they were on this could not have have been better, and the rain that soon began to fall kept the sea down. They soon lost *Nampara Girl*, and until they sighted the Manacles there was no other craft to be seen. Then a couple of Newlyn fishing-boats, intermittently visible between the waves, fell behind them as they raced up the Channel.

Somehow Stephen had cajoled a few eggs out of the dour Hoskin brothers, and these, boiled in a pan before they left, they now ate cold, with a tot of white brandy – of which there was still plenty – to wash them down. The lugger was a heavier boat to handle than she should have been, and in the increasing wind she was as much as they could manage. 'She'll be all right unladen,' shouted Stephen. 'Which'll be soon, I pray to God.'

Off Falmouth they sighted a British frigate which made some signal to them, which they pretended not to see. Jeremy was aware that they should have brought a flag or some other evidence of their nationality. However, with this wind increasing to a half gale, it was unlikely anyone would have the attention to spare for them. By noon the clouds had come down to sea level, drifting in dense masses across the tips of the waves. *Philippe* was sluggish and instead of riding the waves began to ship water over her stern. Stephen altered course to try to get a lee from the land.

Both young men were soaked to the skin, and water was swilling around in the bilge among the casks of brandy. Stephen made gestures to Jeremy to shorten sail.

'I don't want to make Mevagissey much before dark,' he shouted.

'If we don't make it soon,' said Jeremy, 'I'm not sure we shall make it at all.'

'I've been looking at me chart.' Stephen fumbled a piece of damp parchment from under his coat, which was at once torn at by the wind. He folded it into a small square and, steadying himself against the swaying mast, contrived to put his finger on the coastline. 'See here. That's Dodman Point. You can see it ahead. We'll have to weather that if we want to reach Mevagissey, and this wind, blowing full inshore . . . There's these two or three inlets first. Know you if there's any place safe to anchor in any of 'em?'

'I've never sailed in this part before. We'd do better to put about and try to slip into Portloe. There'd be shelter of a sort.'

'Couldn't do it. She's too sluggish. I reckon we've got to take a chance.'

This was a different coast from the one they had skirted on the outward journey. Here there were no giant cliffs stranded like monuments and dropping their deep precipices into the sea. But these cliffs, though a quarter the size, with green fields running down to the sea's edge, were almost as dangerous, with submerged reefs of rock jutting out among the waves, sharp enough to tear the keel out of any vessel that ran foul of them. It was the dagger instead of the broadsword.

For some time they ran across the wind, closing the land. Now the inlets were clearly to be seen, but it was a matter of luck whether one chose wisely. If the one selected turned out to offer nothing but submerged rocks there would then be no chance of beating out again.

To port as they came in was a largish, mainly sandy beach, on which the waves were pounding. To starboard a smaller one with little ridges of bursting water where the rocks lay. In between there were three rocky inlets with no evidence of harbour or jetty but the looks of a few yards of navigable water partly protected from the wind. Stephen chose the third, which indented furthest into the land.

Jeremy at the tiller steered his way between fins of rock, Stephen let go the main sail, then the lug sail; for moments they were on a switchback of swell and broken waves, control lessening with momentum. Stephen snatched up an oar, shoved at a rock that rose like a sealion on their port bow; just in time they swung past it and were into the inlet.

They were lucky: there was a minimal stretch of quay half broken with storm and age, a stone-built hut from which half the slate roof was gone; a pebbly stretch beyond on which were some lobster-baskets. The lugger bobbed and lurched as the swell came round and swung them broadside. Jeremy took up another oar. There was a nasty jar as the lugger took the ground, then they were free again. Stephen flung a rope, missed, flung it again and it caught on a granite post; he hauled and pulled the stern round. Jeremy jabbed his oar down, found bottom, pushed. The lugger, so sluggish recently in the open sea, was now like a riderless horse that would not come to rein; it plunged and Jeremy, off balance, had to drop his oar and cling to the side to keep aboard. Another harsh collision of keel and rock, and then Jeremy got a second rope ashore and the vessel was brought heaving and grating against the cork mat that Stephen had interposed between gunnel and jetty.

Stephen pulled off his cap and with it wiped the rain and spray from his face. His mane of yellow hair clung dankly to his skull.

'We're safe, Jeremy boy. Though it's a misbegotten hole we've come into.'

Jeremy was fishing for the lost oar with a marlin spike. The oar floated tantalizingly near him with every swell, then with each recession it slid out of reach again. Presently an extra wave brought it within range and he hauled it up dripping water and seaweed.

'She'll be aground when the tide goes out.'

'It has to rise yet, from the look of the rocks. I doubt this inlet is ever dry.'

They made the lugger as safe as they could. The broken jetty was not ideal but it did offer protection.

They were suddenly in haven, quiet, after all the tossing and pitching of the last hours. Wind still blew, rain fell, the sea still surged inshore foaming at the mouth. But here they were quiet, safe from its worst reach, almost surrounded by low-growing trees, their black branches massed for protection, creaking and hissing in the wind. Nothing human to be seen.

Stephen jumped ashore. 'We can wait a couple of hours, maybe more. Dark'd be better. I didn't like the look of that frigate we passed.'

'You'll not get out of here till the wind drops.' Jeremy followed his friend.

Stephen cast a speculative eye at the hut. 'There's no one about. Though they must come down here – those pots. God's blood, I'm as hungry as the grave! We've nothing left to eat?'

'Not a cursed crumb.'

They moved slowly towards the hut. 'D'you know,' said Stephen, 'if we could get help, this'd be a good enough place to unload the spirit. I wonder how far it is to Mevagissey overland?'

'Five miles, I'll bet.'

'D'you know, it's far from a bad idea.'

Jeremy had come to know Stephen's quick change of mood, his tendency to have a thought and instantly to believe in it.

'What is?' he asked cautiously.

'We could stay here – go over – one of us could go over, get in touch with the right people, deliver the brandy here, on the spot. Mevagissey, I know, has an active band of Brothers; but I'll lay a curse the Brethren don't bring all their cargoes into the port; maybe this is one of the coves they use. Twould be easier, safer, better to sell it and unload it here; *then* bring *Philippe* into port unladen, an innocent prize, for sale, all above board and legal and who's to say nay?'

'Stephen,' Jeremy said, 'to hell with the brandy. What is it in all – twenty ankers? The lugger is your prize. The spirit was in the lugger when you captured her. Let's take it in, tell the Preventive men how it came about, let 'em decide what to do with it. We're at war. You capture a French prize and whatever is in her. You get a third of the valuation, don't you? Who's to say that would be much less than you'd get from the Brethren? The lugger will sell just the same.'

Stephen said: 'Is that a cottage – up the hill – there, back behind those trees? I reckon so. Let's see if there's folk can ease our stomachs first.'

Some of the thatch was missing from the cottage, and the way to it was overgrown with saplings and rank weed; but when they knocked a cloth was pulled from a window and an old woman peered at them. Behind her an arthritic hand held a blunderbuss which wavered in a haphazard way as they bargained for food. But when Jeremy produced silver the old man in the background lowered his gun and they were allowed in. They sat on boxes, their feet on a floor that hadn't been resanded for a year or more and was slippery with mice droppings. They wolfed cold rabbit, watery cabbage soup, four half-mouldy apples, drank a glass of cider.

While they were eating Stephen said: 'Look you, those are not ankers in the boat, they're tubs, which weigh – what? – fifty-six pounds. Half the size of ankers and more negotiable, as you might say. There's not twenty – there's forty-eight of them. Each one, give or take, holds four gallons of white brandy. Diluted to the right strength and some burnt sugar to add the colouring, that makes, give or take, twelve gallons a tub. I was never one to be good at arithmetic but I'd guess that adds to something like six hundred gallons. The Brethren can sell it to householders at 20s. the gallon. They should pay us 10s., I'd say. We

171

couldn't make much less than £300. Is that money you want to throw away?'

'No, you great oaf! My share of that would come in very convenient at the moment. But we take all the risk for how much extra profit? The other way we're on safe ground.'

Stephen hiccupped. 'I reckon we're on safe ground anyway, Jeremy. Safe enough. We'll never get *Philippe* out again while this wind holds – you've said so yourself. Why don't I leave you here, in charge, and go overland; these folk'd know the way, could direct me. With luck – if I met willing men early enough and there was a mule train available – I could come back with them; they'd unload through the night, this coming night, and be all clear away before dawn.'

Jeremy rubbed a hand through his drying hair and yawned. The two old people were out at the back somewhere, you could hear them scrabbling around but one could only guess whether they were within hearing distance – even, if they heard, whether they could understand. Jeremy knew the type in the scattered hamlets round Nampara, old and infirm, toothless, scarcely articulate, but somehow scraping enough from land or sea or charity to avoid the ultimate separation of the poorhouse.

He said: 'I don't know if you have the measure of the people in the Trade, Stephen. They're suspicious – have to be. I mentioned this before. If a stranger, like you – and non-Cornish – turns up in a village and starts whispering about the brandy he's brought in to a nearby cove, they'll look at him all ways before they'll move. Might even sharpen their knives. Who's to say you're not from the Customs House, leading them into a trap?'

'I have two names. Stoat and Pengelly. They were given me by a shipmate, who's now dead, God rest his soul; but he said they was big in the Trade and would know his name. That's all I can do. D'you know of a better plan?'

'If you're set on running the brandy,' said Jeremy, 'I'd

rather try to unload the stuff first, hide it in some bushes. Then at least you're not such a sitting target for any Preventive men who happen to be strolling past.'

Stephen thought around it, then shook his head. 'You're right, lad, but not yet. If that's done at all it must be done in the dark. There's always eyes in Cornwall. The lugger looks innocent as she is; let her lie there, no one knowing what she carries . . . What's the time now?'

Jeremy took out his watch, listened to see that it was still going. 'Just after four.'

'There's an hour of daylight, then. If I go now I'll be in Mevagissey soon after dark. Just right. Is there a moon tonight? No, I remember. That's right too; they'd never risk a moon. With fair luck I should be back here by midnight with men to do the unloading for us! Will you stop here? These cottagers'll no doubt let you sleep here – for the price of an extra coin.'

'No. I'll stay in the lugger. Better to keep an eye on her.'

'Good man.' Stephen rose. 'Then I'll be off. But first to press these old folk to tell me the shortest route. Can you understand 'em, Jeremy? I'm poxed if I can.'

Chapter Three

I

Jeremy knew that Stephen was greatly underrating the suspicious nature of the Cornish fishermen, especially those who carried on the Trade. They lived in a close-knit community, intermarrying so much that almost everyone was a cousin to the next man, and everyone knew everyone else's business from cradle to grave. A man from a village three miles away was looked on as an outsider. What chance, then, did a stranger stand, coming from up-country, from a port half of them had never heard of, of gaining their confidence? Had so many of them not been Methodists, the most probable result would have been to see Stephen Carrington floating out face down on the next tide.

That being forbidden, and anyhow most of them being pretty good-natured underneath, the likely outcome for Stephen would be blank faces, half-promises that weren't kept, a passing on from one man to another, an assumption of stupidity that would send him angry away.

Jeremy stayed in the cottage for about an hour after Stephen left. He tried to talk with the two old people, but it was slow work. He learned that they lived in the parish of St Michael Caerhays, that the local landlord and lord of the manor was called Trevanion, that the nearest village was Boswinger but that it was men from the farms at Tregavarras and Treveor who owned the lobster-pots. They kept their boat in the ruined hut by the quay, but just now they was all sick with the jolly rant so they'd not been out this week. Jeremy requested a description and came to the conclusion that the jolly rant was probably plain influenza. He asked how far the nearest town was, the nearest coach route, but they had no idea. The name of Grampound was mentioned but they didn't know in which direction it lay. Their horizon hardly extended beyond Mevagissey.

About five-thirty he left the cottage and returned to the lugger. The rain had stopped and cloud over the land flushed red as a wound as the sun set. The wind still blew fiercely off the sea, but now that he was part dried out it did not seem so cold.

He jumped on the lugger and went below. It was going to be a dreary wait but he did not fancy sleep. While the remnants of the daylight lasted he explored the vessel, found some documents in a drawer and the ship's log; regretted he had learned Latin at school and not French. It was in the hold forward of the foremast that most of the brandy was stowed. There was a good deal of water slopping about in here, and he hoped the lugger had not sprung a leak. That would explain her sluggishness. Pity if Stephen succeeded in his mission and returned to find *Philippe* settled in six feet of water.

Jeremy thought with amusement that his own tendencies towards caution had only developed since he associated with Stephen. The Bristol man had an extraordinary conviction that almost anything he wished to happen *would* happen. He could talk his way, work his way, fight his way out of anything. And into it too. Jeremy's reactions were an instinctive counterbalance to Stephen's blind optimism. Yet – one had to confess it with a sense of admiration – if anyone could achieve the highly unlikely and arrive back at midnight with a posse of docile brandy-runners, it was Stephen.

Jeremy went on deck and looked around. There was nothing more to do here. Darkness had come down. Quilted clouds drifted across the sky, obscuring and revealing a few moist stars. The tide was ebbing, but, as Stephen said, it was unlikely to leave the jetty altogether dry. If the lugger grounded she would do no real harm to herself. He returned to the cabin. There was a storm lantern but he thought it unwise to light it. He settled himself at the porthole to wait and watch.

Hours passed, and he dozed, started fitfully awake, dozed again. His eyelids bore all the cares of the world.

He woke with a start to hear someone moving on the deck above him. He was cold now, chilled, and the darkness was intense. He sat still for a while. Sometimes in the first snap of autumn at Nampara a rat would get up into the roof among the thatch and, deep in the night, would begin to explore the warm haven he had found. This was a noise very similar, cautious, stealthy, inquiring. A footstep, a scrape, a shuffle; all probably inaudible to the person or thing that made it, but magnified below deck. Jeremy had a knife but no firearms; it was indeed no more than a jack-knife – one his father had brought back from America a quarter of a century ago – but he pulled it from his pocket, unclasped the blade.

Then he heard a voice, a whisper, gruff and un-compromising. It was answered. The scraping and the movements went on.

Whoever it was, there was little to steal on deck: the sails, a spar or two, a cork raft. His normal impulse would have led him quickly up the ladder to demand the business of the intruders and to challenge their right here; but Stephen's insistence on bringing in the brandy left him unsure of himself, afraid to claim authority lest it should be authority of another sort that was investigating the lugger. If the intruders came down, then he would face them. If he heard them moving casks from the forward hold he would quickly be out to stop them. But just for the moment wait. Lie low and wait.

So one moment led to another, and presently the scraping and the muffled footsteps died and there was silence. He looked at his watch but could not see the face. Once he fancied there was an extra lurch from the boat as if

maybe someone had jumped off it onto the jetty, but
perhaps that was imagining, perhaps that was thinking
what he wanted to think.

Stephen arrived back an hour before dawn. He
whistled, soft but distinct, and Jeremy came up the
companionway to meet him. The sky had quite cleared and
was a net of stars.

'Well?'

'My damned accursed feet! These shoes was not meant
for walking! It seemed like ten miles, not five. Those old
skeletons who directed me did not know the way! But still
. . . All is arranged.'

'*Arranged*?'

'You were right, Jeremy, these fisherfolk are like clams:
you have to force their jaws open with a knife. Mevagissey
was a nightmare; I could find neither Stoat nor Pengelly.
But in the end . . . by judicious use of silver coin. They're
coming tomorrow night.'

'Tomorrow!'

'They said twas too late to organize a run for tonight,
and I must say I saw their problem. You cannot pick up a
score of mules without due preparation. Also they said it
cannot be done obvious, public like. There's a Custom
House in the port, and a look-out on Nare Head. They'll
come tomorrow at eleven in the evening. Roach is the man
I dealt with, Septimus Roach. He's fat and hard and mean
and niggard as a louse but I reckon he'll play fair. He
knows I'd get him if he didn't . . . He wouldn't promise me
more'n 6s. 6d. a gallon, and that only after he's seen and
tasted. Ah well, that will be a handsome return on an
outlay of nothing at all!'

Jeremy rubbed tired eyes. 'And the daylight hours of
today?'

'We'd best get them off. You were right about that.
Find a cache. It shouldn't be hard, God knows; all these
·trees growing down to the water. It'll be work, but if we
get them hid then we're in a better position – can let 'em

see one tub when they come, taste it, pay up before we show 'em where the rest is.'

'This cove may not be so empty as it looks,' Jeremy said. 'Two people came aboard after you had gone, early on in the night, while I was down here. I didn't challenge them.'

Stephen stopped rubbing his heel and stared. 'What were they – men, children?'

'Didn't see 'em, just heard them moving about on deck for about ten minutes. So far as I could tell they carried no light.'

Nare Head was just becoming visible against the creeping dawn.

Stephen said: 'You didn't dream it? Or was it seagulls?'

'I heard them speak. And they didn't sound like children.'

'Holy Mary, I don't like the trim of that . . . But then . . . what's our choice? Wind has taken off a bit – we *might* get out, spend the day just over the horizon. But the old tub has sprung a leak, hasn't she.'

'It's just for'ard of the rudder somewhere. I don't think it's serious. But the pump doesn't work. We could try baling.'

Stephen pulled his boot on again. 'Don't know why these Frenchies let their vessels get captured in such poor condition . . . Still, she's sound over all. And would be a lot easier to handle if lightened of a ton and a half of brandy! I think we'll get it off.'

'Let's start, then,' said Jeremy. 'I'd like to see it all stowed away somewhere before we break our fast!'

II

They got it off. It was specially hard on the hands, for the tubs were rough and there were splinters. Their choice of a hiding-place was necessarily limited by the distance they could carry the tubs. Also by the growing daylight. The dense vegetation all round the tiny inlet had at first given a sense of security, of isolation. But Jeremy's experience changed that. Who knew who was watching?

They considered first the part-ruined hut. It was handy, the door would force easily. If the people using the lobster-pots were sick they would not be likely to want their boat. Just for one day. But after assembling a mountain of tubs by the door they went foraging and found a declivity, as if someone at some time had quarried there – or even mined. By carrying the tubs to the slope they could be rolled gently in, and it was a position quite hidden from the rocky track leading up from the cove.

By the time it was all done the sun was well up, slanting brilliantly into the cove, and *Philippe* rode more buoyantly, as if she had lost both a physical and a moral weight. The wind was from the south, having backed a point or two, but was still firm and strong. They spent half an hour baling and trying to find where the lugger was letting in water; when they came on deck two children of about seven and eight years old were standing on the jetty, fingers in mouths, watching them.

'These your visitors?' said Stephen.

'I doubt it. Their voices haven't broken yet.'

Jeremy spoke to the children, smiling at them, asking what their names were, where they came from. They stared. One took his finger out of his mouth, but it was only to spit. They were in rags, barefoot, skin showing at shoulder and knee. They were filthy. The girl, who was the younger, had a skin disease, scabs about the mouth and chin. When Jeremy went up to them they both backed away.

'I reckon we leave them here while we look for food,' Stephen said. 'They can do no harm.'

'You didn't think to bring food back with you?' Jeremy asked.

'There was little chance. Else I poached a chicken somewhere.'

'I could eat a horse,' said Jeremy. 'I'm fearful those two

old people will have nothing for us. Even money can't conjure up meat where there is none.'

They left the children sucking at their fingers and staring after them. The old woman, who no doubt knew everything they were about, had baked black barley bread and had turned out some apple conserve. She also offered two mackerel the old man had picked up somewhere, but after sniffing at them, they said no. They drank weak tea. The old man sat in a corner of the tiny room by the cloth-covered window and watched them. Jeremy thought they had hardly altered their own situation from the cottage at Tresco. He paid them ten times what the meal was worth, and the old woman became friendly. Would they be staying long? If so, she'd send Alf into Mevagissey to buy fish and potatoes. ('Holy Mary,' said Stephen under his breath, 'can he *walk* that far?') They replied that they would be leaving in the morning but if she could contrive to provide them with *something*, perhaps a few eggs and butter from one of the nearby farms, they would prefer not to trouble her husband to take such a long trip. She nodded and blinked out of eyes crusty with eczema and cupidity, and said: proper job, proper job, she'd send him only to Treveor.

When they had eaten, they walked back to the lugger and Stephen lit a pipe. The children had gone. The wind was dropping all the time, and in the sharp sunshine it was quite warm. Stephen presently put his pipe aside and stretched out on the deck and went to sleep.

Jeremy sat against the hatchway, picking splinters out of the palm of his hand. By now *Nampara Girl* should be home, unless they had been forced to seek shelter in St Ives or St Ann's. He wondered if his father were on his way back from London yet, if he had met Clowance, if the Enyses would return soon. He knew that it was on account of this young man sleeping in the sun beside him that Clowance had gone away. He wondered if he would like Stephen as a brother-in-law, supposing it should all turn out to be as serious as that. He found him engaging company, as so many people did. Particularly as so many women did. For the last week Stephen had been living with the Nanfans, and already there was gossip about him and Beth Nanfan, who was grey-eyed like her mother, and blonde, and twenty-two. (Not, as Jeremy too well knew, that it was possible to *smile* at any one anointed girl in Sawle or Grambler without creating gossip, even scandal.) Stephen was one of those men whose outgoing natures somehow impede a closer acquaintance. He talked freely of his life at sea, answered readily any casual questions about his childhood and youth near Bristol – which he seemed to call Bristow – admitted that he had lived wild and rough; he was generous with his money and with his time; already he had become well known in Sawle and not disliked – which was an achievement for a newcomer in a district nearly as close-knit as Mevagissey.

Time passed and Jeremy, himself short of sleep, dozed, then woke to see someone moving on the track above the creek. He touched Stephen, who woke instantly from a deep sleep, hand on belt where his knife was sheathed. Jeremy pointed.

'Looks like the old woman.'

'She's making some sign. Go see what she wants, Jeremy. Nay, I'll come with you.'

They jumped ashore and strode up the hill. It was indeed the old woman, around her head a dirty silk scarf. She was standing behind a gnarled hawthorn tree, her jaws champing. She said something as they came up that neither could follow. But they understood the finger raised to her lips.

'What is it?' said Jeremy in a lowered voice, bending towards her.

'. . . gers,' she said through her gums.

'Strangers?'

She shook her head impatiently, eyes aglance.

'*Gaugers*?' said Jeremy.

'Ais . . .'

They both straightened up, looked around, taut and apprehensive.

'*Where?*'

She jerked her head over her shoulder.

'At your cottage?'

'Ais . . .'

'God Almighty! We'd best . . .'

Jeremy patted the old woman's hand by way of thanks as they turned to go down again. But it was too late. A boot clinked on a stone. Stephen sank into the bushes with Jeremy beside him. The old woman started up the hill again as two men came round the corner. They wore shabby blue fustian jackets with darker blue barragan breeches and black hats. Each carried a musket and a bandolier.

The taller said: 'What're ee doin', missus, walkin' out takin' the air, eh? Who told you you could slip away, eh? What *you* got to hide?'

The old woman cowered and tried to slink past, but the man caught at her headscarf.

'Where d'ye get this, you? Tedn what you'd belong to find in these parts. Been doin' a bit of running on yer own, ave ee?'

The old woman cringed and clawed and whined.

'What? Twas give ee? Gis along! Who'd give a fine bit o' silk like this to a speary old witch like you? Eh? Eh? I've the good mind to impound it on his Majesty's be'alf.'

'Come along, Tom,' said the shorter, older man. 'We got more important business than she.'

They let her go and went on down towards the boat. She watched them, and when they were out of hearing spat on the ground where they'd stood and bent to make a curious sign in the spittle. She gave no other indication to the two men in hiding but scuttled up the hill towards her cottage, clutching the suspect scarf.

Jeremy stretched a cramped leg that had been folded under him. Stephen caught his arm.

'Hell and damnation, if they find the brandy we're sunk! But if we don't go down they may well impound the lugger.'

'Come over here. There's better cover the other side.'

They dodged across the track and made slowly in the wake of the two Preventive men. From among the bushes they saw the men go out onto the jetty and approach the *Philippe*. One of them shouted, to bring up from below anyone who was on board. When there was no answer the tall one made to jump onto the lugger but the shorter man restrained him. They stood there arguing a few moments. The older man from his gestures could have been pointing out that Customs officers should not board a vessel except in the presence of the owner.

Then the tall one looked down at the jetty and pointed back along it to the stone shed. It is not possible to unload forty-eight tubs of spirit without leaving some traces, and where the two young men had tramped backwards and forwards with their burdens the damp grass was flattened and muddy. It was plain too that some sort of boxes or barrels had recently been stacked before the door of the shed. The men now walked back and up to the shed, tried the door but could not get in. Then together they must both have seen that the beaten muddy tracks did not end at the door but crossed the grassy square, which still had puddles in it from the rain, to where the brambles and dead bracken were broken to make a way off to the left.

Stephen began to curse under his breath. 'What luck! What misbegotten vile filthy devil-invented luck! God damn them to all eternity! Someone must have *brought* them here. That old woman . . .'

'It was not the old woman,' said Jeremy, 'for she warned us just in time.'

'Well, one of her breed! There was someone came

nosing on us last night – you said so. Maybe they watched this morning. Those kids . . .'

'Careful,' said Jeremy. 'Don't stand up or they'll see you.'

'Nay, they're too busy following that trail we left! Look at 'em: heads down like a couple of damned lurchers . . .'

There was a click behind them; they swung round. A man carrying a musket; a shabby, down-at-heel man in a jacket too big for him, a round peakless cap, heavy moustaches. On the sleeve of the jacket was an arm-band.

'Stay where you're to, my dears,' he said, in a high-pitched voice. 'Just to be safe now, stay where you're to. Leave us see what you're about, shall us?'

After a moment Stephen swallowed and said: 'What we're about? *Nothing*; that's what we're about, save watching those two friends of yours down there on their beat. Strolling, we were, though the woods and we saw a couple of yon scavengers and wondered what *they* were about. See. That's all.'

'Ais? There, there, my dears, thou shusn't tell such lies. Nay, nay, let us be honest men, shall us?' He put fingers into his broken teeth and whistled shrilly. 'Nick! Tom! Up here, my dears! I've flushed a little nest o' meaders!'

Jeremy saw the other two Preventive men stop and look up. They turned and began to come back up the path towards them. From where he was standing the third man could not see whether his companions had heard for he put his fingers to his mouth to whistle again. As he did this Stephen kicked the musket out of his hand.

While the musket clattered Stephen jumped; the man aimed a wild blow but Stephen's fist crashed into his face and he fell backwards into the bushes. He half rose and Stephen, grabbing the musket, jabbed at him with the butt. He fell back.

'Come on!'

They began to run, for by now the other two were a bare

184

forty yards away. There was a crack and a ball whistled between them.

'This way!'

They thrust into the thicker-growing trees that surrounded the cove. After a few yards Stephen stopped and discharged the musket back in the direction of the pursuing men.

'That'll make 'em more cautious.' He flung the musket over some bushes, for they had neither powder nor shot.

They were making their way almost due west through the bare sunshot trees with bramble and every sort of undergrowth plucking at their breeches, clutching at hand and hair. They were making too much noise not to be followed, and they could similarly hear their pursuers, occasionally catch a glimpse of blue among the trees. But no more shots were tried.

It was rough going, and Stephen gave a sudden loud grunt, dropped on one knee, got up again.

'What is it?' Jeremy demanded.

'My ankle — some blamed rabbit hole — twisted a bit! Twill be all right.' After a few moments' more running: 'You go on.'

'Damned if I do,' said Jeremy, slowing.

'Damned if you don't! Look you.' Stephen plucked hair out of his eyes. 'Best if we separate — they can't follow both . . . or won't. They'll be too scared — tis toss of a coin which they'll choose — but it's likely they'll follow me. I can look after meself — I'm used to rough dealing — you're not . . .' The trees were thinning and they would have to cross a trickling stream to the next wood. 'Listen, Jeremy — if they catch you give false name — say twas all my doing! If they don't — make for home as best you can . . . *Adios!*'

A minute longer they were together, then Jeremy leapt the stream while Stephen swung sharply right, hobble-running through the thinning trees. Jeremy felt his back was two yards wide waiting for the musket ball. It did not come. One of the gaugers had fallen and the other one was helping him up. More trees, thank God.

He was coming too near the sea for safe cover. He had twisted his own leg in the last jump and was getting winded. No doubt, he thought, so were the gaugers.

Two or three minutes later he came out on a beach. It was one of those they had seen when coming in yesterday. Sand and low sharp-running rocks. If he went on that he was a target; even at a distance they could get him in the legs. Above the beach were more trees part-hiding a house. A great turreted place, surrounded by a ruined wall. Panting, he looked back. Couldn't see the Customs officers but he could hear the occasional crackle of undergrowth. They, like him, were slowing but were not far away. It looked as if their choice had fallen on him. Perhaps this was to be expected as he had run straight; they might not even know they had split up until the trees thinned again.

By the time they came out of the trees perhaps he could follow Stephen's good example and disappear also. The wall surrounding the grounds of the house was a quarter-mile from the house itself. To reach it he would have to sprint a hundred yards without cover – and preferably not be seen at all while he was about it. A high risk, but the alternatives were to run exposed the half-mile of the beach or try to cut up into the fields to the north where cattle were grazing.

He took the risk, forgetting the jarring in his leg, the panting lungs. Fear doubled his stride. The wall was higher than he'd thought; he scrabbled along it, could get no purchase, ran towards the gate, found a broken part of the wall no more than five feet and was over, fell flat into a shallow ditch on the other side, lay there gasping, trying to get in a supply of air before the necessity of having scarcely to breathe at all.

Seconds passed. Look about: the ditch offered no real cover. A bramble or two, a few leafless saplings sprouting, lumps of mortar and broken bricks; not enough. They only had to climb up to look over the wall. Nearby was a shrubbery. He crawled towards it. As he reached it he saw a skirt.

A woman stared at him. She said: 'What are you doing here, boy?'

Before he could answer running feet came. At the wall they stopped, moved along it, past it, came to the gate. The woman walked to the gate.

'Yes?' she said.

'Oh, beg pardon, miss – we was followin', closely followin' two men – two rascals – two miscreants . . .'

It was the shorter of the gaugers, devoid of breath.

The woman said: 'Is it two you are pursuing or six?'

'Two, ma'am. Er – Miss Trevanion. See 'em come this way, did ee?'

'I have seen no two men come this way, Parsons. What do you want them for?'

'Brandy-running, miss – assault on an officer in discharge of 'is duty, miss – failing to stop when called upon to do so. Possession – illegal possession – of a French lugger.'

'Dear soul,' said the girl, for she was young, 'these are serious charges, Parsons. I hope you will find all six of the men.'

'*Two*, miss,' said the taller man, peering through the gate. ''Tis not impossible that when we find these men they will be sent to trial on a capital charge.'

'I hope so,' said the girl.

There was a pause. The shorter man coughed and seemed about to move on. The tall one said: 'Would we 'ave your permission, miss, to come in and search your grounds?'

The woman looked out at the horizon. 'I do not believe my brother would like that.'

'No, miss? It's just that . . .'

'Is it just that you do not believe my word that I have not seen two men fleeing from justice?'

'Not exactly but – '

'Parsons, what is this man's name? I do not think I know him.'

'Tis not *that*, miss,' said the tall man awkwardly. 'But we followed these yur men right to the edge of your beach an' I cann't think as 'ow they've gone elsewhere but somewhere into your grounds. Could well be as ye've not seen 'em but they be hid here whether or no an' just the same.'

'Parsons,' said the girl. 'You are in charge?'

'Yes, Miss Trevanion.'

'Then pray allow me to do this my own way. Go you with this fellow to look on the beach or anywhere else you please to look so long as you do not trespass on our property. In the meantime I will inform our steward who will instruct various of our servants to search the grounds thoroughly. If in half an hour you have found no one, pray come back. By that time the search will be completed, and if two such wicked men as you describe have been found I promise they shall be delivered to you. Is that satisfactory?'

There was a further pause. Clearly it was not satisfactory, certainly not to the tall gauger; but there was nothing more he or his leader could do. They nodded and touched their foreheads – for both had lost their hats in the pursuit – and turned away. The slow tramp of their feet was soon lost in the damp sandy ground outside the gate. The woman leaned on the gate watching them go. At length she turned.

'Well, boy?' she said.

Chapter Four

I

Ross left London with Clowance and the Enyses on the 7th February and they reached home on the evening of the 12th. Demelza was expecting him, for a letter written after the ball had reached her telling her of their plans. All the same, travel was so imprecise that she could not be sure of the time – or even the day – until the horses came clattering over the cobbles.

Demelza wondered if there would come a time when, obese, warty, and dulled by age, she would fail to react to the sight of her husband standing in the doorway, when her hands would not tingle and her stomach not turn over. If so, it hadn't arrived quite yet. There he was, tall as ever, and gaunter for his hard mission, a little greyer, paler of face from the Portuguese influenza, staring at her unsmiling, staring at her, while Gimlett took in the baggage and Jeremy helped Clowance down.

'Well, Ross . . . I was hoping it would be tonight.'

'You had my letter?'

'Oh yes, I got it.'

She took a few steps towards him and he a few towards her. He took her hands, kissed her on the cheek, then almost casually on the mouth. She kissed him back.

'All well?' he asked.

'Yes . . . All well.'

He looked round, reaffirming his memory of familiar things.

'We'd have been earlier, but the coach broke an axle at Grampound. We were delayed two hours.'

For a few moments they were strangers.

'Isabella-Rose?'

'Asleep.'

'She's well?'

'Yes. You'll find her grown.'

'So's Clowance. Grown up, anyway. I couldn't *believe* at that ball.'

'Did she look nice?'

'Lovely. You – didn't want to go to London with her?'

'I was afraid we might miss each other – you going one way, me the other.'

'I hadn't thought of that. I'm *sorry* to have been away so long.'

'Yes. It's been a long time.'

He released her. Jeremy and Clowance hadn't yet come in. He wondered if it was tact.

'Have you supped?' she asked.

'A little. It will do.'

'It need not. Clowance is sure to want something.'

'All right then. It will be a change to eat your food again.'

'I hope not a poor one.'

'You ought to know that.'

There was a pause. She smiled brightly. 'Well, I'll tell Jane, then.'

'There's not *that* much hurry.'

She stopped. He came up behind her, put his face against her cheek and sniffed her, took a deep breath.

'Ross, I . . .'

'Don't speak,' he said, and just held her.

Supper was quite talkative but at first it was only Jeremy and Clowance who chattered, chiefly Jeremy, airily, with news of the mine and the farm, as if nothing else much was of importance. Effie, their middle sow, had had nine piglets last week; Carrie, the old one, was due any day. On Monday they had turned the end of the corn rick and found scores of mice. With his dislike of killing he had quickly absented himself, but Bella, the little horror, had stayed all through and seemed to enjoy it. They should have finished ploughing by now but both Moses Vigus and Dick Cobbledick had been laid low with influenza and Ern Lobb with a quinsy.

In the middle of this inconsequential talk Jeremy broke off, glanced from one to the other and then fell silent.

'And you met Geoffrey Charles, Father?'

Ross told them.

It was the beginning of new conversation in which Ross did most of the talking – about the Battle of Bussaco, about Lisbon, about his return and the crisis of the King's madness. All was listened to, commented on as a family – just like old times. The only thing missing was personal conversation, communication between Ross and Demelza. It was as if they were still frozen, embarrassed in each other's presence. It would take time to go.

Once – just once – Ross looked in a different way at Demelza and she thought: do our children know, are they speculating what will happen when we go upstairs? Do I know myself? Is it the same with him as it always was?

Later, much later, almost in the middle of the night, when it was all right between them and when they were both still awake, she said:

'These absences try me some hard, Ross. They do really. I have slept in this bed so many nights, so long so lonely. I have felt what it must be like to be a widow.'

'And then the bad penny turns up again after all . . . Oh, I know. Don't mistake but that I feel the same . . . At least, there are the pleasures of reunion. Tonight . . .'

'Oh, I know too. I have been so happy tonight. But is there not a risk – just a risk – that someday absence may not make the heart grow fonder?'

Ross said: 'Unless it affects us now, let's meet that problem when it comes . . .'

There was still a candle guttering in the room. It would burn perhaps ten minutes more if the end of the wick didn't fall over into the hot wax.

Ross said: 'Life is all balance, counterbalance, contrast, isn't it. If that sounds sententious I'm sorry, but it happens to be true. By an action voluntarily taken one gains or loses so much, and no one can weigh out all the profit or loss. When I was wounded at the James River in 1783 and they got me into hospital, such as it was, and the surgeon, such as he was, decided not to saw off my foot for the first day or two, he put me on a lowering diet. No food at all, bleedings, purges, a thin watered wine to drink. After five days when no fever had developed he decided I was not going to mortify and could begin to eat again. They brought me first a boiled egg. It was nectar . . . Like no other I'd ever tasted. You see, the very deprivation . . .'

'I *think* I see what you mean,' said Demelza. 'You mean tonight I'm your boiled egg.'

A shaking of the bed indicated that Ross was laughing.

'No,' he said eventually, 'you're my chicken.' He put his fingers through her hair. 'All fluffy and smooth and round . . .'

'If I hatched out when I think I hatched out, I'm an old hen by now and my comb has gone dark for lack of proper husbandry.'

'Well, it shall not for a while now, I promise; I swear; we shall cleave and be of one flesh – '

'Very uncomfortable.'

He picked up her hand. 'Am I a morbid man?'

'Yes, often.'

'Why should one feel morbid, sad, at such a reunion as this?'

'Because it has been too good?'

'In a manner, yes. Perhaps the human mind isn't adapted to complete contentment. Had tonight been partial in some way, as it so easily might have been, as at first – one didn't know . . .'

'You felt that?'

'Earlier, yes. But then . . .'

'But then it wasn't.'

'It wasn't. So – perversely – one feels a choke of melancholy.'

'Let's be melancholy, then.'

He stirred beside her. 'When I was staying with George Canning I picked up a book of poems – a man called Herbert – I've remembered one bit: "Sweet day, so cool, so calm, so bright, the bridal of the earth and sky . . ."' He watched the flickering candle. 'There's been nothing cool and calm about us tonight, but I think there's been both the earth and the sky . . .'

She said lightly, covering the emotion: 'Dear life, I believe that's the nicest thing you've ever said to me.'

'Oh no, there must be others . . .'

'There *have* been others. I keep them all in a special box in my memory, and when I'm feeling neglected I take them out and think them over.' She stopped and was quiet.

'What now?' he asked.

'What you say's true, though, isn't it. It's not natural – what has been happening between us tonight. It should have cooled off into something else by now. But instead I feel just the same about you as the first time you took me to bed in this room. D'you remember, I was wearing your mother's frock.'

'You seduced me.'

'It didn't feel like it by the time it was over. You lit an extra candle.'

'I meant to know you better by morning.'

She was silent again. 'So perhaps it *is* right to be melancholy . . . That happened twenty-four years ago. Now we have grown children and should know better than to be making love like lovers after all this time. I am prone to bad spells – '

'And I have a lame ankle – '

'How has it been?'

'Neither better nor worse. And your headaches?'

'I was praying to St Peter that you didn't return last week.'

'Well, he answered, didn't he. So there's a good two and a half weeks ahead before we need worry again.'

'After tonight you should be exhausted.'

'I am . . . But do you not think I also have memories when I am away?'

'I hope so.'

'Don't you think I remember the night we came back from the pilchard catch in Sawle? Then it was different. That was the night I fell in love with you. Instead of just the physical thing . . . Without emotion there's nothing, is there. Nothing worth recalling. A shabby exercise. Thank God it's never been that between us since.'

'Let us thank God we are not as other people are.'

'You been reading your Bible?'

'I remember the Pharisees.'

'There's a lot to be said for the Pharisees.' Ross held her hand up to the side of his face.

After a few moments she said: 'Are you listening for something?'

He gurgled with laughter. 'You see – you deflate me. Yes – I *am* listening for something – the beat of your heart.'

'That's not the best place to listen.'

He bent slowly and put his head under her left breast. 'It's still there.' He released her hand and took her breast in his fingers.

'The candle's going out,' she said.

'I know. Does it matter?'

'Nothing matters but you,' she said.

II

Much later still when the moon had risen and was lighting the sky with a false dawn he said:

'I've so much to tell you.'

'Tell me. I don't intend to sleep at all tonight.'

'Before I met Geoffrey Charles . . .'

'Well . . . ?'

'I came across an old friend, an old flame of yours. Captain McNeil.'

'Judas! That all seems so long ago. Was he well?'

'Yes, and a colonel by now.'

'Geoffrey Charles . . . You didn't say much about him tonight.'

'I didn't want Jeremy to feel I was praising or admiring him too much . . . He's lost a little piece off his face. But he looks no worse for it.'

'Do you care for Geoffrey Charles more than you do for Jeremy?'

'Of course not. It's quite different.'

'But you and Geoffrey Charles seem to have an affinity . . .'

'We often seem to think the same, to feel the same.'

'And Jeremy?'

'Well, Jeremy's so much younger.'

She waited for Ross to say more but he did not. In spite of his assurances she could sense the things unsaid, the little reserve.

'And Clowance?' Ross said. 'I hear she has been in some travail about a young man.'

'Who told you?'

'She did. On the way home. The night we spent in Marlborough. I gave her a little more wine and she came up to my room and sat on my bed.'

'Perhaps she told you more than she told me.'

'I doubt it. Clowance is nothing if not honest – with us both.'

'I think she's involved, Ross. Sometimes then it's not possible to be truthful with other people because you don't know what is the truth yourself.'

'She said she'd talked to you and you had advised her to go away for a few weeks.'

'I put it to her, like. She agreed. I think she was afraid – I know I was – that it would go too far too soon.'

'You don't like him?'

Demelza stirred. 'Not *that*. Not as positive as that . . . Maybe I have a peasant's suspicion of a "foreigner".'

'What a strange way of describing yourself! Is this a new humility?'

For once she didn't rise to the bait. 'He came – out of the sea, almost dead; Jeremy and Paul and Ben picked him up. He said first he was in his own ship when it was struck by a storm. Later he said that wasn't the truth; he was gunner on a privateer that had been caught between two French frigates and sunk, the captain killed. He – '

'That does not sound like the truth either,' said Ross.

'Why not?'

'French frigates don't *sink* privateers. They capture 'em and take them into a port as a prize. The French captains are not going to be such fools as to lose their prize money.'

'. . . Even if they were fought to the end?'

'Nobody fights to the end. Not since Grenville.'

A seagull, awakened by the moon, was crying his abandoned cry, as if hope were lost for ever.

Demelza put her head against Ross's arm. 'You've gone thin. Was it the influenza? It has been widespread down here.'

'A few pounds. Nothing. Your cooking will soon give me back my belly.'

'Which you never had. You always fret your weight away.'

'Fret? I might fret if I thought Clowance had fallen in love with a rogue.'

'I don't think he's *that*. I'm almost sure not. Howsoever, perhaps we shall not need to be anxious.'

'Why not?'

'He has disappeared – almost as sudden as he came. He said the privateer he was on had captured a small prize and left it in the Scillies, and he asked Jeremy and Paul and Ben to take him there in *Nampara Girl*. So they did – and Paul and Ben came back in *Nampara Girl*, while Jeremy helped Stephen Carrington bring in his prize. But they made for Mevagissey because Stephen wanted to sell it there, but there was a storm and they came in at a cove in, I believe, Veryan Bay. There they were embayed – is that the word? – for a day, and then Stephen Carrington sent Jeremy off overland alone and he sailed away in the prize. No one has heard or seen anything of him since.'

'Does Clowance know?'

'I reckon Jeremy will have told her by now.'

'So perhaps she went away to good effect.'

'Maybe. Of course, he might turn up again any time.'

Sleep now was coming to their eyelids.

Ross said: 'Clowance made quite a conquest in London.'

'In London? Who?'

'Lord Edward Fitzmaurice. Brother of Lord Lansdowne, a very rich and talented peer. I think the younger man is talented too, though perhaps not so much in politics.'

'So what occurred?'

'They met at a party given by the Duchess of Gordon. He seemed to take a fancy to Clowance and invited her to tea to meet his family.'

'And then?'

'She declined.'

'Oh. Wasn't that a pity?'

'Caroline thought so. Indeed she carried on in such an alarming way when she knew, saying it was simply not socially acceptable to refuse such an invitation, that Clowance was quite subdued into believing her. Of course I don't think it true! Caroline was up to her old games.'

'Well?'

'Caroline insisted on sending a message on the following day to the Lansdowne residence in Berkeley Square saying that she would wish to call on Lady Isabel Petty-Fitzmaurice herself, and might she bring Miss Clowance Poldark? The request was acceded to.'

Demelza let out a gentle breath. 'It's all a long way from the Clowance we know – galloping across the beach on Nero with her long hair flying . . .'

'It is.'

'And did you allow her to be so bullied?'

Ross laughed. 'I allowed her to be so bullied. Saving yourself, Caroline is the strongest-minded woman I've met, and after an initial rejection of the idea, I came to the conclusion that Clowance could come to no harm with such a duenna and that it would broaden her experience to take tea in such refined company.'

'Which I hope it did. Did you hear what happened?'

'Tea was taken.'

'No, Ross, it's too late to tease.'

'I think in fact Fitzmaurice *was* offended by Clowance's refusal; so honour was satisfied all round. His aunt clearly did not dislike our daughter, and Fitzmaurice suggested that, as they would be spending some weeks at their family seat at Bowood in Wiltshire this summer, perhaps Miss Poldark would care to visit them there – suitably escorted, of course.'

Demelza began to wake up. 'I hope you wouldn't want *me* to escort her! Dear life!'

'Who better? But from what Clowance said at Marlborough, she is not sufficiently taken with the idea to accept the invitation even if it is remembered and was not a polite expression of the moment.'

Demelza walked around this in her mind.

'I think if she is asked she should accept . . . Don't you? Caroline would say so.'

He kissed her shoulder. 'Sleep now. The cocks are abroad.'

'Oh, well . . . yes . . .'

Silence fell.

'And the war?' she asked after a while.

'Will continue now – as I said at supper – thanks to the complete turn about of the Prince Regent.'

'I wonder what made him change at the last minute in such a way?'

'I have no idea.'

'Do your friends have?'

'They speculate, of course.'

After a few more moments Demelza said: 'Were you involved in some way?'

'What ever makes you ask that?'

'Just that you kept on putting off coming home – I don't think you would have stayed up there just to vote – and I have a sort of – sort of feeling in my bones that you might have done something. What with your visit to Portugal and . . .'

Ross said: 'If I know those feelings in your bones they'd probably elevate me to being personal adviser to Wellington.'

'I'm crushed,' said Demelza.

'No, you're not . . . So far as the Prince's change of mind is concerned, it was probably because of an accumulation of things – of causes . . . Of course, he might switch back at any time . . . But I have a reasonable hope that he won't now for a little.'

'You want the war to go on?'

'I want peace with honour. But any peace now would be with dishonour.'

'So Geoffrey Charles cannot come home to his inheritance yet.'

'He could come any time. He told me he had leave due; but I question that he'll take it. The casualties have been heavy.'

'That is what I am afraid of,' said Demelza.

Ross lay on his back, hands behind head, looking out at the lightening windows.

III

'Father,' Jeremy said, 'do you know the Trevanions?'

They were walking back from the mine together, Ross having paid his first call at Wheal Grace since his return.

'Who? Trevanions?' Ross was preoccupied by what he had seen and heard and by his examination of the cost books.

'Over at Caerhays.'

'I have met John Trevanion a few times. Major Trevanion. Why?'

'When Stephen Carrington put me ashore, it was near their house. They kindly invited me in . . .'

Ross said after a moment: 'He was Sheriff of Cornwall at some early age – Trevanion, that is; then a member of parliament for Penryn, though he soon gave it up. I came to know him better a couple of years ago. There were meetings at Bodmin and elsewhere in favour of parliamentary reform. He spoke in favour of it. We were in accord in this.'

'You liked him?'

'Yes, I liked him. Though he has the high arrogance of many Whigs that make them seem so much haughtier than the Tories.'

'He wasn't there,' Jeremy said, 'but his – his family invited me in – greatly cared for my comfort, and loaned me a horse. Their house is a huge place, isn't it. A castle!'

'I've never seen it.'

'D'you remember taking us to Windsor five years ago? Well, this house at Caerhays reminds me of Windsor Castle.'

Ross said: 'I remember de Dunstanville telling me the young man was building some great pile – with an expensive London architect under the patronage of the

Prince of Wales . . . It all seems a little grand for Cornwall.'

'It is certainly grand.'

Ross stopped and took a breath, looked around. On this grey February day the natural bareness of the land seemed much more barren because nature was at its lowest ebb. He was dizzy from lack of sleep and excess of love. He would have been completely happy today except for what he found at the mine. But that was how life ran. One scarcely ever threw three sixes. And this morning Jeremy did rather go on about things that were of no importance.

'How often have you been down while I've been away, Jeremy?'

'Grace? Twice a week, as you told me.'

'The north floor is almost bottomed out.'

'I know.'

'The workings are still in ore, but the grade is scarcely worth the lifting.'

'Well, it's done us proud, sir.'

'Oh yes. Thanks to it we've lived so well. And because of it I have a variety of small but useful investments in other things . . . If Grace closed we should not starve.'

'I would not want that to happen,' said Jeremy.

'Do you think I would? Apart from ourselves, more than a hundred people depend on it. God forbid I should ever act like the Warleggans; but once a mine begins to lose money it can eat up capital so rapidly.'

'We need a new engine, Father. Big Beth works well but she is mightily old-fashioned.'

Ross looked at Jeremy. 'I've no doubt there are improvements on her we could still make. Your suggestion that we should steam-jacket the working cylinder by using a worn-out older one of larger size has been a great success. The loss of heat has been dramatically less. But, as an engine, Beth has really no age – twenty years?'

'We could sell her. This would help defray part of the cost of a new one.'

'If the prospects at Grace were better I might agree. But as it is there's nothing to justify the extra outlay.'

'Not even to justify improvements to Beth?'

'Oh, it would depend on the cost.'

'Well, to begin, a new boiler of higher pressure would greatly increase the engine duty.'

'With extra strain on the engine.'

'Not with some money spent on improvements there – the whole pump could be made smoother-acting with less consequent strain on the bob wall – and of course far less coal used.'

Ross said: 'If you could get someone to work the cost out I'd be willing to look at it.'

'I could work the cost out myself,' said Jeremy.

Ross raised an eyebrow but did not comment. They walked on.

'I hear Mr Trevithick is back in Cornwall, Father.'

'Is he . . . Well, you could ask his advice. Unfortunately he only designs engines, he doesn't discover lodes.'

'And there's another man just come – from London, though I think he's of Cornish birth. Arthur Woolf. He advertised in the *Gazette* last month. He has a fine reputation and I believe a deal of new ideas.'

They stopped for a few moments to watch two choughs fighting with two crows. In the end, as always, the crows won and the choughs retreated, flapping their wings in defiant frustration.

Ross said: 'This interest you're showing in the practical side of the working of engines may well be good. But in this instance, looking at Grace only, it is putting the cart before the horse. The most efficiently worked mine in the world is not successful if there is no ore of a respectable grade to bring up.'

Jeremy gazed across at the sulky sea.

'Wheal Leisure never had an engine?'

'No.'

'Wasn't it copper?'

'Red copper mainly. High quality stuff. But it ran thin and the Warleggans closed it to get better prices at their other mines.'

'Does it still belong to them?'

Ross glanced at the few scarred and ruined buildings on the first headland on Hendrawna Beach.

'It may do. Though there's little enough to own.'

Jeremy said: 'The East India Company have offered to take fifteen hundred tons of copper this year. It's bound to put the price up.'

'Not to them. They're getting it at lower than market value. But I take your meaning. Yes . . . demand may exceed supply. Copper has a better future than tin.'

Demelza was in her garden and she waved to them. They waved back. After a suitable pause Jeremy reverted to his former topic.

'This Trevanion family . . .'

'Yes?'

'Major Trevanion must still be young, I suppose. He has recently lost his wife and there are two young children. Also a brother and – and two sisters. And a mother too. A Mrs Bettesworth. Perhaps she has married again.'

'No . . . As I remember it, the male side died out. A surviving Trevanion girl married a Bettesworth; but that was a couple or more generations ago. The present owner – the one with such high ideas about his residence – was born a Bettesworth but changed his name to Trevanion when he came of age. I imagine the others will all be called Bettesworth still.'

'One isn't,' said Jeremy. 'One of his sisters. She's called Trevanion too. Miss Cuby Trevanion.'

IV

She had said to him: 'Well, boy,' and his life had changed.

She scrutinized him, with eyes that were a startling hazel under such coal-dark brows. Her face, round rather than oval and pale like honey, was befringed with darkest brown hair, straight and a little coarse in texture. She was wearing a purple cloak over a plain lavender frock, and the hood of the cloak was thrown back. Her expression was arrogant.

She had said: 'Well, boy;' and he had climbed quickly to his feet trying to brush some of the wet mud and sand from his clothing.

He stretched to see over the wall but could not. 'Thank you, miss; that was most kind.'

'Well, please explain yourself, or my kindness may not last.'

He smiled. 'Those men. They were after me. I did not wish them to catch me.'

She studied his smile, but did not return it. 'I trust it doesn't surprise you to know I'd already come to that conclusion. What is your name?'

Stephen had said not to give it, but this surely was different. 'Poldark. Jeremy Poldark.'

'Never heard of you,' she said.

'No, I am not from these parts.'

'Well, what were you doing *in* these parts, Jeremy Poldark? My brother would not commend me if I were to hide a miscreant – wasn't that the word Parsons used? – a miscreant who has been brandy-running and assaulting Preventive men in the discharge of their duties. And where are your five fellow miscreants? Would you point out the shrubs that conceal them?'

'Not five but one. And he's not here, miss. We parted company among those trees fifteen minutes ago. The men chose to pursue me, so I'd guess he has made his escape.'

She brushed some hair behind her ear. 'You speak like a gentleman. I guessed as much before you opened your mouth. How did I guess? Perhaps it was the hair. Although most of the gentlemen I know have the good manners to shave.'

'It's three days since I left home and we have been at sea

most of the time since then. My friend . . . he wished to pick up this lugger in the Scillies . . .'

Jeremy went on to explain. He was caught anyway if she chose to hand him over to the authorities, so she might as well know the truth. He was aware that he was not making a good job of the explanation, but the reason was every time he glanced at her his tongue stumbled, words not becoming sentences in the easy way they should.

She waited patiently until his voice died away and then said: 'So now you've lost the brandy *and* the lugger. It's the result of being too greedy.'

'Yes, indeed. And but for your extreme kindness I'd now be in custody.'

'And that's not pleasant, Jeremy Poldark. The Customs men are a small matter short-handed, which makes them a small matter short-tempered with those they catch. Even magistrates today are not so lenient as they used to be.'

'Which makes my obligation to you all the greater.'

'Oh, don't jump to the conclusion that you are free! You're in my custody now.'

'I'm happy,' said Jeremy, 'to be at your – your complete disposal.'

The words came out – half joking, meeting her at her own game – but when spoken they took on a serious intent. He felt himself flushing.

She looked away from him, distantly, through the gate. After what seemed a long pause she said: 'Was your lugger brown with red sails?'

He took a few steps until he could see the beach. The *Philippe* was sailing close hauled – and close in – along the beach, only just out of reach of the muskets of the two Customs officers who stood staring at it in anger and frustration.

'He must have doubled back!' Jeremy said. 'Given them the slip and got aboard! Thank Heaven the wind is dropping. But he's looking for *me*!'

'If you show yourself,' said Miss Trevanion curtly, 'there is nothing more I can do to save you from your just deserts.'

The lugger went about and came back along the beach. Though single-handed, Stephen was managing well. A puff and a crack announced that one of the Customs men had fired. As the lugger reached the eastern end of the beach Stephen changed course again, heading out to sea. It must have been plain to him that even if Jeremy could see him there was no way of his getting aboard without the unfriendly attention of the gaugers.

The sea crinkled like silver paper under the winter sun. The lugger receded.

Jeremy turned. 'Miss Trevanion, my home, as I explained, is on the north coast. There's no coaching road nearer to it than seven miles. But if you *could* give me my liberty, to walk the total distance from coast to coast can hardly be greater than twenty-five miles and I could do this easily in a day . . .'

'Mr Poldark, my name is Cuby Trevanion. Having gone so far in frustrating the law, I feel I can deserve no worse by helping you a little more. My brother is away, so I may do this with less risk of his displeasure. In our kitchens there should be food – are you hungry? you look it! – and no doubt in the stables I can find you a nag of sorts. Would you follow me?'

'Certainly. And thank you.'

As she went ahead she added: 'My other brother is away also. We even might be able to lend you a *razor*.'

Up rising ground by a gravel path he followed her, cutting through part of a wood which had recently been felled and the ground excavated. 'To give us a view of the sea,' she explained.

As they approached, the house took on more and more the appearance of a fairy-tale castle, with turrets and bastions and serrated parapets and rounded towers. Jeremy would have been impressed but for the fact that he had really no time for or interest in anything but the scuffing of a skirt in front of him and the appearance and disappearance of a pair of muddy yellow kid ankle boots. Totally lost, like someone hypnotized, he would have followed those boots to the end of the earth.

Chapter Five

I

Between Stippy-Stappy Lane, where the cottages, if poor, were respectable, and the squalor of the Guernseys, where derelict shacks clustered around the beach and the harbour wall, was the one shop of the village of Sawle. No bigger than a cottage, it was distinguished by a small bow window and a painted front door. Aunt Mary Rogers's. Or so it was still known to many people who refused to re-think their ideas even though Aunt Mary had been in Sawle Churchyard for upwards of thirteen years. Since then it had been occupied by the Scobles.

Twenty years ago a man called Whitehead Scoble had married Jinny Carter. He was a miner working at that time at Wheal Leisure, a widower, childless, plump, pink-faced and snowy-haired though only just thirty. She was Zacky Martin's eldest daughter, twenty-three, a widow with three young children whose husband had died of blood poisoning in Launceston gaol. Scoble was much in love with Jinny, she not at all with him; but she had yielded to the advice of her elders, the need for a father for her children, and her own wish to get away from Nampara and Mellin. Scoble had his own cottage at Grambler with a ten-year lease still to run and the marriage had worked well enough until Leisure closed. Then Scoble had gone off on casual work and taken to the bottle. Ross had tried to help them but, for special reasons of her own Jinny had refused. But in '97 when Aunt Mary Rogers had reluctantly sold her last quarter of hardbake and been carried up the hill to Sawle Church, Ross had deviously persuaded Zacky Martin to put in an offer for the shop and its sparse contents; and Zacky with a good deal of bland-faced lying had convinced his daughter that he had made enough money out of his employment as factor to the Poldark estate to be able to finance her to take it over.

Soon after this Whitehead Scoble had returned to his wife, suitably chastened after a spell in gaol himself, and since then they had worked together amicably and made a quiet but comfortable living. The lime-ash floor had been replaced with planking, wooden shelves put up, a clean lace curtain to the window, a bell to ring when you came in, scales renewed telling the correct weight, and the shop restocked with better goods. Now sometimes people even walked over from St Ann's because their own shop was not so well supplied.

Once again Whitehead had been childless; it was something he felt strongly about and had motivated his absences and his hard drinking; but as he passed fifty he had become reconciled to his own shortcomings. And he could be father to Jinny's three children even though they would never bear his name. The elder daughter, Mary, was now married and gone. Katie, the younger, was in service at Trevaunance House. The son, Benjy Ross, or Ben as he was now called, still lived at home.

He was an eccentric. Past his twenty-fifth birthday and not yet wed. Bearded in a community which looked on beards as proper only to beggars and destitute old men. Musical but he didn't sing or play in the choir which would be the conventional way of expressing such leanings; instead he had constructed a pipe organ of his own in the back bedroom upstairs and played tunes for himself when he felt in the mood. He had also got his own one-man mine a mile inland from Grambler; here he had found a few pockets of alluvial tin, and he would pursue them underground either until they petered out or the digging filled with water. Sometimes, since the ground was sloping he could go quite deep. He made little enough out of it but he was astute with money and saved enough on good months to tide him over barren ones.

This also enabled him to take a day off when he chose and go fishing with Jeremy Poldark. Jinny was as mystified by these aimless trips as Demelza Poldark was. Jinny was also against his spending so much time at Nampara, though her quiet discouragement made no difference.

Her opposition rose in part from the scabrous old rumour – first spoken of in her presence by Jud Paynter – that Ben was really Ross's son and that the similar sort of scar on his cheek was a judgment, a stamp of the devil, to mark their kinship. As time passed most people forgot the rumour, especially now Ben had grown a beard and the scar was not too noticeable. But there was always, she knew, some withered old crone, sitting before her cottage door who would still whisper: 'Don't ee know why he growed a *beard*? We-ell, tis plain 'nough, I tell ee.' All through the years it had made Jinny defensive in her relationship with the Nampara household, sometimes hostile in her defensiveness, so that she would not accept help from Ross which might lend new life to the evil lie.

The other reason she did not want Ben to be at Nampara too much was because she knew of his obsession for Clowance. That, she knew, was doomed. Though there was no barrier of blood relationship there was the equally insuperable barrier of class. Mrs Poldark had originally, of course, been a miner's daughter and no better than any other, but that fact would not make Mrs Poldark look any more favourably on a union between *her* daughter and a miner's son. Nor Captain Poldark neither. Besides, it was the wrong way round. If a poor girl married a gentleman she stood a good chance of being lifted to his estate. If a rich girl married a workman she descended to his. It was the way of the world.

Of course the friendship was as much of Master Jeremy Poldark's seeking as Ben's. They had an affinity which owed nothing to shared tastes, the tall slim genteel young man reared in semi-luxury and the thin bearded hard and wiry young miner who, if he had never been short of food, had lived hard as soon as he was out of the cradle.

It was on an early March afternoon when, contrary to the reputation both of the month and the county, there was little or no wind, that Jeremy slid off his pony about half a mile from Jonas's Mill and tethered him to the stump of an old hawthorn tree. The ground ahead of him looked like a lawn that a mole has been working on, except that the lawn here was not green, being rough grassy ground with heather and a few patches of gorse. And the soil turned up by this mole was not the fine tilth of a potting shed but ugly yellow stone and the mud and mixed rubble of moorland.

Jeremy whistled a couple of times and presently Ben emerged from one of the holes, shading his eyes against the hazy sun. Together they examined the latest ground Ben had turned up with his spade. At the moment, after the rains of winter, most of the deeper diggings were waterlogged.

Jeremy said: 'There's a trace of tin, I see, but will it even pay for washing?'

'I don't need it to, for you see I'm but shodeing. You sink these here small pits around this hill and watch the way the stones lie when you come 'pon them. If you have the eye you can see what direction they d'come from. The flow of the tin stones spreads out like a turkey's tail, see, and if you trace 'em back to the root you'll come 'pon a single line which lights your way to the parent lode.'

They sat on their haunches looking up the hill.

Jeremy said: 'Ben, I want you to try something else with me.'

'What's that, boy?'

'Sometime soon – today or tomorrow, maybe, I'd like to go down Wheal Leisure, look her over. Will you come? You've the miner's eye and I have not.'

Ben shook some of the rubble in his hand, testing it for weight. 'On Treneglos land? Owned by the Warleggans?'

'The Trenegloses will raise no objection. Young Horrie is a friend of mine and his father cares nothing for it.'

'An' the Warleggans?'

'There's not a man of theirs been around in years. It's six miles from their nearest mine at St Ann's, and they sold every stick and stone there was to sell when they closed down.'

'I mind when she closed,' said Ben. 'I was a tacker at the time. We was in straits then, for Father worked there. Mr Scoble, I mean, not my real father. I was going to work there myself, fetching and carrying for him. I was to be paid three shullun a week. Twas all fixed, and I was real looking forward to'n – my first *real* work for *real* money. Then the news came she was all to shut down.'

He stood up, wiped the mud off the square spade, untied his loose fustian jacket. 'So what do ye seek?'

'What we all seek.'

'Twill be all derelict. Likely a full house of water.'

'Not on that cliff.'

'Tomorra, then. In the morning?'

'Ben, you know at Grace these floors of tin – they've made the Poldarks – made us rich – and the villages around have done well enough; there's been money, wages, always coming in to them. But they're on the way down; no one yet says so openly but everyone whispers it. The south floor is finished, we all know. The north has yielded for nearly eighteen years. You can't ask more than that. It is no fault of my father; for as long as I remember £100 a month has shown on the cost books for paying men to seek other and different bearing ground. We've driven shafts deeper, we've cross cut, we've linked up with old workings – you remember what happened when we unwatered Wheal Maiden by accident and two men were drowned – we've done all possible by way of exploration. So how long shall we be in profit at Grace now? A year maybe, maybe two if the tin price bears up. Then I know my father will go on losing money for another year or two. But I think it is high time we looked altogether elsewhere.'

'Elsewhere being Leisure?'

'Well, we could start something quite new, I suppose. There's some kindly ground at the back of Reath Cottage, but the Viguses tried there and the Baragwanaths. And you've found nothing here that would justify making it a big operation, have you?'

'You can't be sure without the equipment, the money spent,' Ben said cautiously.

'Apart from that in this area,' Jeremy said, 'there's only Grambler, which would take a *fortune* to reopen, and Wheal Penrose, here beyond Jonas's, which failed in a year.'

'What do Cap'n Poldark think of Wheal Leisure?'

'Well, she was his first venture, wasn't she – before I was born. He believed in her then and for a while she paid handsomely. But when the Warleggans gained control he shut her out of his mind, concentrated on Grace, which then was as derelict as Leisure is now. I was asking him about it yesterday. D'you know Leisure never went deeper than thirty fathoms?'

'I know she never had no proper engine.'

'What sort of a yield should we ever have gained from Wheal Grace if we'd never gone deeper in her than that?'

Jeremy's pony was whinnying, so Ben went across and patted his nose. 'An' the Warleggans?' he said again.

'That we'll have to find out, but likely as not they settled up with the Trenegloses and have no further interest. It would be a strange county if every mine that was started belonged to the venturers for ever.'

'Let's hope they've gone, then. For it would be good riddance.'

While this conversation was taking place Ross was visiting Tregothnan and informing his patron that when the country next went to the polls he would not seek re-election. Edward, fourth Viscount Falmouth, accepted this statement without comment and bent to sniff at a magnolia that was just showing colour in the bud. When he straightened up Ross met his eye and smiled grimly.

'Your family has put up with me too long, my lord.'

'Isn't that a matter of our opinion rather than of yours?'

'There must have been many times when I furiously irritated your father and I'm sure he could have wished me to the devil.'

'Few associations are unmarred by differences of opinion. Or few associations which have any value.'

Ross had known the new viscount since he was ten years old, but since his succession two or more years ago they had not had much to do with each other. Edward Boscawen was an altogether taller, heavier built man than his father, fresh complexioned, recently married, still very young in manner. But in their brief meetings Ross had sensed a strong sense of purpose and ambition, a sense of ardent adherence to the strictest principles of Toryism which did not run with his own beliefs. He liked the boy – the young man (he was now twenty-four) – but he did not think when it came to the point that it would be as easy to agree to differ with him as with his father. The third viscount had only been a couple of years older than Ross when he died; their relationship over the years had grown in mutual respect; this clearly would be different.

'Fifteen years as a member,' said Ross, 'is long enough. Also I'm not, as you know, a man of substance, and my constant absences from Cornwall have led me to a neglect of my own affairs.'

'In what respect?'

'Chiefly the mine on which most of my prosperity still rests. But other things too . . .'

'Do you not have an efficient steward or factor?'

Ross half smiled. 'I have tried to be my own. But it has not always worked *in absentia.*'

There was a pause. It seemed to him that Falmouth was waiting for him to explain further.

He said: 'The worst example was in 1802 and 1803. But there have been others.'

'Pray go on. I am interested.'

'Just after my last daughter was born I was away on and off for a long period – first with Dr Dwight Enys in France during the peace, seeking friends there – or the relatives of friends who had died – and later, when I saw that the peace – Napoleon's peace – was false, in London trying with others to persuade Pitt to return before it was too late . . . while I was away a good deal of villainy was going on at Wheal Grace. With my wife preoccupied with her baby, my son barely twelve years old, and my mine manager ill with phthisis, a group of miners concocted a scheme to rob the mine of tin as they brought it up.'

'But did it not have to be smelted?'

'No, they shipped it as tin stuff to France by way of the vessels that went to bring back silks and brandies. The men in the Trade often carry cargoes both ways.'

Falmouth gave a brief grim laugh. 'I never heard of the miscreants being brought to trial. Perhaps I was too young.'

'No. I did not prefer charges.'

'Why not? It's a mistake to allow anyone to feel he can break the law with impunity.'

'I agree – in principle. But it was a period of distress, you'll remember. I got rid of four, who were the ringleaders. The rest – they settled down. Some men are easily led – and not all of them . . . well, do you know what one of them said to me? "We didn't think twas quite so bad, sur, now we're at *peace* wi' France."'

The younger man laughed again, more freely.

'Well, Captain Poldark, so far as all this goes, your absences from Cornwall have always been of your own choosing. They have gone far beyond the needs of your parliamentary membership. I need hardly point out to you that many of your associates at Westminster are country gentlemen who get themselves elected to Parliament just as they are elected to White's or Boodle's and who treat it in much the same way – dropping in when they fancy and staying in the shires when they do not.'

'Oh, I agree. It so happens that these opportunities to travel have come up and they have seemed a worthier contribution to the country while it was at war than – '

'As they have been. No question at all . . . Let's go indoors. This wind blows cold.'

They went in and sipped canary in the gaunt parlour among the coats of armour and the battle flags.

'Those excavations,' Ross said presently. 'Towards the river. Are you building something extra?'

'A new house,' said Falmouth. 'This has become small and inconvenient. Mr Wilkins is to be the architect.'

Ross raised his eyebrows. The present house, though excessively gloomy, could by any standards hardly be called small – unless one considered it as a small mansion. Clearly house-building was in the air among the richer of his neighbours. And among the young and newly-married too. Trevanion had been in his early twenties when he began his castle.

'How is Lady Falmouth?'

'Very well, thank you. I shall be joining her at Woolhampton House next week. You know she is expecting her first child?'

Ross did not, and murmured his congratulations.

They talked of Portugal; then Ross said: 'I've also been aware over the years that my occupying this seat has been a financial loss to your father. Owners of boroughs expect to profit from the members they choose.'

'It is part of the existing system. A system I believe you'd like to change.'

'Yes. Especially when it comes to the point of Sir Christopher Hawkins turning Davies Gilbert out of his seat because John Shelley offered him more money down.'

The young man wrinkled his nose. 'Hawkins brings the system into disrepute. We – that is my father and I and others like us – make a distinction between patronage and corruption. We are not subverting honest men but giving them whatever has been considered their right and proper due over the generations. We do not go around trying to buy votes by offering larger benefits or more money than someone else.'

Ross remembered certain occasions in 1796 and 1797, but forbore to comment. 'It's a fine distinction. I suppose it can even be argued that if you do not pay men with money to vote, you must pay them with promises.'

'However,' said Lord Falmouth, 'I don't think you need to be concerned about our losses, what it may have cost us as a family, that is, to retain you in one of our seats. Since you became a member, and more particularly in these last years, you have earned something of a name at Westminster – oh, I know, not by your performances in the House – and it gave my father satisfaction to feel that you represented his borough, and that it was through this that you were able to take part in the affairs of the nation. So it was not an association without advantages to him of a sort. Nor would I say it is to me.'

'That's very considerate of you,' said Ross.

'However,' said the other. 'However, there were times, I agree, when my father strongly disapproved of the attitudes you took up on certain issues – chiefly, I suppose, when you were so clearly in favour of Catholic Emancipation.'

'Which I still am,' said Ross.

Lord Falmouth sipped his canary and stared at the tattered banners.

'Do you have any family affiliations with the Catholics? A marriage somewhere . . .'

'None at all.'

'And are you not of Huguenot extraction yourself? Someone told me.'

'That was a long time ago,' said Ross with a smile.

'Even so, it makes it the more strange.'

'No . . . I simply feel that today the present laws partly disfranchise and emasculate a large group of talented Englishmen who are as loyal to the Crown as you or I.'

'The remedy is in their own hands!'

'It is not how they see it, my lord. It is not, I'd venture to suggest, how many Protestant Englishmen now see it.'

'Well . . . I have to tell you, Captain Poldark, that I am as unalterably opposed to any relaxation of the present laws as my father was. If anything, more so. I believe that to admit these people to full citizenship – who in the last resort owe their allegiance to a foreign power – would be a national blunder and a national disaster.'

Ross smiled again. 'It's perhaps as well, then, that I offer to resign while the choice is in my hands.'

'It should not, I hope, come to that. Take your time. No election at the moment appears to be pending, so I suggest you allow this parliament to run its term and I will make new arrangements when the time comes.'

There was a pause.

'More canary?'

'Thank you, no, I'd like to be home before dark.'

The young peer got up. 'Talking of elections, what do you make of this duel between Sir Christopher Hawkins and Lord de Dunstanville?'

'What? Hawkins and Basset! I hadn't heard! When was this?'

'While you were away. I thought you would have known of it by now, considering your friendship with de Dunstanville. Though, all things considered, such an affray is little to boast of.'

'When did it happen?'

'In November. In London. I was in London too but I heard nothing of it at the time. It was at some Whig function. Things have been very sore between them for some time – over Penryn, of course. You know of the struggle there – the rivalry. But the quarrel suddenly flared up. Warleggan was there, I'm told, with Hawkins. Their hostess had just been speaking to them when de Dunstanville passed by, and as he went on Hawkins made some audible remark about "these Cornish pyskies clad in green", which was clearly a comment on Francis de Dunstanville's bottle-green coat and diminutive size. De Dunstanville at once challenged Hawkins, the challenge was accepted, and they fought it out behind the Savoy the following week.'

'And the result?'

'Need you ask? They both missed, honour was satisfied – to some extent – they shook hands stiffly, bowed, and the affair was over. But really the quarrel reflected no credit on either man, and there's little wonder they've tried to hush it up.'

Ross followed his host to the door. 'Duelling seldom reflects credit on the parties concerned.'

The other looked up. 'My father told me something of the circumstances of the one in which you were involved. That was quite different surely. An insult offered to your wife . . . Whereas this affray . . .'

'Yes, there was a difference. But in that case the result was fatal.'

The word fatal moved with them through the hall, their boots echoing on the oak floor, out to the front door and into the wintry sunshine. Without Ross's having at all intended it, the word seemed to carry with it a hint of the refractory, the transgressive which had always been a part of his nature. The young peer was silent while Ross was being helped on with his cloak, accepted one himself from the footman. The strong bones of Ross's face had grown a little stronger with the years, a little more grim.

Falmouth said in a lighter tone: 'How is Mrs Poldark? When we return – it will be late July or August, if all goes well – you must come to the christening. We shall, naturally, be giving a party. And my aunt, Mrs Gower, will be coming for it. I know how fond she is of your wife.'

'Thank you. We should be very pleased.'

Edward Boscawen looked across his land. 'From the new house we shall have a better view of the river. But that's in the future. We shall be several years a-building. I believe my father had such an idea in his early years, but when my mother died he lost the incentive.'

'It happened to my father also long ago – of course on a much smaller scale. Nampara – such as it is – was begun in 1765 and never completed until 1797, when my mine was at its most prosperous and I could afford something beyond the ordinary necessities of life.'

A groom had brought Ross's horse.

Falmouth said: 'Surely the Cornish Bank prospers?'

'Oh, yes indeed. But you'll appreciate that while I am a full partner my actual investment in the bank has been quite small. So naturally and fairly my share in its prosperity is small too.'

'I hear Warleggan's Bank is in low water.'

Ross stared at the young man. 'Can you mean that?'

'So I've been told – though it was not in Cornwall that I heard it.'

'But they – they are notorious for never going wrong.'

'I'm told it's Sir George himself who is in some financial straits. Been speculating heavily in the Midlands anticipating a rise in manufacturing prosperity. Instead, of course, it is further than ever in the doldrums and like to remain so.'

'It doesn't sound like George.'

'Well, the story is he's very tight stretched. They're

putting a bold front on it in Truro and on the whole people are believing them.'

'I would in their place.'

'I gather you know Sir George well.'

'It could be described so.'

'I've only met him a few times. I thought him a parvenu, and a rather disagreeable one. My father, of course, detested him.'

'Well, yes. It was partly a consequence of your father's dislike of George Warleggan that I came to occupy your parliamentary seat.'

'Oh, come. You do yourself less than justice. But I know what you mean. Unlike many sons . . .'

Ross waited. 'You were going to say?'

'I was going to say that, unlike many sons, I listened to my father and talked to him extensively. We were in good accord. He told me a deal about the parliamentary boroughs we control and about the personalities involved. Although often in London, he kept a very keen eye on what happened in Truro. He told me, for instance, about the failure of Pascoe's Bank.'

'Indeed.'

'Yes, indeed. And of the rumours and the broadsheets that were effectively circulated at the time to bring this bank down.'

'Oh, that is the truth.'

There was a thoughtful pause. Having come with him as far as the door, his Lordship seemed in no hurry to end the meeting.

'Is your Mr Harris Pascoe dead?'

'Yes, last year, alas.'

'A pity.'

'I agree. But why?'

'I understand he came to have a position of influence in your bank. Banks – any good bank – can exercise destructive power. Perhaps he would have felt like using it.'

Ross stared across the lawns at the shimmering river. 'What are you suggesting?'

'Suggesting? I'm suggesting nothing.'

'Then observing.'

The young Boscawen made a dismissive gesture. 'Your Mr Pascoe might have felt like settling old accounts. That is all.'

Ross's horse, seeing his master standing near, whinnied, ready to be gone.

'And do you, Lord Falmouth?'

'Do I what?'

'Feel like settling old accounts.'

'I have no accounts to settle. I have no idea how my father would have felt. It is all long ago. But in any event the question for me is theoretical. My family's banking interests in Cornwall are small. And our mercantile interests are not of a nature to exert sufficient influence on the matter did we so choose to exert it.'

'Such as the Cornish Bank could do.'

'That is for them to decide, is it not.'

'Indeed. Yes, indeed.' Ross mounted his horse. He raised his hat. 'I wish your Lordship good day. What you have told me will give a new turn to my thoughts on the way home.'

Chapter Six

I

A week after this Sir George Warleggan visited his uncle in the counting house behind the Great House in Truro. Cary had changed little in the last decade. Bradypepsia had long since shredded away any flesh to which he had laid claim in middle life, but bone does not deteriorate. Undressed, he looked like a model of a human body used for the demonstration of anatomical structure; but fortunately no one ever saw him in this pristine state. His skullcap hid the shaven white hair; black clothes hung on him so limply that he might just have been dragged from the sea. But the eyes were as alert as ever behind their thickening spectacles, the brain, attuned only to think of figures, continued to function with the emotional instability of an automaton. In the last month he had taken a keen dislike to his distinguished nephew.

George said: 'Well, have you had your answers?'

'I've had them,' said Cary, 'in so far as I put the questions. And they was not favourable.'

'In so far as you put the questions? What does that mean?'

'It means that the less people know we *need* money the safer we are! That's elementary. A child's horn book would tell you as much. Writing to other banks, sending to other banks, especially at a time like this when everyone's short – tis *spreading* the news. I wrote only in the most general way, and that to three: Carne's of Falmouth; Robins, Foster and Coode of Liskeard; and Bolitho's of Penzance. Twas the same sort of answer, the answer you'd expect, all round.'

'What answer?'

'Excuses. All round. War with France to continue, ruinous losses to exporters, reduction of private paper, diminution of transactions of credit, policy to narrow one's commitments. Could you expect any different? What've we done over the years to build up goodwill with these fellers? Nothing. Because we reckoned we didn't need 'em, never should need 'em. Warleggan's was *safe*, that's what we reckoned, what with the smelting works, tin and copper mines, flour mills, schooners, rolling mills! Who was to know that Nicholas Warleggan's only son – Luke Warleggan's grandson – would take leave of his senses and spend his fortune buying up bankrupt mills in Manchester!'

'We've been through all that,' said George tightly.

'But not through it enough. Not through it enough. When your wife died more 'n a decade ago you was constrained to make one or two unwise speculations – but they was carelessness, and they was *understandable*; you was upset, you put much store by that woman, you didn't know what you were doing. But now! At the height of your powers! . . .'

'Everything I have invested is not lost. In due time there must come an improvement.'

'What's this firm of calico printers – whatever that may be – Ormrod's is it? Bankruptcy! That's not improvement, that's one hundred per cent loss, George, one hundred per cent loss! And you're keeping this Fleming firm alive only by throwing good money after bad. And these commodities you own. You'd as well have invested in attle! There's no one to *buy* them! What was *amiss* with you?'

'The war was certain to end if the Prince Regent remained loyal to his party . . . Was I to know he'd turn his coat at the last hour!'

Cary flipped over the papers on his desk. They all related to George's investments in the North – his iniquities, as Cary considered them.

George said: 'The Prince is nothing more than a vain weathercock. Should the war go badly for us now he might well turn to the Whigs to make peace after all. Then my losses would become the profits they ought to have been. So long, that is, as I am able to hold on to what I have bought.'

Cary's mouth tightened like a crack in the floorboards. 'Sometimes people get too big, get too big-headed, go outside the part of the country they understand, the industries they understand, try expanding where they don't know enough. I'd never have thought it of you, George. Does your mother know?'

'Naturally not. She's too unwell to be worried by such matters.'

'She'll have to be if things go wrong at this end.' Cary peered at his nephew over his spectacles. 'You was never a gambler, George. What caused you to gamble? Was it another woman?'

George took a deep breath. 'Have a care, Uncle. You can go too far.'

'I've heard rumours. Don't think I hear nothing because I never go out. Don't think that. There's been rumours. And you haven't answered my question.'

'Nor will I. You don't command the world from this office; nor do you command me. Tell me what the situation is now, and then I'll leave you to your calculations.'

Cary thrust the papers on one side and opened his note-issue book. Since George became a knight bachelor he had been less amenable to correction, and although the two men often saw eye to eye, when there was a difference of opinion it was more often George who got his way. But of course there had never before been anything like this.

Cary said icily: 'If there came a crisis tomorrow – a run, folk crowding in and banging on the counter and demanding what's theirs – we could cover twenty per cent of our note issue!'

'That's only five per cent more than last week!'

'It's not possible to create assets overnight! If we throw things sudden upon the open market we straight off strike down their value.'

George went to a drawer, unlocked it and drew out a file. In it was a summary of all his possessions.

'Has there been any *sign* of a run today?'

'No big depositors have made a move yet. Brewer Michell came in to renew his notes. I had to refuse. That makes a bad impression, for no doubt he can get them discounted across the way. Symons drew more than his custom, more than half his deposit – but he's small fry.'

'Well, then . . .'

'But there's nervousness about, I can tell you that. I can smell it. I can see it in people's eyes. Tis like a field of gorse after a dry summer – just lying there, just needing the first spark.'

'We have some India stock,' said George, peering at his file. 'We could dispose of those quickly enough and bear the loss . . . But ideally we still need another bank – one of the bigger ones – to re-discount £20,000 worth of sound short bills. That way we should be safe.'

'What about the Cornish Bank?'

'What about it?'

'You were friendly enough with de Dunstanville once. Twould be a neighbourly act.'

'Out of the question.'

'Why?'

'We have hardly been on terms for years. And last November I was involved – innocently involved – in a quarrel between him and Sir Christopher Hawkins. It ended in a duel. I was one of Hawkins's seconds. That would make such an approach now unthinkable.'

'There's always something . . .'

'In any event,' said George, 'to approach the Cornish Bank would do what you were at pains to avoid with the others. Our direct competitors in this town . . .'

'What of Hawkins, then? He's landlord of the great Hallamannin Mine and of the silver-lead mines of the Chiverton valley.'

'Oh, he's a warm man, I'll grant you that. But you would not expect him to respond to a situation like this.'

There was silence.

George said: 'How far can I rely on you, Cary?'

'Rely on *me*?'

'You're a rich man. You are as much involved in the solvency of the bank as I am.'

Cary rubbed his forehead under his skullcap. A white powder of dandruff floated down onto the note-issue book.

'Most of my money is invested. It couldn't be realized in a hurry.'

'You keep a thousand pounds in gold upstairs. My father told me.'

'He had no business to. And it's not as much now.'

George stared at his uncle. 'Suppose the worst happens and somebody puts a spark to the gorse. What should we need?'

'In a real panic? Not less than thirty thousand.'

'Of which we can find twelve. Two more perhaps with loose assets, such as personal cash. Is that right?'

'Near enough.'

George closed his file, carefully locked it away, fingered the key. 'Well, the bank shall not close its doors if *I* can help it. The smelting works at Bissoe would give us all the capital we need.'

'Ye wouldn't sell that! The foundation on which we've built all the rest! I'd remind you I've a third share.'

'And I have fifty-five per cent. It could go if the worst came to the worst.'

'At a knock-down price for a hasty sale – it would be lunacy!'

'Bankers can't always be choosers . . .'

'There's always Cardew,' said Cary.

George looked at Cary with dislike. 'You'd see your sister-in-law turned out – your nephew – your niece?'

Cary knuckled his hands together, then shrugged his shoulders as if throwing off some nightmare in which family loyalty might become involved in the conservation of his personal fortune.

'Well, you said yourself, time is of the essence. These assets we have; ye can't pause to auction a mine or a smelting works – advertised in the newspaper, etcetera – while men are shouting at the counter for their *cash*! It may not happen, George. The man in the street – spite of the rumours, the whispering, he'll take a time to believe it: Warleggan's Bank, he'll say, but they're *always* solid. If we put a bold face on it – show our assets – meet every call willingly. I see now I was wrong not to accommodate Brewer Michell this morning. We got to be expansive, not careful. To liquidate Bissoe or Cardew, to do this would be criminal. My strongest advice to you, George, is to sell your Manchester investments *now*, at once, for what little ye can get. They must be worth something – a few thousand. Get your money out at once – what ye can – in gold – have it brought down here by post-chaise. If tis an eighty per cent loss, that's bad, but a few more thousand on hand during the next two weeks – under the counter, ready to use – it might be just enough to save a banking run . . . and then no cause for all this talk of other sacrifices.'

II

Ross had not yet seen Francis Basset, Baron de Dunstanville. He told himself that his home affairs were too pressing; but he had already found time to visit Lord Falmouth.

The truth was that for the last year or so a coolness had grown up between them, dating from the scandal of the Duke of York's mistress, Mrs Clarke, and her sale of army commissions. This *cause célèbre* had occupied parliamentary time for far too long when so many greater issues had to be decided; but a member of the Commons called Colonel Gwyllym Wardle had persisted in his accusations and had linked it with an attack on the corruption implicit in the rotten parliamentary boroughs. On this Ross had sided with him, making one of his rare speeches in the House, and, when the issue flared up locally he had taken the part of the reformers who had held meetings up and down the county demanding change and an end to bribery and venality. Basset had passionately resented this, had indeed spoken at meetings and gone to great pains to spike the guns of the protesters. Although the agitation had now subsided, and although superficially everyone was again the best of friends, he had never quite forgiven Ross for his support of these Jacobin elements.

It was therefore not a particularly propitious time to discuss the county's affairs and more especially Warleggan's. Nor did Ross know how far Basset would be concerned to vent his resentment on George and his uncle in the way Falmouth had hinted as a possibility. During the last ten years many changes had taken place in the Cornish Bank, the present directors being Mackworth Praed, Stackhouse, Rogers, Tweedy, Poldark and Nankivell. De Dunstanville had chosen to withdraw his name, though everyone knew that his interest, in terms of money, was still the controlling one. There was to be a meeting of the partners next week at Truro. The Warleggan situation would no doubt all be discussed there, since it was difficult to believe that two banks, operating so close to each other in a small town, would not each be sensitive to fluctuations in the other's health and credit. If such a discussion took place what was his, Ross's, attitude to be?

On a sudden morning of brilliant sunshine – which presaged rain before dark – Ross walked out to where Demelza was digging in her garden. Ten years ago, inspired by her visit to Strawberry Hill and oppressed by the way the mine and its workings were encroaching on the land before the house, she had persuaded Ross to have a drystone wall built enclosing and extending the area of the garden she had then cultivated. It lay in a large oblong running up and away from the house, the house and the library comprising an L-shaped joint and part of two sides. With this shelter from the wind miracles had been wrought with daffodils, tulips and other spring and early summer flowers. By July the best was over, for the soil was too light to retain moisture. Also most winters, and often in the spring, the garden was ravaged by storm winds from which even the wall could not guard it. Often everything was broken and blackened as if by a forest fire. Yet in between times the flowers handsomely repaid Demelza and one or two casual helpers for their efforts. She had long since given up trying to grow trees. Hollyhocks were difficult enough.

This morning, as if by coincidence, she was forking round Hugh Armitage's present of more than a decade ago, which had been planted against the wall of the library. She straightened as Ross came up, pushing her hair away from her face with a clean forearm.

He said: 'The Falmouths' two magnolias, which I think came from Carolina at the same time as ours, are twenty feet high, and one already in bud.'

'This poor thing has never been happy here. And it has had a sad winter. I don't think it is ever going to do any good. The soil is wrong.'

They stood looking at the plant. This was quite a casual discussion between them, with only the faintest shadow of Hugh Armitage left.

'Perhaps it should go back,' said Demelza.

'Where? To Tregothnan?'

'A plant that neither dies nor prospers . . . It is out of its element.'

'No, keep it.'

Demelza looked up at him and smiled. The sun made her eyes glint. 'Why?'

'Why keep it? Well . . . it has become part of our lives.' A reminder of past error, his as well as hers, but he did not say as much. It was implicit. And without rancour.

Just at that moment Isabella-Rose came screaming into the garden and went galloping over the grass. A stranger might have thought her scalded, but her parents knew this was just an evidence of high spirits, her way of saluting the joy of being alive. Gambolling along beside her was Farquahar, their English setter spaniel, and they both disappeared through the gate that led to the beach.

Demelza peered after her, but they were not visible, presumably rolling together in the sand below the level of the garden wall.

'She's more like you than either of the other two,' said Ross.

'I swear I never screamed like that!'

'I didn't know you when you were eight. But even at eighteen you had your crazy moments.'

'Nonsense.'

'And later. And later. You were twenty-one or thereabouts when you went out fishing on your own the day before Jeremy was born.'

'There's Jeremy now. Perhaps it was that expedition of mine which has made him so fond of sailing! . . . Where did he come from, Ross? He's not like either of us.'

'I would agree on that!'

'There has been a change in him recently,' Demelza said defensively. 'He seems so high-spirited these last few weeks.'

'Not just flippant?'

'Not just that.'

'Anyway,' Ross said after a moment, 'before he reaches us, let me tell you something about George Warleggan that I heard from Lord Falmouth last Friday . . .'

Jeremy, coming down from the mine and seeing his

mother and father in serious conversation, steered away from them and jumped over the stile to the beach where Isabella-Rose was now throwing a stick for Farquahar to retrieve. Approaching her was a hazardous business, for she took the stick, whirled her body around and let go, so that although its objective was the sea the stick was as likely to fly off in any direction.

Demelza said: 'It is hard to believe. I never thought George would grow to be a speculator . . . But if it's true, it's true. So what are you besting to do?'

'I cannot think that de Dunstanville will have heard nothing at all. No doubt he will have a point of view.'

'But you will have to express a point of view too, Ross. Won't you?'

He rubbed his foot over a worm-cast in the grass. 'Revenge is a sour bed-fellow. Yet it's hard to forget the deliberate way Warleggan's Bank broke Harris Pascoe – not merely by semi-legitimate means but by printing broadsheets and spreading lying rumours. And the number of times before that George has tried to ruin us.'

'Not only in money ways neither.'

'. . . One thinks of the power he has come to wield in Cornwall, the numbers of small men who have gone to the wall because of him. One thinks of his influence for ill. One wonders if in this case it is not so much a matter of paying off old scores as a public duty to bring him down . . .'

'Could you if you tried?'

'I doubt if it would be necessary to do anything so despicable as start a whispering campaign. A rival bank can do so much by making certain moves, and the panic begins of its own accord.'

'So it will much depend on Lord de Dunstanville?'

'And my fellow partners. Mr Rogers has no reason to love the Warleggans. Nor Stackhouse, I believe.'

Demelza tilted her face to the sun. 'Caroline tells me George has been courting some titled lady, Lady Harriet Something. I wonder how this will turn out now.'

He said: 'You don't advise me.'

'On what?'

'On what *I* should do.'

'It won't be in your hands surely.'

'Not entirely, of course. But partly it might. Now Harris Pascoe has died, they look on me as – well, in a manner as his successor.'

'And you ask for my advice? Is it right for me to give it?'

'Very right. You have suffered almost as much at George's hands as I have.'

'But is this not a man's decision?'

'Don't hedge, my dear.'

She looked at him. 'Then I will not hedge, my dear. I should have no part in it.'

'No part in any attempt to bring him down? No part in any pressure applied to Warleggan's Bank?'

'You ask me, and I think not.'

On the beach Isabella-Rose was giggling at the top of her voice. The thin high infectious sound was not quite human; it was like some bibulous nightingale bubbling away.

Ross said: 'When I came to stand trial for my life the Warleggans did all they could to secure a conviction. Without their money, their contrivings . . .'

'What George and his kinsfolk have done they have to live with. What we do *we* have to live with. I look back on my life, Ross; oftentimes when you are away and I have no one to talk to I look back on my life, and I do not remember many shameful things. Perhaps I forget some! But the less of such I have to remember the better it pleases. So in saying have no part in it, it is not of George I think but of ourselves.'

'And you would say that if Mackworth Praed or Rogers or Basset himself suggests any such move I should oppose it?'

Demelza rubbed some of the damp soil off her hands. 'I do not think you have to work *for* the Warleggans, Ross.

But I think, being once so involved, you should stand aside and take no part.'

'Pilate did that.'

'I know. I've always felt sorry for Pilate . . . But not for Caiaphas . . . Nor Judas.'

'Though you often call on him.'

'Do I?' Demelza looked up. 'Now you're teasing.'

'Only because you're my better self. And I have to keep my better self in its place.'

'Seriously . . . do you not agree?'

'I know I ought to. But I regret the temptation has ever arisen. For it is not only George we'd be settling with; it is that odious uncle.'

'He's old,' said Demelza. 'He'll soon be dead. Like so many other people and things. *George* is older too, Ross. People mellow, don't they? Perhaps he has mellowed. Clowance, I think, did not find him so hateful.'

'Clowance? When did she meet him?'

'By accident,' said Demelza, aware she had let it out. 'Near Trenwith. A while ago.'

'I didn't know he ever came.'

'Nor I. You were right to warn Geoffrey Charles that the house was neglected. I do wish he would come home for a while – take some leave. There's been bad news from Portugal, hasn't there?'

Ross refused to be side-tracked. 'Did they speak to each other? Did George know who she was?'

'I believe she informed him. But this was months ago, last summer, before ever you went away.'

'And I was not told?'

'I thought you might worry, and there was no need to worry.'

'Another time allow me to choose.'

'Your mind was already occupied with your coming journey to Portugal. I thought to save you a distraction.'

'You mean you thought to save Clowance a talking-to. Judas, what a deceitful woman you are!'

'Now you've stolen my word again!'

Jeremy had appeared off the beach and was coming through the gate.

Ross took his wife's arm and gave it an admonitory squeeze. 'All the same, it shows how tenderly my good intentions walk the tightrope. You say forgive and forget, and on the whole I agree . . . but, mention of him coming to Trenwith, no doubt gloating over the decay of the house, inciting the Harry brothers to new enormities, and – and *talking with Clowance* – this raises all my hackles over again, and I am ready to – ready to – '

'What is raising your hackles, Father?' Jeremy asked, coming up. 'Who is the one to tremble now?'

Demelza said: 'If there was a little more trembling done among my children, there would be better discipline at Nampara.'

'Oh, pooh, Mama,' said Jeremy. 'You know you love your children far too much not to give them all their own way.'

'Never rely on it,' said Ross, doubling his fist. 'If you – '

'But I do!' said Jeremy. 'Am doing at this very moment. Seriously. Can we be serious for a little while?'

'We were perfectly serious,' Ross said, 'until you turned up.'

Jeremy glanced from one to the other, uncertain whether he had made a tactical error in speaking to them both at the same time. Often in the past he had found it easier for his purpose if he approached one and let that one put his point of view to the other. They would confer, and usually the one he had approached would act as his advocate. At least, that was how he supposed it happened.

But this was probably too important to be treated that way.

'Yesterday morning, Father,' he said, 'I did not go down Grace, as usual. I went the other way – for a walk along the cliffs. Fine views you get from there. Sands are very clean at the moment – no driftwood, no wreckage.

But unfortunately it came on to drizzle. You remember? About ten. And I thought to myself, drot it, this is not good enough. I thought, I'm getting wet, and to no purpose; I must shelter somewhere. So I decided to shelter by going down Wheal Leisure. It just happened to be handy, there on the cliffs. So down I went.'

The brilliant morning was nearly over. Wisps of cloud, like white smoke from a fire, were drifting up from the south-west, unobtrusive as yet; they would darken and thicken by midday.

'I thought I told you not to go down Leisure!'

'I don't remember that, sir. I remember you were a mite discouraging.'

There was a glint of irony in Ross's eye. 'And what did you find there? Gold?'

'It is all in a poor way. Some of the shafts have fallen in, and it was necessary twice to come back and start again. The thirty fathom level is very wet; much of it is in two feet of water, running fast towards the lowest adit.'

'It was dangerous to go on your own,' Demelza said, memories stabbing at her.

'I didn't, Mama. Ben Carter went with me.'

'Who also happened to be just strolling along the cliffs?'

'Exactly . . . Well, in fact we were strolling together.'

'I'm sure. So you went down – getting wetter than you ever could by staying out in the drizzle. What was your feeling about it all?'

'Well, Ben is cleverer than I – ten times more experienced anyhow. He thinks it would pay to sink a couple of shafts deeper – say twenty fathoms deeper.'

'Pay whom?'

'We were working it out together: in this district the lodes usually run in an east–west direction – which means we could strike a continuation of the tin floors we've been working at Wheal Grace – or even pick up some of the old Trevorgie lodes. In any case the copper has only been exhausted so far as the present levels are concerned.'

236

After a moment Ross said: 'There is no way of going deeper without installing pumping gear.'

'In a few months if the spring is dry it should be possible to sink a shaft or two and temporarily drain them with hand pumps until we see if there are any signs of good-quality working ground.'

'And if there are?'

'Then we could build an engine.'

'But surely,' Demelza said, 'Wheal Leisure belongs to the Warleggans.'

'After we'd been down we went to see Horrie Treneglos. Horrie's grandfather was alive, of course, when the mine closed. Horrie asked his father about it; we thought the Warleggan interest might have fallen in altogether. But it seems it did not. The Warleggans by then had bought out most of the other venturers; so they sold off the few things that would fetch anything at all and declared the mine in abeyance, and that's how it has stayed. So far as Mr John Treneglos knows, he owns an eighth share and the Warleggans about seven-eighths, though he thinks there was some relative of Captain Henshawe's who refused to sell a sixty-fourth part . . . It's really all worth nothing at the moment; a few stone buildings and a hole in the ground.'

Ross said: 'Trust the Warleggans to preserve an interest in a hole in the ground.'

'So it still isn't feasible,' said Demelza.

'Well . . .' Jeremy cleared his throat and looked from one to the other. 'I suggested to Horrie that he could perhaps persuade his father to do something – such as call in at Warleggan's Bank when he is next in Truro and say he would like to reopen Leisure with them. They're sure to say conditions aren't favourable – and he could then offer to buy their interest and go ahead on his own. They might very well sell to him where they'd not be willing to sell to us.'

Ross said to Demelza: 'The boy is developing an instinct

for commerce. And this deviousness is in the best traditions . . . Are you suggesting that John Treneglos should act as a sort of nominee?'

'Not altogether, Father. We think – if the price isn't too high – he might put up a third.'

'It doesn't sound like the John Treneglos I know.'

'It *could* be profitable. His father did well out of it. And as it's Treneglos land, he's mineral lord and would get his dish if the mine opened; just as we have done all these years from Wheal Grace.'

'In the old days Mr Horace Treneglos only put up one-eighth – and that reluctantly.'

'Well . . . it's like this. Since Vincent went down in his sloop Horrie says his father and mother are passing anxious to keep him home. They would, he thinks, welcome the idea of giving him a mining interest.'

'And the other two-thirds?'

'I thought you might take up a third, Father, and the other third we could advertise. With your name and Mr Treneglos's heading the list I don't think we should be hard set to find a few investors.'

Ross said after a few moments: 'You are of a sudden very practical and enterprising. It is somewhat of a change.'

Jeremy flushed. 'I simply thought it a good thing, with Wheal Grace nearing exhaustion . . .' His voice ended in a mumble. Demelza eyed him.

Ross said: 'Twenty years ago when Cousin Francis and I opened Wheal Grace it cost us about twelve hundred pounds. Today that would no doubt be fifteen hundred without the cost of having to buy the mine back. I know the expense would not come all at once; but the engine itself – if it came to that, as it surely would – would cost in the neighbourhood of a thousand pounds.'

The first real smudge of cloud moved across the sun. All the lights of the day were lowered; then they came on again.

Jeremy said: 'I have been studying pumping engines. While you have been away. I believe I could design a suitable engine – with Aaron Nanfan and one of the Curnows to advise. Of course that would not reduce the cost of manufacture, but it would be a considerable saving over all.'

Ross stared at his son, then at his wife.

'*Has* he?'

'If he says he has, Ross, he has.'

Ross said at length: 'But, Jeremy, it cannot all be learned in a few months, however much you have been studying; nor all by diagrams.'

'It has not all been diagrams.'

'I shall need to be convinced of that. In any case it would not reduce the cost by more than – fifteen per cent?'

'I thought twenty, Father.'

'Even so, it would not do to build an engine which by some perhaps small flaw in design would put the other eighty per cent at risk. However,' he went on as Jeremy was about to speak, 'we can consider that later. Supposing we should come to look on this reopening as a practical idea – and clearly there'd have to be a deal of consideration before we came to that point – two hurdles must be cleared first. Thoughts of an engine must wait on those. First, is the prospect of the mine as good as Ben seems to think? Though I dislike the thought of trespassing on Warleggan property, I'd want to go down myself. And if Zacky Martin be well enough I'd wish him to go with me. Second, if we are convinced of a fair prospect, will the Warleggans sell?'

'Yes,' agreed Jeremy, satisfied with progress so far. 'That's the order of things.'

Ross frowned at the rising wind and perhaps a little also at his son's tone of voice. 'We've stopped your gardening, my dear.'

'Oh, I shall go on for a little bit yet.'

'I'll help you,' said Jeremy.

'Well, you can try to pull that stroil out from among the fuchsia,' said Demelza. 'It's a horrid job and it hurts my fingers . . .' She looked up, pushing away her hair again. 'D'you think George really *would* sell his interest, Ross?'

They stared at each other. 'It's possible now,' he said. 'We might even get it at a bargain price.'

'And that,' Demelza said, 'would not be playing Caiaphas.'

'Well, I shall be seeing John Treneglos on Friday. We'll talk it over then.'

When Ross had gone in Jeremy said: 'You two have a secret language which defeats me even yet. Damn it, what was this supposed to mean – this biblical thing? It was Caiaphas you said?'

'Never mind,' said his mother. 'Sometimes it is more proper to be obscure . . .'

'Especially in front of your children . . . Mother.'

'Yes?'

'I would like to be away next Saturday night.'

'Not for the Scillies again?'

'No. Though it springs from that. The Trevanions – who were so kind when I landed near their house – are giving a small party on Saturday evening and have invited me to spend the night there.'

'How nice . . . They did not invite Clowance?'

'No . . . I'm not sure if they know I have a sister.'

'Inform them sometime. She needs taking out of herself.'

'Yes, I know. I'm sorry. But – well – perhaps I could ask one of them – Miss Cuby Trevanion – to spend a night here sometime towards the end of the month? As we had no party at Christmas, with Father being away, it wouldn't come amiss to have one now. I don't mean a big one. Perhaps a dozen or fifteen?'

'Easter is early this year. We might do something as soon as Lent is over. Have you met Miss Trevanion's parents?'

'Her father's been dead a long time. I've met her mother. Her brother – her elder brother, Major John Trevanion, that is – was away when I was there last. He is head of the family; but he has lost his wife recently, very young. Another brother, Captain George Bettesworth, was killed in Holland. There's a third brother, Augustus, whom I also haven't yet met, and another sister, Clemency.'

Demelza sat back on her heels and watched him tugging absent-mindedly at the couch grass. 'I would not have expected them to be party-spirited at such a time.'

'Oh, it is a music party. Clemency plays the harpsichord, and I believe some neighbours are coming in.'

'Does Cuby play?'

He looked up, flushing again. 'No. She sings a little.'

'That's nice,' said Demelza. 'Please tell her I would much like to meet her.'

She *knew* now what had been wrong – or what had been right – with Jeremy these last few weeks. He had been striding about, acting as if galvanized by one of those electric charges one read about in the newspaper. Also – wasn't it true? – she fancied she had heard him shouting out at the top of his voice just now with Isabella-Rose on the beach. Did not Miss Cuby Trevanion explain everything?

Chapter Seven

I

The girl with the face like a new-opened ox-eye daisy, as her mother had once described it, was not being quite so open with her family as her reputation suggested. On Friday, having seen young Lobb – son of old Lobb – riding down the valley with the post, she had intercepted him, not for the first time, to ask if there were any letters for her. And on this occasion there had been.

Having opened her letter and read it, she had not announced at dinner – as she well could have done – that she had just received a note from Stephen Carrington. After all, everyone at the table would have been interested to hear. Instead she had slipped it into the pocket of her skirt, buried it with a handkerchief, and mentioned it not at all.

Miss Clowance, dear Clowance, [it ran]
You will have wondered what has become of me. Since we was near caught by the Preventive men and I wonder even now if Jeremy escaped safe, I have bin most of this time in Bristow. There was trouble with my lugger Phillipe because they said I had no right to my prize or could not pruve my right. So I am still in Bristow in Argument and trouble over this. I am sartin I shall not give way for no one has a better Right than me to the prize Money. When tis settled I shall come back to Nampara where my own love is. Miss Clowance I put the tips of my fingers on your cool skin. I beg to remane respectfully Yours.
Stephen Carrington.

A strange letter from a strange man. Imagine her *father* getting hold of it! Clowance was lost in cross-currents of feeling. But a darker one than all the others moved in that stream.

By the following day, which was the Saturday Jeremy was going to Caerhays, Clowance knew the letter by heart. She repeated some of the phrases over to herself as she walked towards Sawle through the damp misty sunlight with comforts for the Paynters. 'Back to Nampara where my own love is.' 'Where my own love is.' 'My own love.' 'Miss Clowance, I put the tips of my fingers.' 'Miss Clowance, dear Clowance.' 'I put the tips of my fingers on your cool skin.' 'Back to Nampara.' 'Back to Nampara where my own love is.'

As she came near to the first shabby cottage in Grambler village she gave her head a defiant shake, almost unseating the pink straw hat she was wearing. It was a motion more suitable to a swimmer coming up through a wave than to the young lady of the manor out on a charitable visit. But that, to Clowance, was what it amounted to, a shrugging away, a throwing off, of some dark beast that clutched at her vitals and made her blood run thick, her heart pulsate. For the moment let it be forgotten. 'Back to Nampara where my own love is.'

She saw that Jud Paynter had been put out to air. Put out was a literal fact these days, for at the age of about seventy-eight he had become almost immobile. Prudie, a mere girl ten years his junior, was still active, if activity could ever have been called a characteristic of hers. She was now totally in charge, for Jud could only totter a few steps with a stick, clinging fiercely to her arm. He had lost weight in the body, but his face had become fuller, as it swelled with age and rage and inebriety. Today, it being still March though very mild, he was wrapped in so many old sacks that he looked like a bull frog sitting on a stone. Clowance was relieved to see him out of doors because with luck her business might be concluded there and she would be saved the need to go inside where the smells were strong.

Jud spat as she came up and stared at her with bloodshot eyes, half concealed among a pie-crust of wrinkles.

'Miss Clowance, now. Where's yer mammy today, an? Reckon as she's becoming tired of we. Reckon as she's thought to give us the by-go. Not surprised. When ye get nashed and allish, that's when ye d'come to know yer friends . . .'

'I've brought you some cakes, Jud,' Clowance said cheerfully. 'And a drop of toddy. And one or two things for Prudie.'

The sound of voices had penetrated the open door, for Prudie came out, wiping her hands on her filthy apron and all smiles, followed by a duck which trailed eight tiny goslings behind her.

'So they've hatched!' exclaimed Clowance. 'All safe? When?'

'Ah, twas some time we 'ad wi' 'em. Nosy didn' have 'nough feathers to cover 'em all. She were restless as a whitneck, turning back and forth. So seems me if she was to hatch all eight twer fitty she should be 'elped. So I hatched three myself.'

'How do you mean?'

'Down 'ere.' Prudie pointed at her fat bosom. 'Kept 'em thur night and day, night and day. Twer not uncomfortable day times, but night I was feared I should overlay them.'

'Proper Johnny Fortnight she looked,' Jud said. 'And what 'bout me? What 'bout me? She paid scant 'eed. Never a moment but what she wur thinking of her eggs. "Cann't do that there," she'd say, "else I'll crush me eggs." "Don't shake me when I help ee up, else ye'll shake me eggs." "Cann't go out today, cos I've got to sit wi' me eggs." Great purgy!'

Prudie said: 'I wish ye'd been buried in a stone box and put away alive; that's what did oughter 've been done to ee, twenty year agone when you almost was! Come inside, Miss Clowance, and I'll make ee a dish o' tay.'

'I'm going on to Pally's Shop,' said Clowance. 'But thank you.'

'And look at 'em now they'm hatched!' Jud went on. 'Squirty little things. Hens an't so durty. Hens ye can live with. Hens *drop* their droppings like a gentleman, like you'd expect. Ducks *squirt*. Look at our kitchen floor already, lampered all over wi duck squirtings!'

'Hold thi clack!' said Prudie, getting annoyed. 'Else I'll leave ee there to freeze when the sun d'go down. Miss Clowance 'ave better things to do than to listen to ee grumbling away!'

'Tedn right,' shouted Jud. 'Tedn proper. Tedn fitty. All them ducks squirting anywhere where they've the mind to squirt. Tedn *decent*!'

The two women, to his consuming annoyance, walked out of hearing, where Clowance handed Prudie the half-sovereign Demelza had sent. Prudie as usual was so pleased, already translating it into quarts of gin, that she accompanied Miss Poldark a little way down the track through the village, making comments on life as she went.

Chief targets were her immediate neighbours, the three brothers Thomas, who had not only committed the crime of coming to Sawle from Porthtowan a few years ago but had compounded it by closing down the gin shop that had always been there, since they were teetotallers and Wesleyans. However, their religion and their abstention from strong drink did not excuse their sinfulness in other ways, particularly, according to Prudie, their common lechery.

Every day of his life John, the eldest, whose name often evoked ribald comment, visited Winky Mitchell in her cottage on the other side of Sawle: regular as a clock when he was not at sea, five of an evening, tramp the moorland, regular as a clock home he came at ten. What went on there didn't bear thinking of, for Winky Mitchell, who had an affection of one eye and a deaf and bed-ridden husband, was known for her shameless wanton ways. As for Art Thomas, he was paying an outrageous courtship to Aunt Edie Permewan, who was thirty years olderer than him and as fat and round as a saffron bun. Of course everyone knew what he was about, for with no children to carry on the tanner's business since Joe died, a strong young man was just what was needed to pull it together again. Twould not be that bad except Art was known to be lickerish after girls; and who thought if he wed Aunt Edie he'd be content with what she had to offer? As for Music Thomas, the youngest, who was a stable boy at Place House, Prudie considered him the most dangerous of the three, because he hadn't ever actually been *caught* doing anything. But to be eighteen and still singing treble in the choir, and to walk on tiptoe all the time as if he was a fly . . .

'Some folk,' said Prudie, scratching, 'd'think he's a Peeping Tom. Let'n be catched is all I d'say and he'd be tarred and feathered afore you could say knife!'

So it continued until, complaining of her feet, Prudie turned and slopped her way home. Clowance went on, aware that Prudie's mutterings only lit up a few dark corners of scandal in the village. As for most, she knew it already. Though she lived away from them, distant at Nampara, the villagers were too close not to be personally known. Captain Poldark – though a landed gentleman and now, with Trenwith empty, the only squire around – had always been on closer terms than normal. It could have happened that his wife – a miner's daughter – might have sought to create a greater distance between them so that there should be no risk of presumption; in fact it hadn't happened that way. That one of her brothers was the local preacher and had married a girl from Sawle only served to reaffirm the peculiar friendly relationship.

Clowance knew them all. Next to the Thomases was the elderly Miss Prout – about whom Prudie darkly muttered: '*Her* mother was Miss Prout, and *her* mother was Miss

Prout' – a large loose jolly woman with no teeth. Then a brood of Triggs, tumbling over each other in the rags and the dirt. At the pump two girls drawing water and giggling, Annie Coad and Nell Rowe, one pock-marked and thin, the other with the wide hips and short legs of a farmer's daughter. They smiled and half curtsied and whispered together as she passed. On the opposite side Jane Bottrell was standing at the doorway (sister-in-law of Ned) with ragged black curls, eccentric eyebrows and big yellow teeth – her husband had died in a smuggling venture; of five children one survived and worked at Wheal Grace. No one stirred in the next cottage though everyone knew it was full of Billings. Further on came the Stevenses, the Bices, Permewan's tannery, the field with the goats straggling up to the first empty buildings of Grambler mine. Other cottages were dotted about. Clowance knew them all: she knew the smell of the place, goats and pigs here instead of the rotting fish of Sawle; and of course the open catchpits that emitted wafts offensive to all but the strongest nose. Fortunately, for nine days in ten, a cool clean wind blew.

It was in this village Stephen Carrington had made his home after leaving Nampara; the Nanfan cottage was a bit further on, near the village pond. After years the Thomases were still looked on with suspicion by Prudie and her like, yet Stephen Carrington had been accepted with good grace. Of course he was different; a sailor saved from drowning and recuperating here, not expected to stay and make his home, so arousing sympathy and kindness, not assessment and wariness. He had soon come to be on drinking terms with the men and – possibly – on flirting terms with the women. She had heard whispers. But no village could exist without whispers. What if he came back and really made his home here? How would they take it then? And how would *she* take it? Her skin crawled at the thought. Quite clearly from his letter he was coming back.

Jeremy left a bit later riding Hollyhock, the little mare Demelza and Sam had bought one day in Truro, and taking with him the pony he had been loaned. He went via Marasanvose, Zelah, St Allen and St Erme, crossing the main turnpike road from Truro to St Austell at Tregony and then riding down the leafy lanes and tracks towards the southern sea.

It was a cobwebby day: after heavy rain very mild with smears of mist and sun, the whole countryside beautifully, wonderfully damp, with pools of clear water and rushing soaking streams. Everywhere the bare twigs of trees and shrubs were festooned in cobwebs picked out in molecules of shining water. Demelza always said the spiders had a bad time when it was like this because no fly would be stupid enough to blunder into nets so plain for everyone to see.

She walked a way up the valley with Jeremy, as far as Wheal Maiden and the Meeting House, wishing as long as possible to share in his excitement and pleasure. Though knowing she was no part of it, she savoured seeing him so vitalized, so tense, so ready to be irritable or to be jolly at the least thing. Not like her Jeremy at all, who, though high-strung in childhood and prone to every minor ailment, had developed into this light-weight young man who seemed to prefer to observe life rather than get involved in it.

From the top of the hill she watched him go. Well, now for better or worse he was involved. The agony and the joy. She only hoped Miss Cuby would be worthy of him. She hoped too she would be kind. Girls could so easily cut deep with their sharp little knives, often not even meaning to. At such a time one was so vulnerable. What did Ross think of it all? He said little unless probed. His elder daughter who had half lost her heart to a handsome sailor of dubious character, and who almost concurrently was considering an interest shown in her by Lord Edward Fitzmaurice – a letter from him had just arrived. His son riding away to see his first girl; in his case a very eligible girl with a beautiful home and an ancient ancestry. It was all happening at the same time. Perhaps that was how it always was: two children, the younger, being a girl, more grown up, so both in the same year coming to sudden maturity and all the travail that that was likely to involve.

As Jeremy's figure dwindled into the distance and then disappeared around a turn in the ground Demelza looked towards Grambler and saw her daughter returning with her aunt. Demelza's sister-in-law was leading a young bull calf by a cord round its neck and nose, and Clowance was bringing up the rear, giving the calf a friendly shove when it chose to be obstinate, as it frequently did.

Years ago when it seemed that her brother Drake was breaking his heart over his lost Morwenna, who was hideously and irrevocably married to the Reverend Osborne Whitworth, Demelza had thought to save him by introducing him to the pretty young Rosina Hoblyn, the surprisingly intelligent and refined daughter of Jacka. Drake had presently agreed to marry Rosina, but an accident to Mr Whitworth had intervened, sadly for Rosina but in the end joyfully for Drake, and the planned wedding had never taken place. After the break-up Demelza had continued to befriend Rosina but had studiously avoided putting her into social contact with Sam, her other brother, who was smarting under a broken love-affair of his own. Enough was enough. Matchmakers could be a danger to the community. She had burned her fingers.

Sam, indeed, with Salvation to sustain him, went joyfully on his way, without an apparent thought for any other woman than his lost Emma (and precious few one would imagine for her). When Drake and Morwenna moved to Looe, Drake to take over management of Ross's boat-building yard, Ross had offered Pally's Shop to Sam. Sam had prayed about it and refused. His flock was centred round Nampara, Mellin and Sawle, the Meeting House on Poldark land. It would take him too far away. Better to remain a humble miner, not become a tradesman, putting himself in a superior position to most of his Society. Apart from which, he was no wheelwright and none too smart a carpenter.

So for a while Pally's Shop remained empty and its fields fallow.

But whatever the joyous certainty of salvation and glory in the life to come, this life has to be lived, and Sam, though doggedly sustained by his convictions, suffered from his loss more than people realized, and often felt his loneliness in the cheerlessness of Reath Cottage. And one day, walking to Sawle on a mission of hope, he fell into step with Rosina Hoblyn and her married sister Parthesia, and could not help noticing the great difference between the two sisters. Parthesia younger, noisy, tooth-gapped and laughing, clutching two dirty children and followed by a third, while Rosina was so quiet, so well-mannered, and yet capable-seeming, with a certainty and a strength of mind that much impressed him. He already knew that Rosina was not of his religious persuasion but was nevertheless a steady attender at church. Almost as an after-observation, he took in the fact that the girl was attractive, dark-eyed, small-featured, soft-cheeked, with clean tidy black hair and a slow but winning smile.

So, very gradually, with Demelza holding her breath and crossing her fingers but scrupulously doing nothing to help, an attachment had built up. Rosina, twice jilted through no fault of her own, thirty years old in 1803, too refined to be a common miner's wife but not well-bred enough to attract a gentleman, was the ideal wife for a Methodist preacher who himself was low born but through his sister related to the Poldarks. Not to mention his special relationship with God. But for all his high-flown language which verged on the pretentious, a truly good man in the absolute sense of the word. And in the autumn of 1805, a month before Trafalgar, and after a two years' courtship, they married.

As a wedding present Ross had again offered Sam the now dilapidated Pally's Shop, and this time it was accepted. So in the end Demelza came to have a sister-in-law living there as she had once planned. It was all very strange and strangely very satisfying. Since then, in five and a half years, Sam had re-established the business – though it was never the skilled trade it had been in Drake's hands – and Rosina, her true character and energies released at last, had transformed the house and turned the six acres into a small-holding crammed with corn, vegetables and livestock.

Hence the present procession. Although they had no children – a sad disappointment for them both – a bull calf had recently been born into their establishment and Ross had offered to buy it from them. It was now on the way.

A bull calf is a naturally perverse animal and progress was made in stops and starts. It seemed from a distance that Rosina, the gentler of the two young women, was less determined in pulling at his head than Clowance was in shoving at his hindquarters. As they came up the rise towards the pine trees Demelza could see them exchanging pleasantries and laughing. She wondered with a twinge whether this was not the life most suitable for Clowance as well as Rosina: simple, hard-working, uncomplicated, close to the earth and the sea, ruled by daylight and the dark, the wind and the weather, the crop and the harvest, the cycles of the seasons. Was there any better life than this, if in partnership with the man you loved? But the last was the qualifying factor. Rosina had had a hard life before she came safely to this harbour. Perhaps Clowance would be luckier. Pray Clowance would be luckier.

'Mama!' Clowance said. 'I thought you were baking today! Not a headache?'

'Not a headache,' said Demelza smiling, and kissed Rosina. 'How are you? Are you bringing Eddie or is Eddie bringing you?'

'So you remember his name!' said Rosina. 'Reckon I shall be glad to get'n off my hands, he's so thrustful, gracious knows what he'll be up to next!'

Rosina was not at all fat, but contentment and rewarding work had given her slender body a compactness and solidity. Her limp was only just detectable, her skin glowed with health and her beautiful eyes had become less expressive and more mundane with the achievement of marriage and position. Demelza did not think it had ever been a love-match between her and Sam but it had worked for them both.

'How's Sam?' she asked.

'Handsome 'andsome. He was to've brought Eddie, but Clowance called in just in time, so I said we'd come, her and me, Sam being wrought with other things.'

Rosina had been 'saved' six years ago, and though her language never matched Sam's, her phrases had taken on some of the same colour. The three women turned together to escort Eddie back to Nampara. As they did so the little calf came snuffling up to Demelza and licked her hand and arm with its soft wet mouth. For a moment she felt very queer, faint; for she was taken back a quarter of a century to the night when she had come to the conclusion that her only way of remaining at Nampara when her father wanted her home was to induce Ross to take her into his bed. It had been in the evening, and she was out meating the calves for Prudie, and there in the back of the byre with the calves tumbling around her and their wet mealy mouths plucking at her frock and hands she had had the idea. He had been away, in Truro, trying to save Jim Carter from a prison sentence, and when he came home she had gone into him and made pretty plain to him what she had in mind.

So it had happened, and a few months later he had

married her, and they had had four children – one lost – and now the middle two were in the grip of the same overpowering emotion she had felt that night. Perhaps it was only just stirring in them, a sea dragon moving as yet sluggishly in the depths of the pool. But once roused it would not sleep again. It would not sleep until old age – sometimes, from what she'd heard people say, not altogether even then. But in youth an over-mastering impulse which knew no barrier of reason. An emotion causing half the trouble of the world, and half the joy.

'Are you sure you're well, Mama?' Clowance asked. 'You don't look well?'

'I'm very well, thank you,' said Demelza. 'Just something walking over my grave.'

III

It was, to begin, a small party at Caerhays: just the family and Jeremy and Joanna Bird, a friend of Clemency's, who was staying for some time. Jeremy was flattered.

Not that it was such a very great house when one got inside; it was shallow, the impressive ramparts deceptive. Nor was it quite like home, where everyone talked incessantly at meals and joked with each other and passed the food round and everyone behaved, within reasonably polite limits, according to how they felt at that moment. Here, it seemed, the mood was decided by Major Trevanion, whose position at the head of the table was no nominal one. A florid-faced man, though still in his early thirties, with blue eyes gone bloodshot and fair starched hair growing thin at the front, he wore a plain black silk coat and tight fawn-coloured ankle-button trousers. He seemed untalkative, or was temporarily in an untalkative mood, and this was the cue for the rest of them, all except Cuby, the youngest, who wasn't quite so altogether subdued. Old Mrs Bettesworth, his mother, though she didn't look very old, was tight-lipped and made no effort to brighten the meal. Food was different: pea soup, a codfish with cucumber and shrimp sauce, grilled oysters, a green goose roasted and for dessert apples and oranges and nuts and raisins.

After dinner there was still a little daylight and Jeremy daringly suggested Cuby might accompany him in a walk to the seashore.

She said: 'It's raining.'

'I believe it has almost stopped.'

'Well, I have a fancy for the rain.'

Mrs Bettesworth looked up from her sampler. 'Joanna and Clemency will go with you. The air will do them both good.'

The other girls were none too willing, but when Augustus Bettesworth said he would go too there was a change of heart. Presently the five young people left the castle and began to walk down the muddy garden path beside the lake towards the sea. Jeremy had been right, the brief flurry of rain had moved on, leaving pools luminous in the early twilight. A half moon was veiled in gauzy cloud. After the north coast the sea seemed docile, unobtrusive.

'What do you do, Poldark?' Augustus asked. He was about twenty-eight. A good-looking young man with a fine head of fair hair tied in a queue, boots that creaked even in the damp; flat feet.

'I help my father,' said Jeremy. 'Chiefly in the mine.'

'Your father had a big reputation in Cornwall a few years ago. Still has, I s'pose. Members of Parliament are two a penny, but few enough live in the damn county. It says in the *Gazette* he's just back from a mission. What's a mission? Where has he been?'

'It was government business,' said Jeremy shortly. 'Portugal, I believe.'

'Well, thank God we're still fighting the Froggies. I thought when Prinny took over it would all change. Wish we had a few good generals, though.'

'My father speaks highly of Wellington.'

'That Sepoy general! I doubt if he understands British troops! As for Chatham: he's no more a leader of men than a stone statue on a plinth covered with pigeon droppings! Look at the mess he made at Walcheren, where my brother died! We'll never beat Boney till we breed a few Marlboroughs again.'

'I'm also interested in the development of steam,' said Jeremy.

'Steam? What d'you mean, man? The sort you make in a kettle?'

The girls laughed.

'Very much like that,' said Jeremy, refusing to be provoked. 'Only it can be put to better use. As it is in our mine engines. As I believe it will be in time on our roads.'

Augustus stopped and stirred a puddle with his stick. Because he was in the lead and the path narrow, the others had to stop too.

'My dear Poldark, you can't be serious. You mean a road carriage of some sort with a big kettle in the middle and a fire under it.'

'That sort of thing.'

'Driving the wheels?'

'Yes.'

'It couldn't be done. You'd have to build so big a kettle that the wheels would collapse under the weight!'

More laughter.

'If you used atmospheric pressure only,' said Jeremy, 'what you say would be true. It was true twenty years ago. But if you increase the strength of your kettle so that instead of its bearing 4 lbs pressure per square inch it can bear 100 lbs, then you increase its power against its size beyond all belief.'

'Ha!' said Augustus. 'Beyond all belief! Beyond *my* belief of a certainty.' He went on, marching towards the sea.

'It already has been done,' said Jeremy to Cuby. 'Ten years ago.'

'Hey, what's that you say?' Augustus stopped again. 'Has been done, d'you say? Only by that lunatic – what's his damn name? – Trevithick. I heard tell of that. Nigh on blew himself up, didn't he? Killed people right and left. It's what you'd expect, isn't it. Let your kettle – or boiler, or whatever you like to call it – let your kettle be subjected to *that* sort of pressure and *zonk!* it explodes like a charge of gunpowder someone's dropped a spark in! Stands to reason, unless you're an unreasonable man.'

'A safety-valve is built in,' said Jeremy. 'Then if the pressure rises too high, this blows out to let off the excess of steam.'

'But it killed people, didn't it. Didn't it?'

'In London, yes. The engine was neglected by the man looking after it and he left the valves closed. After that Mr Trevithick added a second safety-valve, and there was no more trouble.'

'But folk have been killed in Cornwall by it! It's a lunatic business, suitable only for lunatics!'

'I'm obliged to you for the compliment,' said Jeremy, touching his forelock.

'Augustus means nothing,' said Cuby. She lifted her cowl against the wind. 'Augustus would have the half of England confined to Bedlam for the smallest of offences against his prejudices.'

'And a larger proportion of Cornwall,' said Augustus. They had at last reached the gate where Jeremy had first hidden. Now they crossed onto the beach. In the soft damp twilight Cuby hopped, skipped and broke into a run towards the sea. It soon became a race, with Jeremy's long legs making him a clear winner. Panting they turned to walk towards the low cliffs on their right and went by two and three.

'It's so different from the north coast,' said Jeremy.

'The fields are greener, the cattle fatter, the trees . . . well, we have no trees such as these.'

'Last year I was going to Padstow,' said Cuby, 'but it rained and blew so hard we abandoned the visit.'

'You must come and see our piece of coast. My mother said she would like to meet you. If we gave a little party, would you come?'

'What, on my own?'

'I would fetch you.'

'I'm not sure that my mother would approve of that.'

'Perhaps Clemency would come with you? Or even Augustus.'

Cuby laughed. 'He barks easily, Augustus. Even growls sometimes. But his teeth are not so very sharp. I'm sorry if he offended you.'

'I'm too content to be here,' said Jeremy; 'and too happy to be here. I believe no one could offend me.'

'I'm glad you shaved this morning. Your looks are improved by it.'

'Do you think Gauger Parsons would recognize me?'

'Dear soul, I hadn't thought of that! Shall we turn for home at once?'

'It will soon be dark. The risk is worth it.'

'Mr Poldark, do we have to take such long strides? I do not believe myself to be short in the leg or disproportionately built but – '

He slowed immediately. 'Forgive me. It was no more than following my natural instinct.'

'Which is what, may I ask?'

'The instinct to outpace your brother and sister, so that I may speak to you alone.'

'Well, they are well back. Shall we wait for them?'

'Not willingly.'

They had reached the cliffs at the side of the narrow bay and now turned back towards the castle in an arc, their footsteps showing blacker against the darkening sand.

'Now that you have me alone,' she said after a glance, 'why do you not say anything?'

'Because I'm tongue-tied.'

'That always has seemed to me a stupid expression. Have you ever tried to tie up anyone's tongue, Mr Poldark? With a piece of string, or elastic, or a ribbon? It really isn't possible.'

'To begin, then, may I ask you not to call me Mr Poldark?'

'I used to call you "boy", didn't I? But that would be discourteous now that I know you to be a gentleman. Mr Jeremy?'

'Jeremy, please.'

'My mother would think that very forward of me.'

'Then in private?'

She looked at him. 'Do you suppose we are going to have many conversations in private?'

'I pray so.'

'To whom do you pray, boy?'

'I think it must be Eros.'

They came to the rocks. In the half-light Cuby sprang ahead of him, clambering, long-skirted but fleet-footed, over the boulders. He tried to keep up with her, to overtake her; his foot slipped on a seaweedy rock and he blundered into the water. He laughed and limped splashing out of the pool, sat on a boulder and held his foot, rubbing it.

She came back and looked down at him accusingly.

'You've hurt your foot again! You are always doing it!'

'I'm always, it seems, running away from someone or running after someone.'

'Which is it this time?'

'Running after.'

The light from the sky, reflected in the pool, was reflected again in her eyes.

'I think I like you, boy,' she said.

Chapter Eight

I

For the musical evening the other guests were a young married couple – he on leave from his regiment: a Captain and Mrs Octavius Temple, from Carvossa in Truro; also a Lady Whitworth with her fifteen-year-old grandson, Conan. Then came the Hon. John-Evelyn Boscawen, and with him was Nicholas Carveth, brother of Mrs Temple, and making up the party Sir Christopher Hawkins and Sir George Warleggan with Valentine his son.

Clemency played the harpsichord, Joanna Bird the English guitar, Nicholas Carveth the clarinet, in its improved form just introduced by Iwan Muller, John-Evelyn Boscawen sang a little, and accompanied Cuby when she sang. It was all a trifle high-society for Jeremy who, with an aching ankle carefully and delightfully bound up by Cuby, was content to sit and applaud and shake his head and smile when anyone looked expectantly towards him for some musical excellence.

He observed then very distinctly what a man of humours Major Trevanion was; from the grim and silent mood of dinner he had swung to become talkative, charming and jolly; the good host intent on seeing that his guests were comfortable and well fed and well wined. He made a great fuss of everyone, including his own sisters.

Although nominal neighbours, and distantly related by marriage to Valentine Warleggan, Jeremy had not set eyes on the other for three years and they had not spoken for six. Valentine was now a tall young man of seventeen with one slightly bowed leg, broad of shoulder but spindly of ankle and wrist, dark-haired with strong features and a narrowness of eye that marred his good looks. He seemed always to be looking down his long slim nose. He was elegantly dressed for one so young, and clearly no expense was grudged to enable him to turn himself out like this.

Jeremy and Sir George had seen one another even less, and each eyed the other askance. George, with devious aims in view, was irritated to see this gangling young man, the first of the next generation of the obtrusive Poldarks, at such a gathering – and Jeremy had none of the sexual charm of Clowance to soften George's rancour. As for Jeremy's view of Sir George, he thought him aged, and stouter in an unhealthy way. Jeremy was just old enough to have overheard and innocently participated in his parents' references to the Warleggans and therefore to have an inbuilt aversion for the breed. He saw him now as the owner of the mine he wished to acquire, the obstacle who must be placated or surmounted before Wheal Leisure could become a working property again.

George's irritation increased as the evening went on because he became convinced he recognized this young man from some occasion when they had been together and he had not known the other's name. George prided himself on his memory for faces, but this time the link escaped him.

Jeremy was differently perplexed about Lady Whitworth; he certainly had never seen her before but the name was familiar in the back of his memory. She was a very old woman and very stout, with a curly wig of chocolate-coloured hair, eyes like fire-blackened walnuts, sagging cheeks so crusted in powder that one supposed if she shook her head her gown would be covered in dust; a powerful voice, a fan. The last created difficulty, for she so wielded it throughout the music that John-Evelyn Boscawen had to ask her to stop, for he was losing the beat. Had this request been made by any other than the brother of a viscount, one's imagination shrank from the thought of what its reception would have been, but in the circumstances she reluctantly lowered her false baton.

As for her grandson, he was big for his age, and thick-lipped and clumsy and generally orotund. He had dark brown hair, growing very fine and close to his scalp like mouse fur; his short-sighted hazel eyes were small and made smaller by the fat around them. His whole face was pale and fat as if it had recently been modelled out of pastry and not yet put in the oven. All through the music he bit his nails, possibly because there was nothing else to eat.

However, Jeremy only took all this in absent-mindedly, for he had more disturbing matters to observe. Not only did young Boscawen accompany Cuby when she sang, he accompanied her during the refreshments by sitting beside her on a window-seat not large enough for three. And clearly he was not finding the proximity unpleasing. As for Cuby, she was in pale green tonight, a simple frock of sprig muslin with flat bows of emerald green ribbon on the shoulders, a little circlet of brilliants in her dark straight hair, green velvet shoes. Her face which in repose suggested sulkiness or arrogance was brilliantly illumined when she smiled. It was like a conjuring trick, a miracle; everything about her lit up and sparkled. Once or twice she met Jeremy's anxious gaze and lifted an amused eyebrow; but whether her amusement was at the attentions of young Boscawen or at Jeremy's obvious concern he could not tell.

Valentine sauntered up to Jeremy with a pastry cake in one hand and a glass of madeira in the other.

'Well, Jeremy, not out fighting the Frenchies yet?'

'No . . . So far I have left it to Geoffrey Charles.'

'I conceit he's still in Portugal or somewhere. More fool he. No one will thank him for it when it's over.'

'I don't suppose he really wants to be thanked . . . Shouldn't you be at Eton?'

'Yes; I've been rusticated for a term. Got me tutor's

favourite chambermaid with child. I don't believe twould have been held so much against me if she had·not so obviously preferred me to him.'

'When d'you go to Cambridge?'

'Next year. St John's. I wonder what the chambermaids are like there.'

'They're mostly men.'

'God forbid. Incidentally, that Cuby girl over there is of a very good colour and shape. I wouldn't at all object to having her after the refreshments.'

'That I think to be unlikely.'

Valentine squinted across at his cousin. 'A little feeling there? Have a taking for her yourself, do you?'

Jeremy picked up his glass and sipped it.

'Watch the way she breathes,' said Valentine. 'Doesn't it give one pretty fancies? Just a pull at that ribbon . . .'

Cuby was smiling brilliantly at something John-Evelyn had said.

'Ever read history?' Valentine asked.

'Why?'

'Soon as a prince or princess comes to marriageable age – and often before – the king tries to pair off the son or daughter with some other son or daughter, to cement an alliance, to join land and property, to heal a feud; some such nonsense. Well, my father – that man over there – finding his beloved son already seventeen and ripe for conquest among the women of the world, now begins to calculate how this son may take or be given in marriage with precisely those ends. Too bad if the son has other ideas!'

'And have you?'

Valentine fingered his stock. 'I have ideas not to be caught yet for a number of years. However much the gold ring and the marriage bed may be a matter of convention lightly to be set aside, it does cramp one's best endeavours to have a sour little Mrs Warleggan waiting at home or watching one from across the room. And a good girl –

some of them are attractive in spite of being good – will not take so kindly to a little amorous exploration if they know a fellow is married. Don't you agree?'

'I agree,' said Jeremy. 'It's a millstone.'

'And tell me about yourself, cousin. Do you have a woman, and does your father have a beneficial marriage in mind for you too? You're a pretty fellow, and I should think most of the girls of Sawle and Mellin will willingly fall down on their backs before you.'

'Haytime is the best,' said Jeremy. 'It makes the most comfortable cushion.'

'Aren't the local girls a bit short and thick in the leg, eh? I reckon. Well, I suppose you get your oats elsewhere. The Poldarks always were secretive about that kind of thing. Oh God, the music is about to begin again. I wonder if I can devise a seat next to Miss Cuby.'

II

Jeremy left the next day after church but before dinner. In the hour before he left Cuby showed him the rest of the house and grounds. The west wing of the castle was as yet unfinished, and as a contrast with the elegant and dignified lay-out in front, the back was a sea of mud and stone and timber, carts and wheelbarrows and hods and piles of slate. Not only was no one working, which was to be expected on a Sunday, but it did not look as if anyone had been there recently. Nothing looked newly dug or newly deposited, and some of the iron was rusty.

'Do the workmen come every day?' Jeremy asked, looking at the pools of yellow water.

'They have not been this winter. My brother thinks they waste their time in the bad weather. It will start again in May.'

'How long has the castle been building?'

'Four years. There was, of course, a house here before.'

'Your brother was very young to start such a venture.'

'I believe sometimes he has wished he had not begun! Yet it is an elegant house now.'

'Magnificent.'

'Mr Nash has made several mistakes in the design, which have added to the expense. As you will see, the castle was built on a slope, and Mr Nash designed the great wall on which one can stroll in the summer after dinner and survey the lake and the park – and also to act as a retaining wall for the foundations of the house. Alas, in the rains of last spring there were not enough drainage holes, and the pressure of the waterlogged ground caused the whole wall to collapse! I remember waking in the night to such a thunderous sound I thought it had been an earthquake! The very walls of the castle shook, and in the morning we beheld a *ruin*. Thereafter it has all had to be rebuilt twice as thick as before!'

They finished their walk at the church where they had recently heard prayers read and a short sermon. Now it was empty.

Cuby said: 'Explain something to me. Last night you spoke ardently of steam.'

'Did I?' he said, remembering the laughter.

'You know you did. You answered most warmly when Augustus challenged you about it.'

'Well, yes. With the latest developments it is surely one of the most exciting discoveries ever made. Isn't it.'

'I don't know. You tell me so. But what is it to you?'

'What it will be to all of us! In time it will transform our lives.'

'In what way?'

He looked at the girl. The dimples beside her mouth were mournful crescents in repose, as now. But give the mouth cause to change, to smile . . . He lost his mind in looking at her.

'In what way?' she said again. 'Instruct me.'

'Well . . .' He swallowed and recollected himself. 'It is the power that steam will give us. Until now we have had to depend on horses and oxen and wind and water – all things not totally under our control. And not created artificially by us, as steam is. When this power is properly developed we can have steam to heat our houses, to propel carts along the roads, to thresh our corn, perhaps to sail our ships. It may even come to be used in war in place of gunpowder.'

'But steam has been used for years . . .'

'Not strong steam with high pressure boilers. This will make all the difference.'

'But as Augustus was saying last night, is there not a great danger?'

'There is risk – as in many new inventions. It has already been almost overcome.'

'Will all these things happen in our lifetime?'

'I believe they could. Also I think it will help the poor and needy by assisting in the cheap manufactures of many things they cannot now afford . . .'

They moved on round the church. Jeremy stopped at one of the monuments

> CHARLOTTE TREVANION, obit 20 February, 1810, aged 27 years.
> To the memory of a beloved wife whose remains are deposited in the family vault; this tribute of a husband's affection is erected by John Bettesworth Trevanion Esqr. From the protracted sufferings of a lingering disease; from the admiration of all who knew her; from children who loved; from a husband who adored; it pleased the Almighty disposer of events to call her.
> Sacred also to the memory of Charlotte Agnes, infant and only daughter of Charlotte and J. B. Trevanion, who died 8 May, 1809; aged 2 years 8 months.

Jeremy said: 'That was your brother's wife and child?'

'Yes.'

'So young. What did she die of?'

'The surgeon called it fungus haematoides. It was – not pretty to see her die in that way.'

Cuby moved on as if glad to do so.

'Little wonder your brother is sad – or sad at times.'

'Before Charlotte's death he was always optimistic, ambitious, high-spirited. Now his high spirits – that you saw last night – do not seem to me ever to come from the heart. There is something overwrought, hectic about them. As if he is grasping at that which now always eludes him.'

'Do you think he will marry again?'

'No. *Never.*'

'With two children to bring up?'

'*We* can do it.'

'You are a close-knit family.'

'That I cannot say. I suppose it is true . . . Perhaps in adversity.'

'You seem very fond of each other.'

'Oh yes. Oh yes, that, of a certainty.'

They moved a few paces.

'Cuby . . .'

'Yes?'

'Talking of fondness . . . What you said to me last evening . . .'

'What was that?'

'You must remember. Or does it mean so little to you?'

'On the beach?'

'Yes.'

'I said, "I think I like you, boy." Does that mean so much?'

'It means so much to me.'

'Oh, tut, boy.' She glanced up at him and then moved on. He followed.

'Did you – '

'You must not take on so.'

'Did you not mean it?'

'Yes,' she said. 'I meant it.'

'I do not believe you have said that to many men.'

She laughed lightly. 'How well you think you know me!'

Jeremy swallowed. 'How well I think I love you.'

They had stopped in the nave. She looked up towards one of the stained-glass windows.

After a while she said: 'That would be a dangerous thing to think, Jeremy.'

'Why?'

'Because I might be tempted to believe you.'

He touched her hand. 'Whatever else you doubt – don't doubt that.'

She withdrew her hand. 'Look, there are other ancestors over here. Here's another John Trevanion. And William Trevanion. And Anne Trevanion – '

'The only Trevanion I'm concerned for is Cuby.'

'Yes, well. But Jeremy, we – we do not live in isolation . . . *any* of us. We are not hermits. Would that we might be!' She looked at him and then away, but he had caught the glint of emotion in her eyes. '*No*,' she said. 'We have said all that can be said – just yet. Yet awhile . . . Look, the sun is coming out. You will have a pleasant ride home.'

'I don't wish to ride home at all. I . . . have an apprehension.'

'Tut, there are few footpads these days.'

'It's not footpads on the way home I'm afraid of. It is footpads here. And I'm frightened for what they may steal.'

'What might they steal?'

'Last night I was in agony half the time because of the greatest of a fuss young Boscawen was making of you! It drove me to a pretty pass of jealousy and despair!'

'. . . Would you have him hanged, then, for looking at me?'

'If his looks meant what I thought they meant. Yes.'

'Oh, my dear . . . you confuse me.' The dimples lost a little of their mournfulness. '*And* flatter me. And we have already met *three times*! You and I must know each other *extremely* well, must we not!'

'Well enough.'

'You do not know my family nor I yours. Nothing of them. It is not straightforward. Nothing is straightforward. Let us go by little and by little. No more now.'

'And Boscawen?'

She fingered the silver buckle on her cloak.

'I do not think you have to fear for him.'

'Give me some proof.'

'What can I give you?'

He bent to kiss her. She turned her cheek to him, and for a moment his lips brushed her sweet-smelling skin. Then, as he was about to lift his head, she turned her head and kissed him on the mouth. A second or two later she was walking away.

He caught her at the door of the church.

'No more now,' she said again, brusquely, having flushed in spite of herself.

'Cuby, Cuby, Cuby, Cuby, Cuby, Cuby . . .'

'Soon you will know my name.'

'It will be the first thing I think of every morning. And the last one at night.'

They went out into the churchyard.

Cuby said: 'Look how the sun is breaking through. Are we not so much luckier than the people lying here? Spring's coming and we're young! *Young!* Ride home, dear Jeremy, and never think hard of me.'

'Why should I – how could I ever?'

'Not ever please. And come again one day.'

III

Some weeks later a group of gentlemen were dining at

Pearce's Hotel in Truro. At the head of the table was Lord de Dunstanville of Tehidy, formerly Sir Francis Basset, one of the richest men in the county – particularly since the reopening of Dolcoath Mine – and also one of the most enlightened. Present also were his brother-in-law, Mr John Rogers, of Penrose, and Mr Mackworth Praed, Mr Ephraim Tweedy, Mr Edward Stackhouse, Mr Arthur Nankivell, Captain Ross Poldark.

The meal was being taken in the upstairs dining-room, which was private and looked out upon the tongue of the Truro river that licked up at high tide past the Town Quay and the backs of the large private houses of Prince's Street. It was a dusty room and always smelt of camphor. Heavy crimson flock wallpaper was hung with faded water-colours of stag-hunting.

Dinner was over and the port circulating.

Lord de Dunstanville said: 'Only one matter remains outstanding, gentlemen, as it did at the end of the meeting. I said, let us leave it until dinner is over so that we should all have a little further time for reflection. Well, that time is spent. Shall I go round the table for your thoughts?'

Nobody spoke. Stackhouse, who was holding the round-based port bottle, filled his glass and passed it on.

'Don't look at me, Francis,' John Rogers said. He was a short fat man with a paunch that made sitting close to the table difficult. He was also deaf and generally spoke loud enough to hear himself. 'I have nothing to add. I am, as you know, no friend of people like the Warleggans, but fortunately they have never been in a position to hurt me, so I feel possibly less involved in the outcome.'

'Well, I don't know that there has been much personal conflict between them and me,' said Tweedy, a Falmouth solicitor who had become wealthy acting for wealthier clients. 'But their name is always cropping up. This small business man or that goes to the wall because the Warleggans come to hold too many of his bills and it will advantage them to close him down. *And* if he says too much against them they'll see he doesn't open up again, scarce anywhere else in Cornwall! Also I believe – or it is strongly held – that they have been behind this move of the Cornish Copper Company to block Harvey & Co's access to the estuary at Hayle. And the litigation betwixt the two mines at Scorrier – United Partners and Wheal Tolgus – is part their doing. I don't know. There is always something. They seem to have a finger in every pie, and it's a dirty finger at that!'

A waiter came in to take some of the used plates. After a few moments Lord de Dunstanville waved him away. A squeaky shoe was followed by the click of the closing latch.

'So you would be in favour of our making some move?'

Tweedy shifted uncomfortably. Largely for business reasons, he had made himself a leader of the church community in the Falmouth district, and a great charity organizer. 'I – if it may be done honourably, without reflection on our own good name.'

'It is difficult to determine what may be done "honourably" these days in the mercantile world,' de Dunstanville said drily. 'Moral values are sadly changing . . . And you, Stackhouse?'

'I don't like *them*,' said Stackhouse. 'But I don't like the expedients which might help to get rid of 'em. I would do nothing; allow commercial and financial forces to have their way.'

The port decanter came to rest in the table hollow designed to contain it. Because the decanter would not stand up anywhere else, no one could forget to pass it on. From where he sat Ross could see a sail being raised on a mast, the mast angling as the breeze caught it. He wanted to be out there with it. He had felt more at home at Bussaco than he did in this room.

'All this moral business,' said Mackworth Praed, sniffing through his long, bent, aristocratic nose. 'I see nothing to trouble our sleep in this. The proposal as I see it simply involves removing a competitor. Or *hoping* to remove him. It is what many do – in smaller ways; probably in larger too if we consider dynasties and nations. I'll lay a crown there was no insomnia among the Warleggans when they brought Pascoe's Bank down.'

'So you would vote for it.'

'Certainly. Of course. A simple commercial step. Without any sort of heart-searching. Amen. Pass the port.'

Arthur Nankivell, who had married a Scobell and so come into lands and property near Redruth, was a brisk, pale little man much pock-marked about the mouth and chin. It was not his turn to speak but he said:

'A great pity Harris Pascoe is not still alive. Twould be informative, my lord, to have his feelings . . . Captain Poldark, you were Pascoe's closest friend – and the most deeply affected by his bank's failure. At the meeting you were – *seemed*, at least, not anxious to commit yourself. Can you not tell us your views?'

Ross turned his glass round and round. Because he had poured clumsily last time, a semi-circle marked the table where his glass had been.

'Perhaps I am a little too close, a little too deeply involved. This should be a business matter, not a means of paying off old scores.'

'*They* are not above it,' said Tweedy.

'Indeed not. I believe it was for malice as much as for commercial gain that they brought Pascoe down.'

Lord de Dunstanville rang the bell. When the waiter came he said: 'Have the goodness to bring me writing materials.'

'Very good, my lord.'

When these came and his lordship had wrinkled his nose distastefully at the soiled feather of the pen, he said:

'Let it be informally recorded. John?'

Mr Rogers put both hands on his stomach and moved it. 'Yea or nay?'

'Yea or nay.'

'Then nay. Conditions are bleak enough in the county this year. If the Warleggans come down it might bring others too.'

'Tweedy?'

'If it can be done discreetly, then yea.'

'Praed?'

'Yea, of a surety. Conditions are certainly bad, which gives us a better chance of success. For my part I think there'd be a sigh of relief throughout the whole county, just to be rid of 'em.'

'Nankivell?'

'How do you propose to vote, my lord?'

'As I am no longer an active partner in the Cornish Bank I shall not feel called upon to vote at all – unless without me there is an even split of three a side.'

The little man scratched his pitted chin. 'Then nay. I have met Sir George Warleggan on several occasions and have found him agreeable enough. No doubt if we had crossed swords over some venture I might feel different and judge different.'

Francis de Dunstanville made a mark. 'I think you would, Mr Nankivell, I think you would.'

Knowing it was his turn, Ross made an excuse and got up, went to the window. The tide was almost full. Cattle were standing knee deep in water at the edge of the river. Water almost surrounded the old bridge leading out of the town. A new one was projected, would, they said, be built soon, making the coaching road to Falmouth easier of access; also the houses that were beginning to go up, good, handsome houses, square built, made to last, and spaced out across a wide street ascending the hill. Half way up the hill were the officers' quarters of the Brecon and Monmouth Militia who were at present stationed here and in Falmouth to keep the peace.

Ross had heard that the Burgesses had only just been successful in turning down a proposition to call this handsome new road Warleggan Street.

'Poldark?' said de Dunstanville.

George, the parvenu, coming almost to own Francis Poldark, and later, on Francis's death, marrying Elizabeth, Francis's beautiful widow, once promised to Ross; George sneering in the Red Lion Inn at the time of the failure of the Carnmore Copper Co, and the fight they had had, Ross gripping his neckcloth, till George fell over the stairs, breaking a table in his fall and damned near breaking his neck. George, elected as a member of parliament for Truro on a majority of one vote – their meeting with Basset and Lord Devoran and Sir William Molesworth, again in the Red Lion, and the bitter enmity almost leading to another fight. George's persecution of Drake Carne, Demelza's brother, so that his bullies beat him up and left him for dead. George and Monk Adderley sneering at the London reception, George, one suspected, egging Monk Adderley on to make an attempt on Demelza's virtue and the duel following that resulted in Adderley's death.

His *greatest* enemy. His only enemy. Always George had been here, in Cornwall, at receptions, at meetings, his *neighbour*, always too powerful, too rich. By the strangest turn of events it seemed now as if George were in his hands.

What had Demelza said? What George and his kinsfolk have done they have to live with. What we do *we* have to live with. I should have no part in it.

Yet Mackworth Praed looked on it as a simple commercial transaction – *nothing* to be ashamed of, nothing to *have* to live with.

Rogers had said: Conditions are bad in the county (which was true enough). If the Warleggans come down it might bring others too (which might also be true).

'Poldark?' said de Dunstanville.

The brig was moving off, luffing away from the quay, making for the wider expanses of the river beyond. Swans moved lazily out of its way.

People mellow, don't they?

Ross turned and frowned. 'I feel convinced, my lord, that the proper thing for me is not to vote at all.'

IV

Ross spent the night in Truro, so it was eleven the following morning before he returned home. He found Demelza alone in the kitchen.

'My, Ross. I didn't expect you so soon! Have you broken your fast?'

'Oh yes. I was up betimes . . . What are you doing?'

Demelza sneezed. 'We have lice in our poultry. It doesn't at all please me.'

'It's a common condition.'

'Well, I'm beating up these black peppercorns. When they are small enough I shall mix 'em with warm water and wash the hens with it. It'll kill all kinds of vermin.'

'How do you know?'

'I don't remember. It came to me this morning.'

'I sometimes wonder if you've lived another life apart from being first a miner's brat and then the lady of Nampara. Else, how do you know these things? What with curing cows of "tail-shot"; and you seem often to know as much as Dwight about the treatment of the homelier ills.'

Demelza wiped her nose. 'Doesn't this stand to reason, what I'm doing now? The lice won't like it.'

'Will the chickens?'

'It won't kill 'em.'

'One thing you haven't learned after all these years, and that is getting your servants to do the dirty jobs for you.'

She smiled. 'If I didn't do this, what else should I do? Besides, I like it. How did your meeting go yesterday?'

'Like most of 'em.' 'I was not born to be a banker, Demelza. Talk of canal shares and accommodation bills and India stock soon sets me yawning, though out of politeness I swallow the yawns at birth and don't let them see the light.'

'Ah yes. But what else?'

'The Warleggans, you mean.'

'Of *course*.'

'Well, they all knew about it. It's whispered knowledge in the banking world. Whether in the world of commerce I don't know; but I'd guess it is hard to stop the rumours spreading.'

'And what did your partners think?'

'We discussed it first at the meeting – then broke off at Francis de Dunstanville's suggestion and left it for decision until after dinner. Some were for doing something, others not.'

'What sort of something?'

'More or less what Lord Falmouth hinted at. Instructions to our clerks as to what to say when being offered Warleggan bills or when paying money out. A few comments in indiscreet quarters about the increase in their note issue and the fact that they hold a vast quantity of pawned stock . . . Followed if need be by anony-mous handbills, as was done in the crisis over Pascoe's Bank . . .'

'And Lord de Dunstanville? Did he approve of all that?'

'His lordship said that, because he was no longer an active partner in the bank, he would not take sides. Or, at least, he said he would give a casting vote only if the six active partners were to be equally divided.'

'And were they?'

'No.'

Demelza waited. 'And so?'

'Rogers said no. He felt that the fall of Warleggan's Bank, if it were accomplished, would have a bad effect on the whole banking and industrial world – especially at a time of depression such as this – ' Ross sat on the edge of the table. 'Praed said yes. We should put all the weight of the Cornish Bank behind an attempt to tip the scales against them. Stackhouse – to my surprise – said no. Nankivell – not at all to my surprise, because he has interests in some of the Warleggan projects – said no. Tweedy said yes. It was then left to me.'

'And what did you say?'

'I spoke exactly as you had instructed me.'

'*Instructed* you!'

'Suggested, then. That, since we – that is the Poldarks – were far too closely involved, even having a sort of relationship by marriage, I would absolutely refuse to vote on such an issue. Pilate, as you suggested, could do no more.'

'So . . . So nothing was decided?'

'Of course, everything was decided. The active partners had voted three to two against any move – with me abstaining. I know de Dunstanville was greatly relieved not have to make the casting vote.'

There was silence.

Ross sneezed. 'That damned pepper!'

Demelza said: 'You are the most lamentable of husbands!'

'What? What have I done now?'

'You have so contrived it – or so contrived your story – that you have somehow placed the *whole* responsibility for the survival of Warleggan's Bank upon my shoulders! If anything goes wrong now betwixt him and you – if he wields his power and money in some wicked way in the future it will all be my fault!'

'No, no. But that was what we agreed!'

Demelza banged the peppercorns. 'You asked my *advice*. I gave it to you. But what you do – how you choose to act – that is your doing, not mine! I will not accept to have this all thrust upon me!'

He moved to put his arm round her. 'Then it shall not be so.'

She shrugged his arm away. 'Be sure it is not so.'

'I have told you.'

'Promise.'

'I promise.' Ross sneezed.

'Do you not have a handkerchief?'

'I'll use my sleeve.'

'How you provoke me! Here's mine.'

He took it. 'I must have lost the one you gave me.'

'You always do.'

'Well, for me what is the purpose of 'em? I never sneeze from one year's end to the next. And I don't expect this sort of assault in my own house.'

'It will soon be over.' Demelza sneezed again. 'Go and sit in the parlour. I'll join you for tea.'

Ross eased himself off the table but made no other move to go. In spite of the half jocular exchange counterpointing Demelza's indignation, Ross knew that she was right. A decision had been taken in Truro yesterday which might have no consequences for them at all; or the consequences might in some way yet unforeseen be of vital importance. The shadow of George Warleggan had lain across them so heavily in the past, and for so long a time, that no one could lightly dismiss the opportunity of removing it for ever. It was true that for the last ten years they had succeeded in avoiding each other and so avoiding conflict. It was true that they were all growing older. It was true that revenge was un-Christian and uncomfortable to live with. Perhaps in a few months Ross would feel happy and relieved that he had not seized this chance of repayment in kind. At the moment he was full of doubt, and Demelza's reaction had shown that she was having doubts too.

Of course it would be all right. Since Elizabeth's death there had really been no cause for open conflict. Spite – yes, there was always spite on George's side and a hackle-raising hostility on Ross's. But even these instinctive reactions had become a little weary with the passing of the years. Live and let live – just so long as they never met . . .

'Demelza,' he said.

'Yes, Ross?'

'Of course, we've made the right decision.'

'And if we have made the wrong?' she asked starkly.

'Then no regrets.'

She half smiled at him. 'It's the only way to live.'

He stood by the door and watched her. She began to spoon up the crushed pepper and put it into the bucket.

'One other thing,' Ross said, glad he could change the subject. 'Coming by Grace I met Horrie Treneglos. He'd been to see Jeremy but apparently Jeremy has gone fishing again.'

'Yes. I told him.'

'Did he tell you why he came?'

'No.'

'It seems that John, his father, has called on George in Truro and has put the proposition to him that they should reopen Wheal Leisure. George, as expected, declined to have any part in the project, saying conditions were unfavourable and that he couldn't see his way to advancing any money, so John made him an offer for the mine as it stands. George pretended reluctance and then, after some haggling, said he could probably accept five hundred pounds. Mr Treneglos offered three hundred and fifty, and there the matter stands.'

'Until?'

'Well, John's astuter than I thought. It clearly doesn't do to look too eager, otherwise George would smell a rat and raise his price – or decide to hang on.'

'What I'm still not so sure of is what rat there is to smell?'

'Nor I for certain. Of course I have a sentimental attachment for Wheal Leisure. Jeremy's proposal touched a chord.'

'Zacky Martin thought well of the idea?'

'So far as he went. But his breathing was troubling him so I did not press him to go too far. Some of the old lodes are certainly alive, but squeezed and compressed between hard strata so that they run barely an inch wide. By following a rib down one might soon come into better ground. Others lie flat or horizontal, so they don't bear so good an aspect. There's little more we can do until the dry weather sets in.'

'But if John gets the Warleggan share for, say, four hundred pounds, you will open then?'

'Not certainly.'

'It is a lot to spend if you don't proceed.'

'There's no other way.'

Demelza put the kettle on the fire.

Ross said: 'It's a fair risk in my view. We'll be guided by events. If we did open we might save considerably by buying a second-hand engine, if one should be available of the right size and price.'

'Jeremy would be very disappointed over that.'

'I know.'

'This idea of opening Wheal Leisure and his work on the engine has given him a new purpose in life, Ross.'

'I know that too.'

'I think it is that and something else also,' Demelza said. 'Both happening together.'

Ross looked up. 'You mean you really think he has fallen in love?'

'I told you.'

'And you believe it to be serious?'

'Yes, I do.'

'In that case, good luck to him. When are we to see the girl?'

'I wrote to her mother last Wednesday. Jeremy wants to give a little party in Easter week.'

The kettle was boiling. As she took it off, Ross said:

'I hope and trust you're not intending to wash the chickens all by yourself. Even if you hesitate to trouble the servants, you might get Clowance to help you.'

'Sarcasm never becomes you, Ross. Perhaps you'd like to hold the chickens for me?'

'Gladly. If you'll explain to me why my son wastes at least a day a week on these fishing expeditions – especially in this weather.'

'Why don't you ask him?'

'I have. He's as evasive as a pilchard. I have even offered to accompany him, but he has indicated that he prefers to go with Ben or Paul.'

Ena Daniel came into the kitchen.

'Oh, beg pardon, sir. Mum. I didn't know you was both 'ere. Post's just come, mum. And the paper. Shall I bring 'n in 'ere?'

'No, Captain Poldark is just returning to the parlour. No doubt all the letters are for him.'

'No, mum. Leastwise, I think not. The top letter says "Mrs Poldark", I do b'lave.'

Demelza rubbed her hands on her apron. 'Then you may bring that one in here, Ena.'

When she had gone, Ross said: 'Don't let her escape.'

'What d'you mean?'

'Do your servants a kindness and allow them a little of the pleasure of catching and washing the hens.'

It was too late to reply as she wanted. She turned her back as Ena came in.

'Ena.'

'Sur?'

'Your mistress needs help.'

'Yes, sur.'

Ross sneezed as he went out.

A large flowing hand on the outside of the letter. Demelza broke the seal. The letter was signed Frances Bettesworth.

My dear Mrs Poldark,

Your gracious Invitation to my daughter, Miss Cuby Trevanion, to visit you at your home in Nampara and to spend two nights, has been kindly received.

Unfortunately, at the present time, she has so many other engagements – and Commitments towards her recently widowed brother that I feel I must refuse on her behalf; much as I understand the Disappointment this will give to all consarned.

I remain, my dear Mrs Poldark, with most respectful compliments, yours ever Sincerely,
Frances Bettesworth.

Chapter Nine

I

Jeremy said: 'Yes, well, we've done as much as we can now. There's no doubt that adding those two feet to the length of the carriage would enable this to be fitted. It's the greatest good fortune.'

'If we can have it,' said Paul Kellow.

Jeremy looked at Simon Pole, who pursed his lips and made a noncommittal face.

'You mentioned it to Mr Harvey again?'

'Oh yes. I told 'im what you said.'

'And he said?'

'Didn't say much. I reckon he was halfy-halfy.'

They were staring at a boiler propped up on wooden trestles where they had lifted it two weeks ago. The fourth young man was Ben Carter and they were standing in a corner of Harvey's Foundry, which was fifteen-odd miles south along the coast from Nampara.

Jeremy said: 'Well, there's no doubt this is exactly what we want – what we *need*. That it should be sitting here, neglected, all these years . . . Let's go through it again. Have you the dimensions, Simon?'

'Four and a quarter feet in diameter and eight from end to end.'

'Go on.'

The parchment crackled in Pole's fingers as he unfolded it. 'The casting be $1\frac{1}{2}$ inches thick overall and the flange is secured by 26 wrought-iron bolts. The interior diameter will be about 48 inches.'

Jeremy wiped his hands on a piece of waste. The monotonous clanging of a hammer stopped as a workman nearby paused to ease his muscles.

'Well, from what you tell me – or from what I've learned here – the cohesive strength of cast iron has to be 15,000 lbs to tear apart a bar one inch square. So . . .' Jeremy took out a pencil and a piece of paper on which he had been working at home. He stared at it. 'You'd need an internal pressure outwards of over 900 lbs per square inch to make this boiler burst. The safety-valve is loaded to what?'

'Fifty lbs per square inch.'

'God save us! So it would require steam accumulated to near on twenty times the elasticity determined by the safety-valve to burst the boiler.'

'The cylindrical part, yes,' said Paul. 'What about the flange bolts and fire tubes?'

'Well,' said Jeremy. 'The safety of the fire tubes particularly has to be considered. But I've made calculations. Perhaps you ought to check the result with your own figures.'

Paul took the paper over to a table and began to do sums of his own.

'This is all too much fur me,' said Ben. 'It seems me the safety be ample for any purpose that we d'want.'

Pole looked round. 'It is as much as you want. But I reckon twill be another matter to get it.'

'Somehow we must get it,' said Jeremy. 'You can't afford to turn down gifts from on high!'

Jeremy joined Paul, and after a long consultation they returned. 'It comes out roughly the same. The bolts are five-sixths of their diameter solid iron. So it would seem to need around 750 lbs pressure per square inch to carry away the end of the boiler. Fifteen times the load on the safety-valve. The margin of safety is beyond any normal precautions . . . We could well re-set the safety-valve to 120 and raise the steam pressure to 100 without the slightest risk. Even then we're covered seven times over.'

''Tis five years old. Mr Trevithick has not been here to look at him in all that time.'

'Well, it no longer belongs to him,' said Jeremy. 'I must see Mr Harvey again. Do my best to persuade him.'

'Think there's a chance?' said Paul.

'Yes . . . I've a card up my sleeve I didn't have last time.'

The others stayed in the foundry: by common consent any negotiations were left to Jeremy, for he was genteel born.

It was raining slightly in a light east wind. He skirted the forges, the boring mill, the fitting shops, the coal yard, on the way to the two-storey timber building that served as offices. He knocked on a door and was told to enter.

Henry Harvey was thirty-six, a stocky man with straight hair worn in a downward quiff over his forehead, corpulent in a dark serge tail suit and a cream silk neckcloth. He did not look too delighted when he perceived who was calling on him.

For best part of a year now Jeremy Poldark, first introduced by Andrew Vivian, had been visiting his foundry about twice a week. With the name of Captain Poldark still one to conjure with in the county, he'd welcomed the son and looked with pleasure and surprise on the way the boy had actually got down to practical work. It wasn't usual. When he'd said yes to the idea he'd expected young Poldark to be interested only in the theory like most gentlemen, and unwilling to soil his hands. Let the engineer-inventor do the work while the gentle-man watched and encouraged. But not at all. Poldark had worked like one of his own men in the foundry and in the ancillary shops, marrying theory with practice all through.

With him had come two other young men who'd also studied and worked – though they had conformed more nearly to type: the slender one called Kellow tending to stand back from the harder labour, the bearded one called Carter matching his rougher clothes and voice. Anyway, they had worked alongside his own men, and Mr Harvey, with enough troubles and disputes on his hands, had not been displeased at the free help offered him; and the young men got on well with his own work-force, which was important. With a law-suit hanging fire and influential friends not too thick on the ground, Mr Harvey had also felt that a Poldark on his side would do no harm at all. That Jeremy asked him not to mention his visits Mr Harvey took to be an example of youthful modesty that could be easily thrown off if need be.

But recently Mr Poldark had been spreading his wings. He had admitted to Mr Harvey that his chief interest was not so much in mining machinery as in locomotive travel. He had, it seemed, followed Mr Trevithick's career from an early age and was fascinated by his achievements and not at all put off by his failures.

So he wanted – he asked – if he might be given leave to construct in Harvey's foundry the basic four wheels, frame and carriage which eventually might grow into a locomotive vehicle like Trevithick's. He would, he said, pay for the ironwork and woodwork, etc. if they could be permitted to spend part of their time constructing it. Henry Harvey had agreed and had looked in once or twice to watch the progress.

It was still a long way from any sort of completion; but two weeks ago, rooting about the works, Jeremy had unearthed this boiler which with some adjustment of the carriage might serve. It was covered in dirt and muck and more than a trifle rusty and had lain unregarded in a corner of the foundry for several years; but they could hardly believe their luck as they hauled it out and began cleaning it. It was a strong steam 'breeches' boiler – so named from the shape of the wrought-iron tube within it – and designed by Trevithick himself, probably for a threshing machine. It lay now on its trestles like a fat baby whale that had lost its mother.

Jeremy had seen Henry Harvey last week and asked him if he would 'lease' the boiler to the three young men for their experiment, since they hadn't enough money to buy it. On this Henry Harvey had not been encouraging. Privately he thought all this secrecy was overdone and that Captain Poldark, if approached, could well afford to pay for his son's whims.

'Have you a few minutes of your time, Mr Harvey?'

'Well, Mr Poldark, there *is* pressing business to attend to; but it can wait the few minutes that you suggest. Pray sit down.'

Jeremy took the edge of a chair. 'I expect you'll know from Mr Pole earlier this week that we have cleaned and examined the boiler even more thoroughly, and it so fits our requirements that we can hardly believe our good fortune in finding it.'

'Pole told me what was going on,' Harvey said cautiously. 'All the same, it hardly removes the prime obstacle . . .'

'In fact,' Jeremy said, 'it is not about that that I actually came to speak to you, sir. It's related, of course, because we have been trying, as you know, experimentally to construct this carriage, but the lack of a high-pressure boiler was one of the greatest problems. If this can be providentially solved we can . . .' Jeremy paused and let the sentence float in the air.

Mr Harvey shifted. 'Yes, well. Let me say I understand your position; no more. But you tell me that this boiler is *not* what you have come to me about . . .'

Jeremy looked out of the window. From here you could see the brig *Henry* lying drunkenly against the wharf, two of her sails still hanging from the masts like drowned butterflies. She had come in on the spring tide this morning, but the sea had all gone away and left a great expanse of sand threaded by three or four narrow snakes of shallow water twisting among the banks. In one of these little channels *Nampara Girl* was anchored so that they could escape at any time. But the brig, unless she could be got away on the morning tide, might be imprisoned here until the new moon in two weeks' time. Over in the distance were the great Towans where the blown sand reached pinnacles two hundred feet above the sea. It was a crying pity that this natural harbour, the safest along the north coast, should be virtually unusable because of the sand.

Jeremy said: 'Almost adjoining my father's mine is one which has been derelict for years. We are thinking of reopening it. And though previously it was self-draining we shall now need an engine . . .'

'Indeed.'

'I believe, from what I have learned here, from the books I have read, and from my knowledge of the mine to be reopened, that I should have a pretty fair notion as to the size and sort of engine which would best suit us.' Ross would have been surprised at the confidence with which Jeremy spoke.

'It could be so,' said Harvey.

'And since I have this obligation to Harvey's, it's clear to me that we should wish to have the engine made here.'

Henry Harvey brushed the quill of his pen along his cheekbone. It was a habit of his when business loomed.

'What had you in mind?'

'Subject to agreement with my father and the other venturers, I thought a 36-inch cylinder to go, say, a 9-feet stroke. The boiler to be of wrought iron, something like 18 feet long by 5 feet with an oval tube $3\frac{1}{2}$ feet at the fire end and maybe 3 feet at the chimney end. Weighing, I'd conject, about 7 tons.'

Harvey made a note. 'And the pump rods?'

'Of Dantzig pine. It is generally the most reliable.'

'And the beam?'

'I'd like it to be of cast iron.'

Harvey looked up. 'That's a departure, Mr Poldark. I know it has been done, but I'm not sure I should advise it for an engine of that size.'

'Why not?'

'Well, largely the difficulty of manufacture. With good

sound oak there is room enough for error. If it is of cast iron the dimensions would be critical.'

Jeremy bit his thumb. 'Cast iron *must* be so much more efficient. A wood beam shrinks and expands, needs constant adjustment, as we all know. The bolts get out of truth. With iron – if the dimensions are once correct . . .'

'Yes, if they are. I understand your feeling. But its size and weight make it a very awkward undertaking.'

'You have the plant,' Jeremy said; 'in the new equipment brought in earlier this year.'

Harvey got up and went to the window, hands behind coat-tails. 'You have me there, Mr Poldark. Well, I'll discuss this with Mr West . . . Have you your father's authority to place this order?'

'No, sir. As I said, it is subject to his approval. I hope over the next few weeks to make a full series of diagrams and have them commented on by my father, also by the others I've mentioned. When we agree the plans I shall bring them to you and invite your advice. Also then we shall have to go into the costs.'

'Who is to be your engineer?'

'I hope to be.'

'You?' Harvey coughed into his fist to hide his surprise. 'Well, yes, I must confess you've shown unusual aptitude . . .'

'Naturally, I won't be on my own. But if we dispense with a skilled engineer we shall save considerably on costs. We should probably have to pay twenty per cent on top of the costs for a good man – that's including his design and supervising the construction. I believe we could do without him if all the parts were made here.'

Henry Harvey nodded his head at the compliment.

'So your father knows now of these visits you have been paying us?'

'Not yet. I expect he will have to know soon.'

'Surely. Surely.'

'In the meantime,' said Jeremy, 'I hope you'll not

dispose of the Trevithick boiler that we have been working on – at least without letting me know of another interest.'

'Agreed,' said Harvey.

'I even might hope that, if this pumping engine is built, you could look more favourably on our wish to lease the boiler and certain other of the parts necessary to construct the carriage . . .'

Henry Harvey's coat-tails swung as regularly as a metronome.

'I seriously don't think, Mr Poldark, that a leasing agreement would amount to a suitable arrangement on either side. But supposing this mine engine is built here, I would be prepared to sell you the boiler at half the price I paid Mr Trevithick for it six years ago. And all other material and labour at cost. Would that be a help?'

'A great help,' said Jeremy. 'May I ask what you paid Mr Trevithick for the boiler?'

'Well, in fact I made this boiler for Mr Trevithick under licence. Later I took it over from him in discharge of a debt. It was – a gesture of goodwill. He is, after all, my brother-in-law. I don't think he would in any way object if I now sold it to you for thirty pounds.'

'That would be a great help,' said Jeremy.

Harvey turned, showing his stomach in profile. 'You've never explained to me the cause of this secrecy between you and your father. Why you adopt this subterfuge of coming by sea on – what is it? – a so-called fishing expedition? By coming for one week in six and staying in Hayle you would have accomplished the study in half the time. Is your mother party to the deception?'

'She knows nothing. The reason is, my father forbade me to have any dealings with high-pressure steam.'

'Oh . . . But why?'

'For one thing, your elder brother, Mr Harvey.'

The other stared. 'Francis? Oh, you mean the danger.

Yes, it's true he was killed by a bursting boiler, but that was in one of the earlier experiments.'

'My father knew your brother. Then there was the explosion at Woolwich when a boiler burst killing four – was it? – and gravely injuring three or four others. And only a year or so ago the tragedy at Wheal Noah with so many scaldings from the exploding steam . . .'

Harvey looked across at his visitor. 'All that you may say. But still . . . A man may fall from his horse and break his neck; that does not condemn horse-riding.'

'It is what I would say to him if it came to an argument. But I thought this was a way of avoiding the argument – at least until there is something to show.'

Henry Harvey went back to his seat. 'Yes, well.' The thought occurred to him that when Captain Poldark knew of his son's disobedience *he* might come into disfavour instead of receiving the compliments he'd expected. 'Well, I must go now, Mr Poldark. We're trying to unload and reload by the morning. It will mean working most of the night, but we shall have a moon. Kindly bring me the diagrams when you have drawn them and they've been approved, and I'll work out an approximate costing.'

Jeremy rose. 'In a few weeks, I hope. It depends how quickly other things move.'

'What is your new mine to be called?'

'Er . . . Wheal Maiden.' Just in time Jeremy remembered that he had once seen Sir George Warleggan at the Hayle Foundry and that Wheal Leisure was still not officially in their hands.

II

They left soon after. The sun would set around six-thirty and with a light following breeze they would reach Nampara in about two hours, which would allow them ample daylight. They had done what they had come to do and were ready to go.

Jeremy was in great spirits. The steam carriage had come nearer. And if the mine went ahead, there would be further interesting work and all the adventurousness of constructing the engine and reviving the old workings. But his chief reason for being anxious to get home was to see if Cuby's mother had yet replied to his mother's invitation for her to come and stay at Nampara. That was the most exciting prospect of all.

Once they were out of the Hayle Estuary and out of sound of the land, Jeremy opened a firkin of ale and led his friends in singing ribald songs. After they had used these up Ben changed the mood by starting them off on hymns, and that lasted for half an hour longer. Then Jeremy, feeling drunkenly sentimental on very little liquor, sang them the song which was a favourite of his mother's.

> 'I d' pluck a fair rose for my love;
> I d' pluck a red rose blowing.
> Love's in my heart, a-trying so to prove
> What your heart's knowing.

> 'I d' pluck a finger on a thorn
> I d' pluck a finger bleeding.
> Red is my heart a-wounded and forlorn
> And your heart needing.

> 'I d' hold a finger to my tongue
> I d' hold a finger waiting.
> My heart is sore until it joins in song
> Wi' your heart mating.'

They too joined in song while the little gig cut steadily through the quiet sea, and the soft drizzle fell on them all.

Book Three

Chapter One

I

By the beginning of May startling news reached England. British and Portuguese troops had not only broken out of the narrow confines of the fortifications around Lisbon but, after a series of manoeuvres and counter-manoeuvres interspaced with some of the bloodiest battles of the war, had driven the French totally off Portuguese soil. Masséna, one of France's greatest generals, in command of the largest army Napoleon had ever entrusted to one of his lieutenants, had been comprehensively defeated. In four weeks the British had advanced 300 miles and inflicted 25,000 casualties on the enemy for a loss to themselves of about 4,000. In a characteristically dry proclamation Lord Wellington announced to the Portuguese that the cruel enemy had retired across the Agueda and the inhabitants of the country were at liberty to return to their homes.

The critics at last were silenced. Even the fiercest Whigs, who had for so long been crying doom and disaster, indiscipline and incompetence, changed their views. A vote of thanks was passed in both Houses for the campaign, and the speakers had scarcely ever been more unanimous. As Canning wrote to Ross: 'But for Prinny's change of mind – and heart – all this would have been lost.'

A few diehards, such as the Reverend Dr Halse of Truro, predicted that Napoleon would now take the campaign into his own hands and sweep the 'Johnnies' back into the sea; but nothing could prevent a national upsurge of pride and optimism. Overnight the abused General Wellington became an international figure.

It was not in Sir George Warleggan's nature to rejoice on any matter which did not personally concern him; but as he drove through High Cross in his post-chaise and saw the bonfire leaping up he felt his own spirits rising with the sparks. At the door of the Great House he walked briskly up the steps and was greeted by a bewigged footman.

This was the time more than any other when he missed Elizabeth – still missed her after so long. Someone had recently said in his hearing – a newly widowed man such as he had once been – 'possessions are no use if one can only possess 'em on one's own,' and he knew the bitter truth of this. The upturn in his fortunes now, after two months of the gravest anxiety, was something not to be kept to oneself. Yet his mother and Valentine and little Ursula were at Cardew; and in any case his mother was unwell and had *no* business head – one sometimes wondered how she had bred him – while Valentine was still too young – and withdrawn and sophisticated and sardonic – to share one's fears and relief with.

What George needed was that slim beautiful creature who now was no more than earth and bone – dead in childbirth eleven years ago. She, for all her patrician breeding, would have understood; they would have been pleased *together*. (Someday, he thought, God willing, and someday not perhaps so far distant, he might have another woman to confide in. He had not seen Harriet Carter since the Gordons' soirée; he had had no right to seek her out when he had only a possible bankruptcy to offer her by way of a marriage settlement.)

The only person of his flesh and blood in this house – if it were proper to think of him as having any of either – was old Cary. And he, certainly, would understand more truly than anyone the reason for his satisfaction. But there would be nothing responsive there; it would be like talking to a balance sheet.

He went into the parlour and warmed his hands at the

fire. The thought of going in search of his uncle was distasteful. He pulled the bell-cord.

'Sur?'

'Fetch me the brandy. The 1801. You will find a half-used decanter in my study. And, Baker, ask my uncle if he will be good enough to step this way. If he has already retired, ask him to come down.'

'Yes, sur.'

While he waited George eased his back with the warmth. Even with the introduction of turnpike roads a long coach ride was an ordeal. Another footman arrived with the brandy. It was known throughout the servants' quarters that it was no good helping oneself to any form of liquor: Sir George would always know the level at which the decanter had been left and the exact number of bottles in the cellar.

George took the glass and drank. Cary came shuffling in. He had not retired, but the black alpaca coat he wore would have done well enough for a dressing-gown.

'So you're back. It's high time.' He sniffed. 'Four days gallivanting. We've lost six thousand in four days. On Wednesday it was almost a *run*. Farmers and the like coming in for market day. The rest of your northern properties will have to go – even at a knockdown.'

'It has never been a run,' George corrected. 'A constant drain. Loss of confidence, nothing more. These are exacting times for any bank.'

'It would not have been exacting for us if it had not been for your folly! Over and over, d'ye know, this last week, customers have refused our notes and asked for gold! And the shopkeepers, I'd have you know, the shopkeepers of this town, prefer to be paid in the notes of the Cornish Bank better 'n ours!'

'It will all end now.'

'I've heard cases,' said Cary, his long nose quivering, 'in *this* town, where shopkeepers have made an *excuse* – said they had not enough change – so as to be able to refuse to give silver and copper for a note of ours! . . . What d'ye mean – it will all end now?'

'I have spent the last three nights with Sir Humphry Willyams,' George said, 'at his house in Saltash. He is the chief partner in the Devon and Cornwall Bank of Plymouth, and a man of great substance. We've agreed to an accommodation.'

'I know all about Humphry Willyams.' Cary then fell silent, his hand plucking at the edge of his gown. One could almost hear the wheels clicking. 'What sort of an accommodation?'

'That we shall work in partnership. A loose yet binding partnership, each giving guarantees of support to the other; to an upper limit, of course, though this need not be published.'

'How much?'

'Initially twenty thousand pounds.'

'How can we guarantee that, in our present state?'

'The rest of my – northern properties, as you call them, will part cover it. You told me to sell them, and now I have sold them. Every last one! Does that satisfy you? Let me get you a drink.'

Cary waved this suggestion away as if it were a troublesome mosquito. 'But to have any effect on the public . . .'

'Something must be published. Of course. That is the whole point of the arrangement. Such an announcement will immediately restore confidence. The Devon and Cornwall Bank is well known even in this western part of the county.'

There was a pause. George went to the window and looked out. You couldn't see the bonfire from here but there was a flickering light reflected from the steeple of St Mary's Church.

'And what have *they* to gain?' Cary asked.

'Sir Humphry has often wanted to extend his interests.

Being in constant touch with us will enable his bank to extend its business to cover most of Cornwall.'

From outside came a burst of cheering. 'You'd think we'd *won* the war,' said Cary. 'We're still outnumbered twenty to one. I'd lay they'd drive us out again, if I didn't begin to have some expectations of this man Wellesley.'

'Wellington.'

'Wellesley. That's how he began. So now at last you're free of all those insane investments.'

'I shall regret it, I know. Even this war can't last for ever. There would have been big profit in the long term. But now our foundations are made secure. Full confidence will be restored.'

Cary scratched under his skullcap. 'You expect me to be pleased, I suppose. But I'm suspicious. I suspect – interference by these fellows in our affairs.'

'There'll be none. That is agreed. We go our own ways in all except the guaranteed accommodation.' George poured himself a second brandy. The first had gone down, warming his heart and stomach. The heat of the fire was easing his back. 'We have not yet decided on one point, and that is on a change of name.'

'*What?*'

George carefully drank, rubbed his chin, looked out of the window, then hunched his shoulders and turned.

'It has not been decided. Sir Humphry suggested – in view of the fact that his own name is not on his own bank, and in view of the fact that it is such a distinguished one in the county – and I cannot cavil at that – he has suggested "Warleggan & Willyams".'

Cary was breathing fast through his nose.

'By God, George, if your father was alive!'

'He is not, Uncle Cary. And I do not suppose in the exceptional circumstances that he would have greatly opposed it. There was a time – and don't forget this – when we should have considered the name of Willyams an honour to have in association with our own!'

'You know how he felt about our name! Ye well know it, George! An' I thought you was the same! Always so proud of it, so determined the name Warleggan should be respected – aye, and feared!'

'You'll notice,' said George, 'that I am not proposing to abandon it. I'm proposing to link another with it – and a notable one at that. And our name is to be first . . . It is a time – apart from any ill-considered investments I may have made – for combining together. The age of the small bank is passing. There have been at least four failures in Cornwall this year: Robinson's of Fowey and Captain Cudlipp's at Launceston – '

'Small fry!' snarled Cary. 'Small fry! We was not *small* – not small like that. But for your gross blunders . . . Besides . . . I should have been consulted. I *must* be consulted before this combination goes through!'

'You talk of our name,' said George. 'But who is to carry it on? You're seventy-one. I shall shortly be fifty-two. There is only Valentine. In five years he may wish to join the firm, but I see no signs of it yet. Indeed, I'm not sure that his temperament will ever enable him to take over the reins. I have frequently to discipline him. Indeed, I have more *confidence* in little Ursula – but she'll not stay a Warleggan all her life. We have trained no one for ultimate responsibility – which has been a choice of our own, for we have never wished to delegate – but we have need of new blood now. This link – this accommodation is the first step.'

Cary coughed and spat in the fire. The spittle hissed bubbling on the bars.

'I get catarrh,' he muttered. 'Always I get catarrh. I remind meself of your father.'

'You should take more rest, more exercise. More time off.'

'Who wants more time off?' Cary said peevishly. 'I shall have time enough off when I'm dead – which can't be long, as you so surely predict. Then the name of Warleggan can go to the devil for all I care!'

'Maybe it will,' said George under his breath.

'Eh? What's that? What's that?'

'Whatever you may feel at this moment, Uncle, you will, I'm sure, become accustomed to the idea of such a union. I tell you, it will not only allay nervousness in the county, it will give us greater freedom to use our own money commercially without a half-uttered threat at our backs. Have you noticed the Cornish Bank trying to blow on the little flame of nervousness? I believe I have!'

'They've certainly done nothing to help us. I'm not surprised with your friend Poldark in the partnership.'

George poured himself another half glass. It never did any good to overdrink, even for such a celebration as this. And it *was* a celebration. Whatever Cary might say, it was for him an emergence from a dark and ominous corridor. The money he had tragically lost was not retrieved; but he could begin to build again. And he only had to look at the industries and merchantries he possessed around this county to know that they were ninety per cent sound and had good prospects for the future. Often during these last few terrible months he had wondered quite as sincerely as Uncle Cary what devil of recklessness had made him plunge so deeply into an area he did not know, why he had not been content to let Lady Harriet choose him or refuse him with the fortune he then had.

Now with his base secure he could begin to rebuild.

Some comment Cary had made, some word he had dropped was stirring useasily at the back of his consciousness, a tiny worm in the bud, hardly worth considering but not altogether to be ignored. He identified it.

'A pity,' he said.

'What?'

'I sold the shares in Wheal Leisure to John Treneglos for four hundred pounds. Had we been less tight I would have held on to them.'

301

'They were no use to you,' said Cary scathingly. 'Who else would give you that for a derelict mine?'

George finished his drink. 'Come, Uncle, a nightcap to see you to bed.'

'Oh, well. If you insist. But I warn you it gives me heartburn.'

'Four hundred pounds for a hole in the ground. I doubt if it's more. But it's near Poldark property, and I've heard Wheal Grace is yielding none too well. I suspect Poldark is behind Treneglos in this. I would have preferred to have blocked his activities.'

II

Letter from Captain Geoffrey Charles Poldark of the 43rd Monmouthshires to Captain Ross Poldark, Nampara, Cornwall.

Before Almeida, 18th April 1811.
My dear Uncle Ross,

It was only during a lull in the fighting, when we were standing side by side among the bullets on that misty hillside of Bussaco that it occurred to me formally that you were not really my uncle at all but my cousin – or cousin once removed, I conject, to be quite Accurate. However, uncle it first was and uncle it must now remain.

D'you remember how we stood that September morning, after the Charge? I believe it was disobedience of orders amounting almost to mutiny when you joined in, biting at your cartridges, leaping like a boy over boulders and dead Frenchmen alike and firing and stabbing with the best. I was lucky that I found you a Regimental Jacket – tight though it was on you, and split at the shoulder seams, I discovered later – else you might have been spitted from behind by one of our excited lads! I thought to myself that day, 'two Poldark *cousins* are fighting together in this battle, and I'm damned if I know which is the more out of breath!' Killing and being killed is not a pretty business, but I estimate there was an element of Inspiration in us all that day!

I have been re-reading your letter from London and am happy you reached home safe; and ashamed I am not to have written in Reply. It has been a hard Winter for us all, with many of our best officers sick or wounded and some of our Worst applying for – and receiving! – leave to return home. The inactivity – for a time – and the sickness were equally Tedious, but since early March we have been advancing and fighting, advancing and fighting day after day in the most arduous, brilliant and bitter Fashion.

Alas, it has not been a happy time; for our continuing victories have been poisoned by the horrors we have found in the Villages and Towns we have been re-possessing. Do you know, Cousin – there I've called you that for a change! – do you know until now I have always felt myself fighting a ferocious but a brave and chivalrous Enemy? I have come across numerous instances of respect and friendship shown between English and French. Often it has been difficult to prevent the ordinary soldiers fraternizing before and after battle. Like pugilists in a boxing ring, once the bout is over . . . And among the generals. Soult putting up the monument to Moore at Corunna is but a case in point. But *here* – towards the Portuguese! We have walked, marched, tramped for miles through a Charnel house, of putrid corpses, violated and tortured women, children hanged upside down, polluted churches, mutilated priests, men with their eyes gouged out . . . It has changed my feelings. Can a just war turn into a war of revenge? It certainly has for the Portuguese.

Now we are Encamped before Almeida. The French have left a Garrison behind, and it will be the devil's own job to winkle them out. And you will observe I am back on that River once again where I lost a chip of my jaw bone. So far I have survived this winter with all the luck of a bad egg, though I have lost my good friend Saunders; *and* Partridge, who was decapitated by a shell one morning shortly after we had finished breakfast. You met them both, you will remember. Partridge was the one with the long fair hair.

By the way, your War Office has slightly relaxed its grip on promotions, and Brevet Colonel Hector McNeil has been awarded his lieutenant-colonelcy! I have met him more than once since you left, and he is an Estimable man but full of stories about the bad old days when every Cornishman – in his view – was a smuggler!

My warmest love to Aunt Demelza, to Jeremy, Clowance and Isabella-Rose, to *Drake*, to Morwenna, to Sam, to Zacky Martin, to Ben Carter, Jacka Hoblyn, Jud and Prudie Paynter – if they are all still alive – and to any other friend of yours who you think will remember me and to whom I may be safely commended.

I too could obtain leave now if I so requested. I don't so request – partly because the war in the Peninsula is entering, I believe, a Victorious phase, partly because it somehow doesn't seem suitable – meet is the biblical word! – for me to return. I know I would have so many welcoming friends, but it is somehow not yet meet, right or my bounden duty.

All the same, may that time roll on!

As ever your affectionate nephew, (Cousin – Second Cousin?)

Geoffrey Charles.

III

Advertisement in the *Royal Cornwall Gazette* for Saturday the 18th May, 1811.

As from next Monday, the 20th May, 1811, Warleggan's

Bank announces its conjuncture with the Devon & Cornwall Bank of Plymouth, Saltash, Bodmin and Liskeard. The activities and note issue of Warleggan's Bank, Truro, will remain unchanged in every respect, except that the interests of its clients will be still more safely secured and the facilities of the Bank more usefully extended. Henceforward, Warleggan's Bank will be known as Warleggan & Willyams Bank. Partners will be Sir George Warleggan, Sir Humphry Willyams, Mr Cary Warleggan and Mr Rupert Croft.

IV

Letter from Lord Edward Fitzmaurice to Miss Clowance Poldark, 16th June, 1811.

Dear Miss Poldark,

I venture to write to you again, having persuaded myself that my first letter may have gone astray, and to renew, if only in the formality of a letter, our friendship of February and to say I hope you reached home safely and have been enjoying the many and diverse pleasures of spring and summer there. Cornwall is so very far away, and though in a sense a West Countryman myself I was never in your county and only once as far west as Exeter.

By this post, or shortly to follow, will come a letter from my aunt inviting you to spend time with us in Bowood in late July. It is the custom of the family – to which so far I have willingly acceded – to see the greater part of the Season through in London, then to spend a few weeks in Wiltshire before going up to our lodge in Scotland for the grouse. This means a very delightful period at Bowood, where most of the Family foregather and where my aunt and I would be most Happy to welcome you. Although far distant from Cornwall, it is but half the Way to London and I trust we may be able to persuade you that the journey would be worth while.

Naturally my aunt's letter will be addressed to your Mother, and will include an invitation to her too, so that you may not feel unchaperoned.

Believe me, my dear Miss Poldark, it would give pleasure, if you were able to come, to

Yours most sincerely,
Edward Petty-Fitzmaurice.

Chapter Two

I

On the last Friday in May Jeremy told his mother he proposed to ride over and call on Miss Trevanion.

Demelza had said: 'Have you heard from her?'

'No.'

'Did you write?'

'Yes, once. She hasn't replied.'

Demelza looked at her tall son. His eyes were blank in the way youth can make its eyes blank when it is in trouble.

'Your father was annoyed at Mrs Bettesworth's letter.'

'I know. But I've left it nine weeks. I think I have a right to call.'

'Of course. Shall I tell your father?'

'When I'm gone.'

'I don't think he would object.'

'Would *he* have waited nine weeks?' Jeremy asked.

Demelza smiled obliquely. 'No.'

They walked to the stables. 'You had a horse called Caerhays once,' Jeremy said. 'That was before I was born, wasn't it?'

'Yes, and before our – prosperity. We sold him when we needed money.'

'How did he come by his name? Did you know the Trevanions then?'

'I think he was so named when we bought him. You must ask your father.'

'Sometime.' Jeremy began to saddle his best horse, a strawberry roan called Colley (short for Collingwood). He had been bought for Jeremy as a hunter, but Jeremy's distaste for the sport had grown with the years and the horse was now used mainly for a fast gallop over the moors. Demelza noticed how well Jeremy was dressed today, more smart than she had ever seen him before.

'Jeremy . . .'

'Yes?'

She helped tighten one of the girths. 'I know you have been – greatly upset; and I cannot help you. It grieves me that I cannot help you. I cann't even give you *advice*!'

'Nobody can.'

'For you would not take it. Quite right. It is hopeless for older people to tell younger ones – particularly their own children – that they have been through the same thing. Such information is no use at *all*! It *bounces* off one's own grief – or jealousy or distress. If we are all born the same we are also all born unique – we all go through torments nobody else has ever had.'

Jeremy patted her hand.

Demelza said: 'But one thing, Jeremy. Never forget you are a Poldark.'

Colley was becoming restive at the prospect of exercise. Jeremy stroked his nose.

'Little likelihood of that.'

'I mean – ' Demelza hesitated – 'think of your father's family in this matter, not of mine. It would be distressful to me if me being a miner's daughter should hinder your chances.' So now it was out.

Jeremy looked out of the stables, his eyes still blank. 'You take me to church now and again. We go as a family half a dozen times a year, don't we?'

'Well?'

'It says there "honour thy father and thy mother." That's a commandment I happen to obey. Understand? And no trouble. Not half of it but the whole of it. It gives me no trouble at all. If anyone should think to teach me different, it should not be you.'

'I only mean . . .'

'I know what you only mean. Now go about your busi-

ness, Mama, and leave me to go about mine. No girl . . .'
He stopped.

'It may not be her. It may be her parents.'

Jeremy looked at his mother and smiled wryly.

'That us'll see, shann't us.'

II

The castle swam in a sea of bluebells. Laced above the bluebells was an embroidery of young beech leaves and silver birch. A limpid sea winked in the bay.

The older footman, who always seemed to have wrinkled stockings, let him in.

'I'll go 'n see, sir. I'm not certain sure whereabout Miss Cuby is exactly at this moment, sir. Kindly take a seat, sir.'

Jeremy did not accept the invitation. Instead he walked about the big hall-like drawing-room where they had made music in March. Clemency's harpsichord was open, with some music splayed on the top. There were shoes in the fireplace, where a fire declared its will to live by sending up thin spirals of smoke. Four shotguns leaned against a wall. Two London newspapers, *The Times* and the *Morning Post*, lay open on a settle. Paintings of earlier Trevanions gazed absent-mindedly at each other across the room.

After a long wait a door opened and two spaniels came barking and romping round his feet and legs.

'My dear Poldark!' It was Major John Trevanion, his tight-lipped face arranged in the lineaments of welcome. 'Good of you to call. How are you? There's been a devilish lot of sickness about. Pray come in here. It's altogether more cosy.'

He led the way back into the study, a smaller, lighter room with a view over the terrace. As usual it was in a considerable litter. In a corner by the fire Mrs Bettesworth sat working at her sampler. She smiled, as tight-lipped as her son, and found time from her work to extend a hand, which Jeremy bowed over.

They exchanged conversation about the weather, about the influenza, about the shortage of horses because of the war, about the difficulty of getting good masons to work on the castle, about the forthcoming Bodmin races, of which the Major seemed to have an extensive knowledge. This was not a field of battle of Jeremy's choice. Indeed, he could not have devised a worse, but he refused to be either over-awed or talked down.

Eventually he said: 'In fact I called to see how Miss Cuby was, as it is nine or ten weeks since we met.'

After a brief silence Trevanion said: 'Cuby's very well, but just for the moment is away. She's visiting cousins in Tregony. But I'll tell her you've called. I'll give her any – er – message you would like to leave.'

'Tell her,' said Jeremy, 'that I was disappointed she was not allowed to visit my family on the north coast at Easter.'

'Not *allowed*?' Major Trevanion blinked in a bloodshot way at his mother, who took no notice at all. 'I think she had previous engagements. Isn't that it? Well, well, I'm sorry about that, Poldark. We're all sorry. In fact, if the truth be known, my mother keeps a very firm hand on her children and does not allow them the freedom many modern girls crave.'

'Would she have the freedom to come on some other occasion – possibly with Augustus?'

'Augustus is in London,' said Major Trevanion. 'He has found himself a post in the Treasury where I think his talents will be well employed. He writes amusing letters.'

'Mr Poldark,' said Mrs Bettesworth. 'I wonder if you would be so kind as to pass me the green silk?'

Jeremy hastened to oblige.

'He writes amusing letters,' said Trevanion, laughing before he had got to the joke. 'Travelled in a hackney coach, he said, in which there was straw on the floor in place of carpet. Went to service in Westminster Abbey, he said, at which there was only *one* other worshipper apart.

from himself. The shops, he says, are full of insulting caricatures of *everyone* in the public eye. French, English, American . . .'

A brief silence fell.

Jeremy said: 'I trust Miss Clemency is well?'

'Very well, thank you. She was in Newton Abbot with me last week when my filly, Roseland, won the Queen Charlotte Stakes . . . Returning, we found the roads around Plymouth crowded with soldiers on foot and in carriages, proceeding for embarkation. These were reinforcements for Portugal and for India. Thank God the war has taken a better turn, for it was time.'

'Indeed,' said Jeremy.

'D'you know, such is the scarcity of men with this endless war that I have to pay £30 a year for a manservant of any quality. And the women are demanding more too. I pay £13 a year for a woman cook. How does your father manage?'

'To tell the truth,' Jeremy said, 'I have not bothered to inquire on these points. Most of our servants have been with us for as long as I can remember. We don't have footmen, but we have chiefly women who help my mother; and two men who are employed about the house in a general way.'

'How many acres does your estate extend to?'

'About a hundred, I believe.'

'We have a thousand here, of which half is farm. Then there is about another five hundred in and around the Roseland peninsula, agricultural land of some richness. But of course the five hundred of the castle and grounds are my principal interest. We are sheltered from many winds, and can grow rare and original shrubs. Had I the time I would show you them.'

'I believe Miss Cuby showed me some of them when I was last here.'

'Did she? Ah, did she.'

Mrs Bettesworth looked up. 'I trust you'll forgive us if

we don't invite you to dine, Mr Poldark. You'll appreciate
that with so reduced a family our arrangements are
necessarily constricted and it would be a thought difficult
to instruct the cook at this late hour.'

Jeremy got up. 'Of course. I understand.' He looked at
his hosts. 'Or perhaps I don't *altogether* understand. You'll
forgive me. I come of a family that – that I believe prides
itself on its candour. As a result it may be I do not enough
esteem that sort of politeness which barely masks
disapproval. To offer the reason for such disapproval
would be to me a more admirable courtesy than – than to
disguise it in meaningless words. Mrs Bettesworth . . .
Major Trevanion: good day to you both.'

He bowed and strode to the door. His hand on the door
trembled with anger.

'Wait, Poldark.' John Trevanion kicked at one of
the spaniels which was fussing round his boots. 'Mama,
these animals need some air. I'll walk Mr Poldark to his
horse.'

'Of course,' she said and paused a moment, needle in
hand. 'Good day, Mr Poldark. I wish you well.'

Jeremy did not notice the hall or the porch as he strode
through them. Beyond the front door, which was on the
sheltered side and away from the sea, was a large open
archway. At the mouth of this he had tethered Colley to a
convenient post.

Trevanion had not kept pace with him but he caught up
with him as he was about to mount. The wind blew
Trevanion's thin brown hair.

He said: 'Not good enough.'

'What?'

'You asked for the reason. Isn't that plain? We don't
consider you good enough for Cuby. The Trevanions have
been in this district, almost on this very spot, for five
hundred years. 1313, to be exact. Makes a difference, you
know. You're a pleasant young feller, Poldark, with a
taking way about you. As a guest in our house you'd be

welcome now an' then. But as a husband for my sister – which is plainly what you're about – you just don't come up to snuff. See? That plain? That clear? We have higher ambitions. Sorry.'

'And Cuby?'

'Oh, Cuby . . . She's a flirt. Didn't you notice? She likes young men. At her age, who would not? She believes in having many strings to her bow. That we are not averse from. Let her have her little romances. But you were becoming too serious. When her young men become serious then *we* become serious. See? She's still very young. In a year or two we shall pick a husband together; she and her mother and I will pick one, and then he will be one suitable to us all.'

The two spaniels, released, were tearing around on the gravel not far from Colley who clapped his foot restively when they approached.

Jeremy said: 'What danger do you suppose there was in my being serious if your sister was not serious?'

'My sister,' said Trevanion, 'is serious two or three times a year. Eh? Eh? There was a stonemason here last autumn on whom she lavished a schoolgirl affection, but she soon outgrew it when she met another young man.' He guffawed. 'That was all quite acceptable because it was *outrageous*. But you are a gentleman and therefore your attentions must be treated on a different level. If you think us discourteous, pray consider the difficulty we are in.'

'The difficulty,' Jeremy said, hardly able to control his voice, 'the difficulty of telling a fellow Cornishman that he is not good enough, because, apparently, although a gentleman, he is too *small* a gentleman.' He mounted. 'It's true. Our acres are not so large as yours – or our pedigree quite as long. But reflect. You are a Bettesworth who *became* a Trevanion. I haven't had to change my name at all.'

The thin florid man sharply flushed. He had been Sheriff

of Cornwall at twenty-four years of age, and no one for long enough had dared to say such a thing to him.

All he said was: 'I'd advise you to clear off, Mr Poldark.'

III

It was five o'clock in the afternoon and Jeremy had not cleared off. He was on high ground, sitting his horse, on a farm track on rising ground half a mile from the castle. It had taken him some time to find this vantage point. From it he could not see the archway protecting the front door of the house but he could see pretty well all the paths and ways that led from it. He had been there two and a half hours now. Colley had made a reasonable meal off the hedges to the lane, but he had not eaten at all. He was not hungry. He was capable, he felt, of staying there another twenty hours if need be.

Twice surly yokels had passed him by. The sun had gone behind drifting clouds. On the opposite side of the hill they were beginning to cut the hay; just four in a very large field, two women in bonnets, two boys. Soon after he left, Major Trevanion had walked round to the back of the house, to the unfinished part. There were no workmen there and there seemed no evidence of progress since before Easter. Trevanion had soon returned and gone indoors. About three a nursemaid had taken his two little boys for a walk along the seashore. They had been out nearly an hour. Apart from this, no one had entered or left the castle all afternoon.

Mrs Bettesworth's voice, thought Jeremy, had a Welsh intonation. Had they been lying about Cuby – was she really from home, or locked – he thought dramatically – perhaps locked in a room upstairs? But they could not have seen him coming in time. And Cuby, however much the youngest of the family, did not look the sort who would suffer such an indignity quietly. She would kick at the door. Yet Jeremy knew the discipline that existed in most such families. Cuby had never known her father, who had died while serving in the Dragoon Guards before she was born; her elder brother had taken over that role. Was Mrs Bettesworth as compliant as she appeared, or was she in fact the power behind it all?

Colley was getting restive at last, tired of supporting his master all this time. Yet if one dismounted one could see too little of the scene.

A puff of dust on the hillside. It was at the top of the lane he had himself come down. The hedges were high and powdered with may blossom, but presently he saw horses passing a gateway. Three. He turned Colley round and moved forward a pace or two. Two women and a man. His heart began to thump. He had recognized one of the women, almost certainly the other. The man was in some sort of uniform.

He moved along the lane, dismounted, unlatched a gate, walked his horse across the next field. Another gate and he was out in the lane. He did not bother to remount.

Voices, and a girl laughing. He could not see them, and they would not see him until they rounded the bend twenty yards up the hill.

Even in this dry weather a little rill of water was bubbling down the side of the lane. The hedge here was like a patriotic emblem: red campion, white milkmaids, and the shiny, gauzy bluebells. Giant ferns were sprouting.

They came into view. It was Clemency and Cuby. The man in uniform – thank God – was a footman.

They stopped. There was no room to get past anyhow. Jeremy took off his hat.

'Good day to you.'

It was Clemency who had been laughing. Unlike Cuby she was a very plain girl, but very amiable. She stopped laughing now, the animation in her face giving way to surprise. Cuby slowly flushed.

'I have been calling to see you,' said Jeremy, 'but alas you were out. I hope you're both well.'

Clemency gave her horse's head a tug. 'Mr Poldark. What a surprise! Isn't it a surprise, Cuby! I declare it is quite a surprise.'

'A great surprise,' said Cuby.

'I saw your mother and your brother,' said Jeremy, 'and we talked of current things for a while. How is Augustus?'

'In London.' Clemency glanced at her sister. 'We are returning for tea. Perhaps . . . you would care to join us now?'

'Thank you, I've already taken my leave. It would seem inappropriate to return.'

The horses were all a little restive, backing and pawing in the narrow lane.

'Wharton,' said Clemency, 'will you ride on with me. I want a word with Mrs Clark at the home farm. Miss Cuby can join us in a few minutes.'

'Yes, miss.'

Clemency leaned down, extending her hand. 'Good day, Mr Poldark. I am sorry we were out. Perhaps another time . . .'

Jeremy kissed her glove. 'Of course.'

He held his horse to one side to allow the others to pass. Cuby remained quite still in her saddle. Her face was at its least animated, most sulky.

When the others had disappeared down the next corner of the lane Jeremy said: 'So you saved me from the Preventive men and now you don't want me.'

She looked at him briefly, then out to sea.

Jeremy said: 'It's the law that anything washed up on his foreshore is the property of the lord of the manor.'

She pushed a wisp of hair under her tricorn hat, kneed her horse so that he could munch at the grass.

Jeremy said: 'Or lady, as the case may be.'

'Don't joke with me, please.'

'I knew a boy at school who always laughed when it hurt most.'

'Why did you come today? Wasn't the letter sufficient?'

'From your mother? No. Why didn't you answer mine?'

'What would have been the good of that?'

'Do you not think I am owed a little personal explanation? When we last met you kissed me and – '

'I did *not*! It was your – '

'*You* kissed *me*. There is no doubt of it! And you called me "dear Jeremy". And you asked me to come again. However light it may all have been intended – and I don't *believe* it was so intended – a fragment of personal explanation is my due. Or don't you think so?'

She looked at him again, but again briefly, her eyes clouded, embarrassed.

'I was foolish. Just say I am of a flirtatious nature . . .'

'That is what your brother said.'

'*Did* he!'

'Yes. I had a talk with him. In front of your mother it was all polite words spoken with coldness. He came to the door, I asked him to speak out, and he spoke out. He told me that I was not good enough for you. Although that may be what *I* feel, is that what *you* feel?'

'I think I must go now.'

'Is that what you feel?'

She seemed about to move past him, but he took hold of the reins.

'No, of course not,' she said angrily. 'What my brother thinks is his own affair.'

'And your mother?'

'Naturally I listen to what they say.'

'And she clearly agrees with him?'

'I have my own opinions.'

'That's what I would have supposed.' He swallowed, marshalling his thoughts. 'I know – have met – a number of young ladies of about your age in various parts of the county. And I have observed how carefully most of them are watched and controlled. It is "yes, Mama" and "no, Mama" and never step outside a line of good behaviour. Often as not they marry who is chosen for them . . . Of all the girls I have ever met, you are the *least* like that. The very last to have preferences dictated to you. I should never in my worst dreams have thought that you and your mother and your brother would ever sit down together and decide in cold blood whom you were going to marry!'

'Who said that?'

'He did.'

There was silence except for the sound of tearing grass, the munching of teeth, the occasional clink of bridle and bit.

She said: 'I shall marry, within limits, whom I choose. But does that not prove to you what I have been saying, that I do not so much care for you? It was – a little fun to treat you as I did. A – diversion.'

'Upon my soul,' Jeremy said bitterly. 'I am almost come to believe you.'

'Well,' she said, 'now you can let me go! You *fool*! Didn't I *tell* you that last afternoon that nothing was straightforward! Didn't I *tell* you – and ask you – didn't I ask you – never to think hard of me!'

'Now you're speaking like someone who does care.'

'I care that I have hurt you! Isn't that sufficient?'

'Hurt!' said Jeremy. 'I'm so desolate I could die.'

Cuby gulped, then laughed through tears that had started to her eyes. 'No one never died for love. I have it on good authority. The poets make all this up so that it is pretty to cry over.'

'As you are doing now,' said Jeremy, his hand to his own face.

She pulled her horse's head up, touched him with her whip handle, pushed past Jeremy standing in the lane. As they stared, each was blurred to the other.

'Goodbye, boy,' she said. 'Perhaps I did care. But not enough. It is not you who are not good enough, it is I. Remember those people in the churchyard – we are luckier than they. Wouldn't they give anything in the world for our breaking hearts!'

She went on. Her hat nodded, her slim young body swayed to the awkward gait of her horse going down the steep lane. She half turned her head and then deliberately did not look back.

Chapter Three

I

Midsummer Eve – or St John's Eve – the saint being John the Baptist – is a magical night. The height of the summer solstice, when the sun, having reached the tropical points, is at its furthest from the equator and appears to stand still. The time of human sacrifice, of sun worship, of the gathering of serpents, of the breaking of branches, of the foreseeing of death.

Among the Celts of Cornwall it had been a special, a supernatural night back into pre-history; but first Puritanism and then Methodism had frowned on the commemoration of pagan practices, so that gradually it had become a simpler feast, a night for bonfires and courting couples and a few brief ceremonies into which there entered more fun than belief.

All the same, under the jollity, the giggling, the dancing, something spoke to people that was older than the Christian faith, older than atheism, older than unbelief. When the night was fine, as it seemed so often to be, there would be odd silences, whisperings, a starting at shadows, a peering about in the flickering firelight and an occasional glance behind into the looming parti-coloured darkness.

On such nights, of course, it was never quite dark, not all through the night, for the sun was not far enough below the horizon and the sea sent up moon-blue reflections into the sky. Which encouraged people to sit up all night watching for the souls of their friends.

Demelza neither believed nor disbelieved in pagan rights and superstitious practices. She thought there was room for a lot of things in the world and there was no virtue in being dogmatic. If she spilt salt it took but a second to throw a pinch over her left shoulder, and who was the *worse* for it? She never carried may blossom into the house or sat thirteen at table. Also some of the remedies old Meggy Dawes had told her as a child worked remarkably well. One just had to keep an open mind and take things as they came.

But in arranging a special party on this Midsummer Eve and reintroducing some of the old customs, she was only building on a general wish in the district to resume a festival that was almost lost. For years, apart from 1802, Napoleon and his threat of invasion had put a stop to the fires. As when the Armadas of Spain threatened two hundred years before, the lighting of the beacons was to be the alarm signal.

It still was; but since Nelson's great victory the danger had been less. Nursemaids still threatened naughty children with Boney and his terrors; the French Emperor was as invincible as ever; but he had subjugated Europe, not the sea or the navy that commanded it. And this year, especially, there had been *another* victory to celebrate – and on *land*. The first on land in *Europe* almost anyone could remember. There had been bonfires to celebrate it, only seven or eight weeks ago. If one bonfire, why not others?

It could not be quite like the old days with the first fire being lighted at Garrack Zans near Sennen at the Land's End, to be followed by Trencrom and Chapel Carn Brea until fires were blazing on all the hilltops creating a link of light right across Cornwall. But there could be nothing wrong with one or two here and there. The highest point near Nampara was just south of the gaunt buildings of Wheal Maiden, near the new chapel and beyond the cluster of windswept pines, and it was Ben Carter calling to ask if they might build a bonfire there that put it into her head to develop the evening into an outdoor party and feast.

It seemed quite rare that almost everyone she cared

about should be at home and available at one and the same time.

But it was not purely for herself or Ross or for the village folk that she had taken up the villagers' idea. Both her elder children needed livening up, needed 'taking out of themselves'. The Easter party had come to nothing; and various suggestions she had made later had fallen flat. When Jeremy had come home in the dusk of that evening in late May he had found his mother still in the garden and after talking casually for a minute or so had suddenly burst into tears and she had held his head on her shoulder as if he were a little boy again. It was soon over and he snivelled and wiped his nose on her handkerchief, and neither of them had ever or would ever refer to the incident again. She had been glad – proud to be there, but it had shown her the depths of his distress.

In the four weeks since then he had behaved pretty much as usual, but he had been absent from the house a great deal – sometimes up at Wheal Leisure mine and forgetting his mealtimes, but often away on Colley, no one quite knew where, except that it was to do with the mine and the engine he hoped to design and build. He was withdrawn into himself, occupying himself to forget. Quite suddenly grown up, but not in the right way. She almost wished he would resume his interest in Violet or Daisy Kellow – or even begin to see something in the narrow-eyed eccentric Agneta Treneglos.

As for Clowance, nothing in her life had run quite right since Stephen Carrington left. The second letter from Lord Edward had crossed post with her belated reply to his first, and, a few days later, the expected invitation from Lady Isabel Petty-Fitzmaurice. The invitation had been commented on when it was received, but nothing had passed between any of them about it since. A reply could not long be delayed.

With the old mine being explored, it brought Ben Carter more often into the house, and he was the only one of

Clowance's immediate suitors to have the advantage of being on the spot. But one pondered how much advantage this really was. It was not in Clowance's nature to be rude to anyone, but she treated him very casually, like a brother – like a fellow miner, for she had been down Wheal Leisure four times herself.

At least, Demelza said to Ross wryly, you got the social gamut with Clowance. The younger brother of one of the richest peers in the land; a thirty-year-old sailor-adventurer with dashing good looks and a shady past, and a penniless bearded miner who happened to be their godson.

'It will all blow over,' Ross said. 'You worry too much. Suddenly in the middle of it all Clowance will rise up and marry someone entirely different.'

'I don't exactly *worry*,' said Demelza. 'Sort of speculate.'

'I suspect – and hope – that with Clowance it will be a long-term occupation. I have faith in her judgment.'

'I wish I had.'

'Don't you?'

'In her common sense, yes, yes. But sometimes women are swayed more strongly by other feelings.'

'And men, for God's sake.'

'Meaning Jeremy.'

'At this moment, yes, for he thinks he has chosen. Of course he'll get over it. But I could kick that man's pretentious backside. Odious little frog. Telling Jeremy there had been a Trevanion there since 1313!'

'Five hundred years is a long time. When did the first Poldark come over from France?'

'1572. It's nothing, Demelza. *Nothing*. I've said this to you before. People who brag of their ancestors are like root vegetables. All their importance is underground.'

'Yes, well –'

'But what does it all matter? Who is to say that *your* ancestor was not here before mine? It is only what you are

323

yourself that counts. Consider it: who has a longer descent than anyone else? Are we not all from Adam?'

'That is not the way the world sees it.'

'Then the world sees it wrong! They attach importance to a *name*. But we all have names! Because Poldark has owned property and Boscawen has owned property and de Dunstanville and Trevanion and the rest . . . Carne and Smith and Carter and Martin and Nanfan . . . and even Paynter; we all come from the same stock in the beginning. That some have had the good fortune, or the cunning, or the skill to climb higher than the others and to continue to ride the wave through the centuries makes them no more deserving of awe, praise or reverence.'

'You're right – of course. Tis all true. Yet . . . I am proud of being a Poldark, if only by marriage. You're proud of it too, Ross; else you would not feel so strongly about the Trevanions' slight of our son.'

'I'd feel strongly about anybody's slight of our son.' Ross said.

Jeremy would have been surprised at this sentiment. He was not sure that his father was proud of him at all.

Midsummer Eve dawned cloudy, and for a while light rain fell. But it was never in earnest, and even pessimists such as Jud, sitting like an extinct volcano emitting a wisp of smoke before his cottage door, agreed that the evening was likely to be fine. And it was. The sun set into a sea of blue milk, and the crowd around the bonfire at Wheal Maiden gathered in pleasant anticipation. The only one who disapproved was Demelza's brother, Sam, who could not see it as part of the Christian festival, but he had been bribed – if such a word could possibly be applied to him – by the promise that he would be invited to say a prayer before the bonfire was lighted.

Paul Kellow had brought his sister Daisy, but Violet was confined to her room. The Pope sisters had come, in charge of a groom, but the pretty young blonde wayward-eyed Mrs Pope was staying in with her husband. Horrie

324

Treneglos and Agneta and the other two boys, and the Enyses with their two daughters, made up the gentry of the occasion. There were about thirty elderly villagers from Mellin, Sawle and Grambler already assembled round the bonfire; the young and the more able-bodied would make up the procession, which was to start from old Grambler mine.

Trestle tables had been set up, on which were piled buns and saffron cakes and shortcakes and ginger biscuits, and seedy cakes, also two huge buttermilk cakes as big as the wheels of a cart. And three casks of ale. And a mound of potatoes to roast when the fire had died down. Behind these tables, when the time came, the dowagers of the village – Mrs Zacky Martin, Mrs Char Nanfan, Mrs Beth Daniel – would stand on sentry-go making sure everyone got a fair share and waited his turn.

'Else they'd be like to overturn the tables,' said Demelza, 'grabbing at everything and the strongest to the fore.'

'It would be no worse than I once saw at a Lord Mayor's banquet,' Ross said. 'Those at the top table behaved with some dignity but as for the rest, it became a scramble and within five minutes of the guests taking up their stations all the dishes were cleared, ten folk pulling all ways at a goose or a rib of beef and tearing it to pieces. Once the liquor was served, bottles and glasses were flying from side to side without intermission. The heat and the noise were worse than a battle.'

Demelza laughed. 'Well, here at least we shall have fresh air.'

The torch procession began at ten. A wild young man called Sephus Billing led the way, accompanied by Music Thomas, singing at the top of his alto voice. Following them came three fiddlers, two borrowed from the church choir, and then a group of young women all singing. These were surrounded by more young men jumping about and waving their torches in circles. Some said the circles were supposed to represent the path of the sun, but mostly it was just a way of making the torches look more effective. Behind the torch-bearers followed about fifty stragglers, talking and laughing and trying to join in the songs.

Three tin barrels were at the heart of the bonfire, and a tent-shaped frame had been made of wood from used pit-props, spars, broken masts and old planks washed up by the tide. It was wasteful; in four or five months every family would be glad of this firewood, but that was how it went. None of them would have said thank you for the distribution now. Since in the nature of the festivity the bonfire must look superficially green, youths had been a few miles inland to collect fir branches and hawthorn and sycamore and elm. These clothed the framework, so that the whole thing looked like a woodland pyramid.

As the torch procession could be seen – and heard – in the distance against the dying light, Daisy Kellow, who had her arm linked with Clowance, said to Jeremy: 'When it is over, why do we not go to the churchyard?'

'Why?' said Jeremy.

'Tis the old belief, isn't it. If we stand by the church door we shall see all the people who are going to die in the next twelve months. Their shades will come up and knock on the church door one by one, and they shall enter in the order in which they shall die.'

'If we saw them, would it profit us?'

'No, but twould give us a perfect *frisson*.'

Ben Carter, who was next to Clowance, but not daring to link, said: 'There is another belief, that the souls of everyone will leave their bodies and wander off to where they be going to die, whether twill be by land or sea.'

'It all seems a thought morbid to me,' said Clowance. 'Should we not concern ourselves with the living?'

'But these *are* the living,' said Daisy. 'That is what makes it so exciting. I believe if I saw myself going in at the church door I should faint right away!'

Her brother said: 'She would faint right away if she saw herself going in at the church door with the wrong man!'

'Paul! I didn't know you were by! How horrid to come creeping up and eavesdropping! This was a *serious* discussion!'

'When Jud was gravedigger,' said Jeremy, 'he was always complaining of scooping up the casual kneecap or skull. When my time comes I shall hope at least to have room to turn over whenever someone says something bad of me.'

Daisy said: 'When my eldest sister died I could not sleep of nights for thinking of her in the cold clay of St Erme.'

'And at her funeral,' Paul said, 'the vicar was drunk as a haddock. Kept reeling against the altar rail as if he was at sea in a storm.'

'Paul, don't!'

The procession was approaching, the torches describing flickering yellow semi-circles in the blue air.

> 'Robin Hood and Little John
> They both are gone to the fair – O;
> And we will to the merry green wood
> To see what they do there – O.'

'What a pretty sight,' said Daisy. 'I wish Violet had come; she so loves such celebrations.'

'She's not well again?'

'Oh, it is the same cough as always, and a light fever. But I do believe she coddles herself – and Mama is bad with her too; having lost one stepchild, she is fearful for another. But the night air is so light and mild I believe it could do no harm.'

> 'As for St George – O
> St George he was a knight – O
> Of all the kings in Christendom
> King George he is the right – O
> And send us peace in merry England
> Every day and night – O . . .'

As the singers came up they surrounded the bonfire, the torches wobbling and uncertain. The voices petered out in coughs and giggles, the singers having become self-conscious in the presence of the gentry. Ross made a sign to Sam, who stepped forward and said his prayer.

'O Lord Jesus Christ, the True Light. Who dost enlighten every man that cometh into the world, do Thou bless this bonfire which in our gladness we light to honour the Nativity of St John the Baptist; and grant to us, being lighted by Thy grace and fired with Thy love, that we may come to Thee. Whom that Holy Forerunner did announce beforehand as the Saviour of the world. Who livest and reignest with the Father in Heaven, ever one God, world without end. Amen.'

Caroline Enys had been persuaded much against her will by Demelza to be the Lady of the Flowers. When Sam had finished his prayer, Ross gave a nod and Music Thomas and Sephus Billing plunged their torches into the green pyramid. A dozen others followed suit, with yells of delight that seemed to come from further back in time than the Christian prayer that had just been uttered. Sam hunched his shoulders in discomfort, and was glad of Rosina's consoling hand on his arm.

Just before the flames reached the tin barrels, Caroline stepped forward and threw a bunch of flowers and herbs into the fire. It contained a collection of good herbs and bad, the good in this instance being St John's wort, elder, oak, clover and foxglove; the bad were ivy, nettle, bramble, dock and corn cockle. Caroline had sworn that no power on earth would induce her to speak the bizarre Cornish words, but the one power on earth that could do so, Demelza, had contrived to worm its way round her protests and she had reluctantly learned them, though she had only the vaguest idea what they meant.

'Otta kelmys yn-kemysks
Blesyow, may fons-y cowl leskys,
Ha'n da, ha'n drok.

Re dartho an da myl egyn,
Glan re bo dyswres pup dregyn,
   Yn tan, yn mok!'

There had been silence while she spoke, but the moment
she stepped back – and none too soon, for the flames were
suddenly out of hand – there was a scream of satisfaction
from the spectators and they began to dance around the
fire, the wild flaring light making demons of them all. A
little drinking had been going on beforehand.

Jeremy drew in a sharp breath and frowned into the
lurching scalding light. One person just withdrawing into
the shadows of the old mine looked so much like . . . He
put out a hand to draw Clowance's attention, but
Clowance was talking animatedly to Ben, and in time her
brother withheld his hand . . .

Many of the girls in their best summer smocks had
joined in the dance, and thirty or forty people held hands
swirling round the bonfire. Once more Jeremy saw the
man, but the third time he was no longer there. A phantom
spirit appearing, as Ben said, at the location where he
would eventually die?

After a while Ross touched his arm: 'The fire is sinking . . .'

Fireworks were a sophisticated touch the villagers had
not expected, and for the next twenty minutes Jeremy and
Ben and Paul Kellow and Horrie Treneglos set off rockets
and squibs and serpents and gerbs and crackers to the
gasps and screams and laughter of the watchers. In the
middle of it the bonfire collapsed and sent up its own
cascade of sparks into the quiet evening air.

Jeremy and Paul had also manufactured some of their
own fireworks. In metal saucers they had contrived a
mixture of chlorate of potash, nitrate of strontia, sulphur
and lampblack, which produced a brilliant light that
bathed the whole scene in demonic red. After these had
died down, to a long sigh and a burst of applause, another

group of saucers was lit containing chlorate of potash, chloride of lead, nitrate of baryta, sulphur and resin, and the night became as brilliantly green.

'How *marvellous* you are!' Daisy said to Jeremy. 'What are they called?'

'They are supposed to be Bengal lights, but don't quite approximate, I believe.'

'Paul says you are a *genius*. He has told me about all your experimentations at Harvey's Foundry.'

'Paul is up the pole. But it's still a *secret* what we do! He should not have told you!'

'Does Clowance know?'

'*No.*'

'So now I am party to this special secret! Delicious! Have no fear: it shall go no further.'

'I think, my child, it will soon have to go further, but for the moment, if you don't mind . . .'

'Of course, Paul is fascinated, with my father opening his new stage to Penzance. He thinks there is a future for a steam engine replacing the horses. Do you?'

'In ten years why not?' Jeremy was loath to discuss it with her here.

'Are you going to be an inventor?'

Jeremy screwed up his eyes, staring at the dancers again. 'Oh, phoo. I'm practical. Not an inventor. I try to see the future – pinch other people's best notions.'

'Would you take me sometime?'

'Where?'

'Fishing . . .'

'You mean – *our* fishing.'

'Of course . . .'

'Well, I . . .'

'Since I knew, I have asked Paul several times but he says no, it is not for women. I wonder why? Your mother has told me she went a ride on that engine in London – what was it called? I do not think women should be disentitled to take an interest in the latest mechanical notion.'

Jeremy looked into her eyes. She passed the tip of her tongue across her lips and smiled at him.

He said: 'There's precious little as yet to see at Hayle.'

'What is there?'

'Just nuts and bolts.'

'No, tell me.'

'A boiler. A few wheels. A piston or two. A frame made in the shape of a bed. A tall funnel which eventually will emit steam: *puff, puff, puff, puff.*'

'How quaint!'

'Yes: it is Trevithick's idea – I told you I pinched 'em. Instead of condensing the steam one *thrusts* it out, dispenses with it.'

'But is the carriage not all yet joined together, assembled?'

'No. Nor will be for a while. For the time being it is all on the shelf while we discuss a more conventional engine.'

'But could I still come?'

'If you wish. But I am now visiting the foundry officially to talk of such an engine. No need to fish. The only obstacle now is a twenty-mile ride.'

'I shall look forward to that,' she said. 'And don't think I can't ride just as fast as you.'

'Oh, I know, I know. I've seen you and Clowance riding hell-for-leather on the sands. It is a wonder you've not come a cropper in a water pit.'

Ben and Clowance came up to them. ''Tis time for the last procession afore supper. Come on!'

The villagers round the fire were linking hands, and Music Thomas and Sephus Billing were crying 'An eye! An eye!' Ben and Clowance pulled Jeremy and Daisy towards the end of the chain, the three Trenegloses closely following. The procession moved off, away from the hot deep glow of the fire, threading among the trees, out to Wheal Maiden, back around the Wesleyan Meeting House, down the hill towards the lights of Wheal Grace where the engine was still about its lonely clanging and sighing, the engine house silhouetted against the candescent night sky. Down, down they went, to Nampara House and on to the beach, thrusting through the thistles and the tall tree mallows, still shouting 'An eye! An eye!' Across the beach almost to the cliffs under Wheal Leisure; there, the arbitrary choice of the two leaders coinciding, the procession turned in a sharp semi-circle and began to jog back towards where the bonfire smoked on the hill.

Past Nampara, across the stream, up the wooded lane, leaving Wheal Grace on their left. At the top of the lane, a few hundred yards from the food and the ale and the smouldering bonfire, the two leaders stopped and formed an arch – an 'eye' – by joining hands above their heads; and under this arch, or through this eye the procession of sixty-odd people had to pass. Once they were through, they scattered like starlings, all making for the trestle tables and the waiting matrons.

The Enyses had a glass of ale and a saffron bun with the Poldarks before leaving with their two little girls and the nurse. Before they left, Caroline said to Demelza: 'I have bad news. My aunt Sarah has at last conquered her lifelong inclination to faint at the thought of coming to see me in this savage county. She has written to say she will be with us in two or three weeks' time. But, my dear, it is an entourage! Not only is she bringing a footman and a maid but Colonel Hector Webb to dance attendance! Clowance met Colonel Webb while she was staying with us. My aunt, though now visibly ageing, cannot bear to be without a courtier.'

'But Mrs Pelham is a delightful person,' Demelza said. 'I shall be happy to meet her again.'

'Well, make no mistake, you shall. We shall *rely* on you and Ross to help us entertain this delightful (I agree) but relentlessly urban lady. I do not suppose she has been west of Basingstoke in her life . . . But stay – I trust this will not clash with your visit to Bowood. When is that?'

'*Late* July. But *nothing* is decided yet, Caroline. I don't even know if Clowance really wants to go. And, of course, if she did, we have no one to send with her. We sadly lack close relatives.'

'I assumed you would go yourself.'

'I should be away for more than three weeks! What would Ross do?'

'What no doubt he does when separated from you for as many months on end. But has Clowance not given you any indication of her feelings about this?'

'Not yet.'

'Then ask her. It is a mother's privilege.'

'Don't tease. How – even if she agreed to go – how could I go into a great house like that remembering I am nothing but a miner's daughter?'

'My dear, you have braved many social ordeals. Unless you arrive at the door wearing a metal hat with a candle stuck in it, I do not suppose they would readily guess, do you?'

'You think it amusing, Caroline, but it is not at all amusing. There are all sort of pitfalls I might tumble into. And I should dearly hate Clowance to feel embarrassed for me.'

'You are far more likely to feel embarrassed for Clowance, who has a distinct habit of calling a spade a spade! Seriously, you must get to know her true feelings. Then if she likes to go, you must take her.'

Demelza said: 'Could you not take her, Caroline?'

The crowds at the trestle tables were long and noisy. Some young men were competing with others in leaping over the fire.

Caroline said: 'Mrs Pelham would make it impossible. But in any case if Clowance goes, then it's right – right for you as well as for her – that you should be the one to go with her.'

'But you *enjoy* these things!'

'So would you if you went. And I promise, I'll lend you Enid.'

'*Enid*? Your *maid*?'

'Yes. Who else? You could not possibly go without one. You like her and she likes you. I'm sure she'd be happy to go.'

'Caroline, you know I *cannot* pretend to like being waited on hand and foot, and sitting about and doing needle-point and – and taking a turn in the park and talking prettily about Mr Scott's latest novel! Now we are so much more comfortably circumstanced ourselves, I believe Ross would sometimes have me more genteel; but I am as I was born and it is too late to change.'

'I'm relieved to know it,' said Caroline.

II

The evening was almost over. The great spread of cakes and buns had been swept clean, the ale casks emptied, the trestles and the tables stacked against an old mine wall until they could be carried down in the light of day. The fire, occasionally replenished by spitting fir branches or a spar of driftwood, had died down till it was a mass of charred embers. Most of the potatoes had been roasted (three-quarters hauled impatiently out too soon and eaten, with many a gasp and cry at their heat, half raw). The old people and the children and the gentry had gone to bed. But a few of the young, of those in their teens and early twenties, stayed squatting on their haunches around the ruins of the fire with the last few potatoes. And others wandered arm in arm in the gathering dark: lovers, courting couples, or a man and a girl responding to a momentary attraction. Not of course among the more respectable, not among the Methodists, and not of course any whose movements had not been closely observed by one or other of the elders, with a nod and whisper and sly nudge. It would be about the village tomorrow that Nellie Bunt was no better than she should be, or that Will Parsons was stepping out at last, or that if Katie Carter thought she was going to do any good for herself with Music Thomas she should think again.

Among those resolute to see the new day in were Jeremy's and Clowance's friends. Jeremy after a few pints of ale had a sudden sickening resurgence of the memory of his last meeting with Cuby and would willingly have tramped off to bed, but the others, laughing and joking, jollied him along. Horrie Treneglos had taken up Daisy's suggestion, and after a while they found themselves outside the lychgate of Sawle Church. They sat outside for a while on the grass telling each other ghost stories and generally getting themselves into a mood more suitable for All Hallows than Midsummer Day. From where they squatted the square leaning tower of the church was scarcely visible against the darkness settled upon the land, but seawards the short night was indigo and cobalt, the stars faint and withdrawn.

They had to some extent paired off. Ben was in his seventh heaven, having companioned Clowance all night; and she had been warmer towards him than ever before, in a way that suggested a greater awareness of him as a man. Jeremy was with Daisy, and Daisy was making progress. The hurt and the ale and the long sadness were twisting his attentions towards this vivacious girl who he could see was offering herself to him if he would but make the first move. Horrie Treneglos was with Letitia Pope, the plain one, but he didn't seem to mind. Paul Kellow was with Maud, the pretty one. Paul, with his air of being so much one of the landed gentry – which he was not – had bribed the groom handsomely to wait at the gates of Trevaunance House 'to escort his charges home'. Agneta Treneglos was with the son of her father's bailiff. The two younger brothers had disappeared with two of the village girls.

Nobody knew the time but nobody cared. Paul was

enjoying himself making Maud's flesh creep, and to that end edged her into the churchyard, where they sat on a grassy grave and he whispered a horrible story to her. She pushed him away but, after laughter, claimed that she had not been made afraid by the story, only that his lips moving against her cheek tickled her. The others wanted to hear the story and presently they were sitting on other gravestones, chatting and whispering together.

Ben said to Clowance: 'I don't really b'lieve these here old tales about rottin' corpses coming to life. I'm not that convinced there's even going to be another world after we d'die, but if there be, twill be well removed from this. I don't reckon graves will ever open.'

'You're an unbeliever, Ben. Yet it was you, was it not, who told that on Midsummer Eve the souls of everyone will leave their bodies and wander to the places where they are going to die?'

'I *told* of it. Tis not to say I believe 'n. Any more than Miss Daisy's story of apparitions entering the church porch showing who's to die during the year. Old wives' tales, I d'truly b'lieve. Do you think aught of them?'

Clowance said: 'There are more things in heaven and earth, Horatio . . .'

'What do that mean?'

'It's from a play I learned at school, Ben. The girls all got it off and misquoted it disgracefully.'

After a pause he said: 'I've never asked; did you like your time in London?'

'Well enough. But there is no air to breathe. And too many people to breathe it. And too many houses, too many shops, too many carts and wagons and horses and – oh, everything.'

'Should you like to live there?'

'It is all so strange,' Clowance said. 'Folk do not really drink milk in London – it is used in tea and coffee and the like but in *such* small quantities. The milkmaids come early in the morning. They carry a yoke to fit their shoulders and ring at every door with their measures of milk and cream. But even though you are wakened *you* do not get up early; no one seems to stir until ten, and even then there is little movement in the house. It is three or four in the afternoon before the gentlefolk bestir themselves in earnest – and then it goes on until the early hours of the next morning.'

'Tis turning night into day,' said Ben.

'Well, yes, when there *is* any day. I was there in the coldest time, of course, and all the fires going created a great cloud over everything. Sometimes at midday you can hardly see to the end of the street, and if the sun chances to come through it is yellow like a transparent guinea. Soot floats in the air and your clothes are all dirty in no time.'

'I think you're better at Nampara,' Ben said.

Clowance yawned. 'I'm not sure what I think – except that I am sleepy, that's what I think. Soon I'll be snoring like an owl. Yet I *won't* go to bed till dawn. How long do you think?'

'Maybe an hour,' said Ben with pleasure. 'Maybe two before sun up. But it is at its darkest now.'

Jeremy was sitting crosslegged on another distant mound, listening to Daisy who was giving a light-hearted account of a party she had been to in Redruth where all the guests had dressed up as animals. Jeremy and Daisy were separated from the rest of the group by a tall rectangular headstone erected in the year of Trafalgar to the memory of Sir John Trevaunance; they were in fact nearest to the overgrown path which led to the church. The darkness and the isolation and the enchantment of the moment were taking hold of the young man. Daisy was in white, with a trailing lawn mantle over a light wool dress, which gave her an ethereal quality. Even in the dark her brilliant eyes picked up some gleam, her face a slender oval, her voice light and pretty and full of fun. So much better-*looking* than Cuby. So much more *versatile*, *vivacious*, *animated*. To *hell* with Cuby!

With some sort of hell in his heart Jeremy knelt

suddenly beside the girl, took her in his arms and began to kiss her. Her lips, after a first surprised gasp, were yielding, her body was yielding; her fine black hair came unloosed and tumbled down. It was the most delicious sexual experience.

After about a minute she part pushed him away, he part released her; but they continued holding each other lightly at half arm's length.

'Jeremy!' she said. 'Well, Jeremy! You *surprised* me! I had no thought of any such *thing*! I did not think you thought of it! You are so surprising – so *startling*!'

'Midsummer Eve,' said Jeremy. 'Why leave it all to the ghosts?'

She looked up at the sky. 'Midsummer Day now. It must have been for an hour or more.'

Her arms were soft and comfortable in his hands. The little breeze had dropped and it was very quiet.

She whispered: 'You startled me, Jeremy. So – so passionate. You almost bruised my lips.'

'Oh, I trust not.'

'You quite *frightened* me. My heart is still beating fast. Feel my heart beating.'

She took his hand and put it against her frock. By judicious misdirection it rested and closed upon her breast.

She laughed quietly. 'No, *lower* than that. I believe you mistake where my heart is.'

'I believe I catch the beat,' said Jeremy, 'but it is very faint.'

She was gently moving against him again, her lips reaching up for his. In the utter silence it was as if a cold air stirred beside them. They both noticed it and paused. Her eyes went beyond his shoulder and fixed themselves and glazed over with fear. He turned slowly to look. Although there was now only the stars and the light from the sea, their night-accustomed eyes could make out details of the churchyard.

Coming towards them – almost floating – walking

silently on the grass beside the path, was Violet Kellow, the sick sister. Unlike Daisy she was in something dark, with a dark cloak over it. But her walk, her face, the long slim hand at her throat, were unmistakable. She passed them by, ten yards away, walking towards the church porch.

Following her, just as silently, his big tawny head silhouetted against the stars, was Stephen Carrington.

Chapter Four

I

There were many thick heads in Sawle and Grambler the following day. Some men wished they hadn't and some girls wished they hadn't, and the older people were disgruntled with life for more mundane reasons; but in spite of this everyone agreed it had been a proper job, best St John's Eve ever they had spent.

Stephen Carrington's return to Sawle became the talk of the villages. He had turned up at Widow Tregothnan's kiddley about eight on the evening of the 23rd. Talking to the widow and Tholly Tregirls and to their customers, he had learned all the news, and in answer to their questions had told them he had landed at St Ives a couple of days ago and was hoping he might again lodge at Will Nanfan's until he could find something more permanent. Learning that there was to be a bonfire feast, he had asked if he might watch it. At Sally 'Chill-Offs' he had as usual been free with his money. Whatever flaws there might be in his character, he was not ungenerous.

Unfortunately for his suit – if he intended to pursue it – Clowance had also seen his appearance in the churchyard. And however eerie and premonitory that appearance had been, Clowance did not believe that it was only his ghost she had seen following Violet to the church door.

It had been a great shock to Clowance; not so much morally, however severe that had been; not so much supernaturally, for the horrid chill of the moment had been superseded by burning anger; but physically. Her body and spirit had leapt at the sight of him. It was a revelation to her, and in view of his apparent misbehaviour, a frightening revelation. If you fancy you may be in love with someone and he turns up and his appearance confirms it, that, whatever the obstacles and complications, is not unwelcome. If however he is clearly in pursuit of another woman and may or may not care a button for you at all, and *still* your whole being leaps and comes alive when you see him again, then you are in the valley of the shadow. Tormented, you loathe and detest his very existence, you can't bear to hear him spoken of, you will not *see* him; all your love is turned inside out like some eviscerated animal, and your life is scarcely to be borne.

On the night Daisy had almost fainted. Created in less sceptical mould than Clowance, she had at first seen her sister as the apparition predicting her early death; and even after it was over she could not rid herself of the superstition that, however much the beings walking in the churchyard were three-dimensional and of warm flesh and blood, the prophecy of their appearance might still be fulfilled in the year to come. Keenly as she wanted to secure Jeremy, the two people gliding among the starlit graves had, for her, wrecked the opportunity for enticing him to declare himself. Partly perceiving this, Jeremy, who was no fool where girls were concerned (apart from Cuby), had liked Daisy all the better for it. Looking back, he saw well enough that his own mood might have led him into indiscretion from which it would have been difficult to withdraw. Now the moment had passed. But he felt sorry for Daisy and warmed to her.

On June 24th, late night or not, Jeremy rode with his father into Truro where they met John and Horrie Treneglos and drew up the legal deed whereby Wheal Leisure became a working mine again. Over the last month and more, while the weather had been dry, they had cleared out the deads of the mine and gone deeper in it, deeper by ten fathoms than ever before and had used makeshift mule-driven pumps to keep the water down. There were definite signs of good copper, but it was impossible to expose the ore in depth without blocking out the lodes section by section.

Before it was finally decided to go ahead there had been several meetings between the two young men and their fathers, with others such as Zacky Martin and Ben Carter called in for consultation – though Ross once or twice superstitiously wondered if, in spite of his apparent caution, he had not set his mind on the venture almost as soon as the proposition was put to him. The sight of the derelict mine on the cliff across the beach from Nampara had subconsciously irked him only a little less than when it had been in full production under the Warleggans. So now the die was cast.

The notary, a young man called Barrington Burdett, had only recently put up his brass plate in Pydar Street, but Ross had met him and liked the look of him, so they went to him. The adventuring money in Wheal Leisure was to be divided into thirty-six parts. Ross and John Treneglos were taking up five parts each; Jeremy and Horrie the same; the remaining sixteen parts would be open to investment from outside. John had been for throwing a larger number on the open market, but Ross had uneasy memories of when he had found himself in a minority before, and insisted they should keep full control. For the moment they would advertise the parts at £20 a share, with another £20 payable in three months' time. Since neither Jeremy nor Horrie had money of their own it meant a big outlay for the two fathers. Warleggans had finally parted with their rights for £400. The prosy Mr King of the Cornish Bank had pointed out that the bank would have to carry Mr John Treneglos's investment, since John, though landed, was always broke, but with Ross a partner in the bank it was hard for Mr King to be as prosy as he would have wished.

They had dinner at the White Hart, during which Jeremy and Horrie tried not to go to sleep and John drank too much. Ross enjoyed his wines and his brandy, but generally restrained his indulgences when out, with a two-hour ride home. Ross did not in fact much like John. In the early days he and Francis had fought John and his brothers; it had been a boys' feud that had gone on a long time. The old man, Horace, John's father, had been a cheerful kindly soul and something of a Greek scholar; but he had bred an uncouth, hard-riding, hard-drinking lot. Then twenty-four-odd years ago the clumsy John, who had always had an eye for Demelza, had married Ruth Teague, who had always had an eye for Ross, and this did not make for an easy relationship. Ruth had tended to be spiteful towards Demelza, and John, at a long-remembered ball at the Bodrugans, had once come, he swore, within an ace of getting Demelza into bed with him, being frustrated at the last by old Hugh Bodrugan himself and that damned Scotsman, McNeil, both on the same scent.

There was also a notable occasion in 1802 when they had been dining at the same house and staying the night, when John had put it to Ross that they should swap wives for the night. After all, he said, it was hard in the country to get anything fresh except the occasional village girl or a guinea hen in Truro; and it stood to reason however much one stood by one's dear wife in a crisis – and no one, no one, could ever say he'd ever let little Ruthie down – a bit of a change, a different sort of a ride, did nobody any harm. As for Ruth, he'd wager there'd be no objection there; because once years ago when there'd been a quarrel between them, a real set-to, all on account of him having got into bed in his riding breeches, Ruthie had let out that she didn't care if she never saw him again, so long as Ross was only a couple of miles away over the fields and the sand-dunes. And concerning Mrs Poldark, she had more than once made it clear that she thought him, John, a handsome, randy sort of fellow, and he could guarantee he'd give her the greatest of satisfaction. Some women had said, well, I can tell you, old friend, what some women had said about me being like a red hot poker . . .

343

Ross had declined, then climbed the stairs to break the news to Demelza. Demelza was highly indignant. 'But you know how I've always fancied him, Ross. How *could* you refuse? Think of the conversations we might have tomorrow, comparing notes!'

However, the passage of time, the cooling of passion, the growing up of the children, good-neighbourliness in a district where neighbours were few, had brought them more often into each other's company. John's sandy hair had turned grey, he had given up some of the more active outdoor sports, his deep-set eyes were seldom properly open, as if he had spent too much of his life squinting into the sun looking for foxes. Ruth, surrounded by her children, had occasionally called on Demelza and sometimes even invited her back to tea to ask her advice about Agneta, who was a problem child.

So now Wheal Leisure, the mine Ross had started more than a quarter of a century ago, was in being again, the company and its shares and its capital properly incorporated in a legal document, and the four men were riding home on a draughty, cloudy afternoon not at all foreshadowed by the beautiful sunrise. Two and two they rode, Horrie and Jeremy a hundred yards in the van.

After a substantial dinner and a fair amount of ale the two young men, though well satisfied with the morning's work, had nothing whatever to say to each other. They rode by instinct, blinking their lids to prevent sleep. Behind them there was more talk, chiefly from John, though he occasionally swayed in his saddle and twice nearly lost his hat.

'Damn me,' he said, 'these upstarts. That fellow King in your bank! I wonder you keep him. It might be *his* money he was advancing, out of his own store hid under the bed. I'd ha' thought you'd have employed some manager of better address and breeding in your bank.'

Ross said: 'It is not precisely my bank, John. Indeed if it were my fortunes on which our clients depended for their confidence and reassurance, there would be an instant run and we would be putting up our shutters tomorrow.'

John grunted and swayed. 'What was this gossip I heard about Warleggan's? God's blood! *Them* in straits! Seems not possible. Stone me, I only wish they *was*, damage they've done to the small man.'

'George plunged recklessly on the expectation of an early end to the war. So I believe it has been touch and go. Banking is confidence as much as anything else, and in the end the run did not quite sufficiently develop in time. But their linking themselves with this Plymouth bank is the outcome. They're safe enough now.'

'Well, I suppose that's how we got the mine cheap. I never thought twould work. I only went because Ruth and Horrie plagued me so.'

They jogged on a way in silence.

'D'you have any trouble with your boy?' John asked, nodding his head at the figures in front. His hat fell over his eyes.

'Trouble?'

'Getting entangled. *I* never got entangled until I picked on Ruth. Horrie goes about the county getting himself entangled.' John straightened his hat. 'Hope he doesn't take up seriously with this damned Pope girl. They're no class and their father's so full of himself I wonder he don't burst. Horrie was with her last night, wasn't he?'

'I don't know. They were all together at the bonfire. I think Jeremy was chiefly with Daisy Kellow.'

'Huh. Well, she's no catch neither, is she. Though at least she's good to look at and would squeeze nicely.'

Ross looked at his companion and new partner. Such a pity that it could not have been Cousin Francis. Wheal Grace had claimed Francis so many years ago and thus precipitated all the trouble between himself and George Warleggan.

On impulse he said: 'Jeremy was recently much taken with one of the Trevanion girls but it fell through.'

'Trevanion? You mean those at Caerhays?'

'Yes.'

John stared up at the sky. 'Damn me, it's going to rain. Never can tell in this damn county. Weather's as fickle as any woman . . . What went wrong?'

'With Jeremy? Nothing. But the girl's brother said no to it. You know, Major Trevanion.'

'Course I know him. We're related.'

'Oh?'

'Well, sort of. My cousin Betty married his uncle. They've a place near Callington. Betty Bettesworth. Silly name, ain't it!' John laughed heartily, and his hat wobbled again.

'Well, your Major Trevanion said no to it, and he apparently rules the house.'

'Oh, he rules it, sure enough. But he's not *my* Major Trevanion. Only see him about twice a year. Used to see more of his brother when I was in the Militia. You was never in the Militia, was you. His brother was in it, so I used to see him. Damned farce, most of it.'

In a few minutes they would come to the parting of the ways. Probably if he were invited John would come in to tea, but really, in his present state . . .

'Well, of course,' Treneglos said, losing his stirrup and finding it again, 'I can see what John was on about.'

'What? What d'you mean?'

Treneglos raised an eyebrow at Ross's tone.

'Well – nothing wrong with the boy, Ross. But they wouldn't want a Poldark.'

Ross said icily: 'I gather the gentleman reminded my son that there had been Trevanions there since 1313. Fortunately Jeremy had the wit –'

He was interrupted by Treneglos's harsh bark. ''Tisn't *that*, man . . . You know me – know my family. Traces back to Robert of Mortain and Sir Henry de Tyes. Can't go much further than that. Can't go much further than *that*! But d'you think Trevanion'd welcome Horrie as a son-in-law? He'd spit in his face! He don't want breeding now, he wants *money*.'

'Well, no doubt some of each does not come amiss –'

'Nay, nay, tisn't that. The madman's nigh on bankrupt. He's spent his fortune on that damned castle – can't finish it, can't pay the men's wages nor buy the materials. And he gambles on the nags. Why, he's been selling land for years. Two or three years ago my brother-in-law, that banker fellow from St Austell, bought three pieces off him, near Tregony, and at St Erme and Veryan. He's raised mortgages right and left, parted with stuff the family's had since Bosworth. Now he's at his wits' end. If he could get one of his sisters wed off to a rich man who would lend him a helping hand he wouldn't care where he came from. Give Jeremy twenty thousand pounds and he'd be the most welcome suitor in Great Britain!'

Ahead the two young men had stopped at the fork in the track. Left you turned for Killewarren where Dwight and Caroline Enys lived, right and you skirted Bodrugan land before taking a wide semi-circle behind Mellin to come to Mingoose House.

John Treneglos fumbled with his reins and laughed. 'Anyhow, there's plenty more about for Jeremy to pick. Don't do to get fixed up too young. I was near thirty afore Ruth hooked me. Any time you think one of my brood is good enough – Agneta or Faith or Paula, just leave me know! And maybe Jeremy will make money in time, eh? They say he's quite the genius.'

'Who, Jeremy?'

'Yes. So Horrie says. Goes over couple of times a week to the Hayle Foundry learning about strong steam. So Horrie says. He's offered to set up this engine, hasn't he? Design it, more or less. Full of ideas, Horrie says. What have you or I done? D'you know one end of a boiler from t'other? Curse me if *I* do. Doubt if Horrie knows much, but he's been over with Jeremy and that Paul Kellow and young Ben Carter – been over four times now in your

347

damned fishing-boat. Seems Jeremy's been doing it for more'n a year. But you'll know all about it. And – and tell the lad – tell the lad from me there's plenty of frilly petticoats to lift in the world without having to mope around Trevanion's sallow sisters.'

II

There was no road or track from this fork heading directly to Nampara, but by jumping a couple of low hedges and fording a bubbling brook one came on rough moor-land that led to the Gatehouse and thence to Poldark land.

Jeremy had temporarily ridden his sleep out of him and was feeling a little less deathly. His grief about Cuby was just the other side of a wall he had laboriously built for himself; it was flimsy and could break under the least pressure, but for the moment he concentrated on the mine and the interest and the work that was entailed as an outcome of the document signed in the presence of Barrington Burdett this morning. And when his mind turned to more personal issues he thought of last night and the extreme excitement he had got out of kissing and fondling another girl. And he knew he could do this again any time he wanted. And maybe next time there would be no apparition to stop them from going a little further. And a little further. And a little further. There was the whole of a young pretty female body to explore.

Beside him his father was silent, but since Ross was not ever really a talkative man except when under the stimulus of his wife's company Jeremy did not think anything of this.

Ross said abruptly: 'You have hinted much of wishing to design the engine for the mine.'

'Yes, Father.'

'And I have always postponed the issue by saying that this was the third item to be considered, and that there was small purpose in discussing it before the other two had been negotiated. Well, now they have been.'

'Yes, Father.'

Ross eyed his son with a long measuring look of appraisal.

'I gather you have been undertaking some practical study in engine building as well as theoretical.'

'Who told you that?'

'You did. When we discussed it first.'

Jeremy said obliquely: 'Did I? Oh yes, of course. I had forgot.'

'On that occasion you remember I said I'd need to be convinced of your ability to design such an engine before we agreed to it. Clearly, a single error might cost us more than what we saved in not employing one of the recognized engineers.'

'Yes, you said that also.'

'And?'

'I quite agree, sir. It is a question of whether, after inquiry, you will feel convinced that it is worth the risk.'

'Can you convince me that it is?'

'I can try . . .' Jeremy hesitated. 'I think the best thing is if I bring you a plan, a design. Perhaps you will not feel willing to say yes or no without some second opinion. But that I'm quite willing to accept.'

They rode on. Ross said: 'How have you come to know so much?'

Jeremy hesitated. 'I have been about mine engines ever since I was old enough to walk.'

'Oh yes, in a general way. But – '

'On this I've had Peter Curnow's advice. Also Aaron Nanfan who, as you know, was twenty years engineer at Wheal Anna. And of course I've discussed the proposition with Mr Henry Harvey of Hayle. He has made his own suggestions. It is not just a – a fancy thing.'

'I didn't suppose so.'

Jeremy struggled with his reluctance to speak of things

349

which previously had been secret to himself. 'Dr Enys –
Uncle Dwight – has helped as well.'

'Dwight? How on earth?'

'He has bought Rees's *Cyclopaedia* as it came out. I have
borrowed it from him regularly.'

'I've heard of it – no more.'

'Dr Abraham Rees is publishing it. It is not yet
complete, but there are many articles that have been
useful.'

'I never saw you reading them.'

'I read them upstairs in bed. It was – easier to
concentrate there.'

Ross studied his son.

Jeremy said: 'I've read other things as well, of course.
'*A Treatise of Mechanics*'. And a separate piece of it, '*An
Account of Steam Engines*' was published independently a
couple of years ago. I wrote to Dr Gregory – the author.
We have corresponded regularly since. Also I have written
to Mr Trevithick a few times.'

'You've been very secretive in all this,' Ross said.

'I'm sorry . . .'

'Have you seen Trevithick since he returned?'

'No. I rode over twice but unhappily he was from home.
I have seen Mr Arthur Woolf, though.'

'Woolf?'

'I mentioned him, you remember. I called on him and he
was – most helpful. With advice and counsel. I'd originally
. . . Shall I go on?'

'Of course.'

'A few months ago I would have thought of designing
an engine on Mr Trevithick's plunger pole principle. It
seems to simplify construction and to reduce greatly the
number of working parts. I still believe it to be a brilliant
idea; but Mr Woolf has convinced me – and a Mr Sims of
Gwennap, whom I also had the opportunity to call on and
who has perhaps the greatest practical experience of them
all – they both think it is over-simplified, that there will be

excess wear on the piston from its constant exposure to the atmosphere and that there will be too much loss of steam because of the absence of a condenser. Taking into account . . . Do you follow me, Father?'

'A little way, yes.'

'Taking into account that they are both rivals of Mr Trevithick, yet I still see too much force in their arguments to ignore them. So I am hoping to design a somewhat more traditional engine, but with high-pressure steam and all the improvements that have been tried and tested.'

'Did these gentlemen make you altogether free of their own ideas?'

Jeremy laughed shortly. 'By no means. Both were very close. But both have engines working which may be examined; and I fear I traded on your name as an influential mine owner.'

'In other words they thought you were going to offer them a commission to design the engine?'

'I can't be sure what they thought. I never made any such offer. We parted on good terms.'

'And there is no patent being infringed?'

'No . . . I have agreed to pay Mr Woolf a consultancy fee. But that is not likely to be large.'

They jogged on. The rain was setting in.

Jeremy said sharply: 'But when it comes time to place the order, I'll agree not to press my own designs, if when you've given them full consideration you don't think well of them – or prefer to play safe. I'm as much concerned for the success of the venture as anyone.'

Ross said: 'Who is that coming across from Wheal Grace?'

'Lord . . . it's Stephen Carrington! You remember I told you he turned up last night.'

'I remember very well.'

'I wonder if he's coming from Nampara.'

The weather did not appear to have subdued Stephen's

spirits as he trotted towards them. He smiled and waved and leapt a gate to come up with the horses.

'Jeremy! This is properly met! I'd hoped you might be at the mine.'

'Stephen. I'm glad to see you.' They shook hands. Jeremy would have dismounted but Stephen was beside him too soon. 'No, we have been to Truro. Father, may I introduce Stephen Carrington to you. This is my father, Captain Poldark.'

They too shook hands. Stephen had a firm grip – almost too firm.

Ross said pleasantly: 'I have heard much about you from my family.'

'Which you would not have,' said Stephen, 'if it had not been for your son.' When Ross looked questioning he added: 'I was pulled out of the water like a hooked herring. Jeremy saved me life.'

'Dramatic but not wholly accurate,' Jeremy said. 'You were in a bad way, but lying on a half-submerged raft. All we did was transfer you to a sounder vessel and bring you ashore.'

'Whereupon the ladies of Nampara cared for me so well until I could care for meself. Sir, however you may look at it, I am still much in your debt.'

'Well, no doubt you'll find some way to discharge it,' said Ross. 'You're visiting the district again?'

'I promised to come back, sir. I promised meself – as well as others. But whether it be for long or short depends.'

'Have you just come from Nampara?' Jeremy asked.

'No. I thought twould be more seemly, seeing as the head of the household was home and as I didn't know him, if I was to ask his permission first.'

'Good God, that's a thought delicate,' said Ross. 'Of course you may call at Nampara when you wish. But I appreciate the courtesy.' Did he? Well, it was graciously meant. Or was the young man in fact obliquely asking permission to pay court to Clowance?

'Thank you, sir. I hear you've another mine a-growing, Jeremy. If I came over tomorrow in the forenoon, could you show it me?'

'You can see it from here. So far we have done little more than clear out the old workings and sink a few experimental shafts at a greater depth. The next step is to build an engine.'

Stephen stared across through the rain. His thick mane was collecting beads of water, but for the most part it seemed ro run off him as if there were a natural oil in the hair similar to that in a duck's feathers.

'The amount I know of mining would not commend me as an adviser, but I've a fancy to take an interest in anything new.'

'Come at eleven,' said Jeremy, 'and take a bite to eat with us afterwards.'

Stephen looked up expectantly at Ross, who smiled and tapped his horse and rode on.

'Then I'll be glad to come,' said Stephen.

III

At about this time Demelza came on Clowance as she was repairing a rent in her underskirt where it had caught on a bramble the night before. They talked for a few minutes about the Midsummer Eve feast, each carefully avoiding mention of Stephen Carrington's return. Eventually Demelza said:

'Clowance, I have to answer this letter to Lady Isabel Petty-Fitzmaurice. To leave it even another week would be impolite . . .'

Her daughter went on with her stitching.

'Clowance . . .'

'I heard you, Mama, but what are you to reply?'

'Only you can say that.'

'At least you might help me. What does acceptance

mean – that I am taking Lord Edward's approaches seriously? In that case . . .'

'I imagine it means that you will spend two weeks in the Lansdowne household. I imagine it means no more'n that. If Lord Edward has some slight fancy for you, no doubt it will help him to decide the degree of it. It might help you too to consider how much or how little you like him. As you know, I was never ever in my life in this situation before, so I can hardly properly advise. But it is – a friendly visit. You may read no more into it than that.'

Clowance turned the skirt over. 'D'you know I hardly ever use any of that fancy work I learned at Mrs Gratton's? Herringbone, cross-stitch, back-stitch. I could well have done without it.' She looked up. 'Will that do?'

'Proper. But you have another snag in the other hem.'

'Damnation,' said Clowance.

'Not,' said her mother, 'an expression that'd be expected of you in Bowood.'

'That's what I'm afraid! Mama, I think it would be all wrong for me to go. Lord Edward is an agreeable young man. Not good-looking exactly, but most agreeable. Kind, I'd think. And very honourable. Papa has a high opinion of the family, and you know Papa does not have a high opinion of too many families of his own kind. But there are two things against my going; and you must know them both! First, what would the younger brother of a marquis be doing paying attentions to an unknown young woman from the farthest depths of a county like Cornwall, and she without money or land or position? His whole family would be totally against it! I would be likely to come in for some sizing up, some cold glances, some sneering asides, if I went up to Wiltshire! Secondly, I do not know if he appeals to me that way . . .'

Demelza went to the window of the bedroom and watched the beads of rain accumulating on the gutter. They formed up, edging towards each other like soldiers in line abreast, then one by one dropping off like soldiers under fire.

'I think you should forget all the first. *All* of it. As for our position, remember your father has become known in the world. It may well be he is better esteemed in London – or the London of parliamentary life – even more than he is here.' Demelza's mind ran sulphurously for a few moments over the insufferable arrogance of Major John Trevanion. 'Your father has been close to Mr Canning, to Mr Perceval, lots of others. He is not a nobody, and because he is not, you are not. And, look at it, who sent the invitation? *We* didn't ask for it. It was sent by his aunt, who because of his mother's death, has been in place of his mother. You told me this. So I think you should forget all those first thoughts *completely*. As for not knowing if you feel "that way" about Lord Edward, you could argue all manner of ways around it. It could be said that because nothing is at stake for you, you would enjoy a visit far more than if there was. Or of course you could feel that – being so honest as you are – you would not be able to hide any feelings you had and would have to make it clear to him soon enough that he didn't appeal to you. If you feel this, then you shouldn't go – indeed, you must not go, for twould be uncivil and unmannerly so to behave.'

Clowance said: 'Would *you* like to go?'

'No!'

'But you would go to companion me?'

'. . . Yes.'

'We should be a pretty pair.'

'I tried to persuade Caroline last night that if you went she should go in my place.'

'And what did she say?'

'That only I was the right one.'

Clowance bit the cotton between her teeth.

'It would cost a great deal. It would cost too much, for we could not go barefoot.'

'I'm glad to see for once you are stockinged today . . .

Clowance, do not consider the smaller things. Whether *I* want to go; or what we should wear. You must decide only on what matters.'

Clowance sighed. 'Yes. I suppose. Well, Mama . . .'

'Yes?'

'Give me until tomorrow. One more day. I promise faithfully to say yea or nay in four and twenty hours from now.'

'Very well.'

'And, Mama.'

Demelza had turned to go.

Clowance smiled for the first time that day. 'Thank you.'

IV

Stephen called at the house next day and he and Jeremy walked over to Wheal Leisure. The drizzle had gone again, and it was warm and sultry, with the sun falling in shafts through clouds as white and curly as a full-bottomed wig. The sea cracked and mumbled as they crossed the beach.

It was, Stephen said, his first ever time down a mine, and he had soon had enough.

'Christmas, I'd not be a miner, not for all the gold in the East Indies! When you get down tis as if the rocks be pressing on ye from all sides. And ready to fall! That's what affrights me. It is as if the earth only has to breathe once too often and you're squeezed down for ever – under tons of dripping rock!'

'It's only what happens when you're dead,' said Jeremy, whose thoughts had temporarily strayed to a girl he had been kissing two nights ago in a churchyard.

'Well, not while I'm *alive*, thank you kindly. Give me the sea and the wind and the rain. I'd sooner face a full gale in a leaky schooner!'

'What happened to *Philippe*? In the end.'

'I had to split the proceeds with the widow of Captain Fraser. She was an old bitch. Tried to bring proceedings against me for robbery. If she'd had the chance she'd have accused *me* of killing the old man – not the French! But in the end I did come away with a little store in me purse. I have hid it away temporary under the planchin in Will Nanfan's bedroom. Now I'm looking for some useful investment that'll double me capital.'

'And coming back here to look for it?' Jeremy asked.

Stephen laughed. 'Well, yes, maybe. Know you any such investment?'

'Not of this moment.'

'In truth, Jeremy, I came back here because I wanted to come back. It has a great attraction. All you Cornish folk are very kind and friendly. I've scarce known such friendliness ever before. Your own family in particular . . .'

They sat on the edge of the cliffs, which were not high here. A path wound its way among the sand and the rock down to the beach. Although a still day, the sea was majestic, tumbling over itself in ever re-created mountains of white surf.

Stephen said: 'The open air's for me, no doubt about that. Look at that sea! Isn't it noble! . . . You know the sort of investment I want?'

'Another boat?'

'You've guessed. But not just a lugger like *Philippe*. Something the size of the schooner I was in when we ran foul of the French.'

'That'd cost a lot.'

'I know. Far more than I have up to now. But you're telling me about this mine, this Wheal Leisure we've been crawling through like blind moles. You all take shares. Your father, you, these Trenegloses – and others. What I'd like is to buy a ship that way. Shares. Me a quarter, you a quarter; Paul, if he has any money –'

'He hasn't. Neither have I!'

'Ah . . . pity. But you wouldn't object to some?'

'Assuredly not.'

'I tell you, Jeremy, that's the way many privateers

operate. Respectable merchants put up the money; hire a captain; he hires the crew. Off they go looking for adventure. Anything foreign's fair game. Then if you get a big prize the crew gets a share and the merchants pocket the rest. I knew a captain who in the end made enough to buy his investors out.'

'Privateering. Hmm.'

'All's fair in war. You know that. Anyway, it's what I'd like to do. Failing that, maybe I'll become a miner!'

Jeremy laughed. 'Seriously . . . If you're looking for investors, had you not a better chance of finding them in Bristol?'

'I tried. But it was not to be. That bitch, Captain Fraser's widow . . . She'd poisoned folks' minds. Spreading stories. Lying rumours about me. Some folk believed her, thought I was not to be trusted. So I bethought meself of me Cornish friends and tried no more.'

'Falmouth would be your place in Cornwall, not here. Here there is nothing. We do not even have a harbour.'

Stephen said: 'There's real money to be made, Jeremy. Big money. Prize money. While the war's on. It won't last for ever.'

'I hope not.'

'I hope not too. But you have to admit it: war's a nasty thing but it is a time of opportunity – for men to climb, make money, make the *best* of themselves. Things you do in peacetime they'd hang you for. In wartime they call you a hero . . .'

Jeremy did not reply, thinking of his own causes for bitter dissatisfaction. In the last few weeks he had dreamed of achieving some sudden distinction – raiding a fort in France, as his father had done – or joining the army and achieving rapid promotion; or becoming vastly rich through Wheal Leisure and able to buy himself a title. Then he would call at Caerhays one day and ask to see Cuby . . .

He said: 'Stephen.'

'Yes?'

'That day we were being chased by the gaugers. Did you go lame on purpose?'

Stephen hesitated, then grinned. 'In a sort of way, Jeremy. Though I did twist me ankle. I thought twas the only way of maybe saving the lugger.'

'Ah . . .'

'I did come to look for you along the coast.'

'Yes, I know . . . Did you see anything of the third gauger when you doubled back – the one you knocked down?'

'Yes.' Stephen laughed. 'I knocked him down again – he was guarding the lugger.'

'Oh, you did . . .' Jeremy eyed his friend askance.

After a few moments Stephen said: 'There was no other way. He was there by the boat shed. He hadn't found his musket – you mind I threw it in the bushes – but he was standing there with his knife out looking after his mates. I saw him before he saw me and came round the wrong way of the shed. He was out – just stirring – when I left.'

'Ah,' said Jeremy again.

Stephen looked back at his friend. 'It was a gamble anyhow, wasn't it. Whether I could dodge 'em and get away. The others might have taken a fancy to follow me instead of you when I doubled back.'

Jeremy laughed. 'I suppose so.'

There was a further pause.

Stephen said: 'Well, I know what I fancy just at the moment: that's a swim.'

'I wouldn't quarrel with the idea. But you'd do well to keep inshore today. This swell isn't to be trifled with.'

They clambered down the steep and slippery path, turned into the cave at the bottom and stripped off. Stephen was a little short in the leg for his height, but otherwise splendidly proportioned. Fine golden hair curled on his chest, diminishing to a narrow point at his navel. He had two wound marks, one on his right thigh, one on his ribs. The second looked recent.

'That the gauger?' Jeremy asked, pointing.

'What? Oh yes. He left his sting.'

They ran naked into the sea and were engulfed by it. Taking no notice of Jeremy's warning, Stephen dived into the first breaker and emerged beyond it. He swam to the second, was turned upside down and came to the surface laughing and spitting. Another wave engulfed him. After being knocked over once Jeremy swam easily after him, dodging the big waves, swimming across their crests or sliding into their bellies before they broke. He suddenly felt glad that Stephen was back. In spite of his strong sexual feelings for Daisy Kellow, nothing really had moved the black ache from his heart. Not work nor play nor food nor drink nor lust. Perhaps for a little while Stephen could cure it. His attitude to life, full of enterprise and empty of caution, was in itself a tonic. If you were in the company of a man who didn't care a curse for anything, it helped you to a similar view.

They were in the sea twenty minutes. The water was still cold for the time of year but its movement so boisterous that one came out glowing. And the sultry air dried them as they ran a mile up the beach and back. They collapsed at the entrance to their cave breathless and laughing, for they had just been able to avoid Beth and Mary Daniel coming along high-water mark picking over the flotsam of the tide. Both ladies would have been a thought indignant at the sight.

One of the sun's shafts pierced the cloud cover and fell on the two young men, and both dragged on their breeches and lay back in the sand enjoying the heat.

Stephen said: 'D'you know, this is the life, Jeremy. You're the most fortunate of human beings, aren't you.'

'Am I?'

'To be *born* here, beside this sea, and into a home where there's money enough. You're not rich but you want for naught. Think of waking up every morning since you were born and looking out on this sea, this sand, these cliffs. There's nothing dirty or ugly or underhand about them. All you get is *clean* things: sun and rain and wind and fresh clouds scudding over. If I had seventy years I'd want nothing better than to spend them all here!'

'After a few you might get tired of it and want to move. You've not got a placid nature, you know. You'd want to be out fighting the world.'

Stephen leaned back on his hands. 'Who knows? Maybe. But when I think of me own life . . . Oh, there are plenty worse; I worked on a farm, was learned to read and write. But don't you think your nature's formed by the way you live? Mine's been all fighting – *having* to fight to survive, sometimes having to cheat and lie. Who'd want to cheat and lie here?'

'There seems to be a modest degree of it in these parts just the same.'

'Perhaps it's not in human nature to be happy. Ecod, given an opportunity, I'd make a try here.'

Some small birds were twittering in the back of the cave. Presently Stephen said: 'And how is Miss Clowance?'

'Well enough, I think.'

'Will she think the worse of me?'

'For what?'

'For what happened the night afore last.'

'No doubt you'll be able to judge at dinner.'

'Has she spoke much of me?'

'From time to time.'

'I mean – since she knew I was back.'

Jeremy brushed some sand off his chest. 'Stephen, I do not know what affection you have for Clowance or she for you. I do not even know if it is the sort that would – would take amiss the sight of you in the company of Violet Kellow on the night of your return. If all that is a little heavy sounding, I'm sorry. Why don't –'

'She saw me, then. Or did someone tell her?'

'She saw you. I saw you.'

Stephen sighed. '*Pity* . . . You know me, Jeremy. I do things on impulse, like. Like going in that sea just now. I don't hum and har. Maybe I don't think enough. But that's how it is. Then I curse meself for an impulsive fool. D'you know it's God's truth that when I got to Grambler two nights ago me first thought was I must go see the Poldarks first thing. Who wouldn't? Isn't it natural? You were me true friends. But then I thought, what if I turn up on your doorstep, I thought, with nowhere to sleep? Twill look as if I expect *you* to put me up. So I went first to Nanfan's and learned there of the bonfire. Right, I say to meself, I'll call at Nampara and see if maybe Jeremy and Clowance are there and I can join them at the bonfire. So I walked up with the procession but cut away from it when I saw you *all* there. You were with Daisy Kellow and Miss Clowance was with that Ben Carter, and each one was paired off nicely, so I think to meself, no one will want *me* ramming me way in; and I see this tall man and someone says he's Captain Poldark and I think, well, there's better times to turn up like a bad penny than at a Midsummer Eve bonfire when everyone's busy, and maybe, I think, I'll be better off waiting till the light of morning. So off I walk back to Nanfan's to get an early night.'

He paused. The two women were abreast of them on the beach and Jeremy waved. They waved back.

Stephen said: 'I've told you, I'm an impulse man. I have to pass the gates of Fernmore, and there was lights burning, so I go in, and Mr Kellow's away and Mrs Kellow and Miss Kellow have got their cloaks on and are arguing back and forth because Violet has said first she's not well enough to go to the bonfire and then changed her mind and says she is. So I say to Mrs Kellow, I say, Mrs Kellow, if you'll give me leave, I'll take Miss Violet to join her sister at the bonfire and there's no need for you to turn out at all. So after a bit of persuasion that's how it was.'

Jeremy reached for his jacket and took out his watch. 'But you didn't bring her to join her sister.'

'Well, I reckon you know the Miss Kellows better than me, Jeremy. Control them, can you, either one or the other of 'em? Like runaway horses. I say to Miss Violet when we get nigh the bonfire and she looks to be walking past it, I say to her, "Miss Violet, that path leads to the beach," and she says in that taunting high mettlesome way she has, "Shut your mouth, fellow, and follow me." '

Jeremy pulled on his shirt. 'It's almost time for dinner. You can come up to my room first and tidy up.'

'You know me,' said Stephen. 'Don't look a gift horse in the mouth, do I. Maybe I should, but it's not me nature. Violet's a pretty piece and out for a lark. You know what both those Kellow girls are.'

'Yes,' said Jeremy uncomfortably. 'I think we should go.'

V

Stephen was at his best at dinner, talking enough to be polite but not monopolizing the conversation. He answered Ross's questions about the *Philippe* in such detail as seemed necessary. He explained that his ship's fight with the two French warships had taken place during a storm. Captain Fraser had been killed by a direct hit from one of the French vessels and the rest of the crew had at once decided to surrender. But the cannon shot that killed Captain Fraser had wrecked their foremast, and before the French could help them they took the ground in high seas on what he supposed were the Western Rocks of the Scillies. He supposed the rest of the crew drowned, for there had only been himself and Harrison and Mordu to get away on the raft.

He also took a lively interest in Wheal Leisure, the mine itself, the probable disposition of the lodes, the way the lodes were worked, the problem of water and the process by which it was pumped away. He showed a quick intelligence and a grasp of what he was told.

Ross thought him probably the sort of young man who would bring an intense concentration to a subject that suddenly interested him, absorbing more, and more quickly, than someone who had studied for a long time. But he thought possibly the interest might, on occasion, as suddenly die.

Jeremy's long fingers, he noticed, were not so artistic as they had once been, and in replying to Stephen and explaining things to him there was a flicker of passion in his face. What had John Treneglos said? 'Horrie says your boy's a genius.' Horrie, not being the brightest of young men, would be easily impressed, of course. Yet it meant something. Why hadn't he, Ross, perceived more to his son than his apparent carelessness, his seemingly detached, feckless, facile attitude to life? Surely since his return home Jeremy's conversations with him might have given him a hint of what was going on in the young man's mind. He'd been short-sighted. Short-sighted in a way fathers so often were short-sighted, falling into the sort of trap Ross had prided himself he was immune from.

Sitting there listening to the two young men, he admitted the fault in himself, yet he could not suppress his resentment with Jeremy for being so damned secretive about everything and leading him into such a false position.

Ross had not told Demelza yet about the 'fishing'. He must first tackle Jeremy on his own . . .

Altogether the dinner was quite a success, except for Stephen. Clowance claimed a bilious attack and begged to be excused putting in an appearance. Half an hour before dinner-time she had told her mother she would accept the invitation to spend a holiday at Bowood with the Lansdownes.

Chapter Five

I

The building of the engine house for Wheal Leisure began in early July. Much thought had gone into the positioning of the engine, for, although up to now all the buildings of the mine were situated at the top of the cliff, if the engine could be built at a lower level, some of the natural drainage could still take place and the engine would have a shorter distance to operate its main pump-rods. So a lower piece of cliff had been chosen some 100 yards from the mine, and a platform created by digging and blasting. There would be little enough room for everything, but it would do. Having then worked out and measured out the exact position of the engine and the boiler, a cellar was dug some nine feet deep, and thereafter another three feet dug round the cellar's edge for the foundation of the house itself.

An old quarry behind Jonas's Mill was reopened, and for three weeks before the first stone was laid a succession of mule carts traversed the moors and the scrubland and the sand dunes in continuous train all the daylight hours. What they carried was killas or clay-slate, which was the most reliable and the most workable stone to hand. Even so, the last of the Wheal Maiden walls disappeared, for some part of them was of granite; Ross was also in negotiation with a granite quarry near St Michael to obtain more, for they would probably need 400 tons of the better stone to build the bob-wall which took most of the vibration and the strain. The difficulty with opening a mine which required an engine and an engine house was that it all had to be built strong enough to last and large enough to accommodate success. There had been occasions of engine houses collapsing because the foundations were not upon an adequate base or because the beat of the engine imposed too great a strain. Nobody knew whether in two years Wheal Leisure might again be derelict; but when building one had to prepare for the best.

So having taken care to provide adequate drainage, they laid the first walls on the broad foundations, course by course, interspersing them with thin lime mortar, the largest and longest granite stones placed at the base and resting always on their broadest sides, with bars of iron running through it all to lend additional strength. When the walls were higher, high enough to accommodate the lintel of the door, more iron bars 10 or 12 feet long would be used, reaching through the thickness of the wall and bolted together at their ends so that they held the walls in their metallic grasp. At the level of the upper cylinder beams, holes had to be left in the walls for their ends, with room to move them laterally so that the cylinder could be got in. Later would come the larger aperture for the fitting of the bob-stools to accommodate the great balance beam. Above this would come the third floor, the slated roof and the tall brick-built chimney stack.

The house would take at least two months to complete, even if there were no serious hitches and the weather stayed un-foul. A large shed also had to be built for coal, and Jeremy was trying to pick a suitable declivity in the sand dunes behind the house which he could have beaten down and laid with a mixture of lime, sand, water and pebbles to form a rain-water reservoir to supply the mine; otherwise it meant carrying barrels from the Mellingey stream which at its nearest was more than a mile away. In the blown sand and rock of the cliff and dunes they had so far been unable to find any spring, and there was no possibility of cutting a leat from the Mellingey unless one started miles back, for they were on higher ground here. The unfortunate paradox existed that, while all this trouble and expense was being gone to to drain water out of the earth, the water they brought up could not be used to create the steam to work the engine, for the minerals in it would quickly corrode the boiler. Such water of course could be used for the washing floors or buddles, or to work any stamp which might be required if some quantity of tin were mined. The original mine out-buildings could be utilized for the remaining offices.

In order to increase his work force as little as possible Ross withdrew twenty tut-workers and masons from Wheal Grace. The tut-workers were the less skilled and the less well paid of the underground men, most of their work being the sinking and linking of shafts, the opening of new ground, binding, and the general maintenance of the mine. They were the worker ants of the mining world.

As soon as news of the reopening got about, Nampara was besieged by miners looking for work. Ross took on a few but explained to them all that any sort of full recruitment would have to wait for the installation of the engine and the proving of the mine. Apart from constructing the house the main work at the moment was labourers' work, sinking the shaft which was to drain the rest of the mine.

The day after it all began Stephen said to Jeremy he would like to lend a hand. He didn't mind, he said, what he did – lead a mule, mix cement, lay a course of stone, dig a drain; it was just something to occupy himself while he looked for permanent work. As Jeremy was hesitating he added:

'I don't want pay, of course.'

'Why ever not?'

'You at Nampara were all very good to me. I'd like to give a trifle of something in return. I have good muscles – don't concern yourself for that.'

Jeremy stared at the workers, who were busy on the plateau below them. 'There's no reason to repay anything.'

Stephen said: 'You do a fair measure of rough work

yourself, helping here, helping there. Do you take wages for it?'

'No . . . But –'

'But you're the owner's son. Eh? Well, I'm the owner's son's friend. Does that not seem reasonable? Besides . . .'

'Besides what?'

'Well, to tell the truth of it I do not think I wish to be bound six days a week. I want time to look around, borrow a pony from you, see if there be anything promising in the neighbourhood. I want a bit of freedom, like, maybe two days a week to go off, perhaps local, perhaps to Falmouth, who knows. But when I'm here I'm here and I don't like to be idle. So what could be better than helping with the new mine and assisting you?'

Jeremy still thought of it. 'Come when you wish, then,' he said. 'I'll tell Ben and Zacky Martin, so if I'm not here they'll know. Wages – they're poor enough, God knows – but you shall get paid by the day. It will be a few shillings. I think it is right that way. I think we should all want it.'

Stephen hesitated and then shrugged. 'If that's how you wish it, then I give way. Can I start tomorrow? Six in the morning like the rest?'

II

Sir George Warleggan was surprised to receive an invitation from Dr and Mrs Dwight Enys to dinner on Tuesday the 23rd of July at 4 p.m. Since calling on them in January in London he had nourished a bitter resentment against Dwight for giving him the advice that he did. He had included Dwight in the curses he heaped upon everyone connected with his disastrous speculations. It was only after some months that his sense of objectivity reasserted itself and he had to admit to himself that Dwight had in fact been entirely correct in what he said. The old King, though still very much alive, had *not* recovered his sanity, he was *not* able to resume his rightful authority as monarch; Dwight's answers to his questions had been borne out by events. The use to which he put those answers was his own affair, his own fault. But that made it all the more galling, and a resentment remained.

It was only after he had read the letter and pondered on the best excuse he could make to refuse that he turned the paper over and saw that Caroline had written on the back: 'If Valentine is home, pray bring him with you. My Aunt, Mrs Pelham, is staying with us for two weeks. Hence this party to welcome in the Dog Days.'

He rode up to Killewarren a little before four accompanied by his son and a groom, and noted that for all her wealth and youth and enterprise Caroline had done little to improve the building since that old skinflint her Uncle Ray had lived there. Strange that Dwight Enys, so forward-looking in his physical theories, still young and energetic and in contact with many of the best medical and scientific brains in the country, should not have torn down that wing and put up something more modern or even razed the place and started over again. It did not occur to George that anyone might really like it that way.

The first persons he saw when he went into the big parlour were two Poldarks. Not, thank God, Ross and Demelza – even Caroline Enys would be beyond such a fox paw, as old Hugh Bodrugan used to call it – but the son and daughter, which was bad enough. And whom were they talking to? George was a man of composed character and there were few emotions which could stir him deeply. But now it was as if the book of his feelings was laid open and a wind were riffling the pages.

Lady Harriet Carter was smiling at something that Clowance had said, and her brilliant teeth were just hinted at between the upcurved lips. She was in a saffron-coloured frock with cream lace at the throat and cuffs. A topaz brooch and earrings. Her hair gleamed, as always; as black as Elizabeth's had once been fair. George just noticed the other people in the room, greeted Mrs Pelham, Colonel Webb; someone with a long neck and a face like Robespierre whose name was Pope, with a pretty blonde young wife who seemed scarcely older than the two simpering girls who seemed also to be his. And a dark smooth slim young man called Kellow or some such.

He was bowing over Harriet's hand. Momentarily she was by herself.

'Sir George.' She was cold but not at all put out. 'The last time we met was at the Duchess of Gordon's, when you were about to take me to see Admiral Pellew's white lion.'

'True, ma'am. I – '

'Alas, then, all of a sudden, as if you'd seen a ghost, an apparition, a spectre, an *affrite*, you made your excuses and left. Business, you said. Business. Which has taken six months.'

'That must have seemed grossly impolite on my part – '

'Well, yes, it did. Yes, it has. Naturally, since I am a clear-sighted person, a simple explanation presents itself.'

'Lady Harriet, I can assure you that would be very far from the truth. Indeed, the contrary.'

'What contrary applies? Pray enlighten me.'

George took a breath. 'I sincerely wish I could explain in a few words all that has passed. Alas, it would take an hour, perhaps more. Perhaps I could never *quite* explain how it came about – '

He stopped. She raised her eyebrows. 'How it came about?'

He glanced at Clowance, but she was talking to Valentine. Jeremy had turned away.

'Explain,' he said, 'that my agitation that evening was the outcome of negotiations I had entered into – nay, completed – because of my wish to stand more – more substantially in the eyes of your family . . .'

'My *family*? What the pox have they to do with it?'

A hint of caution crossed his mind. She had been a little disingenuous there. 'You must understand.'

'Indeed, I do not.'

'Then one day I will explain.'

'Why not now?'

'Because the time isn't ripe. Because this moment is hardly the most propitious moment . . . surrounded as we are . . .'

She looked around, eyes taking in the company, a hint of humour at the back.

'Well, Sir George, you write the most diverting letters . . . Unless by chance you should sit next to me this afternoon . . .'

III

They were at dinner, and Harriet, by Caroline's design, did sit next to George. Clowance sat next to his son. She'd seen Valentine twice in ten years. He was enormously changed; good-looking in a decadent way. A lock of hair constantly fell across his brow; his eyes were too knowledgeable in one so young; but he had great charm.

'I met Jeremy at the Trevanions'. But not little Clowance. When last I saw you you really *were* little Clowance. Not so any longer.'

His eyes lingered on her, and she felt that he had already known other women and had a fair idea of what she would look like without her clothes on. It was not totally an unpleasant feeling. Something about his cheerful grin robbed it of its offence, made it friendly, sexual, but unashamed.

'Are you home from Eton?'

'Yes, m'dear. We're much of an age, aren't we? One or other of us scrambled to get out into the world before the world used up all its fun! I b'lieve I was first by a few months, wasn't I? Born under a "black moon", they say. Very unlucky, they say. How's your luck been of late?'

He might have been asking her some intimate questions about her personal life. She said: 'Are you staying at Cardew?'

'Betwixt there and Truro. I must confess to you, dear cousin, I must confess the local scene seems a little barren of lively young people. Why don't you trot over? You and Jeremy. I believe we should find interests in common.'

'I don't know if we should be welcome . . .'

'This stupid feud. It's best dead and buried, isn't it. Is that why your parents aren't here tonight?'

'They came last night. Aunt Caroline thought . . .'

'I know exactly what she thought. Your father and my father, always swearing at each other like two alley cats. Yet they've never fought a duel. Why not, I wonder? Twould clear the air. Indeed it might clear one or t'other out of the way and make for a friendlier life altogether. I expect my father has been the slow coach. Not a one for firearms, is Papa. One rather for the heavy hand in which the money-bags are barely concealed. Whereas I always picture your father riding to the wars with a gun on his shoulder.'

Valentine looked across at Sir George, who was talking to the dark handsome woman on his right. They had had a right-down set-to before they came out, he and his father. He had spent a week in London on his way home from Eton and had added greatly to his debts; this news he had allowed to leak out slowly, and the worst of it had only broken today. Sir George had been furious – perhaps more angry than he had ever seen him before. Some casual remark of Valentine's near the end, some casual reference to the bullion in the bank, had set Sir George off and he had called Valentine an indolent, lecherous, good-for-nothing who'd be better off taking the King's shilling and plodding it out in the ranks of the army than acting the posturing, simpering roué, a disgrace to his family and his name.

It had been harshly said and harshly meant. Most times

Valentine was able to trade upon his father's natural pride in him to soften the anger at his dissolute behaviour. Not this time. Something had gone wrong in his calculations and the alarm he felt disguised itself as reciprocal anger. When he answered back the third time he thought Sir George was going to strike him. So his remark to Clowance about the duel and its possible consequences was not unmeant. He would not have been at all grieved at this moment to see his distinguished and powerful father stretched in a pool of blood on some lonely heath while a surgeon knelt over him and gravely shook his head.

Instead he was seated across the table talking earnestly to this woman. Who was she, and what was his father being so zealous about? Had the lady rolling mills to sell? Or a foundry? Or a blowing house? Did she represent some banking interest he was anxious to acquire? Nothing else surely could ever engage his attention so completely. (Valentine knew so well his father's social manner when, although engaged in conversation with one person, his eyes would roam about the room seeing if there were better pastures to graze in.)

And then Valentine caught a look in his father's eye and realized with a shock that there was one other interest which could invoke earnest conversation, though it was an utter revelation to discover that his father was likely to be so caught up. Valentine had long since concluded that nothing could be further from his father's thoughts than any interest in any woman at any time. For herself, that was. But unless he had totally and crassly misread Sir George's look of a moment ago, this was for herself.

She was very handsome, certainly; mature but very handsome. But his father was so *old* . . .

'Shall you?' said Clowance, eyeing him candidly.

'Shall I what?' He coughed to hide his own expression.

'You were speaking just now of riding to the wars.'

'Like my half-brother? It depends. I frequently go shooting, you know; but then, the birds don't shoot back, do they. I think at the moment I have too much of a fancy to enjoy life to put it wantonly at risk. Though my father was suggesting tonight that I might like to join a line regiment.'

'Seriously?'

'I'm not sure. It was not intended as an inducement but as a sort of a threat.'

'Why should he threaten you?'

'Because I have been living above my means.'

'At Eton?'

'And in London. I have friends in London and we know how to make merry. I am not to be allowed to return there at the end of this vacation, but must post straight back to school. In truth, Clowance . . .'

'What?'

'I was serious just now. Why should you and Jeremy not come and spend a day or two with me next week? It will greatly alleviate my feeling of imprisonment, and Father will be away then so you need have no fear of embarrassment.'

'I'm sorry. Jeremy will be here, but I leave for Wiltshire tomorrow.'

'For a visit? To see friends?'

'Yes.'

'For long?'

'It will be three weeks, I suppose, there and back.'

'Do you have a sweetheart in Wiltshire, then?'

'Yes.'

'There I think you deceive me. For if it were true, wouldn't there have been a moment's hesitation, some mantling of the girlish cheeks?'

'My cheeks don't mantle.'

'I wager we might try someday.' Valentine laughed. 'You have to remember you're not really my cousin, Cousin . . . By the way – ' he lowered his voice – 'what is the name of my other neighbour?'

'Mrs Pope. Mrs Selina Pope.'

'Is she the daughter-in-law of that tall thin old feller?'

'No, his wife.'

'God's wounds.'

. . . Further up the table his father said: 'Well, madam, you ask an explanation, and it is your right. But how to begin it here? . . .'

'You may have noticed, Sir George, that confessions at the dinner table are seldom overheard by anyone except the person for whom they are intended, since everyone else talks so loud anyhow. But pray do not let me press you.'

George took a gulp of wine. Normally he drank with caution, as if fearing someone might be going to take advantage of him.

'Since you are clear-sighted, Lady Harriet, it cannot have escaped your notice that I had thoughts about you of a warmer nature than mere friendship. When I called to see your brother, the Duke, he made it clear that he did not think me of a birth or breeding suitably elevated to entertain such thoughts. After due consideration I persuaded myself that rich commoners are not infrequently admitted as equals in the highest society, if their wealth is but of sufficient extent and substance.'

A servant put a new plate in front of him, and he was helped to poached turbot.

'So far I have followed you quite clearly, Sir George. Am I right in supposing that the business you are now involved in . . . ?'

'Was involved in. For it proved a business of a disastrous nature. My lack of communication with you since then has been because of a knowledge that, far from improving my claims, this speculation has reduced them to almost nothing.'

. . . Caroline said to Jeremy: 'So they are off tomorrow.'

'Yes. Yes, we leave at six, and will ride in with them, to see them take the coach and bring their horses back.'

'I believe it will be of benefit to them both. You know, of course, I love them dearly.'

'Yes. I do.'

'Especially your mother, whom I have known the longer! Would you believe that when we first met, and for quite a while, we looked on each other with the gravest suspicion and an element of distrust.'

'I didn't know.'

'We came of such different worlds. I from an artificial, elegant and social existence in Oxfordshire and in London. She, in the most delightful way, was of the earth, earthy. When our friendship grew it was the stronger for having roots in both worlds. That is why I badly wanted them to accept this invitation.'

'I don't follow.'

'Clowance is in common sense as earthy as your mother, though in a somewhat different way. Edward Fitzmaurice, who seems to have taken this fancy to her, is elegant, sophisticated, lives in a world of convention and fashion. Whether they will like each other more or less from longer contact I cannot prophesy. But they will do each other *good*. Each will have an eye opened to another view of life. I do not suppose Edward will ever before have met a girl like Clowance, who says what she *thinks*. And she has just glimpsed his style of life in London and will benefit by seeing more. As for your mother . . . She went into society quite often when she was younger – never without the greatest of a success. Of late years your father has been often away and her visits to London rare. She still has doubts about herself sometimes, especially without Ross.'

'But you have none?'

'Do you?'

Jeremy considered and then smiled. 'No,' he said.

Chapter Six

I

Mrs Pelham, who was sitting next to Colonel Webb but found him temporarily occupied with the beguiling, willowy Mrs Selina Pope, turned to her other neighbour, placed there naughtily by Caroline because she knew her aunt adored the company of handsome young men.

'And pray, Mr Kellow, what is your profession? I take it you are not in the Services?'

'No, ma'am, not yet. Though I have a promise of a commission next year. For the present I help my father. He owns and runs most of the coaches in Cornwall.' Paul was never above a little exaggeration.

'Do you mean public coaches?'

'Yes, ma'am, in the main. He operates three coaches a week each way from Falmouth to Plymouth. And others from Helston, Truro and St Austell. We hope shortly to begin a service to and from Penzance, but there are difficulties with the road across the tidal estuary.'

'*All* the roads are difficult,' said Mrs Pelham with feeling.

'Did you come by stage coach, ma'am?'

'No, by post-chaise.'

'Then you may have used some of our horses.'

'The horses, so far as I was able to observe, were excellent.'

'But not the roads? No, ma'am, but I assure you they are improved even from five years ago. Of course what I hope someday . . .'

'Yes?'

'You must find this a tedious conversation after London.'

'You were saying you hoped someday . . . It is never tedious to hear a young man's hopes.'

Paul smiled. 'Even though his hopes may seem dull in the telling? . . . What I hope is that before long we may be able to dispense with many of the horses – thus enabling the coaches to go three and four times the distance before stopping, and thus making the distances seem half as far – by introducing the steam-propelled carriage.'

Sarah Pelham suppressed a shudder. 'You really believe that that would someday be practical?'

'I'm sure of it.'

She looked at his slim, dark, feline face, composed in the confident planes of youth. 'You think people will accept the greater discomfort and the greater danger?'

'I should not suppose there would be an increase of either, ma'am. The saving in time will be very substantial.'

'When there is all the added risk of overturning? And the dangers of being scalded by escaping steam!'

'The roads must be improved, of a certainty. But that will have to happen in any case so soon as the war is over. In Ayrshire there is a man called Macadam using new methods. As for the dangers of steam, they are exaggerated. I have,' Paul said casually, 'been working on an engine recently, and you will see I am suffering no scalds.'

'And your father is a believer in all this too? He is hoping to introduce steam carriages on the roads of Cornwall?'

'My father is not privy to it as yet. He comes of an old family and does not perhaps see commerce as younger men do. Nor innovations. I am working, planning, for ten years ahead. In five years it will be time enough to show him the advantage of steam and how the business of Royal Mail coaches and land transport should be run.'

The red-nosed flatulent seedy man who overdrank and was always in debt would no doubt have been flattered to have been described as coming of an old family, but Paul, speaking to a stranger who would soon return to London, felt he could allow himself a little licence even beyond the usual.

Breast of veal in white wine was served, with young carrots and fresh raspberries.

... Valentine said: 'Mrs Pope, you have been neglecting me.'

Selina Pope turned: 'On the contrary, I think, Mr – er – Warleggan. You have been so engaged with Miss Poldark that I have hardly got a look in.'

'Miss Poldark is a sort of cousin of mine – though the relationship is very complex.'

'Pray explain it to me.'

'Well, her father's cousin was married to my mother. Then he was killed in an accident and my mother married Sir George, and eventually I came along.'

Mrs Pope said: 'I wouldn't call that a relationship at all.'

'That is what I was telling Miss Poldark.'

Selina Pope was blonde and slender, with small, elegant features, a high forehead and little wisps of curl falling down over her face. For a sudden startled moment Valentine was reminded of his own mother. He blinked.

'What is it?' said Mrs Pope. 'Do I distress you in some way?'

'Indeed you do,' said Valentine, recovering. 'That I should ever be accused, even in jest, of neglecting such charm and beauty.'

'Oh, thank you,' said Mrs Pope. 'But my accusation was not in jest, it was in earnest!'

When she smiled the resemblance disappeared. The mouth was more wilful, the eyes a little aslant, the expression less composed.

'Well,' said Valentine, 'since I am accused, committed and condemned without a trial, what is my sentence?'

'Oh, sir, I'm not the judge; I'm the victim.'

'Then if I may pass sentence on myself it is to be in constant attendance on you for the rest of the evening.'

Selina Pope delicately passed the tip of her tongue over her lips. This young man was so mature and so forward of manner that the dozen-odd years that she was his senior hardly seemed to count.

He said innocently: 'Is that your father-in-law?'

'No, my husband.'

'Oh, I'm sorry. And the two young ladies?'

'His daughters by a former wife.'

'And do you live in this neighbourhood, Mrs Pope?'

'At Place House. It used to belong to the Trevaunances.'

'Oh, I know it. Do you come into society much?'

'We are seldom invited,' said Mrs Pope candidly.

'Then should I be permitted to call?'

'On my two stepdaughters?'

Valentine looked her un-innocently in the eye. 'Of course . . .'

The low sun was coming round into the dining-room: motes floated in the sunbeams as the noise of conversation rose and fell . . .

Lady Harriet said: 'I do not know whether to take your confession to me as a great compliment, Sir George, or as a greater insult.'

'Insult? How could that be?'

'That your feelings towards me must have been most sincere I fully acknowledge. Since you must be aware of what people say of you, it cannot offend you to know that I am the more impressed that you should risk your fortune for me, having in mind the reputation that you bear. For caution. For mercantile shrewdness. For – even – sometimes – parsimony.'

George stared at the food put before him but did not touch it.

'Well?'

'Well?' she said.

'Is that reason for insult?'

'No, for an acknowledgment of the compliment. What insults me, dear Sir George, is that you suppose I am like so many other things in your life and may be *bought*.'

'Not so! That was not my intention at all!'

'Then pray how do you interpret it?'

Like a goaded bull George glowered round the table, but everyone seemed preoccupied with their own food and conversations.

'I have already explained, Lady Harriet. I did not think your brother, the Duke, approved of my addressing my attentions to you. I felt that with greater wealth I would merit more serious consideration. I have already done my best to explain this . . .'

'Indeed you have. So far as money is concerned, much would have more and lost all. Is that the truth of it?'

'Not *all*. I am now just solvent; it will be the work of some considerable time before the situation is fully repaired. But I am not *better* off; I am, I must confess, much *worse* off; in other words I have not improved my position or circumstances in *any* way which would stand me in better stead either with you or with your brother, the Duke. Hence my predicament, hence my reluctance to impose myself on you in any way during the last six months . . .'

'Sir George, I wish you would not call him my brother, the Duke. The former is true and has some relevance. The latter, though true, none at all. This is all very interesting . . .' Lady Harriet went on with her food for a moment. 'All very interesting. Do you know how old I am?'

'No, madam.'

'I am thirty. And a widow. The widow of a hard-drinking, hard-riding, hard-swearing *oaf*. Yes, dear Sir George, oaf, even though his pedigree was impeccable. I am not a docile gentle girl, Sir George. I was not to him. I never would be to any man. Still less would I be so to my brother, who has his own life to live, and may good fortune attend on him. For what he believes or thinks I care not a snap of the fingers. If he found me some rich and aristocratic husband I would consider the matter entirely on its merits without regard to my brother's feelings. Similarly, if I should ever contemplate taking a husband without first informing "my brother the Duke", it would not matter a curse whether he approved of it or not . . . So, Sir George, if you are at present in straitened circumstances, take heed that you have done yourself no good by speculating in order to *impress* me, nor special harm by losing a fortune in the *attempt* to impress me. That is all I can say now. Pray turn to the lady on your left. She is anxious to speak to you about something. No doubt she wants your opinion on her stocks and shares.'

. . . Colonel Webb was telling Caroline that in spite of the cheerful newspapers he was of the opinion that the Peninsular Army was bogged down and deadlocked in front of Badajoz and the River Guadiana. Wellington could not move safely fore or back. Neither indeed could Marmont. Personally he felt sorry for troops pinned down in such a pestilential part of the world.

'God help them all,' said Webb, wiping his moustache. 'What with the heat and the flies and the fevers − not to mention the snakes − there'll be no need for fighting to fill the hospitals and the graves.'

'So long as the French are in like position . . .'

'Oh, worse, for they are subject always to those cutthroat brigands who infest every inaccessible corner of the countryside and, calling themselves the Spanish army, descend on any French outpost with the utmost ferocity. They say the French lose on average a couple of hundred men a week − and have done so for years − by these tactics. There is one man, I forget his name − nay, it's Sanchez − who whenever he catches a courier sends his head and his dispatches to Wellington by special messenger.'

'I have never met a Spaniard. No doubt they are a cruel race.'

'Alas, they have good reason, ma'am. The atrocities of the French upon *them* shall be nameless. Sometimes one thinks God sleeps.'

Colonel Webb was addressed across the table by Dwight, and Caroline turned again to Jeremy.

'Has Clowance seen much of Stephen Carrington, do you know?'

'Not to my knowledge. Only twice when I have been there, and I have seen a lot of Stephen . . .'

'You like him?'

Jeremy wrinkled his eyebrows. 'Yes. But my parents have also asked me this. That it should be necessary to ask seems to put the answer in doubt.'

'What do you like about him?'

'Oh, pooh, what does one like about a man? His company. One doesn't fall asleep when he's about.'

Caroline forked at a piece of flimsy-light pastry. 'D'you know there's an old Cornish saying; Dwight was reminding me of it yesterday on another matter. It goes:

> "Save a stranger from the sea
> And he will turn your enemee."'

Jeremy said: 'I can't imagine that ever happening with Stephen. He's a warm-hearted fellow, and I think he would do a lot *not* to become my enemy.'

'Does Clowance like him?'

'Oh yes.'

'A little bit more than that?'

'You must ask her yourself, Aunt Caroline.'

'I wouldn't dare!'

Jeremy laughed, and Clowance, as if sensing some mention of herself, looked up the table at them.

'What a very handsome woman Mrs Enys is,' said Valentine to her. 'Thin for my preference, but I fancy her colouring. And of course her arrogance. Are you arrogant, Clowance? It gives a girl an added sparkle.'

'I'll remember.'

'But don't approve?'

'Oh, it is not for me to say . . .'

'You think my tastes too catholic?'

'I have not thought about it.'

'Well, it is such a pleasure to come to a dinner-party at which there are so *many* good-looking women. I seldom remember a better. Not counting Mrs Pelham because she is elderly, there are: one, two, three, four, five! Do you realize how many thousands of depressingly plain women there are in the world? And hundreds downright *ugly*. Pretty ones stand out like – like beacons . . .' Valentine waved his fork extravagantly and then said in a newer, quieter voice: 'Your mother is pretty, isn't she.'

'Yes, I think so.'

'I remember, though it's years since I saw her. There was some duel fought over her in London, wasn't there.'

'That was a long time ago.'

'1799. The year *my* mother died.'

'Was it? I didn't remember. I'm sorry.'

'I was only five then – same as you.' Valentine screwed up his eyes as if in some effort of recollection. 'I think my mother was something *more*. I think she was beautiful. I remember her quite well. There are of course two portraits of her that hang at Cardew to remind me. Why do you not come and see them?'

'I'd like to,' said Clowance. 'In September, perhaps, before you go back to Eton?'

'And we'll have a Christmas party,' said Valentine. 'Will you also come to that?'

Just before the ladies rose George said: 'When may I call on you, ma'am?'

Harriet held a wine glass to her lips, letting the glass gently touch her teeth. 'I am busy this month.'

'Indeed.'

'Yes, it is a surprisingly busy time. Even though there is no hunting there is much to do. I lead a social life, Sir George.'

'I'm sure you do.'

'In the close-knit Cornish world one becomes too well known in too short a time.'

'Indeed,' said George again, more coldly.

After an appropriate pause, Harriet put down her glass. 'But August is easier. I could be free in August.'

'Then . . .'

'Is Saturday a suitable day?'

'I will make it so.'

'Come to tea on the second Saturday in August.'

'It will be a party?'

'If you wish it.'

'No, I do not wish it.'

'Very well,' said Harriet. 'Pray come at five. I shall be alone and will call in Dundee to act as chaperone.'

II

Ben Carter had been offered the post of underground captain at Wheal Leisure, to take effect as soon as there was anything substantial underground to supervise. He had always been one on his own, a solitary, and it was against his instincts to accept. But his grandfather added his persuasion to Jeremy's.

'Tedn't just any old job,' Zacky had said. 'I've worked for the Poldarks most all my life, an' shall be purser to this new venture if my health permits. I know your mother better prefers to keep her distance, but that be because of strange-fangled notions she have of her own and is no reflection. Indeed if you but ask her she'd tell ee the same. Captain Poldark put his health and position at risk trying to save your father.'

'Tedn that 'tall,' said Ben. 'There's no one in the land I'd sooner prefer to work for if I'm to work for anyone. Tis just that I've grown up to be my own man.'

'That I well d'know. An' it suits you, Ben. But if you live on your own an' work on your own *all* your life, like as not you'll end up not knowing where you're to. Half saved. Egg-centric. So my advice is, take this and see how you d'get on. Your fishing, your own mine – they won't run away. If things build up wrong you can always leave.'

'Yes,' said Ben thoughtfully. 'Reckon that's true.'

So for the time being he worked with the others in building the mine house and sinking the shaft. With 40s. a month coming in he was better off than he had ever been in his life. Not that he needed the money. He had a contempt for money and could have lived off the land.

One of the unspoken inducements to his working there was his chance of seeing more of Clowance. One of the dampening surprises was the discovery that Stephen Carrington was to work there also. There had never actually been words between them, but all Ben's hackles were raised when he saw Stephen assembling with the others one morning to begin digging the shaft. There was something about him he couldn't *stand*. Stephen was too big in his manner, too open-handed, too easy and too confident on nothing. What *was* he, for God's sake? An out-of-work sailor. Yet he might have been the youngest captain in His Majesty's navy the way he bore himself. And – the unforgivable sin – he had an eye for Clowance; and, horror of horrors, she seemed as if she might have an eye for him. Was it credible that she should be attracted by his big bold face and curly blond hair and expansive manner? Was it credible that Clowance, the clear-sighted, the candid, the down-to-earth and totally honest girl whom Ben revered, should be taken in by such a man?

To sink an engine shaft nine feet by nine feet required eight men in relays of four working six hours each. It was calculated that in the hard ground they were in it would take about a month to sink five fathoms. This meant that by the time the house was finished they would be down sixty feet, and if it took a further month to install the engine they would by then be below the lowest levels so far. It then remained only to link up by means of an underground tunnel.

Ben watched jealously how Stephen worked but could find no cause for complaint. Unfortunately for Ben the other young man was strong and willing and capable. Furthermore, Ben saw little of Clowance, for she was still avoiding Stephen. She took care to make her appearances when he was not at the mine or when there were others about.

Of course she knew she would have to confront him sometime . . . unless he should eventually get tired and clear off again. Did she want that? It certainly seemed that she wanted it. But, she asked herself, might it not be better to *send* him away, having confronted him, than just see him become discouraged and go of his own accord? There was anyway, in Jeremy's conversation, no hint of his thinking of going. Did she not perhaps, in her belief that she could dismiss him, send him away in disgrace, presuppose her having a greater importance in his life than she really had?

But a week before the dinner-party there was a meeting.

Daisy Kellow had called at Nampara in the evening and, hearing that all the men were at Wheal Leisure, had suggested to Clowance they should walk up. But when Daisy got there she found the dust from the work getting on her chest and retreated with Paul who had returned early from two days attending to his father's coaching work in Truro and had strolled up on his own. Clowance decided it was too early to go home, and the fact that Stephen was there wielding a pick could be no bar to her staying. So she stayed, rather obviously talking to Ben, and, when he was busy, to Jeremy, not totally ignoring Stephen but generally hovering out of speaking distance. They were building the second of the low walls to carry the cylinder beams. The ends of these beams would be lodged in the walls; but the platform would not be built on them until the house was otherwise finished. She expected Jeremy would walk home with her to supper but he said:

'Tell Mama I shall be another half-hour. I want to use the last daylight. D'you mind? Or stay if you like.'

'No, I'd better go. Otherwise they will be wondering.'

Ben came up to her shoulder. 'Come with you, shall I?'

'No, Ben, I wouldn't drag you away.'

'Twouldn't be dragging no one away. He's near complete.'

'No,' she laughed. 'See you in the morning.'

'Aye. I hope so.'

She slipped and slithered down the cliff path to the beach. The twilight stretched emptily over the wide sands. The sea was half-tide and quiet. A few pools reflected the sky's evening frown.

'Can I walk with you?' said a voice behind her as she was about to jump on to the sand.

Her nerves lurched. He must have seen her leave and at once downed tools. Or perhaps he had been leaving anyhow.

She said: 'I'm just going home.'

She jumped and he jumped after her. 'I know,' he said.

He fell into step beside her. She had tried to make her voice noncommittal, neither friendly nor cold.

He said: 'I've seen little of you, Miss Clowance.'

'Really? Oh . . .'

There was one light showing in Nampara, in her parents' bedroom. But lights in the parlour would not show from here; they were blocked off by a shoulder of grass-covered rock.

'I think you've been shunning me,' he said.

'Why should you think that?'

'In near on three weeks we've not seen each other once. Properly, that is. You did not come down to dinner when your folk invited me in. You're *indoors* so much, all this fine weather.'

'Am I?'

'You know you are. And – and when you come out you're always *with* someone.'

He had grown his hair longer since last year and it now touched his shoulders so that he looked more leonine than ever. But there was no surplus flesh – his face was quite thin.

He said: 'Did you get my letter?'

'What letter was that?'

'The one I wrote. Telling you I was coming back.'

'Oh yes.'

'And when I came back it was a mite misfortunate, wasn't it, that you should see me first with Miss Violet Kellow.'

'Why should it be misfortunate?'

He stopped, but as she did not stop he had to take some quick paces to catch up with her.

'I explained to Jeremy. Didn't he explain to you?'

'What was there to explain?'

'You know what there was to explain. Look, Clowance, I thought you were an honest girl . . .'

The sand here was pitted, ridged and corrugated just below the afternoon high-tide mark. Clowance frowned and patted some of the ridges flat with her foot, then went on.

He said: 'I explained to Jeremy. I didn't like to break in on you that night, that first night I came back, with me not knowing your father. And when I came to the bonfire you were chatting and laughing all the time with that fellow Carter. *And* looking at him. *And* looking at him . . . So I went to go home, back to Will Nanfan's to get an early night, and I just met Violet Kellow. She was mad to see the bonfire, though she'd got a fever and a cough on her that would have affrighted most girls. She was gay, hectic-like, headstrong. I felt sorry for her. I went along with her. She's a lively girl and pretty in her way. But she means naught to me. No more that that stone, there! *You're* the one I care about!'

Clowance did not like the picture she was presenting to herself, of a jealous girl stalking away, head held high, while the man followed. Yet to stop and have it out with him here on the beach was impossible.

She did stop.

'You ask me to believe that story!'

'It's God's truth!'

'And you expect me to care?'

'Well, of *course* you care, otherwise you'd not be angry! If it didn't matter twopence to you who you saw me with you'd – you'd just *show* you didn't care. You'd just be as friendly as when I left. Don't you see, you give yourself away?'

Clowance stared back at the lanterns being lit now about the mine. They flickered and winked against the cliff and the darkening sky. She looked towards them and drew comfort from them. They represented calmness, normality, friendship, an absence of pain. Similarly in the house ahead, her mother and father and sister were sitting down to supper. A known and loving family; no conflict, no distress. Between them here she was with this man, in a situation where cross-currents of emotion could sweep her off her feet. As if the tide had risen and was racing in. All sorts of anguish gripped her. Yet it was not all anguish or she would have turned and gone. She wanted at the same time to hurt him and to heal him.

Her own hurt was so strong. She said: 'All right, Stephen, I do care. You do mean something to me. How much I don't yet know. But something, yes. You tell me I mean something to you – '

'Everything.' He took a step towards her but she backed away.

'You say you care for me. Whatever your story about meeting Violet Kellow – whatever is the truth of it – it is not the way I should have behaved. If *I* cared – *if* I cared for you, and was coming back after a long absence and had not yet seen you, d'you think I should have gone off with the first man I met and spent all the dark of the night walking with him – on beaches and in graveyards? D'you think I should have shown how much I cared by doing something like that!' Her anger rose as she spoke, struggling to express the fierce, bitter distress in her heart.

'No,' he said. 'No. You're certain right. And I'm sorry, sorry. And maybe I don't deserve anything better than the cold shoulder. But I assure you, twas not meant that way. I – I do things on impulse, like, on the spur of the moment. She came out, and I said "Hallo, Miss Violet," and then I was saddled.'

'Was she saddled too?' Clowance asked, surprising herself.

'Now, now, you don't want to think anything like *that*! I was no more'n friendly! Why, curse it, a sick girl, you couldn't lay hands on her! It wouldn't have been fair . . .'

Having heard whispers about Miss Kellow, Clowance doubted this reassurance. Indeed, she was not sure about something in his voice which, because it was too soothing, abraded her sharp senses. Unfortunately for her cooler judgment, his close presence had a trancing quality that undermined reason. His teeth were good but there was one broken eye tooth which always caught her attention when he smiled. His hands were short-fingered and strong but not big, the nails cut close, kept clean in spite of his labouring work. His throat above the open neck of his shirt was columnar. The tawny hair curled about his ears like fine gold wire. The high cheekbones, firm warm mouth above a cleft chin; the blue-grey eyes, almost the colour of her father's but more open, the *experience* in that face, reflecting so much that he had seen and done, together with her knowledge that he desired her . . .

'Oh,' she said, 'it is all so *petty* . . . A *petty* quarrel over a *petty* adventure. I am not only angry with you but ashamed for myself. Let us leave it for a time. If you are staying . . .'

'Gladly, me love. Gladly I'll leave it, and, more than that, I'll forget it . . .'

He put his hands on her shoulders and drew her to him, kissed her, his lips moving sensuously over hers.

'You know there's no one but you – could never be anyone but you . . .'

'*Why* should I know that?'

'Because I tell you so. Don't you feel it to be so?'

He put his hand to the bow at the neck of her frock. She slapped his face.

He drew back, putting the back of his hand across his cheek. It had all been too fast, he saw that now, and cursed himself for making a wrong move. But his own temper was roused.

He said: 'That's something more for me to forget, eh? You've got strong arms, Miss Clowance.'

'I'm sorry if it is different with other ladies you have known. Do none of them have a mind of their own?'

He took his hand away and looked at the back of it, as if expecting blood.

'Strong arms . . . One day, Miss Clowance, I'll kiss them. And bite them. And lick them. That is, when you belong to me. When we belong to each other. I think it will happen. Don't you?'

He turned and left her, stalking silently and angrily away over the sand. She watched him until he disappeared.

While they had been talking the twilight had faded and it was dark.

Chapter Seven

I

Bereft of their womenfolk for three weeks, the Poldark household went along much as usual. The summer was a fair one and the wheat and the oats were cut early. Hay was ricked. Potatoes were drawn and stored. The apples and the pears and the quinces were filling and ripening. Turf and furze was cut and stacked for the winter. Altogether a poor time of year to be away from the farm – not to mention the hollyhocks – and Demelza had almost cried off at the last moment.

'No,' said Ross. 'This is the time to test the training you have given 'em. Everyone depends too much on you for the ultimate decision; and much more beside. Let 'em do it by themselves for once. And if the worst comes to the worst I shall be here to make sure the roof does not fall in.'

'Really it is two hands short. Clowance is as busy as I am in the summer.'

'All the more reason for you both to take a holiday.'

Demelza thought of the two trunks lying packed upstairs. 'And we have *spent* so much! It doesn't seem right – just for two weeks – when we are no longer so well off as we used to be.'

'No, it's a disgrace,' said Ross.

She eyed him carefully. 'But you told us to!'

'Would you have your daughter go into society dressed like a balmaiden? And as for you – could you possibly be allowed to look like a poor relation?'

'. . . The more reason for me not to go.'

'Anyway, Caroline has lent you both so much. Shawls, fans, reticules, favours.'

'And a veil, a parasol, a French watch, a capuchin cloak, a turban bonnet. *That* is quite disgraceful, what we have borrowed from her! Her drawers and cupboards must be empty!'

'She has enjoyed doing it. You know that. She is taking a vicarious pleasure in the whole trip. You must both try to enjoy it for her sake, if not for mine.'

'Oh, we'll *try*,' said Demelza. 'I promise we'll *try*.'

With both the women gone and only little Isabella-Rose to lighten their way Ross had more time alone with Jeremy. His son was out and about early and late, full of energy and enterprise, riding here and there on matters to do with Wheal Leisure; but it was all powered by some other fuel than the high spirits with which it had begun. Several times he thought to tell Jeremy of his conversation with John Treneglos riding home on the afternoon of Midsummer Day. But he felt it might seem that he was trying further to blacken the Trevanions and by implication Cuby in Jeremy's eyes. He remembered once as an eighteen-year-old boy when he had fallen in love for the first time, with a young girl from Tregony, that his father had tried to give him a bit of sage advice and how utterly he had hated it. Even his father mentioning the girl's name was like a foot bruising a lily. The very words destroyed the delicacy of the relationship they were offering counsel on.

Not, of course, that his father had been the most tactful of men. But was *he*? It seemed that he was out of step with Jeremy all along the line. And didn't all young persons resent their parents' involving themselves, even merely *interesting* themselves, in their love-affairs? Particularly a broken one.

Out of step with Jeremy? It still was so somehow, in spite of the decision to open the mine together. Nothing overt, certainly. Their day-to-day contacts were frequent now and not unfriendly. Ross had said nothing about the fishing trips, feeling it was Jeremy's responsibility to tell *him*. Jeremy still said nothing. Perhaps he intended never to say anything. Did he not suppose that Ross would be curious as to how he had acquired so much knowledge? And why the subterfuge, for God's sake? Were his father and mother ogres that he had to do this all by stealth? Or fools, to be so ignored?

Yet was this not the time, now, while they shared the house more or less alone, to have it out, to find out what was behind it all?

After supper on the first Tuesday Jeremy gave him an opportunity of a sort by making a passing reference to Caerhays.

Ross said: 'Horrie's father was rather in his cups the day we rode home from signing the agreement. I mentioned the name of Trevanion to him, saying you'd been over there, and he began to talk about them. Did you know they were related?'

'Who?'

'The Tregloses and the Trevanions.'

'No.'

So Ross repeated most of what had passed. When he had finished – and what was to be said could be said quite briefly – he waited, but Jeremy did not comment. His face expressionless, he helped himself to a glass of port.

'I thought you should know,' Ross said. 'For what good it is . . . This perhaps makes Major Trevanion's attitude more understandable – if no more admirable . . . I should have guessed something of the sort.'

'Why?'

'Well, money counts everywhere these days, particularly among the landed gentry of Cornwall, where by and large there is so little of it. Family is a consideration but fortune is a much greater one. It's the more regrettable in this case that people with so much property as the Trevanions should be in such a plight. It is not ill-fortune that has beset them but over-weening pride, the pretentiousness of one man in building such a place.'

'You say it makes Trevanion's attitude more under-standable. I don't think it does Cuby's.' A rictus of pain crossed Jeremy's face as he spoke the name. But at least he had spoken it, seemed prepared to discuss the matter.

'Trevanion's much older than she is. Eleven or twelve years, is it? For long enough he must have taken the place of her father. If her mother agrees with him it would be difficult for a gently-born girl to go against their wishes.'

Jeremy gulped his port. 'You haven't met her, Father . . .'

'No,' said Ross peaceably. 'Of course not.'

Jeremy poured out a second glass and looked across the table. Ross nodded and the port bottle came into his hand. There was a long silence, not a very friendly one.

'In what way should I revise my opinion?'

Jeremy said reluctantly: 'Oh, I don't know . . .'

'She's very young, isn't she?'

'Yes.'

'Doesn't that have a bearing?'

'She's young, but I do not believe she would be persuaded – even brow-beaten – into accepting their plans for her . . . unless she were willing.'

'She has an elder sister?'

'Yes. A sweet girl.'

'I mean . . .'

'I know what you mean, Father. But Clemency's very plain. I don't think she would attract rich men.'

'Even Cuby yet may not,' Ross said. 'However pretty and charming. Pray don't take that wrong. But there's a great dearth of young men in the county – or even old men – with large fortunes. Remember it is usually the other way round – the men who are the fortune-seekers. Trevanion will have to find someone not only with a considerable fortune but also willing to lend a substantial part of it to him, or to take over the house, or make some such arrangement. It won't be easy.'

Jeremy finished his port again. 'Are you trying to comfort me?'

There was anger in his voice, sarcasm.

'Well, it may be that now we know the true objection we can at least assay the situation afresh.'

'Find me a fortune and all will be well.'

'Ah, there's the rub.'

'But *will* it be well? If I went to India and came back a rich man, should I be enchanted to marry a girl who was marrying me only because I was the highest bidder?'

After a moment Ross said: 'You must not think too harshly too soon. As I said, there are family pressures, even on the strongest-minded of young girls. And it remains a fact that she is not married to anyone else yet, nor in any way attached. The best laid plans . . .'

Jeremy got up from the table and walked to the open window where the plum purple of the night was stained by the lantern shafts of Wheal Grace. A moth batted its way into the room, flying drunkenly from one obstacle to another.

'But I *do* think harshly.'

'Not more so, surely?'

'Yes, more so.'

'Then I'm sorry I told you . . . I think you're wrong, Jeremy.'

'You're entitled to your view, Father.'

'Of course.'

There was another taut silence. Ross was determined not to let Jeremy's anger affect him.

'There may even be a change in Trevanion's fortunes.'

The moth had reached the candle and, having singed itself, lay fluttering on the table, beating one wing and trying to become airborne again.

'And now,' Jeremy said, 'I think I will go to bed.'

Ross watched him cross the room, pick up an open book, find a spill to use as a bookmark. This was probably as unpropitious a moment as there could be for going on to the other subject, yet he chose to do so.

'Perhaps you will spare me a moment longer.'

'Father, I'm not in a mood to discuss this any more.'

'No. Nor I. It's essentially your own affair, and I mentioned it only because I thought you ought to know what John Treneglos had said. Something else.'

'We've both had a long day . . .'

'That day I was talking to John Treneglos he said something more to me. He said that these fishing trips you have been taking for so long were all a mask, a deception as it were for other ends. Those ends being regular visits to Harvey's of Hayle to learn the practical side of engineering and the properties and potentials of high-pressure steam.'

Jeremy put the book down again, closing it over the spill.

'Is it true?' Ross said.

'Yes, that's true.'

'What was the particular object in the subterfuge?'

'Does it matter?'

'Yes. I think it does.'

'Why?'

'Because it seems you have gone out of your way to hide this from me all along. And from your mother too. Your study of the theory of steam and steam engines, the books you've read, the letters you've written and received – and more particularly, the practical experience you've been gaining. You even told Dwight not to mention the books he was lending you. Don't you think I'm entitled to an explanation?'

Jeremy was a long time before he spoke again. 'You thought all such experimentation dangerous,' he muttered.

'When? Did I say so?'

'Yes. And you have never believed in the possibilities of strong steam.'

'I don't yet know what the possibilities are. Perhaps no one does. Certainly there are dangers.'

'So, when I showed an interest you told me to keep away from it.'

'Did I? . . . Yes.' With the corner of his spoon Ross lifted the moth, and it began to flutter around again. 'Yes, on recollection, I did. So you thought, what the eye does not see, the heart does not grieve. Is that it?'

'I had not thought of it in perhaps those disagreeable terms. But yes.'

'I suppose you realize it has put me in a false position?'

'I hadn't realized, no.'

'Well, as you've grown up, come to manhood, you have seemed to me to have too little purpose . . . interest, direction.'

'Does Mother feel the same?'

'Should she not? Of course your mother – like most mothers – tends to see only the best. I tried to. I told myself I was expecting too much too soon. But sometimes your way of treating things came to irritate me. In spite of efforts to the contrary. You may have noticed.'

'Yes.'

'Sometimes I have shown – or at least felt – less than admirable patience with what you have had to say. I don't think I'm altogether deficient in a sense of humour . . . but this – this aimless flippancy . . .'

'It's just a different *sort* of humour,' Jeremy said.

'Maybe. But you see, however flippant, it wouldn't have seemed aimless if . . . I find my judgments – opinions of you – call them what you will – were built on wrong information – or rather *lack* of information. Few things are more galling than to feel one has been . . . made a monkey of.'

'I see what you mean. If it's my fault I'm sorry.'

'Perhaps it does not matter that you don't sound it.'

'Well, would you have been better pleased if you had known I was disobeying your strict orders not to do what I wanted to do?'

'For God's sake, boy, are your parents tyrants that you have to scheme and lie to get your own way! Could there not at least have been a discussion on it?'

399

'You'd said no. What more could you say?'

'I'm not sure I meant it as irrevocably as you took it.'

'Well, I so took it.'

Ross said: 'I knew Francis Harvey well and liked him. If you have a boy who is just growing up and he shows a tendency to play with a dangerous thing which has killed a friend you say to him, "don't do that! you'll injure yourself." So I did to you with high-pressure steam, just as I would tell you to beware the vellows on the beach, or keep away from the cow just after she's calved, or don't go down that mine, it's been closed for years and the planks will be rotten. If when you grow older you don't understand that as a filial impulse, you'll make a bad father!'

'I think it was a little more than that.'

'It's hard to recollect my exact feelings after several years. Perhaps I was afraid of your becoming too fascinated by Trevithick.'

Jeremy blew out a breath. 'That's possible.'

Ross said: 'His inventions are so high-flying and then come to naught. The collapse of his demonstration in London, fascinating though it was, did not surprise me. Nor did the explosion that killed those men. And since then, what has he done?'

'The wonderful experiment at Pen-y-Daren, when his locomotive drew five waggons with ten tons of iron and carried seventy men a distance of ten miles. That was a marvel.'

'That was before the London experiment.'

'Maybe.' Jeremy was disconcerted at his father's memory. 'But it was still a marvel and has yet to be equalled.'

Ross said: 'Trevithick is now a sick man. Back in Cornwall and little advanced for all his years in London. As you told me, you were unable to get to see him.' He added as Jeremy was about to speak: 'That is not meant to be a prejudiced view. Nothing would please me more than to see him succeed triumphantly – '

'Mr Woolf,' said Jeremy, 'is just as committed to strong steam. Only he is not interested in developing the road carriage.'

'Well, I must ask myself then, was there any other reason apart from consideration for your physical safety that made me dislike the idea of your becoming involved on a *practical* level.'

'Does it matter now? Why ask these questions? What do you want me to do?'

'Nothing, of course. Except to take me into your confidence a little more freely.'

'I'm sorry again,' Jeremy said, but sulkily.

Ross said: 'It could have been an instance of false pride.'

Jeremy was surprised enough to look at his father.

'What, in you?'

'Yes, possibly. In spite of oneself one sometimes nurtures false notions of what a man of our position shall do. As you will have observed, throughout my life I have worked alongside my workers and cared not a curse for calloused fingers or dirty nails in seeing to the mine or farm. But studying the principles of steam and motion at a practical level is a little like becoming a – a refined blacksmith.'

'Does that matter either?'

'Well, what other young man of your position has wanted to do this? Quite different from standing by and taking an intelligent interest and encouraging the working inventor. It is somewhat akin to entering the forces without becoming an officer.' Ross put out one of the candles in an attempt to discourage the moth. 'Dear God, how consequential and old-fashioned this sounds! Pray don't think I agree with it; I am trying to explore my own motives and give them a public airing.'

Jeremy poured himself a third glass of port.

'I came across this view when I first went to Harvey's,

Father. Mr Henry Harvey was quite pleased to entertain me as the son of Captain Poldark who had called to look round his works; but he could not quite believe that I wished to work on the nuts and bolts. Twasn't *done*, my dee-ur!'

His lapse into the comic vernacular was a first sign of lessening tension.

Ross said: 'Even now I am not quite sure what the fascination is.'

'Of steam? For me, you mean?'

'Of course.'

Jeremy shut one of the windows and latched it. 'I must have told you this before.'

'Others perhaps. You never bothered to inform me.'

The young man raised his eyebrows at this bitterness escaping.

'It's too late tonight, Father.'

'I don't think so.'

Jeremy hesitated, aware of the clash of wills.

'Is this a condition of some sort?'

'Of course not. Of course not.'

Still he hesitated. 'Well . . . isn't it obvious? Strong steam is the most remarkable discovery since the wheel . . .'

'Is it?'

'Well . . . consider its power. And, unlike gunpowder, its peaceful uses are limitless. In the end it will provide light and heat and replace the horse and the sail. It will transform civilization!'

Ross said: 'For the better?'

'I believe so. Anyway its power has come to stay. We cannot turn back. If we don't develop it, others will.'

Ross looked at his son, who was now, much against its wishes, helping the injured moth out of the other window before he closed it.

'With Saturday's meeting coming on, it's important I should know as much on all this as I can.'

'But that's just it; I don't want the decision on the engine to be influenced in any way by my being your son! The choice should be made quite indifferently.'

'So it shall be. But let us be practical. Saving the presence of some complete outsider, some engineer from Truro or Redruth, the decision ultimately has to be mine. What do the Tregloses know? And the Curnows and Aaron Nanfan have already been consulted by you . . .'

'Mr Harvey and Mr West will be here.'

'Yes – I'm relying a good deal on that.'

There was a pause. Jeremy finished his port and inelegantly wiped his mouth on the back of his hand.

'Well, let us see when Saturday comes, Father.'

Ross put out another of the candles.

'Lately I have been looking again at our old engine at Wheal Grace, and I have been talking to Peter Curnow. You've made many unfavourable comparisons during the last weeks with what can be built now. But Beth was put up by Trevithick, or at least to Trevithick's designs. Have his ideas changed so radically in twenty years?'

'When Beth was built the Watt patent of his separate condenser had some years to run; and if other engineers infringed it they courted a lawsuit. Watt was pretty unscrupulous, wasn't he?'

'So I've been told.'

'At Grace we have a Boulton & Watt type of engine working at only a few pounds above the pressure of the atmosphere, with some improvements, of course, by Bull and Trevithick, and it is a good engine, will work for years if properly treated. There are many such about. Indeed many of them are working at far below their proper efficiency because of ignorance and neglect. I wouldn't say that about Beth. But her best is just not good enough.'

Ross put out the third candle. From the last he lit two carrying candlesticks.

Jeremy said: 'When the Boulton & Watt patent firstly ran out they took away all their experienced engineers and agents. Murdock left the year before, and so many mines depended on him . . . It seems as if for a few years there weren't enough Cornishmen to go round who knew the science of it or had the experience. Isn't that so? You must know it better than I do . . .'

'It was that, I suppose. And also there was no rivalry – Boulton & Watt against anti-Boulton & Watt. Whatever the reason, things fell apart for a while, I know.'

'But it didn't stop invention, did it. People went on experimenting. Of course the basis of the biggest advance lies in the high-pressure boiler and the new ideas incorporated in that; but there are others. Much of the advance lies in the accuracy of the manufacturing.'

'Which Harvey's seem confident of achieving.'

'Yes . . . Oh, yes. My – this engine for Wheal Leisure is not so different from others they have recently made; but as you will have seen from the measurements, it is *much* smaller than that at Grace. Yet you'll find it more powerful and much cheaper to run.'

Ross handed one of the carrying candlesticks to Jeremy. He thought of saying more but decided not.

'I wonder how your mother and Clowance are faring.'

'Very well, I should guess.'

'So should I,' said Ross.

In a state of embattled but increasing amity the two men climbed the stairs to bed.

II

On Saturday in a discussion that lasted from eleven till one it was decided to proceed with the engine designed by the chief venturer's son. Afterwards dinner was taken – a purely masculine meal – and then Mr Henry Harvey and Mr William West set off on their long ride home. Three times the following week the chief venturer's son rode to Hayle, twice with Horrie Treneglos as companion, the last time with Paul and Daisy Kellow.

There was, of course, nothing whatever to see as yet,

404

and in any event, even when completed, the engine would be shipped piecemeal – by sea, given the right weather – and would be totally assembled only on the site. Paul was chiefly interested in the road machine, and Daisy similarly, though there was precious little of this to see either, as Jeremy had warned her on Midsummer Eve. Still, she seemed to find enough to occupy her while Jeremy was deep in discussion with Messrs Harvey, West and Pole.

As they mounted to return home Daisy said to him: 'What does it all mean, Jeremy? "A neck joint to be made with a dovetail spigot and socket and iron cement?" Is that not what I heard you say?'

'I'm sorry, Daisy. I told you it was all very tedious.'

'Yes, but what did it mean?'

'Mr West believes that such heating tubes may sometimes crack but will never burst. Is that not of sufficient importance?'

She lowered her eyes. 'I'm sorry if *I* am tedious to you asking such stupid questions.'

'You could never be tedious.'

'Well,' she said, glimmering a smile at him, 'since St John's Eve you have given me little opportunity to be so.'

'Then it is my concern to be sorry, Daisy, not yours, for I have been so engaged with plans for the mine and for the engine that I have had little time for anything else.' Which was only true in so far as he had deliberately sought the absorption. He had come so close to seeking the counter-irritant of a love-affair with Daisy. But she was not a girl to be lightly had – or if lightly had not to be lightly discarded – and he had just retained sufficient common sense to perceive that taking another girl on the rebound was not the recipe for a happy marriage.

Even as it was the relationship was difficult enough; he genuinely liked her and found her good company. One side of him also wanted her. She was an altogether attractive young woman with a lively, challenging, sparkling manner and a pretty figure. He knew he only had to nod. So keeping her at a friendly distance without offending her was a matter of balance and a cause of frustrating self-restraint.

And all because of a girl who had discarded him and was waiting around to marry someone with money. His father, it seemed, had expected him to take comfort from what he had told him of the Trevanions' situation. He had found no comfort in it at all. The obstacle between him and Cuby was now greater because it was more assessable. Fundamentally the first objection had been ludicrously and offensively slight. But money was another matter. This was something you could set down on paper and add to or subtract from. To add to golden numbers golden numbers. It was a precise barrier which could precisely, but only in one way, be removed.

Jeremy saw no way whatsoever of even making a start to remove it. He had never previously felt any special desire to be rich. Of his two projects, the steam carriage would be likely to be years coming to practical fruition – if it ever did. As for the mine, that was a gamble; but unless they struck another Dolcoath it would be unlikely to put him in the category of rich man the Trevanions were looking for.

And if some miracle should occur, what, as he had said to his father, was the attraction of marrying a girl and into a family that only wanted his money?

So while he rode home with Daisy and joked with her and allowed a new little flirtation to develop, another part of his mind was allowing itself the brief luxury of thinking of Cuby – brief and seldom consciously permitted because it bred such bitterness and devastation in his heart. And as the day faded and he left Daisy and Paul at Fernmore with a promise that they should meet again on the morrow, so his last hopes, his last pretences faded too. It had to be faced. Life without Cuby Trevanion had to be faced – not for this week or for this year but for good. She was not for him. There must be other girls in the world. Daisy, even. But he could never see Cuby again. It would only tear him apart if he met her again. She was not for him – ever.

He was home before the sun set, but could not bring himself to go in. He felt so deathly tired and full of a misery and a pain more awful than before. He decided to walk up to Wheal Leisure, since this might for a few minutes take his attention away from himself. To one of the other men . . .

His father was there.

Jeremy's first instinct was to avoid him, to dodge away so that there was no risk of his own mood being perceived. Somehow his father knew him both too well and not well enough . . .

But he checked the impulse. Ross greeted him with a smile and a raised hand and went on with his inspection of the building. Presently Jeremy joined him.

At least something, Jeremy thought, had come out of this miserable week. That talk, that non-quarrel they had had, had somehow begun to clear the air. For the first time he had been able to see his father as a vulnerable man. Previous to this he had seemed so formidable, secure in his position and in his accomplishments. His father and mother were such a *pair* – complete within themselves, self-contained, they seemed capable of dealing with any problem or emergency. At that supper talk he was sure his father had pretended a lesser knowledge of the development of the mine engine than he really had. But nevertheless the nature of that pretence – if it was such – and the nature of the whole conversation had suggested . . . Perhaps his invulnerable father was vulnerable in one respect only – to the feelings and happiness of his children. It was a new thought.

The house was now up to the second floor. Even in its site on the lower shelf of the cliff it was already showing against the skyline. When it was finished, with its arched door and windows, its sharply canted slate roof and cylindrical brick chimney, it would conform to an architectural tradition that blended use and dignity.

After a while Ross said: 'Is something amiss?'

'No . . .' This question was just what he had been afraid of.

'I mean – more amiss than usual.'

Jeremy smiled wryly. 'No.'

Ross looked up at the building. 'She will look somewhat grander than Grace has ever done. When we put up that house we were living hand to mouth in all respects. Seeking, ever seeking copper and never finding it. I was negotiating with the venturers of Wheal Radiant to sell them the engine when we at last found tin. I remember Henshawe's face, how he looked when he brought those samples to show me . . .' He paused. 'Don't forget I can have a fellow feeling, Jeremy. I was once in the same boat.'

'What boat?'

'Perhaps I should more properly call it a shipwreck . . . I mean the boat of loving a woman and losing her.'

'History repeating itself . . . But you found . . .'

'Someone better, I know. But it's hard to think that at the time.'

Jeremy stirred the rubble with his foot. 'A pity Captain Henshawe left. He had the keenest eye for a lode.'

'Oh, and still profits from it. But the offer from Wales was too good. I could not stand in his way.'

'I think Ben will do well.'

'I hope so. It will come different when he has thirty or forty men to see to. There are many like him in the county – eccentrics by nature. It is an aspect of the Cornish temperament.'

'I don't think I like some aspects of the Cornish temperament.'

'Oh, if it is the aspect I think you're thinking of, it is not peculiar to Cornwall. Indeed, the further east you go the more pronounced it becomes.'

Jeremy said: 'Perhaps it is just human nature I detest.'

'Some parts of it, no doubt.'

Jeremy said suddenly, roughly: 'Did Aunt Elizabeth marry your cousin Francis Poldark because he had more money?'

Ross blinked. This was straight from the shoulder. But he had invited it.

'Her mother was minded that she should marry him. Elizabeth was much influenced by her parents. But also there was the report – or rumour – that I had died of wounds in America. When I returned she and Francis were engaged . . . It is a very complex subject.'

'All such subjects are, Father.' Jeremy gave a short laugh. Abruptly he turned away. 'Ben was a long time making up his mind to accept our offer. I think in the end it was on account of Clowance he took it.'

Ross frowned. 'What mystery now?'

'None . . . You – I expect you know that Ben has always been – well, lost for her.'

'I knew he was fond. Not to that extent.'

'Oh yes. I don't think he has any hopes, but he may feel that if other things do not work out and by some miracle – miracle for him – she should turn to him, he would have more of a position, be earning money of a sort, be more in step, as it were.'

After a moment Ross said: 'God, we are a wry lot.'

'I echo that.'

As they returned home the sand was soft, recently washed by the tide; their feet crunched in it like walking over new-fallen snow.

Ross said: 'Tell me, does Bella indulge in any courtship yet?'

'Only with her guinea pig.'

They climbed the stile from the beach and made for the house. Stephen was in the garden examining Demelza's flowers.

'Stephen!' Jeremy said.

'Ah,' Stephen nodded. 'Good evening to you, sir. I trust I'm not intruding, like.'

Ross nodded back. 'Not at all. Pray come in.'

'These tall flowers, sir; these spikes with little roses. I don't recall having seen 'em before.'

'Hollyhocks,' said Ross. 'My wife has a weakness for them, but they get badly treated by the wind.'

Stephen bent to sniff them. 'No smell.'

'Little enough. You wanted to talk to Jeremy?'

'Well, no, not exactly. I wanted a word with you, Captain Poldark, sir. With Jeremy too, if he's the mind to stay. It is just a matter of business, like. I thought to come and have a word wi' you.'

Ross glanced in at the window of Nampara. Mrs Gimlett was just lighting the candles. Isabella-Rose, not yet having seen her father's approach, was dancing round Jane Gimlett. What vitality the child had! Far more even than the other two at that age.

'Business?'

'Well, sir, it is this way. No doubt you know I have been working at Wheal Leisure.'

'Yes, of course.'

Stephen pushed a hand through his mane of hair. 'As you know, Captain Poldark, your son and I, we got well acquainted while you was away; and since I returned to these parts he has told me about Wheal Leisure and what he has planned to do. Well, I've faith in that, Cap'n Poldark, I've faith in that.'

There was a pause.

'Yes?'

'A few weeks ago I went down the mine with Jeremy, and working *in* a mine is not for me! I've never in me life wished meself out of a hole in the ground so quick! But I've been thinking of the venture, *as* a venture; and I'm a bit of a gambling man. You know how it is when you've a feel that something is going to do well? I think Wheal Leisure is going to do well.'

Ross said: 'And the matter of business is . . . ?'

Stephen came closer. He was carrying a small leather bag.

'The business is I'd like to invest in the mine. No doubt Jeremy will have told you that I sold me prize in Bristol. Not that I got what I should've, but I got a share. Well . . . Jeremy has told me you have shares to sell in Wheal Leisure. At £20 a share. I'd like two, if you please.'

The two Poldarks looked at each other. Jeremy made a slight lift of the eyebrows to indicate to his father that this was as much a surprise to him as anyone.

Ross said: 'The shares that are being offered to the public were advertised in the *Royal Cornwall Gazette* of July 13. As stated in the advertisement you would have to apply to a Mr Barrington Burdett of 7, Pydar Street, Truro. I do not know whether they will yet have gone. Of course I should have no objections to your investing, but I must tell you of the pitfalls. You look a young man of experience, Carrington, and worldly wise. But sinking money in a mine carries with it unique risks, and it wouldn't be fair to let you take those risks unwarned. It is all a little safer than staking your money on a horse or on the throw of a card, but not much.'

Stephen looked him in the eye. 'You're doing that, Captain Poldark.'

Ross smiled. 'I have been lucky once, but nearly came to bankruptcy first. Just say it's in my blood.'

'I'm a trifle of a gambler meself.' said Stephen. 'Life, I reckon, is not worth living if you don't take a risk. And working at the mine like I have been has got me interested. I happen to be down here. One way or another I've the hope to work around here. It's a feeling, like. If twere not for your son I'd not be alive, so I've the feeling he's me lucky mascot. So I'd like to take the gamble with me friends.'

Ross said: 'Perhaps Jeremy will have told you how this system is operated. Those who put money into a mine are called the venturers, and each deposits into the purser's fund in accordance with the number of shares he has taken up. If each share is provisionally valued at £20, then I must put in £100, and Mr Treneglos, Jeremy and Horace Treneglos the same. You if you bought two shares would of course pay £40. Wait . . . that is not the end of it. Every three months a meeting is held at which the purser accounts in his cost book for the money spent. When opening a new mine such as this it will be necessary to call for another similar amount to be put in at the first quarterly meeting. That doubles one's investment. There might well be another later. When a venturer can no longer find the money to pay in his share, or is no longer willing to, he puts his holding up for sale. If the mine by then has not been proved he may well have to sell at a very big discount. When enough of the venturers are unable or unwilling to answer further calls then the mine closes down. You understand this?'

'Pretty well,' said Stephen. He swung his little bag against his thigh. 'I reckon I can meet a second call. After that, twould depend on what I have done since. But – '

'My father,' said Jeremy, 'rightly points out the dangers. There is of course the happier side – when the venturers meet quarterly and it is the business of the purser only to distribute the profits. This he does on the spot: in gold, in notes, in bank post bills. I have often thought a successful venturers' meeting would be a suitable target for a highwayman, Father, for many of the venturers on such an occasion get as drunk as a Piraner.'

Ross was going to say something more but he was suddenly overwhelmed as Isabella-Rose came hurtling out of the house in a flurry of curls and ribbons and petticoats and threw herself at her father in great distress. 'Bella, Bella, Bella!' He lifted her in his arms and swung her round.

'Papa-a-a,' she bleated. 'Mrs Kemp says I may not stay up to supper because I have been r-r-rude to her! She says I *pinched* her, when I did *not*! I merely tweaked her skirt, and she says that was r-r-rude too! She wouldn't let me light the candles because she said I dropped grease on the carpet. Have you ever seen me drop grease on the carpet? Have you, Papa – *have* you?'

Ross kissed the delicate cheek, which he noticed was not at all tear-stained.

'My little Bella, Mrs Kemp is a very kind person who, while your mother is away, has *charge* of you, do you understand? Mama cannot be here, so Mrs Kemp is in – authority. Do you know what that means?'

'Yes, Papa, how strange of you to think I should not! But she says I *pinched* her, when I did not, and – '

'Bella, would it not be a nice thing to do: to say you are sorry to Mrs Kemp – oh no, I didn't say you *pinched* her – sorry for tweaking her skirt; and then, perhaps, if you said you were sorry for that, she might be persuaded to let you stay up to supper. See, we have Mr Stephen Carrington to supper, so do you not think you should run in at this minute and make your peace with Mrs Kemp?'

'Thank you, sir,' said Stephen Carrington, as the little girl, after an initial hesitation, went flying in.

'I cannot promise about the shares,' Ross said. 'Food we can guarantee.'

He went in ahead of the two young men. He thought while Clowance was away it would be a good time to see more of one of her suitors and to make up his own mind about him.

Chapter Eight

I

Mrs Poldark and Miss Poldark had been a week at Bowood. Having left Truro early on the Tuesday morning, they arrived at the great house when tea was being taken on Thursday evening.

Mrs Poldark had never been so nervous. There had been many occasions when she had had to face the landed, the rich and the noble, but nothing quite like this. Though far better equipped now than ever in the past in knowledge of the way to behave and the way things were done, this time, for almost the first time ever, she was without Ross. (She excepted in her mind the wild Bodrugan party of the early nineties because then she had been so angry and hurt she didn't care what the devil happened.) On all other occasions Ross had been at her side. Now he was endless miles away, and she was going to meet people she had never seen yet in her life and did not particularly ever want to see. Further, she was going to *stay*, which made it all much more difficult, and was accompanied by a lady's maid who, however sweet and courteous, was an oppressive complement to the party.

Nevertheless, hard as all this was, it could have been shrugged off but for one thing. This time it was not herself she might let down but her daughter.

A matter that concerned her more than a little was the question of accent. Almost as soon as she met Ross, long before he married her and while she was still his kitchen maid, she had listened attentively to how he spoke and had tried to copy his grammar. After they were married she had taught herself to read and write and her quick brain had assimilated everything he said. But while trying to speak correctly, and presently quite succeeding, she had taken less care for her accent. Living in the country where she did, and among countryfolk who knew all about her origins, it had seemed pretentious to assume an accent that was not her own. Of course over the years it had inevitably faded, by small degrees and by small degrees so that now there was comparatively little left. It was scarcely noticeable in Cornwall. Only on her occasional visits to London was she aware of the 'burrs' in her voice still. Even Ross, she suspected, had some. But his was the best of all accents, a resonant, educated voice with a faint regional intonation. Jeremy had more of a Cornish voice than Ross. Clowance's had an apparently unconscious habit of changing with the company she was in. But daughters, she suspected, were more often than not judged by their mothers. (Could it be, a hideous suspicion whispered, that this was precisely why she had been invited?)

They drove that first evening, it seemed endlessly, through a great deer park; and when at last they arrived, wheels crunching on the gravel, before a pillared mansion which itself seemed to go on for ever, she thought some big reception or ball was in progress. People in evening dress thronged the gardens in front of the house and milled about in the hall. It was still light, and somewhere music was playing, strings reedy and lilting in the distance among the conversation and the laughter.

They had hired a post-chaise from Bath, which Demelza had had the presence of mind to pay for in advance, so there was no embarrassment about settling for the conveyance while liveried footmen waited to take down the luggage. The three ladies alighted, Enid standing respectfully in the background with one of the smaller cases. An icy horrid two minutes followed while the luggage was unloaded and a few quizzing-glasses raised and some whispered asides behind fans. Then a tall, rather cumbersome young man ran down the steps.

'My dear Miss Poldark. Mrs Poldark, I assume. A privilege to us, ma'am, that you were able to come. Pray excuse the number of our guests. Thursday is a special day. Pray come in; I trust the journey was not too tedious; my aunt is inside and most anxious to welcome you; did you have rain on the journey? Hawkes, Harris, please see to Mrs Poldark's maid. Let me relieve you of that vanity case, Mrs Poldark. The servants will see to it all. What good fortune that you will be here for tomorrow. Miss Poldark, allow me . . .'

In the hall a stout, homely little woman was emerging from a group of people. Purple silk; a pince-nez dangled on the end of a gold chain and she carried an ear-trumpet. Lady Isabel Petty-Fitzmaurice.

'My dear Mrs Poldark. Miss Poldark. How good of you to travel all this way to see us! You must be fatigued. Eh? Alas, dinner has been over an hour. But you must have something to sustain you. Eh? Chivers, pray take Mrs Poldark and Miss Poldark to their rooms and see that a light meal is served to them there. Eh? Thursday is *such* a busy day here. But in one manner or another we contrive to be occupied *most* of the time!'

A pretty young woman dressed in shimmering white lace floated across to them from another group and absent-mindedly took their hands. But her welcoming smile encompassed them both as Lord Edward introduced them to his sister-in-law, the Marchioness of Lansdowne. In a chatter they were led upstairs and shown into a large bedroom looking over a lake with a smaller bedroom-dressing room leading off. Since the house was rather full, Lady Isabel trusted that they would find the two connecting rooms adequate.

Demelza, the ice all thawed, and instantly taken by the fat little woman, who reminded her of Aunt Betsy Triggs, found the words to offer their appreciation and graceful

416

admiration of the rooms and the view from the rooms; and in what seemed no time, though it was probably half an hour, Enid and another maid had unpacked and disappeared somewhere to eat downstairs while Demelza and Clowance took comfortable small semi-circular arm chairs and faced each other across a table on which were set half a salmon, a roast capon, an uncut ham, a syllabub, a bowl of fruit, a cheddar cheese, and three bottles of Rhenish wine.

'So we are here!' Demelza said, and smiled brilliantly at her daughter over the top of her wineglass.

Clowance, whose expression up to now had remained calm and rather impassive, gave a little ironical grimace of pleasure. 'It seems we shall not starve! Would it not be lovely if we could have all our meals up here!'

'First impressions,' said Demelza. 'Is it bad to take too much heed of first impressions?'

'Not if they are good.'

'Are not yours?'

Clowance laughed. 'Yes.'

'But so many people. Is this a house or a town?'

'Lord Edward explained it was open house on a Thursday. I don't quite understand what that means, except that tomorrow the crowds will be gone. It – it seems to be like a garden party to which almost everyone may come. The Lansdownes are here so small a part of the year, that when they *are* here this is what they do.'

Demelza helped Clowance to the salmon, and took some herself. 'How strange to have so much property that one must spread oneself so thinly! Your father, I fear, would say that it is not quite suitable that one family should own so much. Yet I confess they impress me more favourably than I had ever thought possible on so short an acquaintance.'

Clowance raised her glass. 'It may be all different tomorrow, Mama. So I think we must just drink to first impressions.'

'That I'll gladly do.'

They did it.

Clowance said: 'For the first time – or almost for the first time – I believe I am finding myself somewhat nervous!'

II

The good fortune Lord Edward referred to in their 'arriving in time for tomorrow' was that on Friday the house party went to the Races at Chippenham. They left at midday in dog-carts and chaises and a few more sober barouches, picnicked on the way and spent four hours on the course. Horses were inspected – three running from the Lansdowne stable – bets laid, races watched and cheered, more canary wine was drunk. Demelza was loaned a spy-glass the better to perceive which horse was coming first round the corner, and Lord Edward was assiduous in lending his own glass to Clowance.

The alfresco nature of the picnic and the general atmosphere of the racecourse was well suited for everyone to become acquainted with everyone else; no one was too much concerned to quiz his or her neighbour while there was unimpeachable bloodstock to take the attention. Demelza early confided into Lady Isabel Petty-Fitzmaurice's ear-trumpet that she had never been to a race meeting before, but this evidence of a neglected youth was later somewhat overborne by the fact that she seemed to know a good deal about horses, and animals in general, particularly their complaints. Clowance found two of the young ladies, the Hon. Helena Fairborne and Miss Florence Hastings, a little distant and patronizing; but otherwise it was a very pleasant and informal day.

Twenty made up the party to the races, and by the occasional reference to those left behind it seemed that there were another half-dozen or so guests at home. It was going to be difficult to make sure in a short time the exact position of various people who had been seen wandering around the house after breakfast, whether they ranked as guests or residents, as gentlefolk or as a superior echelon of servant. No attempt was made to divide the race party by sex or age; and indeed with the Marchioness herself only twenty-six and making herself the focus of attention there was little chance to do so. Lady Lansdowne was tall and fair and pretty and flittered vaguely about in loose flowing garments; but when she had occasion to approach you or speak to you direct she looked you in the eye with uncommon straightness and lack of affected dissimulation.

So, for that matter, did Edward. Clowance wished her father might have been here as well·as her mother, for where Demelza's judgments were native and intuitive, his refreshing prejudices added another dimension to the scene. If he said something that was clearly wrong, it gave Clowance a sounding board on which to try out her own judgments.

Demelza thought it probably a deliberate arrangement on the part of the Fitzmaurices to begin their house party with such an outing. Everybody entered into the day with considerable gusto, with some money won – Clowance eight guineas – and some money lost – Demelza four – and everybody warmed and eased with canary wine, and talkative, without regard to the precise social position of their neighbour, and tired on the way home – tired with wine and sun – and eating a comfortable dinner at Bowood without the need to dress, and very soon the ladies were yawning behind their fans and everyone went early to bed.

This, however, was not a typical day, and the typical day which followed conformed more nearly to Demelza's apprehensions.

Breakfast was at about nine-thirty – some two hours later than the normal hour at which the Poldarks sat down. At ten-thirty prayers were read in the hall by the chaplain, Mr Magnus, after which everyone drifted into the magnificent library to discuss plans for the day, or to listen to announced suggestions as to how the time should be spent. This day being Saturday, all the gentlemen went off shooting or fishing and did not return until five. With the custom of dinner growing ever later and supper ceasing to be important, a new meal called luncheon had been introduced at about one, to bridge the gap between breakfast and the formal meal of the day at six-thirty, for which everyone was expected to dress.

So Saturday, when sixteen ladies were left to their own devices, was the testing time. The day fortunately was fine and warm, so there was no need to sit indoors and play cards or work embroidery and make polite conversation. It was indicated that there were certain walks and certain drives which were more or less part of the ritual of a visit to Bowood, the walks describing an inner circle of the park, the drives a much wider circle when various follies and sights were inspected. The suggestion that these should be visited today was greeted with feminine cries of enthusiasm.

Looking down a gentle green slope upon the lake from the opposite side was a Doric Temple, and the tour was so arranged that all should reach there at about one o'clock when a cold meal was served and the ladies sat in wicker chairs under sunshades and ate and drank and chatted and admired the views and the flowers and the water birds.

'Pray, Miss Poldark,' said Miss Hastings, as she was being helped to wine, 'what would you be doing at this time of day if you were at home? For myself I swear I should not be enjoying myself one half so much!'

'On fine days in the summer,' said Clowance, 'it is our custom – my mother's and mine, and sometimes my father and my brother too if they are at home – to take a swim.'

'In the *sea*?' said Miss Fairborne. 'How quaint! But does it not upset one's . . . constitution? One's *arrangements* for the rest of the day?'

'I don't believe so,' said Clowance. 'We are usually busy all morning with matters dealing with our household, and, since it is our custom to dine somewhat early – before three

– it is quite delightful to plunge into the sea for half an hour first. One comes out – braced up . . . and glowing.'

'What a delicious picture,' said Miss Hastings, stifling a yawn. 'But, faith, I think I should be quite discommoded.'

'The Prince Regent has made it all the rage in Brighton,' said Lady Lansdowne. 'You are fortunate to have bathing huts so close, Miss Poldark.'

'Oh, we don't have bathing huts.'

There was a momentary silence.

'We have bathing huts at Penzance,' Clowance went on, 'but that is all of thirty miles away.'

'Then pray tell us the mystery,' said Miss Fairborne. 'Do you use *caves*?'

'We can,' said Clowance, 'but seldom do, for the house is so close. It is a simple matter to wear a cloak.'

'But are you not then liable to be *observed* by the local commoners?'

'There are few commoners to observe anything, and those that are are our tenants.'

(Well done, thought Demelza; so my daughter is not above making things sound for the best.)

'How diverting,' said Miss Hastings. 'To have a house so near the sea one can use it as a bathing hut! I trust the sea never *invades* you, does it?'

'We sometimes have the spray on our windows. But it is not at all dangerous, I assure you.'

'And when you are bathing,' said Miss Fairborne, 'pray what sort of cap do you wear to keep your hair dry?'

'Oh, we don't wear caps,' said Clowance. 'One's hair dries very quickly in the sun.'

There was an intake of breath.

'Ugh! But does it not all become infamously *clogged* and *sticky*?'

'Little enough. It easily washes out later.'

'Some people drink sea water for their health,' interposed Lady Lansdowne. 'It was all the craze a year or so ago.'

Demelza had been nervous lest Clowance should be asked what sort of costume they wore. Not liking personally either to bathe naked or to wear the extraordinary jackets and petticoats illustrated in the fashion papers, she had devised her own costume, which was like a Greek *chiton*, sleeveless, short, and caught at the waist with a piece of cord. She felt that if the ladies here had seen such a garment they would have been greatly shocked.

After luncheon they all visited the Hermit's Cave, which was dank and unimposing compared to the various sea-made hermits' caves which existed at the further end of Hendrawna Beach; and then a splendid Cascade falling in three thunderous tiers – man-made like the lake, but no less beautiful for that. There was also a Lansdowne mausoleum.

In and out of their chaises the ladies stepped with their sweeping frocks and their gaudy parasols, like a flutter of butterflies, laughing and talking and exclaiming at the attractions and peculiarities and beauties of each scene in turn. It was not boring to the Poldarks, for the things to be seen were indeed pretty or odd or interesting; but it was a trifle embarrassing because the other ladies had so much quicker a wit for expressing, however artificially, their pleasure and fascination. Demelza and Clowance seemed always a little to lag behind in finding the words to say so. Once or twice Demelza put in a quick remark ahead of the others, but it was hard work and desperate.

Dinner was the great event of the day and Saturday the first day of their stay when it was to take place with full formality. The ladies were expected to retire at four o'clock to prepare for it and then to come down at six in the utmost finery for polite conversation before 'the procession' from library to dining-room. Lady Isabel, in explaining this to Demelza, said that in the old days of not so very long ago the couples had moved simply from the small drawing-room to the dining-room; but this procedure had been abandoned because it wasn't far enough to walk – it didn't make enough of a 'procession'. She added in an aside that there was another advantage: if the men made a lot of noise when left on their own after dinner, the ladies would not be disturbed by it in the more distant library.

Since it had never in her life taken Demelza more than half an hour to prepare for the extremest function, she spent the first hour writing to Ross and part of the second hour helping Enid to help Clowance.

So far, she thought, their clothes had passed muster. At the races their attire had been a little more sombre than the others and today they had lacked ribbons and laces; but no matter. This evening would be far more important. Not again, if one believed Ross, that matching extravagance with extravagance was all. Good breeding was what counted – and looks and wit and elegance, in which, Ross was confident, they could not find themselves at all deficient. It was all very well for Ross. He was born with an absolute knowledge of where he stood in the world; not everyone had that advantage. Why couldn't *he* have come, presenting his daughter at such an aristocratic house party as this?

Well . . . Caroline had made them spend money – and when Mistress Trelask had been ignorant of the latest trends, or barren of ideas, Caroline had provided them. So Clowance was going down tonight in a Grecian round robe of fine Indian muslin. It had a demi-train, and robe and train were trimmed with a silver fringe. The sleeves Mistress Trelask had called Circassian, and the bosom was trimmed *à la Chemise*. Her hair was dressed rather flat but with curls on the forehead and the fullness of it confined behind with a row of twisted pearls. She wore white satin slippers with silver clasps. She looked, Demelza thought, so beautiful she could hardly be true.

As for herself, as befitted a middle-aged matron, her gown was much more sober, being of Scandinavian blue satin, confined with a cord, and silver buttons all the way down the front.

When they eventually went down Demelza was led in by Mr Magnus, the chaplain, and Clowance by Edward. The dinner went well and was followed by music and cards; but on this evening it was the gentlemen who were swallowing their yawns, and again almost everyone retired early.

Sunday was much the same, except that the gentlemen stayed around, and there was a church parade and other religious matters; but on Sunday evening Clowance was led in by Lord Lansdowne himself – a considerable honour – and her mother by an officer called Colonel Powys-Jones, who was on leave from Portugal and recovering from wounds sustained at Barrosa. Demelza, whose hearing was not of the worst, had heard Colonel Powys-Jones ask who she was the evening before, and to comment on her being a damned pretty woman, so it seemed likely that the arrangement was at his request.

Powys-Jones was about forty-five, short, trim and staccato. His hair was cropped close – 'get used to it; keeps the lice out, ma'am' – his evening garments shiny with use, his skin was yellow – 'thank the Indies for that, ma'am'; but he had an eye as sharp as a cockerel's and with much the same ends in view. (Not that anything scandalous could occur under this so highly respectable roof; but the idea was there.) Demelza with her bright dark eyes, her beautiful mouth and fine skin, was just his cup of tea. That she had a daughter here of nearly eighteen made it all the more interesting. As for Mrs Poldark's feelings, Mrs Poldark had known a fair number of Joneses in her life, and had tended to look on the name of Jones as rather an ordinary one; but apparently the Powys in front of it invested it with some mystic Celtic significance which she didn't, although herself a Celt, at first altogether understand. The Powys-Joneses, it seemed, were in some way descended from the Glendowers and Llewellyns of Welsh regality.

The Colonel told her all about this over dinner while Demelza half listened and half tried to observe how Clowance was faring with their host. Clowance was wearing her second frock tonight, a fine scarlet brocade, which flattered her fair hair and skin. (They had brought only five dinner frocks for Clowance: Caroline had said this was enough, but Demelza was a little concerned about it.)

The Marquess of Lansdowne was a better-looking young man than his brother, perhaps a little too precise, a little too long-necked for perfection; but obviously a very *good* man, intelligent, serious, and conscious of his position only in so far as it spelled out his responsibilities. Little more than a year ago he had been Lord Henry Petty, member of parliament for Camelford, with a distinguished but not necessarily successful parliamentary career ahead of him. Then, because of the death of his half-brother without issue, all this. A marquisate, a large estate and other possessions, three parliamentary seats, an income of twenty-six thousand pounds a year. It took one's breath away.

And a younger brother? Little perhaps in proportion, but he would scarcely be anything but wealthy. What did one wish for one's daughter? Certainly not, certainly *never*, position at the expense of happiness.

But what were the other choices open to her? (Unless she really wanted to, did she have to make *any* decision so soon, while only rising eighteen?)

Was she in fact going to be *asked* for any decision? Perhaps Lord Edward brought many such young ladies here. Perhaps the week would end with the announcement of his betrothal to the Hon. Helena Fairborne, daughter of Lord Fairborne of Tewkesbury. (He was being very attentive to her at this moment.) Or to Miss Florence Hastings, a cousin of the Earl of Sussex. Or did one have to think of the house party in matrimonial terms at *all*? Why

425

should young people not meet without so much absurd speculation?

'Please?' she said to Powys-Jones.

'You've got a soldier husband, I'm told. And a nephew, what, in the 43rd? Damn fine lot, Craufurd's Light Division. Black Bob, they call him. Saved the day at the Coa. Though Wellington was angry with Bob that day. Your husband still abroad?'

'No, he returned home a few months ago.'

Powys-Jones grunted his disappointment. 'You must come and visit me after you've done here. Tis but a day's ride west into Radnorshire. Or mayhap in a coach you would be more comfortable with a day and a half.'

'That's kind of you, Colonel. But you will observe I am with my daughter.'

'You must have been a child bride, ma'am, but God damn the world, bring her as well! I have two lazy sons who'd maybe smarten up a bit at the sight of her. Or you. By damn, or you, ma'am – '

'My husband is expecting me – '

'Oh, fiddle to husbands. After ten years of marriage, what are husbands for? Just to give you a name and a position and a place to live. Pieces of furniture, that's what husbands are – '

'But must you not be one yourself?'

'Was, ma'am, was. Then the lady took it on herself to fly away with my cousin: stupid young oaf; I hope he's got what he deserves. As for tomorrow . . .'

'Tomorrow?' Demelza raised her eyebrows at him. 'Who mentioned tomorrow?'

'I did this minute. You shall come a drive with me.'

'Is that a command?'

'Yes.'

'As one of the 43rd?'

'By damn, yes, if it pleases you.'

'Colonel, I could not. Think of my reputation.'

'Your reputation, ma'am, in the company of an officer and a gentleman, will be in safe hands. Have no fear.'

'And you think our hostess would approve?'

'I'll make damn sure she does.'

'And my daughter?'

'What has she to do with it? Don't say she has such care for her mother. No child is so unnatural.'

'She's devoted to her father.'

Colonel Powys-Jones shrugged. 'Still damned unnatural. Hate family ties. People, in my view, ma'am, should procreate and then separate.'

'It sounds like making cream.'

'Cream?'

'Cornish cream. You heat it up and then you separate it.'

'I know what it is you want, ma'am.'

'What?' Demelza asked provocatively.

The Colonel hesitated and then did not dare say what he was going to say. Instead he looked injured.

'You don't *trust* me. That's the truth of it. You think I am some blackguard from the Welsh marches with designs on your honour, that you do!'

Demelza took a piece of bread. 'As to the first, no, sir. As to the second, haven't you?'

The Colonel sputtered a little food into his napkin trying to conceal a laugh. 'By God, yes.'

Dinner went elegantly on.

Chapter Nine

I

All through the meal Lord Lansdowne had chatted at intervals with Clowance. He led her on, encouraging her to talk of her likes and dislikes and putting seemingly interested questions about life, and her life, in Cornwall. It was, she told herself, the natural good-mannered exercise of a practised host. Only the peculiar circumstances of their visit suggested to her that – since Edward lacked parents – it might also be the inquiring mind of an elder brother concerned to discover more about this young provincial girl Edward was interesting himself in. Was Lord Lansdowne – like Major Trevanion – *in loco parentis*? Would she – like Jeremy – presently be shown the door?

Having talked considerably about her father – on which they were in splendid accord, since they both thought so well of him – conversation moved to her brother, and Clowance mentioned his interest in steam. Amusement getting the better of her shyness, she told of the fishing trips which had puzzled them all, and what he had been really about.

Henry Lansdowne smiled with her. 'When he knew the truth, your father was not at all displeased?'

'I do not know whether he has yet heard! But had my brother asked permission before going I doubt whether my father would have given it. We are all a little nervous as to the risk.'

Lord Lansdowne said: 'In the winter this house is heated by steam. I have recently had it installed.'

'*Really*, sir? I will tell Jeremy. He'll be excited to know it.'

'In the morning I will take you into the cellars and show you how it works. Then you may explain to your brother.'

'Thank you, my lord. That is very kind.'

Lansdowne took a half spoonful of syllabub, savouring it for flavour.

'When this war is over, Miss Poldark, I believe we shall be on the brink of great new developments. The French have undergone a political revolution. Even if Napoleon falls they will never be able to restore the *ancien régime*. Or put the clock back. We in this country, partly by our inventiveness, partly as a result of the war, are undergoing a mechanical revolution of which steam is an important part. I believe it will transform England. All Europe is crying out for our manufactured goods. When they are allowed to buy them there will be a great wave of prosperity running through England. Even though times are so bad, so desperate in the Midlands and in the North, it will change. And although there will be many to decry such developments I believe the ordinary man, the working man, the farm boy who has left home to work in the factories – I believe they will *all* have some share in this prosperity. There will of course still be misery and poverty and injustice, but I believe the *level* will rise. Not only the level at which people live but the level at which people *expect* to live. We are on the brink of a new world.'

Clowance smiled at him. 'I'm sure my brother would be happy to hear what you say, sir. I'm sure he would agree with it all.'

'Perhaps one day,' said Lord Lansdowne, 'we shall meet.'

Which was very gracious of him and suggested that he did not find his dinner companion objectionable to his taste.

The following day was wet, but on the Tuesday, with cloud and sun alternating over the great park, Colonel Owen Powys-Jones returned to the attack and had his way by taking Mrs Poldark for an extended drive. But Demelza also had her way and Clowance came with them. Not only Clowance but Lord Edward Fitzmaurice as well.

They went in an open barouche – not at all what Powys-Jones really wanted; he had had ideas of driving Demelza at a cavalry gallop behind a pair of greys in some light curricle or other; but with four of them it was all far too sedate, and a coachman into the bargain. However, he soon recovered his temper.

'Here, by God,' he said, 'here on this hill your Cornish folk under Hopton and Grenville gave as good as they got in a fine stand-up affray against that damned Presbyterian, Waller, but Grenville died and tis doubtful to this day who was the victor – though Waller it was who withdrew. They say both sides was so exhausted twas a matter of chance which retreated first. Now if we get back into that carriage I'll take you as far as Roundway Down where the Roundheads were really given a beating. Prince Maurice had ridden hard from Oxford and arrived just in time to turn the scales.'

Edward Fitzmaurice said to Clowance: 'We were not here in those days.'

'Which days?'

'Of the Civil War. I think the estate belonged to a man called Bridgeman. Our family has only been here about sixty years. The house was then unfinished. My father really made it what it is today.'

'Are you Irish?' she asked.

'Why?'

'The name of Fitzmaurice sounds . . .'

'The Pettys were drapers in Hampshire. But a clever one

became a professor at Oxford and *he* went to Ireland and acquired an estate there. His son married the daughter of the Earl of Kerry and *their* son inherited, and so the two names became linked and have not since been separated . . . But tell me of your own.'

'My own name? Poldark? I do not quite know. Someone came over with the Huguenots and married into a Cornish family called Trenwith. And then . . .'

'So we are very much the same, Miss Poldark.'

'Are we?'

'Are we not?'

'Well, no; for you have great properties and great possessions. We have little of either.'

'I meant in that the families are blended in rather the same way. But I would point out, Miss Poldark, that the properties and possessions belong to my brother. I am relatively poor. My own house, Bremhill, you must come and see tomorrow – '

'Har – hum!' Colonel Powys cleared his throat. 'We are waiting for you, Fitzmaurice.'

'I beg your pardon.' Lord Edward whispered to Clowance: 'Have you ever practised archery?'

'No. Never.'

'We have a range. No distance from here. I wonder . . .'

'What?'

'If they would excuse us from this longer trip . . . Colonel Powys-Jones.'

'Sir?'

'I wonder if you might excuse us from coming with you to Roundway. I had thought – '

'Gladly, dear boy – '

'What is this?' asked Demelza alertly.

'Mrs Poldark, it happens we are very near the archery range, and I thought your daughter might like to try an arrow or two. I confess I am merely a beginner myself and could very well instruct myself as well as her. But you and

431

Colonel Powys-Jones could proceed to Roundway as arranged and pick us up on the way back . . .'

'Archery,' said Powys-Jones, rubbing his chin. 'Ah yes, archery. Where is it?'

'Just over the next hill. My brother Henry is proficient at it, and it is, I believe, a skilful sport, but I have had little time to play.'

'You have a lawn or something?'

'Oh yes, we have a special lawn. It is all set up. If you would care to take Mrs Poldark as planned to Roundway . . .'

Machinery worked for a moment or two inside the Colonel's shaven head.

'Then we shall all go,' he announced in his usual military way, commanding the expedition.

'Go where?' asked Demelza.

'To try our hand at archery. Damned good idea, I would say.'

'Sir, there is simply no reason for you and Mrs Poldark to alter your arrangements,' said Edward, clearly put out. 'I had only thought that for myself and Miss Poldark . . .'

'Nonsense,' said the Colonel. 'Very interested in archery myself. Very agreeable exercise. How about you, ma'am?'

'Well,' said Demelza, astonished at the Colonel's change of front, for she had thought this division would have suited his purpose, and feeling some sympathy for Edward's wishing to have Clowance to himself for a few minutes, 'Well . . . I confess I had hoped to see Roundway. You have told me yourself, Colonel, of this battle, and I had been much looking forward to seeing the site and hearing your further description . . .'

'Go tomorrow,' said Colonel Powys-Jones.

'But, Colonel, today is a delightful day for a drive.'

'Nonsense . . . Beg pardon, ma'am, but look at those clouds. Any moment now, might be heavy rain. Then where should we be? No . . . Archery. Agreeable exercise. Ever tried it, ma'am?'

432

'No. I know nothing of it.'

'Then you shall be instructed too. Very simple sport, shooting an arrow. Little or no skill required.'

In curious disarray they proceeded to stroll up the hill, Edward biting his thumbnail in chagrin, Clowance walking sedately beside him, fanning her face gently with a pink glove, Powys-Jones extending an arm like an angle iron for Demelza to lay her finger-tips on, and the coachman and the barouche making a detour up a narrow track to be ready for them when they next had need of him.

It was only when they came upon the archery lawn that the mystery of the Colonel's change of mood was solved. Edward took out the bows and arrows from the pavilion and proceeded to fire a few practice shots at the target and then invited them to try. Instruction, it seemed, was a very intimate affair. Demelza could see that Edward, while touching Clowance frequently in the course of his teaching, was indeed behaving impeccably. Colonel Powys-Jones was not. His object clearly was to hold Demelza altogether within his arms while one hand held hers in the bow guard and the other guided her to pull back the string of the bow. Since the instructor was an inch shorter than the instructed the attempt was not a great success, except for the Colonel himself. The first of Demelza's arrows went winging up into the air and missed the target by some forty feet. Starlings rose.

Having her hat pushed out of place, Demelza took it off and dropped it on the grass.

'Really, Colonel, I think twould be better – '

'Nay, hold still, look you. You almost got it then. Allow me.'

The lesson went on, with Demelza taking what evasive action she could. Clowance's second arrow was dead on target but died and took the ground ten feet short.

'Bravo!' said Edward. 'A truly splendid attempt! If we can get the bow a little higher . . .'

'Let Mama have another try.'

Demelza's second arrow went off in quite the opposite direction from the first. This time some sheep scattered. Colonel Powys-Jones licked dry lips with satisfaction and squeezed her arm.

'Once more, m' dear . . .'

Demelza said: 'I wonder why all the sheep round here wear black leggings.'

'Oh, they're not leggings, ma'am,' Lord Edward said. 'It is the breed – ' He stopped.

Clowance bubbled with laughter.

'I beg your pardon,' Edward said to her. 'Your mother . . . I never know quite when she is serious.'

'It has long been a trouble for us all,' Clowance said.

'The trouble for me at this moment,' said Demelza, 'is that the next arrow is entangled with my skirt, and unless the Colonel allows me I will have to tear the stuff or shoot my own foot.'

'Nay, ma'am, I am simply attempting to aid the general direction of your aim! . . . Have a care! See, have a care or the arrow head will scratch your pretty arm. Pray do not remove the guard!'

Given a half chance, Demelza stepped delicately out of his grasp. 'Do you show us, Colonel. There is nothing better for instruction than a good example. Every church commends it.'

'Yes, yes,' said Clowance, coming to her rescue. '*Please*, Edward. It is very warm this morning. Let you two gentlemen hold a contest first, while we learn and admire.'

So in the middle of the green midday, among the hum of bees and with a few lazy birds twittering in the sultry bushes, the two men took off their jackets just as if they were preparing for fisticuffs and shot twenty arrows each for a purse of ten guineas.

In spite of Lord Edward's disclaimer he had the better eye and won by eleven to five, the other four arrows having missed the targets.

Then, money having changed hands, they all sat

together on a stone bench, talking and gossiping until it was time to return to the house for the new meal of luncheon.

While they tidied their hair, Enid having been rapidly dispensed with, Clowance said to her mother: 'Aunt Caroline warned me of this.'

'Of what?'

'She said, have a care, Clowance, have a care lest your mother does not cut you out from all the best attentions by all the best men. It is not her fault, poor woman, she cannot help it.'

'Your Aunt Caroline might have thought of some better advice than that,' Demelza said breathlessly. 'Best, indeed! Would you include Colonel Powys-Jones among the best men? And I request you, have I for one moment *encouraged* him?'

'I should need thought and time to answer that, Mama. But it is not only the Colonel. Look at Mr Magnus on the first night. And Sir John Egerton. And that other man, that young French aristocrat, de Flahault.'

'Dear life, he's young enough to be my son! Or nearly,' Demelza conceded.

'But old enough to be something else.'

'Oh, he's French. Many of them are like that.' Demelza thought of two beautiful Frenchmen she had known sixteen or so years ago, dead long since in an abortive landing on the Biscayan coast, a landing in which her husband had risked his life and her brother nearly lost his.

'All the same,' said Clowance, 'I fully realize for the first time why Papa has to keep you hidden away in Nampara.'

'I conceit you realize,' said Demelza, 'how unbecoming it is in a daughter to offer such remarks to her mother. Far better to consider your own situation.'

'But I am doing so! I am sure you have only to look at Edward in the right way and he will be following you instead of me. Oh, how this tangles!'

Demelza put her comb down. 'Serious, Clowance. Just for a moment. Does it prosper?'

Clowance stopped and stared out of the window. 'Do you want it to prosper?'

'I want *you* to prosper.'

'Ah.'

'And is that different?'

'I wish I knew. I am . . . not in love with him.'

'Are you in love with someone else?'

A shadow crossed her face. 'No-o . . .'

'And is he – Lord Edward, I mean – do you think him serious?'

'The way he looks, I suspect he is.'

'I suspect that also . . . What were you whispering about just before we came in?'

'He was simply saying that he was glad I had at last called him Edward instead of Lord Edward.'

'I don't know the niceties of these things.'

'Well, it was really all your fault,' said Clowance. 'I was so concerned to rescue you from the clutches of your Welsh colonel that the name slipped out unthinking!'

'I see I am to be blamed for everything.'

'He has also asked me to visit his own house. It is quite near here, it seems, and was owned by the Lansdowne family before they bought this estate.'

Demelza put her fingers down the side of her frock to be sure it was straight and in order. 'Clowance . . .'

'Yes, Mama?'

'I don't know how to say this. Or perhaps it is not necessary. Perhaps it is already understood.'

'Well, I do not mind if you put it into words . . .'

Demelza still hesitated, looking at her daughter. 'Clowance, if it should come to some decision that you have to make, don't be influenced . . .'

'By what?'

'I don't want you to be influenced in his favour by the knowledge that Lord Edward is a nobleman and rich and possessed of many things that you would not otherwise ever have.'

'No, Mama.'

'So that means also do not either be prejudiced *against* him because he is the possessor of these things. You have so much of your father in you, and you know well the feeling he has about such matters as wealth and privilege. I – I do not suppose he married me just because I was a miner's daughter, but I believe the irony must have pleased him . . . Yet he is as stiff-backed as the rest in some ways, as you well know . . . It seems that he approves of Lord Lansdowne because they pursue the same ends in Parliament. Therefore . . .' She stopped and looked at Clowance for a long moment. 'Try to judge this as best you may – by your own thoughts and feelings and likings and by the feeling of warmth in your heart and the perception of such warmth in his. Love may grow. But above all try to think of nothing but *Edward* . . .' She shrugged. 'Impossible, I know.'

'But such a marriage – if it came to that – it would make you happy?'

Demelza hesitated. 'I should be happy for the circumstances. But not, Clowance, if they did not please you. I should be happy in the circumstances, yes. What mother would not?'

Clowance began to pull again at a knot in her hair.

'Anyway, I am certain it is all fanciful, Mama. Edward, I am sure, has young ladies here by the score – and teaches them all to shoot arrows. Tomorrow when I go and see his house it will be part of a tour arranged for all the guests at the same time. We shall go home happily together next week having had nothing more important to decide than which hat to wear for the journey!'

'Are you looking forward to going home?'

Clowance thought a moment. 'No. I believe I am enjoying it here.'

'So I think am I.'

Clowance said: 'I saw you invited to play billiards last night. Was it Sir John Egerton?'

'Yes.'

'How did you refuse?'

'I told him I should surely tear the table.'

'Do you suppose, Mama, that instruction in billiards involves such intimacies as instruction at archery?'

'Not with the other ladies looking on.'

III

Demelza had never played whist until Jeremy grew up and developed a temporary passion for it; then both she and Clowance were persuaded to take a hand in order to set up a table at home. Thereafter she had played occasionally when Ross was home. So neither she nor Clowance was able to deny all knowledge of the game and they were drawn in to play on one or two evenings. Clowance, who generally feared nothing, was thrown into a panic by these games and was fairly trembling as she played the cards. Demelza was twice partnered by Powys-Jones and hoped her occasional gaffes would spoil a beautiful friendship; but nothing seemed to injure his high opinion of her. Two evenings there was music, and two evenings music for dancing. These were the least constrained, although, since there were never at the most more than nine or ten couples on the floor, those who danced were not exactly lost in the throng. Clowance for once was grateful for the tuition she had received at Mrs Gratton's, and Demelza, though she did not know the best steps, was light enough of foot to get by. They were pleasant evenings on which one was conscious of being observed but not conscious of being weighed up or criticized. A great deal of the credit for this went to Lady Lansdowne, who, although herself the daughter of an earl, wafted around with an unstudied and absent-minded charm that somehow prevented the starch and stiffness which would have ruined the occasions.

The visit to Bremhill passed off with two other guests, happily but noncommittally. Thursday was another open day; and Friday brought a further visit to the races; on the Saturday, amateur theatricals in which Clowance was persuaded to take a part.

Barefoot Clowance, Demelza thought, thundering across the beach on her black horse at a breakneck pace, blonde hair flying; tomboyish, frank of speech, running away from school simply because she found the curriculum tedious, incapable it seemed of the frivolous chatter in which elegant young ladies were expected to indulge, now preparing to appear before this sophisticated audience playing some character called Maria out of a play named *The School for Scandal*.

Her part, when it came to it, was the most difficult to sustain because the others could make themselves into caricatures, while she had to appear almost as herself. She was loaned an old-fashioned frock of cream and yellow satin, flounced, tight-waisted and of low decolletage, which reminded Demelza of her own first ball frock of nearly a quarter of a century ago. Little powder or paint, but her hair and skin were striking. And she sustained her part better than the others, moving and speaking with ease and only having to be prompted once.

Oh dear, thought Demelza, how strange it all is! Me, sitting here, a mother, like a middle-aged dowager, moving in the best circles, behaving with prim propriety, hands folded on reticule, feet politely together, smiling graciously when spoken to, inclining the head this way and that, the perfect lady; when I've still got two scars on my back from my father's leather strap, and I learned to swear and curse and spit before I was seven, and I crawled with lice and ate what food I could find lying in the gutter, and had six dirty undernourished brothers all younger than me to look after. And although one has died, there are still five: one a blacksmith and Methodist preacher, one a manager of a boat yard, three miners eking out a bare living working under the earth like blind worms. And thank God for gloves, for my hands are not as lily-white as those around me. Indeed it is not two weeks since they were scouring a preserving pan that Ena had not got properly clean. And before that they have had years and years of wear.

I am not of the same *breed* as these women, she thought; I should be *different* in colour or shape. But except for a few rough edges which they graciously ignore . . . Lady Isabel is a dear sweet sight, though I wish one had not to howl everything into her trumpet. And who would have thought Lady Lansdowne was three months forward? I wish I were. I wish Jeremy was three again like her son. I wish I was twenty-six like her and it was all to come again. Life . . . it slips away like sand out of a torn envelope. Well, I'm still not exactly old. But it worries me to see Ross limp, and the lines about his jaw, and many of my friends sick or old or dead.

What *was* Clowance's future, she wondered? Children in their youth blossomed and bloomed; then chance, inclination, heredity all played their part in deciding how that blossom would fruit. A hot sun? A savage wind? A frost? Clearly Clowance did not feel herself out of place among these high gentlefolk, not overawed. There was no folk memory; she had never known Illuggan and the dirt, the disease, the drink. If she married here she would fit in. But had not any of his relatives tried to influence Edward against such a poor match? Perhaps they were doing so every day. As a younger brother he ought to marry money. Perhaps the family was so well founded it did not matter either way.

Edward was playing Charles Surface, better-looking for his handsome white wig. He seemed everything that was admirable in a young man: a little clumsy but kind, just as aware of his responsibilities as his more brilliant brother; automatically in Parliament, Whig in the best sense of favouring a paternal liberalism; now that his brother had gone to the Upper House his own talents might be more quickly appreciated . . . a *thoughtful* husband and a loving one. Could one ask more? Demelza looked back at Nampara, and suddenly the outlook was bleak and cold. Not for her, thank God. For her Ross was everything; and by some miraculous chance she seemed to represent the same to him. But for her children. Jeremy had fallen deep in love with Cuby Trevanion – and while there should not have been any let to his suit, there clearly was. Although prepared to bury himself in his mining engine and his belief in the revolutionary power of steam, he was in fact a hollow man lacking the very sap of life because a young woman with a pretty face had for monetary reasons been denied the privilege of promising herself to him. Here, now here, in this room, was her daughter, just finishing amid considerable applause, a short extract from a play in which the hero was being played by a young man who apparently was interested in *her*. The let here, if there was one, existed only in her daughter's feelings. Home, back home, in that warm lovely home she had made for herself, was no happy or lovely alternative for Clowance, any more than there was for Jeremy.

Of course she was very young; if nothing came of this, the present alternatives at Nampara need not be the be-all and end-all of her choice. But Caroline had been right, she must be shown more of the world.

Demelza came to herself to find a grey-haired handsome man bending over her.

'A delightful interlude, ma'am. And you are to be congratulated on your charming daughter.'

'Thank you, Sir John.'

'May I venture to remind you of a promise you made last evening?'

'What was that?'

'You have so often sworn to tear the cloth if you were once given a billiard cue, that I suspect you of being an expert who fears to shame us with her knowledge of the game. Colonel Powys-Jones and Miss Carlisle are willing to be our opponents, if you would honour me by becoming my partner.'

Demelza had a soft spot for Egerton.

'Sir John, I *swear* I am a beginner. If you have money on this I earnestly would like you to find some other partner. What about Lady Isabel?'

'She could not hear the score.'

'Do you *need* to hear the score? Isn't it more better to hit the balls into the right pockets?'

'There, I told you, you have the essence of the game! See, our opponents are waiting for us at the door.'

So she went to play billiards, a game at which she showed more proficiency than with bows and arrows. For one thing she did not have Colonel Powys-Jones squeezing her into the wrong frame of mind, for another, having mastered the bridge on which her wobbly left hand had to support the cue, she found that by closing one eye like an ancient mariner peering through a spy glass, she could focus her attention so successfully on one ball that she more often than not hit the other ball in the direction intended. This did not always achieve the desired result, but it seemed to please Sir John Egerton and to confound Colonel Powys-Jones and Miss Carlisle often enough to achieve some sort of victory for her side.

In a warm glow of acclamation the game ended, and Powys-Jones said damned if he didn't believe Mrs Poldark didn't have a table of her own down in that outlandish peninsula where she made her home; and he was returning to Radnorshire next Tuesday, and he'd be glad to see as entertaining a game at Clwyd Hall, if the opportunity could come his way. It seemed that Sir John Egerton was returning with Colonel Powys-Jones and spending a few days there on his way to his own home in Cheshire.

Demelza escaped upstairs ahead of Clowance, who came in half an hour later, elated in spite of herself by the way the evening had gone. In the business of learning the lines and

442

dressing up and being rehearsed and the interchanges that went with it there had been more genuine fun and a closer harmony of spirit among the young ladies than before. Even Miss Florence Hastings had been heard to laugh, a means of expression which she normally looked on as bad form.

'I think I may go more often to the play,' Clowance said. 'The trouble in Truro and Redruth is that there are so many melodramas of blood and slaughter. I much better prefer such a social comedy as we have done tonight.'

'Perhaps you should have gone more frequent to London,' Demelza said, 'but often you seemed not to want to.'

'Is there not just as much blood on the stage there?' Clowance asked.

'Every bit. Folk who don't want to bother to go to Tyburn dearly like to see mock hangings instead.'

Clowance unpinned her hair and shook it out. 'I wonder what they are doing at home now.'

'Abed, I would suppose. Unless they are up to some mischief. You know Colonel Powys-Jones and Sir John Egerton want us to go on into Wales with them when this party breaks up on Tuesday.'

Clowance laughed. 'Do you think we should ever come back safe?'

'It depends what you mean by safe,' said Demelza.

'I don't think Papa would approve.'

'Sometime, though, you must listen to Colonel Powys-Jones on the subject of husbands. He sees them as a very unnecessary nuisance.'

'I don't think I should ever want my husband to be that,' Clowance said.

'Nor I for you,' said her mother.

IV

It was planned on the Sunday that after church they should

443

all go on an expedition to Bath to see the Abbey and to drink the waters. The weather had turned fine and warm again, and this would be a final expedition before the house party broke up.

As it happened Demelza, thought looking forward to this outing, was not able to go on it, being attacked by one of her megrims in the early hours of the morning. So she spent the day in bed.

It was while they were in Bath that Lord Edward asked Clowance to be his wife. With as much grace and delicacy as she could muster she refused.

V

The house party ended as arranged on the Tuesday morning. Colonel Powys-Jones, having made a final but abortive effort to capture Demelza for his Welsh fastness, rode off sorrowing with Sir John Egerton. The Hon. Helena Fairborne, accompanied by her maid and groom, left shortly afterwards in her own carriage for the family seat in Dorset. Miss Hastings likewise, though she shared a carriage with a Mr and Mrs Dawson who also had been there. Mrs Poldark and Miss Poldark were a little later, the post-chaise that was to take them to Bath being tardy in arrival. At the last there had to be haste, for the coach leaving Bath for Taunton would not wait for them; this haste was perhaps fortunate, for there was short enough time for leave-taking. At the last Demelza bent and kissed Lady Isabel Fitzmaurice's cheek; the others had all been kind but she had given that extra warmth that was endearing. Very politely but with a little tautness in his manner, Lord Edward came down the steps to see them off. The coach crackled and crunched on the loose gravel as the coachman made a turn, his horse providing a staccato of hooves and snorts as they got under way. As they left, bowling along the fine avenue towards the far distant gates, Edward turned and went up the steps again

444

and walked thoughtfully through the great house. It seemed very quiet after the fuss and bustle of the last two weeks. On Thursday the family would begin to assemble themselves for a Friday departure for Scotland. They would arrive in good time for the twelfth.

In his spacious bedroom looking out over the ornamental gardens Edward went to his desk, opened it and took from a drawer a letter he had written last Friday to Captain Ross Poldark. He read it through a couple of times before tearing it across and across and dropping it into the wastepaper basket. He blew his nose and walked to the window to see if the chaise was out of sight. It was. He went down to rejoin the others.